BLOODSINGER

THE STARCHASER SAGA
BOOK V

To Georgie
Always fight for what
you love

R. DUGAN

WAVE WALKER
press

For information contact:
R. Dugan
PO Box 1265
Martinsville, IN 46151
reneeduganwriting.com

Cover design by Maja Kopunovic
Map by Jessica Khoury
ISBN: 978-1-7339255-6-3

First Edition: December 2021

10 9 8 7 6 5 4 3 2 1

CONTENT WARNING:

This book contains scenes of prolonged fantasy fighting/PTSD, wartime peril, and discussions of pregnancy loss/miscarriage.

Discretion is advised for readers sensitive to these themes.

DEDICATION

To Dustin
Who first traveled the world of Valgard
and believed in the cabal.

And to Mom and Dad,
For coming behind him and reminding me
it was still an adventure worth having.

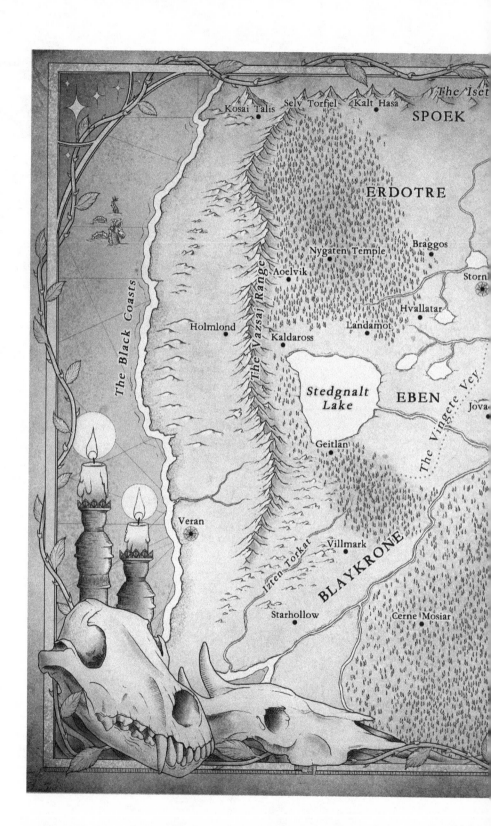

Kosai Talis Selv Torfjel Kalt Hasa

SPOEK

The Iset

ERDOTRE

Nygaten Temple   Braggos

Aoelvik   Storn

Hvallatar

The Black Coasts

Holmlond   Landamot

Kaldaross

Stedgnalt
Lake   EBEN   Jova

Geitlan

The Vingete Vey

Veran

Villmark

Izten Torkat   BLAYKRONE

Starhollow   Cerne Mosiar

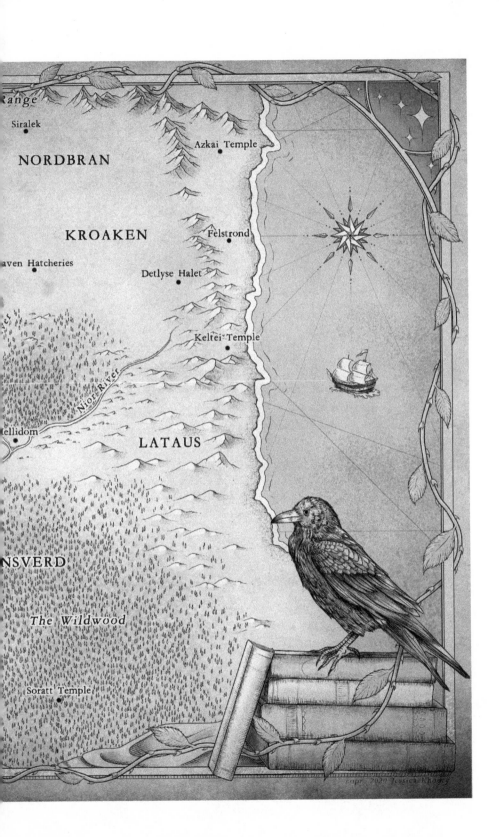

Range

Siralek

NORDBRAN

Azkai Temple

KROAKEN

Felstrond

aven Hatcheries

Detlyse Halet

Keltei Temple

Nior River

ellidom

LATAUS

NSVERD

The Wildwood

Soratt Temple

copr. 2020 Jessica Khoury

TALHEIM

CHAPTER ONE

IT MIGHT HAVE been a lovely day, bright, full of thawing spring sunlight and birdcall melodies. But inside the princess's mind, it was always smoke and scarlet skies, a warmth which did not belong in winter and sickness festering in the air.

This is one of those moments. One I'm going to remember the rest of my life.

Me, walking away from Valgard?

You, walking toward me with love in your eyes.

A kiss that blinded. Shadows that consumed.

I would've loved you for a hundred years. Two hundred. However long the gods gave us.

They had none of that time. Because she had walked away—because he *begged* her to.

Anything for you, Starchaser.

Wildheart.

Wildheart...

"Cistine?"

She jolted, head rising from her fist, focus returning to the Citadel's council chamber. It was indeed a bright day, the meeting table splashed with gold dapples tumbling through the glass roof, and a league of councilors stared at her—lords and ladies of Talheim from estates far and near.

Plainsmen and desert dwellers, fishers and mountaineers.

Cistine felt like she'd been all of them, in another world her mind stole away to whenever she wasn't careful. On days like today, the heat of the room's twin hearths and the monotony of the reports lulled her back to a dream where there was never too little to do; when she was the fulcrum upon which meetings like this hinged. When it was only her standing for Talheim's interests—not her and her father, whose voice drew her back to this meeting.

Cistine sat away from the table, smoothing her hands down the scarlet dress spilling across her knees. It was still difficult to wear gowns like this, even with long sleeves and high collars, at a table full of men; but each time she did, it was to honor Mirassah, her bright-eyed and sharp-witted counselor. She could only imagine how Mira would smile to see her now, dressed in trousers under a full dress, a tiara woven into her hickory hair...conducting royal business like the future queen she was. How proud they would all be. How Thorne—

The thought of him was a blade driven straight through her, wrapped in vines of slick darkness, dread and despair and *illness* tunneling deep into the very bones of the world itself.

Nazvaldolya.

Clenching her molars against a surge of bile that never lessened no matter how many times that sensation came and went, Cistine forced a smile. "I'm sorry, the warmth has me drifting. You were saying about the southern border forts, Lord Petr?"

The elderly lord flashed her a cautious smile. "That there's been no sign of unrest. So far, King Jad remains within Mahasar's borders."

"He'd be a fool not to." At Cistine's left, King's Cadre Warden Rozalie Dohnal cinched her arms and tossed her honeyed hair over her shoulder. "I think we proved well enough in Middleton we won't stand for provocation."

"Be that as it may, we keep the watch on the southern border." Queen Solene Novacek leaned against the table's edge, the softness of her face not in the least belying her piercing green eyes. "We don't need Jad seeing a lapse in our attention as an excuse to start prodding again after the harsh winter we had."

It *had* been harsh, the worst Cistine could ever remember. She wasn't certain if she was simply too distracted to notice them before—wrapped up in books and tea and suitors—or if the vicious snowstorms and shortage of game and plants was a creeping down of the blight from the north, an echo of far more perilous dangers beyond their borders. Whatever the case, she'd spent much of the last three months helping ration out supplies to the neediest towns in Talheim...when she wasn't researching fortifications and sieges, or writing in the tooled leather journal tucked into her belt, never far from reach.

She traced the dimples of horses artfully etched into the cover now, and her heart clenched. If the boy who gave it to her were still alive, he'd either take faint at the words within, or beg to be part of everything she was plotting. Perhaps she was better off not knowing which it would be.

King Cyril Novacek cleared his throat, bringing every eye at the table to him—including Cistine's, to whom he spoke: "Suggestions?"

The direct solicitation no longer made her palms sweat. This was a dance they had mastered by now. Trapping her hands together on the table, she held his stare. "I agree, we don't give ground at the southern forts. But I think we should offer the Wardens there a well-deserved rest. Pleasant as the southern warmth must be compared the snow we've had, I'm sure they're missing their families."

Cyril nodded curtly. "Viktor, see to it."

Viktor Pollack, the acting Commander of the King's Cadre with Rion Bartos retired back to his estate in Practica, dipped his head and offered a fleeting glance to Cistine from the Queen's right. She held that stare when she added carefully, "I think it may be time to offer the Wardens at the northern barracks a reprieve as well."

A hush gathered up the table, as it always did when she mentioned the north. She tried not to blame them—for two decades, her kingdom was mandated to keep silent about Valgard, and none were as comfortable discussing it now as her—but it was an effort not to bristle at those uneasy looks.

"The North has been quiet," her uncle Filip mused, "aside from that gods-forsaken storm. We're left weakened at both sides if we rotate our ranks all at once."

"But the ranks haven't changed in nearly three months." At Cistine's own behest, but Filip didn't need to know that. "It's long past time those Wardens saw their homes again."

"I agree." The shock at Viktor's flash of support was nearly enough to rend Cistine's focus. "Most are exhausted, homesick, and restless, especially at the northern barracks."

All her doing, because Cistine had insisted they be kept there from the moment she returned to Talheim. She shoved away a prickle of guilt that sizzled in her fingertips, reciting a silent mantra to herself: *Wartime necessity. Wartime necessity.*

The chant floated like words off a musty page, ink and old paper soothing her frayed senses. When her focus returned, her father was nodding—both to her and to Filip. "I agree, a rotation in the north is necessary. But it's also true we don't want to change shifts at the borders all at once. We'll compromise—move the southern ranks now, the north in a fortnight."

Cistine fisted her hands in her skirts.

Another fortnight. She could endure it.

When both Cistine and Filip dipped their heads, the King rose, bringing the rest of the table with him. "It's been a long day, my friends. Let's reconvene in the morning, and I'll see about having the hearths stoked less often tomorrow."

A few chuckled, and Cistine shot her father a dry smile he met with a wink—carefully covering for her distraction.

The room slowly emptied, Solene escorting a flock of ladies to the tearoom with a parting kiss blown to Cistine. She returned it, glanced at her father's face again, and stilled; he had that look in his eye, the sort that once heralded discussions of successorship and her duty as future Queen. These days, it lent itself far more to conversations she enjoyed even less, because they required too much delicacy of tongue that erred close to lying. And she did not like to lie to her father.

"I really am tired," she said quickly. "I think I'll nap before supper." A meal that would, thankfully, be attended by every lord and lady from across the kingdom, keeping the conversation shallow and cordial.

She feigned ignorance to the King's heavy sigh when she all but dragged Rozalie from the room, yanking the doors shut behind them. Rozalie offered a grimace while they walked. "That went better than expected."

Cistine kneaded her temples. "Thanks to Viktor's support, of all people."

"I'd rather have the support of a snake sleeping in my bed, but in this case, I think we take it as it is: we're getting the rotation at the northern barracks. It's finally happening."

Excitement veined Rozalie's voice, and Cistine dropped her hands and met the Warden's gleaming stare. "Two more weeks. That's manageable."

"I'd believe you better if you didn't have that murderous look in your eyes."

Cistine stuck out her tongue, and she and Rozalie carried on in silence the rest of the way to the Princess's rooms—not the same ones where she'd lived for her first twenty years. She'd tried to stay in the chamber of her childhood, its balcony stretching above her beloved inner garden where the comforting scents of winter berries and pine waited to embrace her during these long days. But after so many difficult nights reading and writing in her new leather journal—after restless slumber when she woke in cold sweats, sobbing Thorne's name into the darkness, aching for her *selvenar* who was not merely across the hall anymore, but a kingdom away—she found the restlessness was too much, the surroundings too familiar.

The call was too great.

It whispered to her now when she and Rozalie entered her new rooms in the north-facing tower, inhaling scents of lavender, jasmine, and cinnamon from the bouquet on the breakfast table. Shutting the doors and leaning her weight against them, Cistine breathed in until air struck the bottom of her lungs, trapped there while she listened to that quiet growl deep in her spirit.

Come, it urged, as it had all her life. *Come and see.*

But she couldn't. Not yet.

A throaty caw greeted their arrival, and Cistine flashed a tired smile at the sleek black raven roosting on the back of her dining chair. "Hello, Faer."

"*Hello, Cistine.*"

Rozalie shuddered. "I still think it's horrible you taught him to mimic your voice."

"He's a battle bird. He needed something to occupy that clever mind...didn't you, you handsome bag of feathers?" Cistine fed Faer a scrap of beef from her cold breakfast plate. "Besides, it was this, or let him keep stealing necklaces from all the courtiers until Viktor went mad searching for Astoria's newest jewel thief."

"That was a good week." Smiling, Rozalie dumped herself on the bed. "Just don't teach him to say *my* name."

Cistine laughed. "I give you my word."

Rozalie was silent. Cistine turned from feeding Faer, and her heart lurched, then sank like a dropped stone. Rozalie had peeled back the lumpy quilts Cistine ordered untouched by the servants, burying stacks and mounds of books frittered out of the royal library. She should have stashed them under the bed before the council, but after another restless night of bad dreams, she'd slept so late all she could do was throw down a few bites of cheese and run to the meeting hall, leaving the mound where it fell.

"Bit of light reading before bed?" Rozalie's tone tried and failed for mirth. "I didn't think you were researching *this* deeply on battle tactics, Princess."

"I couldn't sleep last night."

Rozalie turned to her, scooping one book from the buried heap. "What is *this* all about?"

"Arithmetic." Cistine sank into the dining chair, and Faer settled on her shoulder. "The average war in Talheimic history consisted of anywhere between six and ten thousand battles, did you know that?"

"I didn't. Nor would anyone who hasn't had their nose buried in books on war theory for the past three months."

Cistine couldn't muster even a smile at her wry tone. "The Bloodwights depleted their store of augments over the last twenty years in the wilds, but they took Stornhaz, which means they have all the flagons the Courts couldn't steal out during the siege. Besides that, they don't need flagons for every battle, they have Blood Hive fighters, too."

"Your point?"

"Let's say the Courts fled with five hundred flagons, generously. If they skirmish with the Bloodwights even twice a week and use as few as five augments every time, they'll only have enough to last a year."

Rozalie shrugged. "Maybe they can win by then."

"Maybe. Except most wars have historically lasted eighteen to twenty-four months."

Now Rozalie set the book side, frowning. "It's not enough."

Cistine slumped forward, resting her head in her hands. "It's nowhere *near* enough. They'll be fighting with steel alone while the Bloodwights still have plenty of flagons to spread around."

"So, what are you thinking?"

"What I always have: that they can't win this war without help." And help was something her father wouldn't be quick to send, something the lords would never agree to. She'd tested those waters her first week back in Talheim and found them fathomless, full of doubt and suspicion.

But then, this wasn't truly a war of able bodies; it was a war of augments. And in such a skirmish, there was no one to plead Valgard's cause. Nothing could be done, except...

Cistine furiously clamped down on the thought, shoving it aside as she did whenever it arose; as deep as she'd stuffed it last night before it manifested once more in her nightmares. "You're free to go, Rozalie. Spread the word to the Wardens and prepare a note for Viktor. If you need to, let him know the names on your roster have my personal support. I'm not certain what his angle was today, but let's use it for all it's worth."

"Consider it done." Rozalie stood and stretched. "I'll see you at the dinner tonight."

The moment she was gone, Cistine latched the door and hurried to the bed. Beneath it, she chiseled a stone loose and opened a cavity in the floor where she'd hidden the last gift from her mentor, Quill: an augment pouch with six flagons inside.

Too dangerous to leave them exposed in a citadel full of those who didn't yet fathom that the augment wells in the North were truly gifted by the gods—the powers within them mere weapons, not the abomination Cistine's grandfather Ivan claimed them to be; those who still believed forcing the Northern Kingdom to seal the Doors to the Gods, depleting their augment stocks dramatically until these six precious flagons had become a gift without measure, was justified. Those like Viktor, tutored to prejudice by Rion Bartos, who might destroy them—and devastate the city and Cistine's heart.

If she was wiser, she wouldn't touch these augments at all. Quill had given them to her in case Valgard fell to the Bloodwights—the twisted and cruel Order of former *visnprests* who keyed the Doors shut and sealed their craft into the Novacek blood—and it was left to Cistine alone to ensure they did not spill her blood or her father's on the Doors and summon enough augments to enslave the world. But handling the flagons calmed her, quieted the call, soothed the ache in her chest. It made her feel powerful again. Training always did.

She perched on the edge of her bed and cradled a flagon in each hand, their separate calls weighing differently on her mind: fire in one, ravaging darkness in the other. She breathed deeply, in and out through pursed lips; then she uncorked the fire, releasing the smallest kernel into her palm.

It bloomed like a flower, not so much as a tendril of heat escaping her command. She let it burn back her sleeves just enough to bare the beginning of the Atrasat inkings that girdled her wrists, extending up along her arms and meeting above her heart. The winking stars flickered in flame, one for each member of her cabal: Quill and Tatiana, Maleck and Ashe, Aden and Ariadne, Baba Kallah and Julian, and Thorne. Every name a blow, every one welcomed for the love that came with the agony. Bringing them back in moments of solitude was the only way she kept them alive.

Sucking in a deep breath, she let the fire bracelet her wrist. Wiggling her fingers, she thumbed open the shadow flagon, its murky purple contents roiling like that deep night when she'd fled Valgard to protect the Key and let the war against the Bloodwights be waged without her.

She poured a seed of darkness into her palm.

The separate augments surged like hounds baying at their leads, racing up her arms, tugging at her will with a violent threat to destroy the entire northern tower in darkness and flame. Pressure built in Cistine's chest, a mixture of panic and power braided together, but she ground her teeth, stopping it in its place with a silent command barked inside her head; at that unspoken word, the storms abated. The fire crawled back down her arm, the darkness returned to sulk within the cage of her fingers.

Sweat sliding down her nape, chest shuddering, Cistine held an augment in each hand.

She'd begun practicing this her first week back in Talheim, when memories of facing the *Aeoprast* in the acolyte temple and a Mahasari spy in the sewers below the City of a Thousand Stars kept her awake long after dark. Curious and still grief-stricken enough to be daring, she had ridden out deep into the heart of the plains one night, halfway to the Calalun Peaks where no one would see what happened next. Then she did what she'd managed twice before, purely on luck and guessing both times: wielding two augments at once.

It should not be possible; the power ought to rip her apart from the outside inward, armored flesh or none. Yet here she sat with a strength she only saw Bloodwights possess, or heard in stories Quill and Tatiana told of treacherous Oadmark and the time they fought the *Aeoprast* there. And while it chipped away at her stamina far more quickly than a single augment, she could cling to them both, and more: she could command them.

Rallying her strength, she rose, cupped her palms, and wove the augments together, an undying heat and a darkness so deep the light did not penetrate it. She watched their hypnotic dance a moment, then spread them out between her fingers and started sparring.

It was strange to do it with the empty air, fire-and-darkened fists leaving glowing paths, then snuffing them out. But she did as Quill taught her, mustering the power and bending it to her will; and while the sunlight climbed down the walls and night beckoned the capital city of Astoria, steadiness filled her middle, soothing the quivering tension of another day spent in long councils that felt like such a waste when war breathed at their backs.

Training reminded her that she *was* doing something for the good of her kingdom. Of *all* kingdoms.

When sweat dripped down her back, her dress destroyed and the augments all but spent, Cistine relented at last. She dispatched the fire into her bedside washbasin with a hiss of steam and scattered the darkness against the stone floor. In the silence, she heaved for breath and twisted her thumb against the black-gold band of her betrothal ring, setting moonlight dancing along the ultramarine opal; a promise from Thorne, a vow for a future he gave up to send her home and keep her safe. She wielded it like an anchor now, kedging her mind back down the channels of question that had distracted her in today's council meeting.

Had the cabal found Pippet yet—Quill's younger sister, ransomed off to the Bloodwights? If they hadn't, how were Quill and Tatiana faring? What of Maleck, facing his brothers on the battlefield again, those masked manifestations of his greatest fears and failures; and Ashe, always a sword and shield, at Maleck's side no matter how terrible things became?

What of Ariadne, the cabal's light and soul, helping shoulder the weight of their spirits in dark hours like these? And Aden, a newly-minted Tribune, taking his position in a war which had to echo so vividly his years in Siralek's Blood Hive arena? They would be perhaps the most focused, the most reliable in the fight, but what if the weight became too great for them to bear?

And what of Thorne, a man who fought for decades for a better future and instead inherited conquesting *visnprests*, stolen children, and the city of his birth set aflame?

Fear licked her insides, and she forced it down. All was not hopeless. She was doing *something*.

Two weeks. Just two more weeks.

A heavy weight banged against the inside of the glass balcony doors, startling Cistine so badly she yelped. Faer picked himself up from his impact with the shimmering surface and strutted before his reflection, offended croaks taking on a deeper cadence—the first name Cistine hadtaught him to mimic. "*Quill. Quill. Quill. Quill.*"

Pain speared through her chest. "Oh, Faer." The raven squirmed when she crouched beside him and lifted him in both hands, brushing her nose against his skull. "I miss him, too. But we can't go back. Not now."

Outside, a faint toll of thunder rattled the Citadel mortar, as if the True God and his vassals agreed to the danger. And yet the very core of Cistine's being—that wild heart of fire reduced to embers but not entirely foundered—ached to go anyway.

Just two more weeks.

CHAPTER TWO

C ISTINE DIDN'T HAVE the heart to tell her parents she hated this glass ballroom.

It was splendid enough, as all the Citadel was, filigreed in silver pigment, the glass dome allowing a clear view of the stars. Chiseled braziers and well-tended hearths kept it warm despite the chilly spring night, and there was food in plenty on the array of tables lining the walls.

But it was not a lack of comfort that rubbed her ill when she entered; it was that they had held her coming-of-age ball here, and among the memories, specters still danced.

Ashe in Warden's garb, blue-and-green eyes full of doubt for their kingdom's safety; Julian Bartos in the full regalia of a Lord's son, asking her to dance; the echo of Jad's threats; and the person Cistine was that night, untested, naïve, but determined, a vision in a blood-red dress, a princess willing to go further and endure more for her people than she ever dreamed.

Whether those people were Talheimic or not no longer mattered.

With Faer perched on the shoulder of a jacket far too large for her, cast over a deep blue dress carelessly chosen to make it through the evening, Cistine stood in the ballroom archway and felt every difference between that long-ago day and this one counting off on the beats of her heart.

The smiles were genuine now; no trace of clandestine war councils dragged down the countenances of distant relatives and unrelated lords. This peace was true—and yet this all felt like a lie, knowing death bore down from the north. She wondered if this was precisely what her parents had felt the night of her birthday celebration, if their smiles tasted just as gritty and false as hers, if it wearied them just as much to pretend.

And now, compounding her despair, pale-haired and sharp-eyed Viktor spotted her across the ballroom and slipped through the crowd to join her. "Princess."

"*Bandayo*," Faer croaked.

Cistine flicked him across the chest. "Good evening, Viktor."

Wary gaze skipping from the raven ruffling up on Cistine's shoulder to her oversized attire, Viktor slowly straightened his spine. "I may be an ignorant man, but even I know that's an interesting choice of fashion."

Cistine glanced down at the jacket—long since worn out of its sandalwood-and-salt scent, her skirt poking out beneath its hem—and shrugged. "It's cold in the Citadel."

"Indeed." Viktor chose a different tack. "It was a good suggestion you made this afternoon, giving the Wardens a reprieve. Most haven't seen their families since Darlaska."

Memories of food and fletching, gifts and snow and battle and *joy*, had Cistine's thumb raking the ring around her finger. "We ought to have a patrol schedule in the south. No one should be there longer than a few weeks. It's not fair to leave them separated from their families." She was careful not to add the same for the north.

"I'll speak to the King about it at once. Perhaps you and I can have conversations about your other strategies over tea sometime?"

Cistine studied this man of sharp angles and cunning smiles, whom Rozalie and Ashe both disliked yet who had supported her so unexpectedly in the meeting today. Her gut gave a hard, uncomfortable twist; it never boded well when unlikeable men became agreeable allies. "Be sure you do speak to the King. And make certain you also tell Lord Rion he already bullied one son into being my suitor. I'm not in any mood to court a second."

Another hard blink, and the scowling Warden emerged from behind the approachable mask. "With how whispers carry in this Citadel, Princess, you may find offers of that nature are in shorter supply than you remember."

She stepped closer, Faer's talons boring the jacket tighter against her shoulder. "I would prefer if they disappeared altogether, seeing as I'm already *betrothed*."

Viktor's gaze dipped dismissively to her hand, a glance harsher than any word or blow. "If you're going to make suggestions about how our ranks assemble, you need the new King's Cadre Commander as a friend. What would your father think if he knew you were reading up on battle strategies and meeting with Dohnal in unsavory places these past few months?"

Fury launched through Cistine, raising the hair on her neck. "Have you been *spying* on me?"

"Consider it careful observation from a concerned subject."

"Yes, a *subject*. One who has no place spying on his future queen!"

"Not a queen yet, Princess. It's a long way from here to the ivory throne, and I'd advise you to think strongly on which allies you want to make along the way. And which enemies."

He turned on polished heel and vanished into the flock of dancers, and Cistine let the steel seep out of her spine while she traced her fingertips over Faer's smooth skull. "I'd give you the whistle and let you strip him bald, except no one here is merciful to you like I am."

In a flirt of dark armor, Rozalie appeared with orange tarts in hand. She offered one to Cistine, eyes glowing. "That was even more satisfying than I envisioned."

"You knew?"

"There've been murmurs among the Wardens for weeks now that Rion was making suggestions to Viktor about asking for your hand."

"And you didn't warn me?"

Rozalie shrugged. "I wanted to see how you'd handle it."

Equal parts gratitude and irritation battling in her stomach, Cistine accepted the tart. "What did he mean about whispers in the Citadel?"

Rozalie fidgeted with her own tart, breaking it in half and licking custard from her smallest finger. "Nothing, just court gossip."

"I live and breathe court gossip, but whatever whispers he means, they haven't reached my ears. Deliberately, I'm guessing."

The Warden shot her a sidelong glance. "It's just unhappy biddies squawking their usual songs—no offense to your raven." Cistine held her stare levelly and let one brow slide up. Rozalie sighed. "They want to know what your betrothal means for Talheim's future, especially when you didn't bring the man home with you."

"They don't want me to know they're gossiping about my affections?"

"Among other things."

A vague, misshapen understanding annealed into focus, whittling away her nerves and appetite. She murmured an excuse to Rozalie, whistled Faer up to the dome's ledge, and slipped away through the crowd of her people— who she'd fought for in the North, who sat with her in meetings like the one today and saw the strength she came home with, the wisdom and leadership she'd battled to attain.

It was almost pitiful how quickly she found the thread of Viktor's whispers in their midst, where wine flowed freely and drowned inhibitions. Three lords were engrossed at the dessert table and didn't even notice the princess picking disinterestedly over the many cakes and mousses, her gossip's ears trained on their conversation.

"I don't see it." Lord Michal, black-bearded and steely-eyed, spoke barely above a growl, but still his voice carried in its harshness. "No matter how much the King claims it."

"Well, of course he wants to believe in her," Lord Boris replied. "She's his only daughter, after all. If she's unfit to rule, who will?"

"And let's not forget," Lord Ambrose added, voice soft as his white hair and beard, "she did secure us the treaty."

"Don't mistake me. I'm grateful," Lord Michal said with the unique ability not to sound grateful at all. "She's a fair diplomat. But as a princess— as a queen? Did you see her in council today?"

Lord Boris scratched his curls. "Not at all different from when she'd get lost in a book during court."

"That's precisely it. The King is making quite the effort to convince us she desires the throne now, that she takes her birthright seriously...and here she is, daydreaming during a council like she always has. And when she does pay attention, it's often to advocate for the North."

"There's still hope," Boris cautioned. "I know things didn't turn out between her and the Bartos boy, gods rest him. But perhaps she'll marry a diplomatic husband, someone the King favors for his interest in the Middle Kingdom."

Ambrose nudged him. "Hoping your Lukas might be a contender?"

Cistine withdrew from the pie she reached for, what remained of her appetite crumbling like the Citadel's foundations below her feet. The table blurred, fanciful dishes swimming like swill, the taste of fury and despair clogging the back of her throat and turning the sweet aftertaste of orange custard to rot.

For three months, she'd been present, putting Talheim's needs first, advising to the best of her might on fortifications and supplies for their cities and people, ensuring the royal family's safety in case of a siege like the one she herself had barely survived in Stornhaz. And yet this was what they were concerned about: a day's slip-up and who her future husband would be.

She stalked away from the lords, from the banquet, before anyone could spot her eavesdropping and console her with pretty words meant for royalty while she knew what lurked in their hearts.

They doubted her. They did not see a woman sitting beside the King, but a girl with her head lost in the stars.

Faer's comforting weight descended on her shoulder at the doorway, and they left the ballroom's brightness for ghostlit corridors, a palette of pink, rose-gold, and blue phosphorescence paving the way through the cold, lonely Citadel. She wasn't going anywhere in particular. She couldn't go where her heart craved, anyway.

"I don't want to do this again, Faer," she whispered. "First I had to prove myself to Valgard, now my own people. Even after *everything*."

After all the battle, imprisonment, and torture she'd suffered from

Chancellor Salvotor; after she won them the treaty that brought them peace. Still they doubted she'd put their interests first, hinging their faith not on her, but on whichever man she would marry.

In one empty hall of a hundred, she slumped to the wall, head resting on the cool stone. Gazing up into the shadowed vault of the ceiling above, she let the heaviness make itself known in her head and heart. Becoming strong enough to be queen was one thing; convincing the people to trust where she led them was entirely another.

It would not bode well that she'd left the banquet, either...they would whisper about that come morning.

Groaning, she buried her face in her hands. "Can I do anything right anymore?"

Faer nipped her earlobe, cross as a finger flick, and she didn't need his mimicry to read intent into the gesture: *Stop that, Stranger.*

She couldn't lurk here in the darkness. She needed a distraction, something purposeful—something *useful*.

Books. The royal library. She knew precisely what to read, like a scream in the face of their doubt, proving herself by choices they would disdain.

She had decided long ago she would not marry a man who made her choices for her, who sought to set her away while he ruled her kingdom. And she was not about to let the Lords cast her aside and put their faith in whomever she wedded, either. If they wanted a proper husband for her, she'd give them a Chancellor instead. And if they longed for a king worth following, she'd give them a queen worth dying for.

She found peace at last, tucked into one of the reading nooks that were her sanctuary as a child reticent of the crown. Faer preened atop the shelves, muttering to himself every so often, and Cistine sipped peppermint tea and thumbed through books of strategy—the diplomatic sort Viktor had likely been reading at Rion's behest before he cornered her tonight.

She found herself here often, perhaps too frequently since she came home. What was once dry theory littering dusty pages now spoke life to her, telling precisely what the cabal was doing, what all her Valgardan allies were entrenched in. Knowing eased the ache; it gave her a sketch of the world she'd left behind and a clear vision of the days to come.

Tonight, she read of a different battlefield—one she'd danced the fringes of since coming home, when thoughts first took seed of destiny and choices and duty. She'd opened these tomes frequently, then shut them just as fast, flushing and muttering to herself that she was being foolish, it wouldn't come to this, it was useless even to look.

But a fortnight was all she had left. And with Michal, Ambrose, and Boris still chattering away in her head, she had to know.

So she stayed and read deep into her family's history, into laws that hadn't mattered before—pages on succession rites and rituals, oathtaking and binding duty, consorts and crowns. At this she paused, her finger grazing the band on her finger again, brow pinching in a frown.

Somewhere deeper in the library, pages rustled.

The hairs rose on Cistine's neck. She shut the book with a snap, sitting up and peering between the long, dark shelves. "Hello?"

Another rustle, fainter this time. Hand to the dagger sheathed under her dress, Cistine slid from the nook and clicked her tongue. Faer took wing, gliding swift and silent as an ink stain. On soundless feet, Cistine stole after him. No sense of imminent destruction hugged these familiar walls. No trace of the Bloodwights, of an enemy, of *Nazvaldolya*, and yet distant darkness brushed her limbs and fear twisted in her stomach.

She rounded a bookcase just as the bang of iron and glass ripped through the library. Her shriek pierced her own ears, pitifully high-pitched, and Faer squawked in response. Not at any danger; a window banging open under the wet breeze. Outside, the clouds emptied themselves in a torrent.

"Rain. Again." Cistine shut the window. "All bow before the future Queen of Talheim, frightened by a storm. Let's go to bed, Faer."

And go they did. But not before Cistine heaped up stacks of books into her arms, checked both ways that Viktor's spies were not watching her, and carried them off like a secret hugged to her heart.

CHAPTER THREE

IN THE DEAD of dark, in Cistine's nightmares, the *Aeoprast* reigned from a throne built on the bodies of her friends.

She climbed a tower of bone and sinew toward them, wading through blood to reach their corpses impaled at the Bloodwight's feet. She yanked at Quill's hands, clung to Tatiana's cold face, screamed for Maleck and Aden, wept when she kissed Ariadne's forehead, and sobbed Ashe's name. She slid Thorne from the jagged pike on which he hung, cradled him, shook him and begged him to come back to her while the *Aeoprast* watched from above, his mandibled mask leering.

"You could have stopped this." His voice was a thready echo of that horrible night in the acolyte temple when he'd turned Chancellor Salvotor to blood mist. "You could have saved them if only you stayed."

She laid Thorne down and lunged to her feet, drawing the sword strapped across her back and flinging herself up to the throne; the *Aeoprast* retaliated with a cut of his hand, blasting her back down the mountain of corpses, and before she struggled to her feet it all plunged into a lightless hall, friends and foe swallowed by the deep. A cavernous echo spiraled around her when she spun left and right, looking ahead and back at broad walls muraled in twists of shadow and ancient glyphs, runic language chiseled like Atrasat inkings on stone skin.

She was deep underground, the scent of cold rock and ancient earth as familiar as the walls of Kalt Hasa. But there was something different about it now; ahead, wreathed in shadows, a pulse thudded in the world's chest, begging to be free.

Blade dipping, Cistine took a cautious step forward. Red tines branched out from her boots like veins all connected to that throbbing heart somewhere far in the distance.

Come. Find. Take.

Fingers brushed the small of her back. "I'm with you, Wildheart. I'm right here."

Cistine twisted with a desperate shout of joy, but just when she caught a glimpse of silver hair and blue eyes looking ahead into the gloom, she gasped awake. Thorne's name burst from inside her as she recognized the darkness of her room and the sound that woke her: the blast of thunder outside her balcony doors, carrying on and on.

Panting and sweating, Cistine pushed aside the books she fell asleep reading and stumbled from the bed, wiping her arm across her eyes, coming away damp with tears. Panic tingled in the tip of her nose and across her lips, and the memory of Mira's instructions hit like a shove from behind— go, move, don't sit and dwell.

Kraut. That would settle her stomach. Managing the nausea would calm her, then she could face the rest.

"Faer," she hissed, and he woke from his roost on the back of her chair and came to her at once. They went down to the kitchens on silent feet, through halls she ran since childhood, striped with lightning tonight. Hands shaking, she piled a bowl with kraut, jutting her jaw to keep her teeth from chattering.

It was just a dream, and dreams were lies—even if Thorne's presence, his noble face turned toward the dark, the touch of his hand were so *real* the small of her back still tingled from it. Even if she wished she could've fallen back asleep, dropped straight back into that place so she could look at him and remember every detail the months made her forget. And that place where he found her...

Strange, how real it felt, less like a fantasy spun from her mind and more like a memory of somewhere she'd been. But that was another lie of a tense mind; that place was the macabre reassembling of Kalt Hasa, nothing more. Even its bones felt the same.

Thunder crooned a morbid lullaby and lightning beckoned in lavender curls echoing other bad dreams when Cistine followed Faer's flight back up to the north tower, bowl in hand. Foregoing the distraction of bed and book, she shouldered through the double-doors onto her balcony. The broad white crescent welcomed her, though she avoided it so often...the tug to its railing and the yearning to gaze northward.

But tonight, stomach rioting and skin tacky with sweat, she could make an exception.

She settled her back to the Citadel stone beneath the eaves shielding her from rain and slid down cross-legged, the bowl of kraut in her lap. While she ate, she watched the storm.

It had begun the night she returned to Talheim, and it never seemed to stop. Though blizzards masked it from time to time, and in the daylight it was little more than a suggestion among thin clouds on the horizon, at night it was inescapable—and utterly unnatural. The augmented power of the Bloodwights punished the world that drove them out after they lost the war against Talheim.

Cistine's shudder racked in tandem to the balcony doors creaking open, and she sat up, fingers clenching tight around her fork. She only relaxed when her father padded out to join her, wreathed in the sugary scent of cookies from his own bowl. He'd removed his kingly regalia, settling for trousers and a loose linen shirt, his hair tied back in a short tail. How he convinced the Queen to let him grow it so long was a mystery Cistine was determined to solve.

"What are you doing awake, Papa?"

"I should ask you the same. It's the dead of night." He settled beside her, mirroring her posture.

"I couldn't sleep anymore."

"Well, neither could I." Cyril offered her a cookie, and when Cistine shook her head, he wrinkled his nose at her bowl. "I don't know how you and your mother can stomach that dreck."

Cistine pondered a joke but chose honesty instead. "It helps the sickness, and that helps me not to panic."

Cyril's eyes moved to her face. "More nightmares?"

She nodded. "And then the storm woke me."

"Me as well." He toasted his cookie to her kraut fork and bit into it, leaning his head back against the wall with a heavy sigh. "But not your mother. She's sleeping like the dead. I wonder if this is just an affliction of the Keys."

Cistine chewed and swallowed. "I think it might be."

He nodded through the railing. "That storm, what do you make of it?"

"I think it's a boundary," Cistine admitted. "The Wardens writing to Rozalie from the north call it the Dreadline...they say it's so thick and terrible they can't get through."

"They've tried?" A tinge of outrage undercut his voice.

"Papa, some of them are hardly older than Julian was when we went to Valgard. What do you think?"

Cyril sighed again, but wisely laid aside the matter of cocky young Wardens. "The Bloodwights want to keep everyone out."

"More likely to keep everyone *in*. Especially if the cabal managed to lay a trail that convinced them I fled into the wilds instead of coming home." She speared more kraut, then tapped her fork tines against the ceramic while she watched the lightning flicker. "Thorne got me through just in time."

The weight of her father's gaze returned to her. "You must miss him terribly."

"With my whole heart." Cistine set aside her bowl and curled back against the wall. "I always knew it would only end one of two ways: either we stood alone, or we fell together. I just didn't expect the thought of falling together would somehow be *easier*."

Cyril frowned, set aside the cookie bowl, and stretched. "Today at the council, where were you?"

A blush spread across her cheeks. "Not listening to Lord Petr's tenth non-report in the past six weeks, that's for certain."

"Cistine. These meetings are important."

"Are they, Papa? More important than what's crouching at our door?"

"It's not at our door. Not yet."

No. Because it was inside Valgard's walls instead—and not just crouched, but ravaging.

"We've done what we can to brace for an attack from the Bloodwights," Cyril added. "*You*'ve done what you can, helping me lay out our defenses and escape routes should it come to that. Those new tunnels will be fortified within the month. You've done *enough*...now I need you to be present at these meetings. You help no one if you come to Talheim's table but leave your mind in Valgard."

The words stung, but there was truth behind them. She'd been more absent lately, the dreams worsening, the storm bearing down on her like a dark harbinger. And it didn't help, the things she overheard at the banquet—that her people doubted her already.

She couldn't afford for the King to doubt her, too. Not knowing what was yet to come.

CHAPTER FOUR

THE REPETITIVE SLAM of fists on fibers drowned out the world. The bob and weave of Cistine's boots on the sandy training floor and the crash of her knuckles against the grainsack mannequin eased the strain of a fortnight's worth of pleasantries and razored smiles gritted like a knife between her lips; of pretty dresses and politicking and sideways glances from lords and ladies she pretended not to see.

Nothing calmed her anymore but the familiar rigors of training, and even then, it was like Mira and Sander had told her: sometimes coping methods worked forever, and sometimes the body adapted too well. After two weeks, this grainsack was becoming less of a distraction; she was more keenly aware of how the Wardens watched her when they came and went from their own training, how they whispered between the pillars: the Princess of books and tea becoming a warrior of rage and bloody knuckles, pounding the dust of anticipation and nightmares from her body while she imagined this grainsack had white-and-black hair and a grin to goad her even on her most exhausted days.

Left hook. Right hook. Now bring up that knee!

Snarling, Cistine slammed her leg into the grainsack, sending it reeling backward on its rope—straight into her mother's waiting hands.

Queen Solene nearly blended between the brick pillars of the undercroft barracks in her dark cardigan and riding trousers, shooting brace and jerkin. The smell of sweat penetrated her crisp perfume. Perhaps Cistine's tendency to release her cares in training was not something learned just from the cabal. "Your father's been looking for you since sunup."

"I've been here a while."

Solene released the bag with a hard shove. "Your knuckles are bleeding."

Cistine punched the bag back to her, unraveling more of the fist-wrappings that had broken down hours ago. "I don't care. I have worse scars in other places."

Solene raised a brow. "Is that what this is about now? Gathering scars?"

"It's about being strong enough that the little hurts don't matter anymore."

Solene swung the bag back to her. "If I didn't know better, I'd say you aren't maintaining your strength, you're growing it for something bigger."

Cistine's next punch broke the fraying rope, sending the grainsack rolling to the Queen's feet. She propped her boot on its edge, holding Cistine's gaze while the Princess bent with hands on her knees, panting. "Is it wrong to want to be stronger than I was?"

Solene tilted her head, and Cistine fell into step with her toward the undercroft steps, cleaning her bloody knuckles on her pants. The dull chime of tools on masonry kept tune with their steps; the smiths were working the stone and mortar still, forging new escape tunnels for the royal family's safety—pure precaution.

"The servants tell me they found you sleepwalking again last night," Solene murmured when they were out of earshot of the workers. "In the northern corner of your room."

Cistine grimaced at the memory of fingers on her shoulder shaking her awake, slumped in the corner, forehead pressed to the wall. "I don't know how Papa endured the call for so many years. It must've terrified him."

"The mind acclimates in time, like with captivity or danger. Or war."

Cistine flexed her fingers while she and Solene mounted the steps into the inner Citadel. "How did *you* acclimate to being under scrutiny from

Papa's allies when you became Queen?"

"I reminded myself I didn't marry two dozen lords. I married a king, and my loyalty was to him, and to the wellbeing of our kingdom...not to making them all love me."

"I didn't expect I'd have to fight this battle. I thought once I embraced my throne, they would embrace *me*."

"Well, they *want* to embrace you, but on their terms. They want you to lay down your sword and bow. They want you to be a princess of peace."

"What if I'm not ready to lay everything else aside? What if it's not my time yet?"

Solene halted and turned to her, green eyes shrewd. "I think you ought to ask yourself very plainly what it is you're still waiting for."

A prickle of unease traced Cistine's spine. It felt like her mother saw through her with that piercing gaze, into the heart she'd kept hidden all this time. "We all choose our battles, I suppose."

"That we do. I chose to stay, to endure their doubt. Which battle will *you* choose, my love?"

Cistine held her mother's gaze and did not answer.

Solene's lips twitched, and she turned up the corridor to walk away, then paused, glancing back. "I will tell you this: you're going to find the greatest battle you face in this life is not against old-fashioned lords or mad kings. It's between the person you have always been, and the person you are becoming. The woman you were born to be."

"I thought I'd already become her."

"Then why are you fighting to be stronger?"

She left Cistine alone with that question unanswered, hanging heavy among the chiming hammers and sinking nails from the tunnel still being forged below.

～～～

Numbers and strategies drilled through Cistine's mind even after she left the Citadel for less-favorable places, the pain of too much planning somehow still preferable to the questions raised in conversation with her mother. Pipesmoke and red ghostlight filled the world whenever she surfaced from her pen and paper, but it might as well have been battlefield skies and the scent of cracked wood and breaking stone—the world falling to pieces beyond her reach.

A tankard slammed down on the table, sending both the journal and Cistine jumping. She wrenched her gaze up from the page she scribbled on, returning to the Talheimic tavern, to her own mead before her, and to Rozalie's face when she slid into the opposite seat. "You're early, Princess."

Early for what?

Then she remembered where they were, and why: this tavern where the walls practically sweated from the heat of the patrons, most of them Wardens. "Well, you're early, too." She braced her forearms on the journal and bent forward. "Ready to begin?"

"I don't think we need to." Rozalie's knee quivered against the table leg, rattling the entire frame.

Unease nicked down Cistine's spine. "Roz, what's wrong?"

"I just spoke to Viktor. He accepted my recommendations for which Wardens should populate the northern barracks—every last one. It's happening, Cistine. They leave at dawn."

She lurched back in her seat, the fire-gilded tavern pulsing at the edges of her vision as shock, elation, and anxiety flooded through her.

It's happening.

The fortnight was over. So swiftly and so slowly, it was done.

She looked around at the familiar walls. *Their* tavern, where she and Rozalie came almost nightly the past three months, reeling in Wardens by the tankard, paying for just enough ale to loosen their tongues, then plying them for their feelings about the treaty with the North. Such a careful winnowing process, so delicate Cistine often wanted to scream while she listened to yet another intoxicated Warden list off all the reasons the northern rat-rompers deserved whatever was happening beyond the Dreadline.

But there were some who'd been in places like Middleton who felt differently; men and women who appreciated the sacrifice Valgard was ready to make to halt King Jad's advances, and thought it was a shame Talheim could not offer aid in return with the straits so dire. Those of such a mind, Cistine and Rozalie took careful note of in the back pages of her journal.

And now all those names were deploying to the northern barracks.

"Did you hear me, Princess?" Rozalie asked.

"I heard you." Cistine numb lips struggled to shape the words.

Rozalie bent forward. "It's time, then?"

She dropped her gaze to the careful ledger she kept, scrawled in a mixture of royal cipher and Valgardan runes. She read it again as if it wasn't already committed to heart, pored over countless times in the past three months. Nearly every row was marked out, every task done, or at least begun—all but two.

The first, she knew how to complete. She knew the outcome, but it was not something to be rushed or trifled with. It would come at the proper time, once she confronted the final question, the last piece unsearched. And she could not find the answer to it within Talheim's walls; she'd tried, though she knew it was hopeless. There was no scrap of such lore to be found in their libraries.

To find out if it was even possible, she had to reach outside their borders again. And there was only one way to do *that*.

"Yes, it's time."

The words severed something within her—not a breaking, but a setting free. For the first time in three months, breath rushed easily into her lungs. Her chest expanded to its fullest, and her heart soared with terror, relief, and determination.

Rozalie shoved her tankard aside. "Be careful out there, Princess. I'll see you soon."

Heart thundering, Cistine watched her rise. "Win me an army, Rozalie."

Her smile was feral at the challenge. "Your Highness." In a whip of dark armor, she was gone.

Cistine gripped the edges of the table to push back from it—then hesitated. Weightlessness dropped through her, a dizzying plunge, her blood pumping so swiftly her face tingled.

She was really doing this. No more daydreaming, no more speculating, no more scheming in the dark. Now was the time for action.

The girl she was a year ago would've cowered from this choice. Even the woman who returned to Talheim three months ago, a traitorous portion of her spirit relieved not to march off to battle, would've considered everything she was about to do insanity to the utmost.

But now she'd done what she learned best to do: she'd trained, breaking down the barriers in her way, destroying her own ignorance and doubt. She spent three months tunneling not just into her kingdom's heart and history, but deep into herself, searching every shadowed crevice of her spirit like an ancient temple, all things consecrated deep in those secret caverns now brought to light.

This would not be easy. The danger was great, the risk as real as the wood biting into her palms, splinters welling up that precious blood in her veins. And she would have to give far more than that to see this through.

But she would do it—because it was right. And because no one else could.

CHAPTER FIVE

T HE CITADEL THRONE room was rendered differently in shadows. Cistine hadn't noticed it when she spied on the war council that first set her on the path to Valgard; but when she shoved the doors open and stepped inside tonight, the scents of the tavern on her dress and the tingle of nervous energy still rioting on her skin, she noticed every plunge of darkness, every glint of moonlight on the council table, the dais, the ivory, ebony, and porcelain thrones...and the man seated on that black throne, waiting for her.

She halted but didn't shrink back, toes curling in her boots. "Papa."

Cyril rested his chin on his fist, his elbow on the armrest. "I wondered when you were going to do it. Truth be told, I'm surprised you waited this long."

As one, their gazes fell to the precious item in her hand, the one she'd removed from her head and stowed in her satchel when she arrived at the tavern: a crown of rose and pearl, flecked in diamonds. Her birthright.

She turned it in both hands. "Who told you?"

"Viktor, by way of several Wardens who caught you reading particular books in the library. Once he told me which ones, it didn't take long to put together what you were scheming."

She blew her forelock from her eyes, scowling. "You ought to have Viktor removed."

"I'd planned on it once the rationing died down. I had a few alternatives in mind, but it seems many will be otherwise detained. Sent off to the northern forts, of all places."

Cistine regarded him warily, saying nothing.

Cyril reclined on the throne, spreading his hands on the armrests. "Tell me what I did wrong."

His tone, so hollow and sad when she expected anger, cracked her heart. "*Nothing.*"

"I know you've been unhappy since you came back. I tried to make the lords see reason, to give grace while you learned. If they said something that pushed you toward this—"

"I never intended to stay." She finally spoke the truth tucked away between the pages of Julian's last gift to her, hidden for months in secret plans and ciphers only she and Rozalie knew until now.

The King's brow creased. "All these things you've pushed for in the council meetings, the Citadel's reinforcements, the rotation to the north...you planned it all?"

She fought not to fidget. "I will *never* neglect my duties to Talheim again. But I have other duties, too, not just to this kingdom."

"Because you're a Key."

It was not a question, nor did he have an argument against it—she carried this burden because of his choice to forge their blood to the Doors. He'd made this her fight long before she was born, before the battle existed in any minds but the Bloodwights', festering in their communal darkness. "Talheim won't miss me, anyway. I've heard what the lords are saying. They'd still put more faith in the man they think I'll marry than in the woman I am."

"And is that woman leaving for the man she *would* marry?"

"Didn't the prince go to Mahasar for the woman he loved?"

A ghost of a smile traced her father's cheek. "Fair point."

"Thorne is part of it." A much larger part than she could articulate even now. "But it's more than that. They're our allies, Papa. They're *my* friends. I came back, I did my duty, I put Talheim first. But now it's time for someone to help *them*."

Cyril's stare bored into her. "And if I forbid you to go?"

Cistine raised her chin. "You can't forbid me. I'm of age."

His brow quirked. Not a king's look, but a father's.

"Besides," she added, much more carefully, "you promised me a year to go where I pleased. That year is not over yet."

Slowly, Cyril reclined again. "So it isn't."

She held his gaze steadily. "I'm asking for your blessing, Papa. Not your permission."

He was silent for so long, she began to fear Wardens would gather at her back. What would she do if this was a mark where her father would not compromise? What would they become?

"You don't have my blessing," Cyril said at last, every word dropping heavily through the thick air. "Only because I can't willfully support a plan that puts you in harm's way. But in this moment, you more fully embody what it is to be a Novacek than you ever have before."

Surprise yanked her head back, cocked in confusion when her father rose and descended the dais toward her.

"Being born Novacek makes you a princess, next in line for the throne. But being our daughter, *my* daughter, means you come from a line of fools who rush into danger for those they love...and who give their love to many, because they have hearts large enough for it." He halted before her, tilting her head up with the tips of his fingers. "I understand better than anyone what calls you, but even then, I know it's different for you. Deeper. Truer. Whatever ache I feel for the North is mere suggestion to yours."

A smile creased his face, full of love, sorrow, and understanding. And something heartachingly like farewell.

"When Jad threatened us, I was prepared to lay my crown on that throne and go to war again, like I did when he took your mother, and when my father and I stormed the North. I never had to because of you, because of Thorne and his people. If a king lets friendship and fealty of that depth go unreturned...well, then thank the gods he has a daughter wise and brave enough to right his wrongs."

He wrapped his arms around her, and Cistine leaned into him, breathing deep of the smell of cider and smoke in his clothes. The scents of home.

When they drew apart, it was the King's face that greeted her—not her father's. "I'll see what I can do about the lords. They'll learn to respect the woman who rides home triumphant. And I'll be certain they know she was braver to leave than they were to sit and gossip behind her back."

"And Viktor?" she asked.

"I'll keep him around for a bit. But I'll need those Wardens back when you're finished with them."

Cistine managed a small, tight smile, her heart picking up speed again. "Thank you, Papa."

He regarded her with a tilted head and narrowed eyes. "Have you spoken about any of this to your mother?"

She bared her teeth sheepishly. "I'm more afraid of her anger than yours, really."

"You will say goodbye to her."

Cistine dipped her head and kept it bowed even when her father's fingers brushed her cheek. Then he was at the throne room door, and through it, letting it whisper shut on its hinges.

The resonation of the clacking latch had not quite faded when Cistine straightened again, facing the thrones—her birthright, sealed and accepted in a vision months ago.

But not today. Today she was the Key, the balance prayed for, the answer sent by the gods to a question not yet fully-formed.

Lightning guttered and thunder purred beyond the throne room's painted windows when Cistine walked to the porcelain throne atop the dais and paused before it—the seat that had once intimidated her, that she hated and then came to crave.

Her future. Not her present.

A cool wind skirled through the Citadel as Cistine Novacek laid her crown on the seat, the echo of a long-ago prince's hands covering hers. Twice in as many years, Cyril had laid aside the duty of his station to go to war for what he loved, his crown remaining on his seat until he came home; and now Cistine set hers down and stepped back from the throne that would someday be hers.

She *would* take it. She would have it all—her birthright, her kingdom, her destiny laid at her feet.

But first, she would go to war.

⁕

Cistine strode through the northern tower in periwinkle stripes of lightning, stepping out of her flats, freeing her hair from its jeweled updo and releasing the clasps of her dress as she went. Ribbons unraveled and buttons undone, she shed the deep brown gown in her doorway, baring the clothing beneath: an armored breastband, reinforced leggings, and the remnants of a dress cropped to a shirt.

She went to her table first and whistled Faer up onto her arm. "Are you ready to see Quill?"

He bobbed and hopped down her arm. "*Quill. Quill, Quill!*"

"I thought so." Cistine laughed breathlessly and sent him to the bed. By the lightning's glow, she dug beneath it for her broken gauntlet, her augment pouch, and the jacket folded neatly into the crevice again; she drew it on and buttoned it across her front, lashed the pouch to her hips, and slid the gauntlet on. Broken or not, it would defend her, the black *Svarkyst* blade jutting out just enough to be dangerous to enemies. A those, she expected to have in plenty.

When she turned away from the bed, armored and outfitted, her mother stood in the doorway, eyes blazing like a hearth. "Your father told me everything."

Cistine froze and drew in her breath to explain.

"You'll need these." Solene slung a bow and quiver from her back and held them out, her jaw firm, her gaze clear.

Hands shaking slightly, Cistine accepted them. "You aren't going to tell me to stay?"

"I would be a poor mother if I hadn't noticed you kept one foot outside the Citadel door since you came back. We are not just royalty, Cistine. We are huntresses from a long line, trained to see every brush of movement in the meadows around us. My body may be soft, but my wits are not. I know exactly what you've been doing these last few months." Her mother's hands enfolded her cheeks, and her lips grazed Cistine's hair. "Thank you for enduring this pain to see to Talheim's needs before your own. I know not all our people will fathom the sacrifice you made, but I do. I did the same when my love went to war without me. And I will always be grateful for every precious second you and I had together."

Tears pricked Cistine's eyes when she and her mother drew apart.

"I will wait for you always," Solene vowed, and before the tears silvering her own lashes could fall, she strode from the room. The door fell shut behind her in a last farewell—a final blessing.

Swallowing, Cistine lashed on the weapons and whistled again; with Faer swooping up to her shoulder, she strode to her balcony and pulled the doors open, stepping out into the lightning-carved night.

There was no doubt the storm had strengthened again. Its utterings were brighter, its thunders louder when she went to the railing and spread her hands on it, studying the dark distance, the path northward—*homeward*, to the piece of herself she'd left behind.

She drew in deep breaths for bravery and exhaled her fear, looking once more at the glistening spread of her city below, slumbering in peace; a peace she and Thorne and their cabal had won together. A peace she'd spent three months shoring up, insuring against almost every possible outcome.

And now the horizon called her again.

Cistine peered up through her lashes at the Dreadline, a volatile boundary daring her to cross into the Bloodwights' arena and take them to battle. Then she plucked Faer from her shoulder and buttoned him inside the jacket; he didn't fight her, still croaking Quill's name.

"That's right," Cistine murmured. "We're going home, Faer."

She broke the wind augment against her body and brought it up along Thorne's jacket, along her inkings, until it consumed her.

The Princess, the Queen, the Key was coming.

THE LAND

OF

ICE AND WAR

CHAPTER
SIX

F ALL BACK! ALL of you, *fall back*!"

The shout burst from Thorne Starchaser's throat, every syllable ragged. Battle hummed in his blood and breath when he wrenched his gore-dulled blade from another augur's chest and bent double, hooking his hands under Aden's arms and dragging his wounded cousin behind the shelter of a boulder knocked free by earth augments—skinning the ground with a spray of blood in their wake.

Darkness stained the battlefield, the gloom of the endless night in which Thorne had prayed they would have some advantage among the shadows. He and Ariadne had discussed it for half a day before they decided when to make their move. But even with full moon's light and the advantage of an unexpected first strike, driving in like a blade against enemy forces at dusk rather than dawn, they were outnumbered and flagging.

And now the blows fell too close to Thorne's heart.

Aden barked with pain when Thorne shoved him back-first to the rock and stripped off the scarf that had kept frostbite from forming over his lips and nose during the long day camped in these hills waiting for the battle to begin. Now that it was upon them, he reeked of so much sweat and blood he wished he could strip shirtless; but those reinforced threads and the

Atrasat inkings below were all that kept him alive.

The scarf, at least, he could spare. He knotted it around the gushing wound on Aden's thigh. "You can't walk on this."

"*Try me.*" Aden's voice was guttural, bloodlust flashing in his gray eyes. Of all the warriors of Kanslar Court, he fought the most brutally in this battle and every one before it, unleashing the Lord of the Hive once traded for fine threads and politicking to become a Tribune. A future Thorne could no longer promise him, or any of them.

Sitting back on his heels, he gripped Aden's shoulder. "You *can't* fight on this wound. If you hadn't wasted your last healing augment—"

"*Do not* start this."

Grimacing, Thorne looked to his right—then shouted, swore, and reached for his sabers again, far too late; an enemy augur bore down on them, hands outstretched, lightning gathering in his palms and aiming for where they crouched in the boulder's shadow.

A furious shout rent the air and steel flashed as Thorne's High Tribune lunged down from the top of the boulder, *Svarkyst* blades whirling. The augur was too focused on bringing down one of the Chancellors; he did not react until it was too late, his hands separating from his body, falling into the bloodsoaked grass. Sander rammed his shoulder into the man's sternum, and with a deft whirl and a backhand thrust, impaled him through the gut and left him to bleed out.

"At last, he shows his face," Aden grated out when the High Tribune slid to his knees in the damp grass beside them.

"Oh, spare me, I've racked up twice as many bodies as you just battling my way down from the crags." Sander palmed blood from his dark, curly beard, face wan beneath its tawny complexion. "It's a massacre out there, Thorne. Like Braggos all over again."

"*Don't,*" Thorne snarled, watching Aden's face turn pale as soured milk. "Not here, not now. *Report.*"

Sander grimaced. "Your assumption proves correct yet again, Chancellor. There is a camp somewhere in the mountains. They're pouring out like desert beetles now."

Thorne lacked the breath even to muster another curse. This was the enemy's goal all along—this deep, dished valley between the spiny gray peaks of the Isetfell Range where their footing was solid while Thorne's forces still acclimated to the terrain. After weeks of tracking this band deeper into the mountains, he'd had no choice but to confront them here, suspicions of a hidden camp be damned; and what had his uncle always taught him but that having no choice was a guarantee of a trap?

"Thorne." Sander clapped him on the shoulder. "We need a command. Give me something I can carry out to the ranks."

Thorne turned his head from his panting, wounded cousin and winded High Tribune, toward the belly of the bowl where battle raged in earnest and warriors of five different Courts all blended: Yager's hunters and Tyve's poisoners weaving in with Skyygan's flighty shadows, Traisende's brawlers and Kanslar's death-gods mustering and driving in against ranks of augurs recruited by the Bloodwights. They fought in blinding augments and slashing steel, with primed bows and hacking axes, but was it enough? If any of these warriors were half as exhausted as Thorne, who hadn't gotten more than a snatch of sleep wondering who would fall in tonight's skirmish, who else they could not afford to lose—

He'd lost sight of his cabal hours ago. Even Ashe's mighty dragon, Bresnyar, was beyond his view, golden scales smeared with soot and stone dust to blend him among the hills before their ambush began. Only Aden had remained at Thorne's side, but the others...had they fallen already? Would this finally be the battle where he shouted for them to report and one did not return to him?

Fierce Tatiana, faithful Ariadne, reckless Quill, valiant Maleck, or savage Ashe—which one's death would finally kick his legs out from under him so hard he'd never rise again?

When they die, the blame is yours. The vicious thought raked through his mind, so familiar now he was powerless to parry its blow. *You brought this on them. On all of us. You chose this fate.*

"*Chancellor!*" Sander's voice cracked. "Give a command!"

Thorne's tongue cleaved to the roof of his mouth. Which order would save the most lives? Which loss was permissible to stanch the free-bleeding wound of these vicious augurs spreading across the northern front? Bravis, Benedikt, Valdemar, and Adeima and Maltadova had entrusted this line to him; and before his very eyes, it was breaking, the warriors of Valgard fleeing toward the cliffsides in terror-stricken retreat. The enemy augurs drew back, power spidering out from their bodies as flagon after flagon broke. Thorne's skin dewed not with blood or sweat, but with augmented water.

They'd drawn his people in close to the very heart of the bowl; now they would flood it and drown them all.

The realization introduced a strange calm to his taxed muscles, soothing the knots. Clarity showed him the way forward, to that back line of augurs, to stop this madness before it killed every man and woman under his command. To make right a portion of what he willfully broke three months ago.

Thorne plunged his sabers into the dirt and stood. "Get Aden out of here."

"Thorne," Aden began.

"No, enough. Sander is my High Tribune, you're a rank beneath him. If I die here, I die. But Kanslar needs leadership in my absence." *Better leadership. More worthy.* He pierced Sander with his fiercest glare. "We're closest to the crags. Get out while there's still time."

Jaw set but mouth wobbling, Sander yanked Aden's arm across his shoulders and pulled him up. Aden wrenched against his hold, fought to stand steady on two legs, but buckled instead. He gripped the boulder's rough face, anguished eyes fixed on Thorne. "Don't do this."

"It's all been borrowed time since Braggos, *Allet*. Time I owe you." Thorne gripped the side of Aden's neck. "You lead them out."

He stepped away, and Aden snarled, reaching for him again—

And then Quill's voice boomed out for the first time in hours, smoke-throttled, taxed by battle, carrying across the killing field.

"*Wildheart!*"

Thorne's feet latched to the rubbled earth, ears ringing, heart stilling. His weary mind did not make sense of that shout—a word none of them ever spoke except Thorne himself, bringing the will to live close to his heart in the darkest dregs of night.

"Wildheart!" Quill roared that Name like a banner raised high in the dark. "*Wildheart!*"

A beacon. A victory cry.

Then another voice took it up: Tatiana, never far from Quill's side. Then Ariadne, like a half-broken prayer. Then Maleck, deep in the thickest of the killing, and Ashe, with exultation and disbelief. Even Bresnyar, his trumpeting bellow sending men scrambling left and right.

"Wildheart," Aden panted, pointing.

Thorne whirled toward the peak of the shale hillside to the south, where the stamp of dawn's first rays showed they had fought all through the night, that they should be dead already.

But they were not. Nor would they die this day.

For there, above the carnage, silhouetted in blazing glory...the Princess had come.

CHAPTER SEVEN

WAR WAS SO much worse than Cistine imagined, worse than her darkest nightmares of King Jad and his Enforcers or her dreams of Kalt Hasa; worse than anything she'd seen before or ever would again.

It was the sheer amount of blood, its hot, iron scent thick above the hollow; the dead bodies heaped on the grass, mercilessly trampled; the screams of rage, agony, and despair; the clatter of blades and the boom of augments riddling the air with shards of power. She did not sense the *Aeoprast*, nor any power like his—no Bloodwights were here—but at the base of the dished valley's opposite slope, she felt augments breaking open in droves. A last strike aimed for Thorne's people below.

Vomit pulsed in the base of her throat. She wanted to turn away, but she couldn't flee from this.

Not from her cabal. Not again.

They were here. Though she couldn't see them from this height, this distance, they screamed her Name like salvation, a prayer pushing back the shadows. It meant nothing to the rest of the battle-gathered; no one else in the valley knew what she was capable of.

Gods, not even the cabal knew, not really. But she'd show them now.

A trace of the wind augment remained in her hands, the power that bore her across Talheim's lands, through the Dreadline with a force like being reborn, pushing her out of darkness into a new and terrifying world. Filaments of shadow and storm still clung to her body, tines of lightning singing over her armored jacket and leggings, singeing the tips of her hair. But when she'd emerged on the other side, she'd moved faster than thought itself, spearing like a fallen star straight to the maelstrom of augments and blood...to the sense of Thorne that beat underneath every pulse of her heart.

Wind brought her to them. Now it would serve her once more.

"Faer," she growled, "find Quill."

At her whistle, the raven was gone, clawing free of the jacket and diving into the massacre below. Cistine rallied the power of wind's destructive might in the palm of one hand; in the other, tucked behind her back, she unleashed fire, calling upon twin storms and taming them to her will. The wind tossed her hair and the fire turned her gaze to embers and her inkings to starlight.

Far below, at the base of the hillside, fleeing Valgardan warriors slammed to a halt and withdrew deeper into the valley, cursing and screaming. She let them fear her, their fright turning them back to the battlefield, to their floundering brothers and sisters; let them feel her wrath at every soul who retreated, including herself; and let them see that after today, fleeing was no longer an option.

They would all stand together—and fall together, if it came to it.

The augments braided, whirling around her body in a chaos fed by conviction, and with a shout she dropped to one knee and slammed her fist into the rock, releasing a roaring pillar of fire and wind that rivaled the light of the sun reborn behind her. Forging within herself a ray of hope, the Princess who promised peace, she released her power on the battlefield.

It soared out from her just as the enemy augurs unleashed a torrent of water from the north slope, an avalanche of waves gushing toward Valgard's ranks. Cistine bellowed with rage and poured out blast after blast of wind-borne flame, smashing into the water before it could reach their ranks.

Steam burst and mixed with the blood on the air, and she gagged on the fume of all different smells, the reek of dirty water and metal and new blood. But she kept rallying and releasing fire, pulling up more and more power from within her until the enemy's tidal surge became a stream, a trickle, a mere mist. Then it stopped altogether.

The augurs shouted in shock when the last of their power sputtered out, and Cistine stood, gasping and heaving, wiping her bloodied nose on her wrist. Fire still cloaked her, though the wind had gone out; and by the light of that fire, the Valgardan army rallied and slashed into the enemy flank again, their hope renewed.

Mustering what strength remained, she slid down the hill to join them.

CHAPTER EIGHT

THORNE TRULY BELIEVED he had nothing more to give. Chest splintered with fear for those under his command, exhausted from this and every fight before it, he had surrendered to the notion that all he had left was that final cleaving into the enemy ranks. Then he would be finished, and it would be over.

Until he saw her.

Suddenly he wanted to live, desperately, with every wild thud of his heart jerking him back into the midst of the warground where his warriors rallied, grouped together by the cabal on every flank. Bresnyar battled loose from a knot of augurs and took wing again, pulsing across the sky like an ember, shaking off his sooty covering and lighting up the dawn with vicious, golden power.

Hope.

Thorne ran with all his might, carving across the battlefield while the augurs swarmed down the opposite slope in a dark tide, robbed of their last mighty strike by Cistine's power, a sight like none he'd ever seen before. Tears still salted his lips from the awe of beholding her raw strength. When she descended the hillside to do battle, only one thought remained: he needed to reach her *now*.

She was easy to find, even in the fight. Their singing *selvenar* bond drew him toward her amid the carnage, hewing through with his *Svarkyst* sabers to where she burned enemies to dust, freeing their army from the anterior attack.

Saving his people. Saving *him.*

She stopped fighting when she saw him slide to a halt on the slick grass, a swath of death and blood between them. They stared at one another for a moment—the only pause the battle allowed.

With a bloodied smile, she shot toward him, and he to her. Feet away, she lunged to close the distance, and he caught her by the waist and spun them both, blade slicing behind him to take the head off an augur who attacked their left flank. Then he swept Cistine low and kissed her.

Around them, flames erupted. Wind screamed. Lightning broke open the sky. His sword thudded to the soil and his broad fingers splayed against her back and tangled in her hair. The world was cracking apart, but he didn't care. His soul was crying out, the song of something once caged set free. *There you are, there you are, I've been waiting for you. All this time, I've been waiting for you.*

The brush of her lips, the heat of her breath, the beat of her heart against his chest were the answer to every prayer he'd offered up these past three months. The iron-and-mint taste of her mouth told him what no dream had ever said, what no reminiscing could ever prove true: this was real. No mirage of battle, no hallucination on the threshold of Nimmus.

There you are, and here I am. And now we are.

She was here. His Wildheart was *here.*

And that was not a wonderful thing. It was terrible.

Thorne released her, eyes shooting open at a furious cry from ahead. He thrust her head down and crossed blades with an augur lunging at her exposed neck; she swiveled out from under his arm and slammed a wreath of fire toward another attacker coming from behind. Whirling to place their backs together, they dueled in tandem, sending the augurs to their knees, then to Nimmus. They pivoted again to face each other, and Thorne stabbed his blade into the bloody soil and gripped her shoulders. "*You shouldn't have come back.*"

"I know!" Cistine shouted over the boom of augments near the shale slopes. "I know why I had to leave, why returning was a terrible idea..."

"Then why did you do it, Wildheart? *Why?*"

She gripped his face and met his gaze fiercely. "This. You." Her voice cracked with wonder and love. "That's all the reason I need."

Bresnyar's ear-shattering roar split the sky, and Cistine and Thorne broke apart, looking up as one.

"The north slope," she murmured. "The strongest augurs are still back there. If we bring them down, will it end the fight?"

"It's worth a try." Thorne studied her pale face, the faint rings of blood inside her nostrils, and his heart lurched. "Can you still wield?"

"I need to catch my breath first."

"Do you have any other augments?"

She shifted, showing him the pouch on her right side. "Lightning, darkness, healing, and one more fire."

Thorne yanked her off to the side of the skirmish, stuck two fingers in his mouth, and whistled; when Bresnyar's answering snarl shattered the calamity of battle, he offered his hand. "Give me the fire augment. We'll bring it to you across the battlefield."

"Are you sure?"

"Trust me."

With a deft nod, she freed the fire flagon from her pouch and tossed it to him. "I'll see you on the other side."

Bresnyar dropped down beside them with a broad cut of his wings, flame churning from his throat. Ashe tilted from his back, offering Cistine her hand. "Honorable steed at your service, Princess."

"I beg your *pardon?*" Bresnyar growled.

"Oh, be quiet, at least I called you *honorable.*"

Cistine grabbed Ashe's arm and swung up behind her, pressing a kiss to the back of her shoulder. With a wicked grin and a shout, Ashe spurred Bresnyar back into the sky. And the race was on.

Thorne whistled again; a raven's shriek pierced the tumult of battle this time, and in a fluster of ink-black feathers Faer swooped into sight. Thorne locked eyes on Quill's trained bird and ran.

They all knew this pattern, had danced it dozens of times; Faer led him straight to Ariadne in the tangle of battle, her eyes blazing, chopped-short dark hair raking her jaw when she spun toward Faer's call. Thorne hurled a portion of the fire augment to her, and she caught it with a backhand twist of her arm, slamming her elbow into an enemy's jaw and catching his face alight. Her sword removed his head as she whirled, falling into stride with Thorne, shouting for Tatiana while they moved.

Dark skin glowing in the dawn light, she broke free of the warriors and lunged to catch the fire Ariadne heaved her way. Thorne shot forward to cover her back while she bolted after Faer, bellowing for Quill.

A continuum bound by power, the cabal traded the fire augment across the battlefield, dividing it among themselves and moving back through the ranks toward the enemy boundary line. If they could just get that far by the time Bresnyar crossed the sky—

Lightning arced out suddenly, so bright it lit a dazzling teal glow across Thorne's eyes; the dragon's thunderous roar might've been from shock or pain. Thorne slid to a halt, head cast back with dread, finding Bresnyar plunging from the sky, scales smoking.

"Thorne, catch!" Quill's voice came from his left, and Thorne reacted without thinking, spinning to palm the flames Quill hurled his way. Through the flock of dueling bodies, Quill slammed to a halt, shouting over his shoulder, "Mal, cover me!"

Sabers whirling in a mortal arc so fast they blurred, Maleck broke down the enemies careening toward Quill's back while he shattered his last wind augment and sent up a burst that lofted Bresnyar just high enough to slow his descent. Cistine and Ashe leaped down from the dragon's back with feet to spare, tucking and rolling upright, and Cistine clapped palms with Tatiana, taking a portion of the fire. Quill and Ariadne skidded up on Tatiana's right, Maleck bursting through the fray on Ashe's left, all facing the bleak northern slope and the augurs who'd nearly drowned their ranks.

The cabal was outnumbered by half a dozen, but those odds didn't matter. Nothing mattered but that they were *here*: Ariadne, Tatiana,

Thorne, and Cistine with fire in their hands; Quill wrapped in wind, braced forward on the balls of his feet, every muscle coiled; Ashe with Odvaya, Maleck with Starfall and Stormfury raised to strike; Bresnyar, hide steaming and tail bleeding, flames glowing in his gullet; and Faer, talons soaked in blood and tatters of skin, perched on Maleck's shoulder with wings ruffled, prepared for flight.

Cistine's head snapped left and right. "Aden? Where's *Aden?*"

"Hurt, but alive," Thorne said. And perhaps the same could be true for all of them now. For the first time since Braggos, he saw victory—a war that could be won. "Let's finish this, Wildheart."

Her posture settled, hands forming fiery fists at her sides. "Together."

With a bellow to break the world, the cabal attacked.

CHAPTER NINE

IN HALF A decade ruling the Blood Hive, breaking himself and others apart one piece at a time, Aden thought he'd witnessed all the ways life could surprise him when it came to conflict and viciousness and what lengths people would go to for survival.

But nothing prepared him for the sight of Talheim's princess, Thorne's *selvenar*, standing on that hilltop in a pillar of flame, a vision of Nimmus at dawn's first light. Nothing—not even his father's stories of the war between Talheim and Valgard—readied his heart for what it might look like when Middle Kingdom royalty took the battlefield.

Nor did he expect her to come straight to him, carried on a dying wind augment, before the last cry went up that the enemy was retreating.

She skidded to a halt in the shelter of a stone overhang where Sander had abandoned him and returned to the fight. Aden had only made it two steps after the stars-damned High Tribune before his injured leg crumbled beneath him. So here he sat, wretched and useless with just a blade in his hand, staring up at Talheim's princess while the wind settled and her wide eyes assessed him.

"Thorne said you were hurt." Her voice wobbled. "May I help?"

Aden grimaced. "Just a flesh wound."

"Your pants are soaked."

His neck heated. "It's blood."

"I know." Lips twitching weakly, she sank down and drew a healing augment from her pouch. "I wouldn't hold it against you if it wasn't, though. I think I need a change of clothes myself after all...*this*."

Reluctant laughter burst from him, dissolving into a hiss when she unbound Thorne's scarf from around his leg. The wound was both wide and deep; it would've needed stitching if not for the salvation of the warm white light swirling over her hands when she uncorked the healing augment and poured a kernel into her palm. He couldn't remember her measuring it so intrinsically before she left them; certainly not when she'd brought an entire stars-forsaken cathedral down on the *Aeoprast's* head.

Her fingers trembled when they grazed his wound, the gentle twines of white light going to work first on the vessels, then the sinew and muscle, then the flesh. Aden had seen this done so many times by his mother's steady medico hands, he didn't need to watch the power of the gods do its work. He watched the Key do hers.

Blood and sweat beaded on her face. Her gaze was downcast, focused on his wound with the intensity of a new Siralek fighter scrubbing off the sand of a first match from her hands. Aden thumbed a trace of something thicker and heavier than sweat from her cheek. "Your first true battle."

"No. I fought the *Aeoprast*."

"But this was your first battle against men who bleed like us."

Cistine raised her damp eyes to him and nodded slowly.

"You saved our lives. Saved your own life." The words were familiar, a litany spoken over new recruits heaving into buckets in dark catacomb corners before he taught himself not to care for their tearstained faces in a place designed to kill them. "The gods do not contempt you for this. War is brutal. Survival is ugly. *You* are neither of those things."

She heaved a deep breath in and out through rounded lips. "If I...if I need someone to speak to about any of this..."

"My ear is yours."

With a last uncomfortable tug, the light knitted him shut. Cistine withdrew her hands and grazed one along her arm, healing some unseen injury there. Gaze less frantic now, she offered her hand to him. "I missed you."

He let her draw him up and leaned with some regret against her when his leg spasmed, a memory of pain racing through the nerves. "And I you, *Logandir*."

Sunlight rippled and blackened, and Bresnyar settled down before them with a grunt, the others sliding from his back—all ruffled, bloodspattered, and limping, but alive. Another miracle to thank the gods for, just like after the Battle of Braggos. He'd never stop being grateful for it.

"Is everything all right?" Ashe demanded.

"Aden peed himself."

He choked. "*Cistine.*"

"I'm joking. It's just blood." She wagged her brows. "So he says."

Aden might've headlocked her and dug his knuckles into her skull until she begged for mercy, except the cabal was staring at them, silent and weary. And though it was not him who held their attention, the scrutiny still made his skin crawl.

A croak splintered through the heavy air, and in a blur of sleek black feathers Faer plummeted from the sky and straight into Quill's chest, knocking him back with a curse while those powerful wings beat in his face. It took him a moment to subdue the bird under his arm. "*Hello* to you, too, you miserable bag of feathers."

"*Hello, hello, hello!*" Faer squawked.

Aden nearly choked again. Quill dropped the raven with a jolt, eyes blowing wide. "*Cistine?*"

She raised her shoulders helplessly. "I read in a book somewhere that ravens can mimic voices, and he was *bored...*"

"You taught Quill's bird to *speak?*" Tatiana rubbed her blood-freckled cheeks. "We're lucky you didn't return him to us an augur and a scholar."

Faer took advantage of Quill's shock to alight on his elbow again, burrowing his head against the warrior's chest. "*Quill. Quill, Quill, Quill.*"

He inhaled harshly and bent his face to Faer's back. "I know, I know. I missed you, too."

Aden had missed *this*: those looks on their faces, the glimmers of hope shattering the dread. He missed them even more when they faded again, replaced by reserve while the cabal took in the sight of Cistine, standing before them in paltry armor, hands fanned out helplessly at her sides.

"Well," she said when the silence stretched on and on, "I'm back."

"Define *back*," Ashe demanded.

Cistine breathed in deeply. "I've been reading books on war—"

"Of course you have," Tatiana muttered.

"I know that doesn't make me fit for battle," she barreled on, "but it doesn't have to. *You* all did that. I've been training, I've been reading, and I'm ready. Whatever comes, we face this together, like we always have."

"We voted," Ariadne reminded her.

"Talheimic royalty doesn't vote." Cistine smiled crookedly, and Ariadne rolled her eyes. "*Please.* Let me help you save your kingdom like you saved mine."

A long silence, frigid with the absence of beating blades and falling blood, and Aden caught a flicker of some strange emotion in Thorne's eyes. Then Quill said, "We all know you're going to stay whether we want you to or not. Might as well be with us...safety in numbers."

Cistine's frown proved this was not the welcome she'd hoped for—not the one Aden expected, either. But he understood it, the same way it made sense the reserve with which they beheld him after he returned from Siralek.

It wasn't his place to tell them how they ought to feel about this; nor did he feel like drawing any attention to himself.

"You came alone?" Ariadne asked.

Cistine nodded. "I only had the one wind augment. And with the Dreadline, moving Talheimic forces into Valgard is impossible right now. Our Wardens would be ripped apart."

Convenient for Talheim, though he didn't dare say that either.

Tatiana stepped forward at last, eyes narrowed on the gauntlet Cistine wore—the gift Aden gave her for Darlaska. "What is this? It's *mangled*, Cistine, what did you do?"

"I didn't do anything! Salvotor—"

"Still blaming him for all our problems, are we?" Tatiana clicked her tongue and tugged the gauntlet off. "*Here*, let me fix it. If I can."

Smiling hesitantly, Cistine flicked her gaze to Quill. "Have you found Pippet?"

The question jabbed into Aden's chest like a blade, his eyes shooting to Quill's. The memory of Pippet's face, already touched somewhat by the cruel grind of passing time, surfaced and disappeared like ripples on a pond.

"We only saw her once since Stornhaz fell." Ariadne laid a hand on Aden's shoulder. "But we haven't stopped searching."

Cistine nodded faintly, and charged expectancy hung in the air when she looked to Maleck, tracing the nervousness in his face. Aden had watched that caginess spread like a disease through Maleck's veins, sealing off his trust, forging this flighty thing in him. In battle, he remained steady; but between conflicts, he was a quieter man, withdrawn, the look of a cornered animal in his eyes, like the world was hunting him and he *knew* it.

Cistine swallowed and forced a smile, stepping toward him. "Hello, Darkwind."

He recoiled, taking himself sharply out of her reach, and she flinched back, too. Happiness soured into discomfort again, and they all looked away from each another.

Thorne cleared his throat first, mercifully breaking the silence. "Bravis and Benedikt will have questions about a Talheimic presence here...what it means for all of us. We should return to the camp before word reaches them from someone else's mouth."

Cistine smoothed her hands down her legs, keeping her gaze carefully averted from Maleck. "I'm ready."

Of that, at least, Aden had very little doubt.

∽⁀∿

They returned by dragon's back to the camp, a makeshift sprawl of stone-gray canvas tossed over innumerable poles, their ends speared to clefts in the tiers of ruthless Isetfell rock Aden had trouble sleeping on at first. It no longer bothered him, but he could see it disturbed the princess. Her wide eyes took in the barren scape of the mountainside, then the population of unfriendly quarters, and paled. "You've all been sleeping *here?*"

"Oh, these accommodations are new," Tatiana said. "Before this, we didn't have much cover at all."

"We've been chasing the *mirothadt* north for weeks," Quill said. "Or maybe they've been leading us somewhere. Hard to say after today."

"*Mirothadt?*" Cistine echoed.

"The criminals," Ariadne said. "The cruel unloved."

Cistine rubbed her arms. "Do they know about this place?"

"No, thanks to this canvas." Tatiana tweaked one of the thick threads weaving the covering together. "One pull, and all this comes down around us. The camp blends into the rock perfectly. It was a gift from *Heimli Nyfadengar.*" Familiar pride and sadness wove in her tone at the mention of her father's inventor guild, hiding in the wilds of Blaykrone territory.

"All of you need to rest," Thorne said. "Cistine and I will join you after we report to the Chancellors."

She smiled unhappily and reached out to squeeze Ashe's gloved hand, then followed Thorne toward the largest vault of gray canvas where the maps and war tables were screened off from view. Aden had spent his share of early days and long nights gathered at those tables over the past few months with Thorne and Sander; he was glad not to stuff his head with any more knowledge today.

Shouts followed the cabal below the canvas roof, questions about the night's battle in Jazva Chasm and whether it was victory or another defeat. Ashe finally barked at the curious warriors to shut their mouths—they'd receive an official report in time—and Aden was glad for that, too. As the Tribune of this very territory, Spoek, it was his responsibility to quiet unrest and smooth out the ranks with a firm hand. But he was too stars-damned tired and achy from bloodloss to do his duty.

A fine Tribune, indeed.

They all settled at last around a dying firepit and built it back up again, and by the light Aden assessed his cabal: all wounded, though none seemed in need of a healing augment like him. It was sorrow more than scars that seamed their faces, exhaustion flowing from every angle of them. Tatiana settled cross-legged on the ground with Cistine's gauntlet in her hands, exploring its mechanisms with a pinched, nauseous look on her face; Quill perched on the log above her, his knees knocking her shoulder, fingers absently stroking Faer when the raven settled on his thigh. Ariadne bent forward, head in hands, blood flaking from her fingers. Ashe sat close to Maleck, arm and leg pressed to the length of his, and Maleck…

Aden did not like that look in his eyes, distant and clouded with memory; or the way his boot heel tapped erratically on the stone, as if at any moment he'd lunge up and start to pace; or how shakily he tore his leather-bound journal from his pocket and angled away from them to sketch in it, giving his hands purpose.

He did that often before the last war, too, when he was still an acolyte of Azkai Temple.

"I'm just going to say it," Quill broke the tense silence, "since I know we're all thinking it: Cistine wielded two augments on that clifftop today, didn't she?"

Maleck flinched, his pen skimming off the page. Ariadne picked her head up sharply, looking left and right, but there was no one nearby.

"It could've just been fire." Defensiveness touched Ashe's voice. "She's been a powerful augur as long as she's been wielding, you've said that yourself. You're the one who trained her."

Quill shook his head. "I didn't teach her *that*. What she was doing, that was fire and wind, I'd bet my life on it. And I've only seen power like that once: with the *Aeoprast*."

Maleck pocketed his journal and lunged to his feet, pacing behind the log seats, dragging his hands through his braids. Ashe shot Quill a look of pure reproach, which he ignored or didn't notice, bending forward to stoke the flames again.

"What does that mean?" Tatiana directed her gaze, and the question, toward Ariadne—formerly a *visnpresta* acolyte, the most knowledgeable of them all about augments. "For her—for this war?"

Ariadne stroked her thumb along her lower lip, ruminative gaze cast to the flames. "I'm not certain. It's entirely possible the Key is fortified to withstand the might of many augments, a strength the Bloodwights replicated by...other means." She flicked a glance at Maleck, trembling slightly while he made another tight circuit around the fire.

"I wonder what else she could do. How far and deep this goes," Tatiana mused. "And how in *Nimmus* she harnessed it that much in just three months."

"If that *is* what happened," Aden said, "Cistine will tell us when she's ready. It serves no one to speculate."

"Mal." Ashe caught his hand when he strode past her. "Come back."

He gazed at her for a long moment, blinked, then shook his head sharply. Breath gusted from him, and he dropped back onto the log, leaning into her side. Concern surged like bile in Aden's throat, easing slowly into gratitude for Asheila Kovar and what she did for his brother not by blood, who carried the weight of this war across his shoulders.

Boots trudged on rock, and the cabal straightened when Sander joined them, flinging himself unceremoniously on Ashe's other side and bending his hands to the fire. "Predictable of you all, leaving *me* to sweep up the mess in the Chasm while you flew back on your dragon."

"The glory of being High Tribune," Tatiana said. "You wanted the title. Welcome to the table." Sander gestured rudely at her, and she shot him a tired smile, their easy camaraderie a reminder that, had Tatiana and Quill not been blended hearts sworn to one another long before they even knew the bond between them as love, she might've become one of the twenty-six women who guarded Sander's *valenar*.

Less than twenty-six now, Aden reminded himself. Only two went with Mira to retreat in the mountains. Few of the others still lived among the lines, sworn to serve a High Tribune whose life was a prize among the *mirothadt*. Aden had helped Sander send the others off on pyres.

"I see your leg didn't fall off." Sander's jab drew Aden from his melancholy. "More's the pity."

"And you still have the power of speech after all this time. A shame."

They swapped vicious smiles over the fire.

"How many did we lose?" Ashe asked—the very question Aden had dreaded ever since Bresnyar carried them from the battleground.

"Fifty-eight," Sander said, "with more on the brink. We managed to carry off most of their augments, but not the bodies this time."

Tatiana blew out a long breath and banded her ringlets back from her brow with both hands. "So. Not quite as bad as Braggos."

"But bad enough," Quill said roughly, and Faer nipped his fingertips.

"Wherever that *mirothadt* camp is in the mountains, we need to root it out," Ariadne said. "It's too great a stronghold. Like Stornhaz all over again."

They were all silent for a time, the pop of kindling all that filled the quiet. Then Aden said, "I'll return to the Chasm at dawn, burn our dead, and search for any hints of where the enemy came from. Or in which direction they fled."

"I'll go with you," Ariadne offered, and Aden nodded. With fifty-eight dead to pray over, he needed her at his side.

"I don't need to tell you two to be careful," Sander warned, "but there was an ill sense about that place when we left today, worse than the feeling after battle...darker. It made my skin crawl, I tell you."

"What did it feel like, precisely?" Ariadne's tone was careful, a blend of the strategist's keenness and the *visnpresta's* alacrity searching out what lay beyond mortal sight and comprehension.

"Like being in the temple below the Blood Hive again."

Tatiana shivered, fingers separating from the gauntlet, and Quill squeezed her shoulder. Maleck's callused palms rasped together furiously, and he bent into the firelight. "Something is coming. A change."

Ashe rested a hand on his back, meeting Aden's gaze across the fire. She didn't need to speak; as with every day since they fought together in Siralek, her intentions conveyed to him with clear certainty even in silence.

There were no coincidences on these killing fields. And with Cistine's arrival today, there was little doubt the change had already begun.

CHAPTER TEN

THE WAR TENT with its map-littered table and circle of braziers was attended already by a pair of Chancellors, hollow-eyed and frowning, who did not look up when Cistine and Thorne arrived until Thorne said, "Is silence any way to greet royalty?"

Both their heads snapped up, and to Cistine's surprise, a smile followed the shock breaking in Bravis's weary gaze. "I don't believe it."

"Shouldn't you be dining and reclining in your peaceful kingdom?" Benedikt's greeting surprised her less.

"Shouldn't we all?" she countered. "That's why I'm here."

Bravis's eyes flicked to Thorne. "What of defending the Key? As I recall, that was the reason Talheim didn't offer aid at the start of this."

"We spent most of the winter fortifying and securing the Key's safety. And safety is why I came back." Cistine met the Chancellors' scrutiny with a level stare. "We all know the Key and our kingdoms won't truly be safe until the Bloodwights are dealt with."

Benedikt's scowl softened slightly. "I see your wits have not dulled during your absence, Princess Cistine."

"And what of aid? What of an army?" Bravis asked. "Has Talheim sent those as well?"

"That's a more difficult subject. Whatever aid Talheim could send won't make it past the border."

Bravis leaned his fists on the table. "That stars-damned storm."

"Did you pass through it?" Eagerness touched Benedikt's tone.

Cistine's skin prickled with the memory of that unnatural tempest digging into her inkings like Bloodwight claws struggling to subdue her. "I did, with a wind augment. But an unarmored Talheimic army never could. Do you know how to break through it?"

Bravis shook his head. "We haven't had the time or strength to spare learning its intricacies. Too many battles being fought elsewhere."

"Speaking of battles," Thorne approached the table and spread his fingers along one of the maps, beckoning Cistine to his side with a tilt of the head, "we routed the enemy forces from Jazva Chasm today, but their numbers were beyond what we reckoned."

"An ambush?" Benedikt asked.

"Reinforcements funneling in from the mountain pass."

Bravis paled except for twin slashes of furious color on his cheekbones. "Where in Nimmus are they *finding* this fresh blood? Before Braggos, we nearly had them stymied!"

"Apparently not." Thorne's tone was curt, his eyes cutting to Cistine, then leaping away. "Or if we did, they're recruiting again."

"Recruiting from *where*?" Benedikt snapped. "They've divested our prisons already, where else could they find *bandayos* mad enough to join their stars-forsaken cause?"

"There are other kinds of prisons. Slave markets, devastated villages, and cities the Courts forgot. I don't think we can underestimate the cruelty our kingdom deals its own people by choice or negligence...or how they might support a cause that gives them a taste of what they might consider retributive justice."

Bravis's jaw flickered. "You're full of opinions as usual, Thorne."

"I'm glad you noticed, because I'd like to offer another." He traced the dark maw of Jazva Chasm to the west. "What we saw today only confirms what I've suspected: there's an enemy stronghold somewhere in these mountains."

"This again?" Benedikt scoffed. "How many times—?"

"What sort of stronghold?" Cistine interrupted, heart thundering with unease.

Thorne's eyes turned to her again. "I'm not certain yet."

"You're not certain because deep down you know there's no sense behind it," Bravis argued. "Why should they sulk within a mountain bastion when they've taken *Stornhaz*? Our city is all the fortress they need!"

"Separate armies could wait in separate places." Thorne had the flat tone of a man used to making this point—and always being cut off at the knees. "It's quicker to reinforce the northern ranks *from* the north rather than the heart of the kingdom."

"But we're not discussing reinforcements, we're discussing a *stronghold*," Benedikt retorted. "Somewhere fortified, likely established some time ago. And we would know if they'd built such a place in our own borders."

"But we saw at the beginning how cunning the Bloodwights are," Cistine pointed out. "Maybe they sent forces ahead to secure a bastion in the mountains. Maybe that's where they built the siege towers, even." Bravis and Benedikt exchanged a glance. Thorne's cheek ticked, fighting a smile. "It makes sense strategically to have more than one stronghold in a kingdom you're trying to conquer."

"I'd forgotten how insufferable the pair of you can be when you have one mind about something." Bravis kneaded the bridge of his nose with a thumb and forefinger. "Young rulers will be the early death of me."

"You give us far too much credit. The war will take us first," Thorne deadpanned. "How does the front hold elsewhere?"

"It doesn't look promising." Benedikt sketched the territory borders with his fingertip. "To the west, Spoek's Tribunes of Yager and Skyygan have resorted to enclosing the fighters in a wide falcate and pushing them back. But if they give even an inch of ground, the *mirothadt* gobble it up within hours."

"And the east is no better," Bravis added. "Traisende, Kanslar, and Tyve hold the line, but barely. They're ready to crumble any moment."

Thorne frowned down at the map. "And the south?"

"Maltadova and Valdemar are hard-pressed not to find themselves trapped between the enemy and that storm. It's a dance—they can hold no ground for too long, and their augment stores are low as it is. Right now, they're focusing their efforts on snatching up children and hiding them away in the Vaszaj Range."

"The Bloodwights are still capturing children?" The words emerged breathless from Cistine's lips.

"Not the Bloodwights themselves. Their criminal allies," Bravis growled. "No, those masked *bandayos* have not been seen in battle since the war began."

The report rang, not like a cymbal of relief, but a warning knell. Cistine had to grip the table to keep herself steady. "*What?*"

"They haven't been in a single skirmish." Thorne's stiff tone matched her unease. "Not one."

"Considering what havoc they wreaked in the siege on Stornhaz, I count that a gift," Benedikt said. "We're better off with them shut up in the city, letting their zealous acolytes do the grim work."

"It is some small relief," Bravis agreed.

One look at Thorne, and Cistine knew he did not share their relief. Nor did she.

"The Chasm was a success, by the sound of things," Bravis went on. "We break camp at week's end and send half our forces to shore up the defenses near Nordbran's border."

Thorne dipped his head. "I'll see to it." He turned to go, eyes storming with thought, and Cistine followed him.

"Princess," Bravis called, and she halted, looking back. "I hope you came with your father's permission. I won't be held responsible for what happens to Talheim's sole heir when she comes to these killing fields of her own accord, seeking the same war-glory as her father."

Thorne jolted a step back toward the table, but Cistine motioned him down with a cut of her hand, holding Bravis's stare. "I know precisely what I'm risking. But so did you when you all signed a treaty agreeing to stand with us against Jad. I hold my kingdom to no lesser duty than that."

She ducked through the thin canvas screen, Thorne in step with her. A low chuckle rumbled through him while they moved between dips in the canvas, heavy with snow, hanging over lonely fire pits and bedrolls spread on the hard rock. "Stars, I'd forgotten how magnificent you are when you stand your ground."

"And I'd forgotten how insufferable Valgardans can be."

"Not all of us, I hope."

She checked his hip with hers. "You're only *occasionally* insufferable."

"Diplomatic as ever." Thorne rubbed a hand back through his silver hair; it had grown long again, spiking wildly behind his ears and licking the nape of his neck. "I wish they'd heed me about that stronghold. I've been asking to investigate it for weeks. But it's always the same pointless battles instead. We aren't striking them where it *matters*."

Cistine halted, cold dread washing down her spine. "Could the Bloodwights be absent because of the false trail you laid? Hunting me?"

He paused as well, brushing his knuckles against the round of her cheek. "It's possible. But let's leave speculation for the morning. Right now, I think we're missed."

And it seemed they were. The entire cabal, Sander included, was gathered at a fire Thorne went to directly like a favorite meeting place; they all looked up at once, their faces carrying that same blend of trepidation, despair, and exhaustion as on the battlefield. Just like then, no one seemed excited to see her.

A gulf of loneliness opened through her chest. Not one embrace from them, not even a smile. They looked at her like an untrustworthy stranger.

Ashe patted the seat next to her, and Cistine settled at her side, trying not to feel stung when Maleck shifted infinitesimally away like she carried an odious stench. "Where's Bres?"

"Hunting, most likely," Ashe said. "We all would've starved weeks ago if not for him. He can bring down a herd of caribou faster than Tatiana destroys a buffet."

"If you're referring to that last feast in Stornhaz, we're all lucky I did." Tatiana patted her middle. "I'm still surviving off the cakes I ate that night."

Aden snorted, and Ariadne laughed outright. Thorne wagged his head slowly, poking the fire, which had gone dim as if the cabal was too preoccupied to stoke it.

"So," Tatiana added. "Why are you really here, *Yani?*"

Anxious energy spiked in Cistine, though Tatiana could not have possibly guessed her mind. "I'm here to help my friends win their war and protect their kingdom. *All* the kingdoms, really."

"And you thought putting yourself in danger was the best way to do that?" Quill's retort hung heavier than the shadowy rings beneath his once-bright eyes.

"You're all putting yourselves in danger every day. Why should I risk any less just because of what I am?"

"What you are," Tatiana scoffed under her breath. "Which *part?*"

"What do you mean?"

"She means the part where you wielded two augments at once today," Quill said. Ashe slapped him upside the head, but it was Thorne Cistine looked at, who stopped tending the fire and raised his eyes to hers.

Slowly, she bent forward, trapping her hands between her knees. "Do you think anyone else realized?"

"Most were too busy fleeing," Sander said, "and they would be deserters or deadmen now if not for you. I'm not eager to call your actions into question, let it be known."

"No one is calling anyone else into question," Thorne said evenly. "This is not a tribunal."

"No, but I'd still like to know what in Nimmus that was," Quill insisted.

Cistine chewed the corner of her lip. "It started with Reema. When I fought her in the sewers, I wielded two augments." Their breaths snagged all at once. "Then again, in the cathedral, with the..." Maleck tensed, and Cistine broke off, looking up at him. He didn't acknowledge her, his gaze fixed on the fire, but blank. Unseeing. She swallowed. "The night I left Stornhaz."

"You've been practicing." As usual, Ariadne's sharp mind found the truth unspoken. Cistine nodded.

"That's not why I gave you those augments," Quill said.

"What did you expect me to do? Go home, sit on my throne, and wait to become Queen while you all suffered and died in battle?" she snapped. "I am *not* going to inherit an unallied kingdom and write all your eulogies when I take the throne. I made all of you a promise, a long time ago, that I would stay and fight and we'd build peace together. So I'm going to find a way to destroy the Dreadline and bring Talheimic forces into this kingdom."

Thorne's head snapped up. "How?"

"I don't know yet, precisely. But Rozalie has a group of Wardens already waiting at the northern barracks who believe in the treaty. We spent the past few months weeding through the ranks, searching for anyone we could trust. As soon as we're able to break through that storm, they'll come to Valgard's aid."

Sander whistled lowly. "Now, that would be a sight."

Cistine couldn't coax volume to her tone, but passion burned and dampened her eyes. "I'm a warrior in this cabal the same as the rest of you, and this is my battle as much as it's anyone's. More, even, given what I can do."

"What you did..." Thorne trailed off, shaking his head. "Cistine, I've never seen anything like that."

"If we didn't have the Bloodwights' attention before, we will now." Tatiana looked up from tinkering with Cistine's gauntlet. "You're the only one besides them I've ever seen wield more than one augment at a time."

Sander inclined forward, chin in hands. "I wonder how *many* you could use at once."

Ashe cursed under her breath, and Aden shot a warning look at the High Tribune. But Cistine held his curious stare, her pulse slowly kicking up. "I don't know. I've never tried more than two."

"And now you can't," Ariadne warned. "It would be too dangerous with the Chancellors so desperate for a way to level the odds against the Bloodwights and the *mirothadt*."

Cistine scratched the hair at her temples. "I'm sorry I didn't tell you about the augments, or...what I was planning when I left. But I'm here now, and I'm going to fight for Valgard. And for all of you, because you're my family as much as Talheim is. I hope you'll respect that. We don't need a different war on our hands."

No one spoke for several heartbeats. The fire popped and crackled, and wind moaned among the passes.

Tatiana, finally, cracked a smile. "Nimmus' teeth, I missed this."

"It's not as if we could pitch you through the storm and back into Talheim," Ashe sighed. "Quill was right, you're safer with us than out there in the wilds, anyway."

"Especially when we don't know what the Bloodwights are up to," he added gruffly.

Cistine leaned around Ashe to meet his eyes. "You mean the way they haven't been seen since the siege?"

Aden nodded. "Nothing bodes well about this. They should be laying waste to our forces, yet they refuse to show their faces in a fight."

"Well, they're criminals and *visnprests*, aren't they? Not warriors."

"That's what Bravis and Benedikt claim," Thorne grunted. "But they could end any threat of fighting much more quickly if they faced us themselves. And they have to know that—they've proven themselves strategic in the past."

"So the question," Sander murmured, "is what could possibly be more important than finishing the conquest they began with the City of a Thousand Stars?"

Maleck shot to his feet and hurried away, vanishing among the canvas roofs. With a heavy sigh, Ashe squeezed Cistine's shoulder and followed him, pausing to kick Sander's tailbone and eliciting a yelp and a wounded curse when he pitched off the log onto his seat before the fire.

Shaking his head, Thorne rose as well. "Make sure you all sleep tonight. Bravis and Benedikt intend to move camp and divide our forces soon. I need you rested for that fight."

While they all broke apart, he beckoned to Cistine with a jerk of his head. Heart aching for Maleck, for Ashe, for all of them, she followed him.

They wove through pockets of the Valgardan army, other fires where warriors gathered in quiet conversation or dull-eyed silence. Cistine's stomach lurched when they passed the makeshift medico's tent where the silver burn of healing augments was absent; instead there was a reek of blood and tinctures and strong spirits, and quiet sobs riddled the air.

Thorne followed her gaze to the broad span of canvas under which the wounded lay, and his frown deepened. "We used the last of the healing augments a month ago. The *mirothadt* stole the rest, along with all the blood augments, not long after Stornhaz fell. They need them to corrupt the children."

Throat tight, Cistine shook her head. "This feels like a nightmare."

"And I wish you didn't have to see it." Thorne halted before a drape in the canvas tugged down to create a makeshift alcove, a semblance of privacy like the war tent. He lifted it aside and nodded her through.

His sleeping space was sparsely furnished, just a beast pelt for a bedroll, a three-legged stool against the rock face at the back, a lonely brazier and a rucksack spewing dark sleep clothes and a small kit for cleaning weapons across the rock. A sturdy post in the center, driven deep into a slit in the stone, forged the illusion of the high ceilings he was used to in the Den and his apartment in Stornhaz.

It smelled like him. Like home.

Cistine wandered to the sheer black rock that made up the back of the alcove, smoothing her hand along its face where thin white scrapes stood out like peeps of bone. "What are these?"

"One mark for every warrior I've lost."

Tongue knotted, she turned and truly looked at him for the first time since the battlefield. He slouched against the tent post, head, shoulder and hip to the wood, eyes half-lidded yet clear and knife-sharp in their focus— fixed on her. Cistine's cheeks warmed at the quiet scrutiny of his stare, and she threaded a loose strand of hair behind her ear, averting her gaze. "What?"

"I thought I'd never see you again."

The admission was soft like a secret, and her vision swam at the anguish in it. "Thorne..."

"I wish you hadn't been called back here. But I'm so stars-damned *glad* you came."

She blinked, her tears evaporating. "You are? Back on the battlefield, you said—"

"I know. I know what I said." His voice roughened. He dragged a hand through his hair. "It's complicated. All of this. The way I feel when I see you standing here, the way I felt when I saw you on that ridge...and I don't have the right to feel any of it."

Frowning, she stepped forward and reached for his hands. "Thorne, you have every right to feel whatever you do."

He snatched his fingers from reach, shaking his head. "No, I don't. Not after what I did. I don't deserve to have everything I want. And you being here...I don't know if it's grace from the gods, or punishment to prove that."

Unease prickled down her spine. "Thorne, what did you do?"

Agonized eyes locked with hers. "I failed my kingdom by loving you."

Cistine's numb arms swung loose at her sides. "*What?*"

He peered down at her, eyes flashing heartbreak in the canvas gloom. "I spent months convincing myself that if by some grace of the stars, I ever won the privilege of holding your heart, I would find a way to balance the weight of that with my duty to my kingdom. But when the time came, when that choice was before me in practice...Cistine, I didn't even hesitate. I sent *you* to safety before I ever thought of Valgard's wellbeing, of what my kingdom needed from you, as the Key, with the power you possess. What it needed *me* as a Chancellor to consider." He dragged a hand back through his hair. "I broke my oath that I would always place my kingdom first."

His brutal honesty left her shaking. "I never asked you to put me before your kingdom. I wanted to *stay*."

"I know. And I should have let you. More than that, I should've called on the treaty and demanded aid from Talheim."

Shock bristled along her hackles. "You know that's not possible with the Dreadline."

"I'm speaking of *before*. Instead of sending you back, I should've been the one pushing to bring them here. But I didn't, because I saw how that notion terrified you. Again, I put you first. And I've lost countless warriors because of that."

Her heart clenched, but anger rode a hot current behind it, flinging itself against her ribs. "Talheim wasn't ready for this fight. Not without armor, not when the treaty is still so fresh."

"Would that have been your argument if the battle was against Mahasar?"

"That's not fair! Jad's forces are one thing, the Bloodwights—"

"This!" Thorne jabbed a finger at her. "This is the same argument I've had with myself, over and over, and that's what makes this so stars-damned difficult. It shouldn't *matter*! We both signed our names to that treaty and we *knew* it wasn't just about stopping Mahasar. Those words we put our oaths behind were for the benefit of *both* kingdoms. We lied and danced around the truth to send you home, and we were wrong. Valgard needed Talheim in this fight. It still does."

"I know that! It's why Rozalie and I did what we did with the Wardens—"

"But they aren't *here*. And I've listened to you make treaties and dance with politicking enough to know you're biding your time to decide what to do with that storm. It could be broken down tomorrow, or never. And if it's *never*..."

"Then you don't have Talheim, you have *me!*" Cistine snapped. "Is that enough? Are you *satisfied* with that?"

"No!" Thorne's voice cracked in a shout. "Because you are not an army, you're a princess! You are *one person,* and that does not measure up to all the lives lost because of my selfish choice!"

The breath gusted out of Cistine's lungs. She'd been less winded the times Quill punched her in the gut. "You think I don't measure up?"

"I didn't say *you* didn't, I said—"

"One person, for all the lives lost." She stepped nearer to him, hands forming fists at her sides. "So if *my* people came and fell in their stead, that would've been enough? Talheimic lives lost instead of Valgardan...that's what you think when you look at me?"

Thorne's jaw shifted, anger blazing in his eyes. "It's not the number of pyres we burn, it's the principle. When the time came for battle, when the words in that treaty mattered most, you couldn't bring yourself to fulfill Talheim's end. And when I saw what it meant to you to face that prospect, I chose you over Valgard."

"So this is *my* fault now—*my* weakness?"

"It's both our faults, and that is the entire problem. If you're putting Talheim's needs first, and I'm thinking of yours, then who protects Valgard? Who protects *them*?" He jerked his chin back toward the camp where his people lived and suffered, awaiting the next battle.

And he was right. Though she'd always planned to return, she hadn't intended to involve Talheim—never to the extent the treaty warranted. All she had was a desperate plan cobbled together from books on war theory and hopes yet to be explored...and a question, hovering at the tip of her tongue, one she'd planned to ask him the moment they were alone.

But this *was* his answer: his heaving chest, his sparking eyes, his agony in choosing her over everything. Her kingdom over his.

She couldn't ask him. Not now, perhaps not ever.

"I'm sorry," she said, and Thorne settled his weight, shoulders loosening, surprise flitting across his face. "You're right. Neither of us fought for Valgard when it mattered...but I'm here now, and I need you to believe in me. I want to find a way to break the Dreadline and bring help. But for now, there's just me. Can we find a way for that to be enough?"

His eyes softened that way she could never bear. His head fell against the tent pole again. "I'm afraid if we do, then it means the gods brought you back just to punish me for letting you go in the first place."

Tongue tingling with secrets, Cistine offered her hands. "Come here."

He obliged this time, taking her hands only to guide her arms around his neck. Then his fingers were against her back, digging desperately into the sturdy jacket folds, pulling her flush against him. He buried his face in her neck and wept in great, broken sobs; in exhaustion and agony and rage, relief and joy and terror. For his fallen warriors, for those who lived to face more danger, for the hopelessness of the battle—and for her, returned to the heart of it all.

The sun's angle through the camp hinted midday when Thorne at last composed himself, released her, and unbuckled his weapons, belts, and armor, hanging them from the tent post. Cistine leaned back against the cold rock, hands folded behind her haunches, and marveled at the sight of him carrying out life as a warrior Chancellor—the man she always knew him to be. He didn't speak until he disrobed to a simple shirt and pants, kicked off his boots for woolen socks, and stoked the brazier. Then he settled cross-legged on the patchy furs and turned his palms upward on his knees—the same invitation she'd given him.

Cistine knelt before him and pushed on his shoulder until they both lay on their backs, arms folded behind their heads, gazing at the canvas roof. "How are the others, really?"

"Tati and Ari have been without equal during this war." Ardent fondness laced Thorne's voice. "They've been the cabal's spine more than ever. Without them, we—*I* would've crumbled long ago."

Cistine smiled. "That's what they do best."

Thorne's cheek ticked in a fleeting smirk. "Quill is...unsteady. He has been ever since Stornhaz. He's pushed himself halfway to Nimmus more times than I care to count. Likely more times than I even know, but trying to wrestle honesty from him these days, I'd have better luck prying prey from a Viperwolf's jaws. And Maleck isn't much better. You saw him. He hardly eats, barely sleeps. When he does, the nightmares plague him."

A shudder wrapped through Cistine at the memory of Maleck's eyes, vacant with only fear blooming in their depths. "What about Ashe?"

"I owe her my life many times over. She and Bresnyar are a reckoning force. But it's no surprise her focus is less on Valgard's fate and more on keeping Maleck sane."

Cistine rolled onto her side to face him. "And Aden?"

"Aden is...everything a Tribune ought to be. But there's something missing." Thorne rocked his head to look at her. "He comes to meetings, he gives his opinion, but I can tell he's holding back. He never argues counterpoints, just agrees with my word. Or Sander's, if he's feeling obstinate that day."

"It must be difficult, inheriting a title just to carry it into war."

"It is," Thorne said. "And I doubt if any of us knows what we'd do until we're standing in it, and then...the proper choice isn't always clear."

Cistine curled closer to his side, resting her head above the strong beat of his heart, and changed the subject. "Thorne, what was it Bravis mentioned...what's Braggos?"

Beneath her cheek, his chest stopped rising and falling. Then he was up, sliding from beneath her, reaching for his weapons and armor again. "I have...there are things I need to see to."

"I'll go with you," she offered, propping herself up on one hand.

"No." His reply was swift and sharp, but the next words softened when his eyes found hers. "Chancellor duties, it's nothing you can help with. You need to rest...I know you're exhausted."

That was true; but the look on his eyes gnawed at her even after he ducked from the tent.

She wasn't the only one keeping secrets.

CHAPTER
ELEVEN

THE SKY WAS grim and gray, thick with the promise of snow, when Aden and Ariadne returned to Jazva Chasm for the bodies of their fallen friends, leading an oxen cart loaded with cut lumber for the pyre through rime ice and drifts of snow.

This had once been a fertile desert east of the Ismalete River; Aden still remembered what it had looked like when his parents brought him here to visit as a boy, full of vineyards in the foothills and burnished bronze sand below—before the Bloodwights fled north with their stash of augments and stomped out ice in their wake, ridding themselves of pursuing warriors desperate to retrieve those precious flagons.

Now all they had was this scarred tundra and the memory of wine festivals and long summer dances, and this new dance they did, which Aden despised: where the *mirothadt* sent the addicted, reckless children to scour the killing fields for any flagons left behind. Like hounds baited by the scent of blood, the young acolytes pushed themselves through harsh climes and over rough terrain, hunting any sense of augmentation. And if they found it...

Stars help him. He still had nightmares of what Braggos had looked like when he and Quill returned to tend the fallen, their penance for that fight; what the children did to those cadavers, how ruthlessly they tore into them to reach their augments. Yet here he was, standing with Ariadne on the same cleft where Cistine had appeared the previous sunrise, knowing he had to do this. It would be worth it if they caught even one child in the act and saved them.

Especially if that child was Pippet.

Aden's hands felt empty without her, his heart a cracked-open cavity where failure and grief fought for dominance on any given day. He could still hear her wild laughter when he taught her hold breaks and she mastered each one, see her smile sassing him from across the room when she pirouetted from his reach, feel the tightness of her embraces knitting pieces of his spirit back together. But they'd lost her. *He'd* lost her, and with that he watched Quill's joy and Tatiana's hope die—a whole future gone up in smoke.

He was her mentor, her guardian, like Quill before her. Two generations of the cabal he'd failed to protect.

He went today for her as much as anyone, trudging through the drifts, the cold biting beneath his armor; for Pippet and any child like her they might have a hope of saving. They had captured so few since the war began, and those they dragged away from the battlefield did not survive the strain of their bodies being parted from augments. Maleck was the only one Aden knew who ever endured it alone, and even he was deathly ill when he'd returned to Stornhaz from the front lines in the war against Talheim.

They would have to be weaned carefully, the medicos said, fed a bit of power here and there until their bodies could manage. What troubled Aden most was that the Chancellors were reluctant to spare the augments to wean the ones they did rescue. They needed more flagons to win this war and save the children—and those were in smaller supply than hope these days.

Even before they reached the snow-swept crevice, Aden knew it was too late this time; he could see it in the tracks of fresh blood along the snow. But it was Ariadne who said it, perching her hands on her waist and squinting down into the valley.

"They've already come and gone." She sighed and shook her head. "I pray Sander and the others gathered all the flagons. Come, let's give our brothers and sisters the end they deserve."

They worked silently, building the pyre the same way they had prepared meals and washed dishes and muddled through Thorne's hastily-written ideas of Sillakove Court a decade ago; a Tribune's son and a *visnpresta* acolyte constructing strategy from the madness while Thorne and Saychelle had curled up on the sofa and dreamed of broader and grander schemes. Much had changed since then, too much for Aden to fathom most days. But not the steel in Ariadne's spine or the way she brought method into the madness of the world. Even moving the dead made more sense at her side.

"How are you faring?" he grunted while they carried a pair of bodies to the heap. It was a question he tried to ask the cabal every day—to show them he cared, that he was trying to make up for the five long years when he wasn't there to ask, and the five years before that when they didn't look at him the same anymore.

"Fair. Exhausted," Ariadne panted. "The same as anyone."

Aden heaved a man's corpse gently onto the pile. "I know this isn't what you hoped to be doing after the trial, after...everything."

"True. I'd rather be training *visnprestas* to fend off attackers and how to blend augmentation and swordplay. But I swore to the True God I would do whatever he asked of me, and if it's to fight alongside my family to my last breath, I'll do it gladly."

"Still the same noble, pious Ariadne."

"Still the same stubborn, mother-hen Aden."

He didn't bother arguing. She always laughed off his attempts at dignity where caring for the cabal was concerned. He would never forget the birthday she'd gifted him an apron, of all things; he'd worn the seams straight out of it.

"I spoke to Ashe last night," Ariadne added while they carried corpses across their shoulders to the heap. "She's worried about Maleck...about how he reacted to Cistine's return."

Aden grimaced. "So am I."

Ariadne slid the woman's body onto the pyre and straightened, ashen as the corpse she had just surrendered. "It's clear all he sees when he looks at her now is how her power resembles his brothers'. He's losing sight of everything but them."

Aden wiped blood from his hands and inhaled deeply, chasing out the reek of old meat and iron from his lungs. "Perhaps, given enough time with her, he'll see things differently."

"Don't be a fool. Cistine will do what she's always done, and train, and continue to test the boundaries of her abilities. If that made Maleck desperate before, what do you think will happen when she doesn't stop? What do you think he'll do if it happens on the wrong day?"

The breath gusted from Aden in a rush; Hive instinct pricked his chest, turning the snow to sand and reminding him of what it was to live in darkness so long everything became a threat—and what became of a man who lived in such a place too long. "Have you spoken to him?"

Ariadne shook her head. "He doesn't want to broach the subject of the Bloodwights with anyone, not even me. That's why I'm telling *you*—you're the closest to a blood brother he has. You've always been best at bringing mercy to his madness."

A humorless smirk carved Aden's face, painful where it hung. "Not in the last decade. I betrayed him as much as anyone. He needs someone like Mira, not someone like me."

Ariadne gave him a long, measured look full of dangerous thought. "Mira's not here." Then she jerked her head. "Let's finish and pray."

They worked in silence apart from the grunts of strain when they heaved the last of the dead warriors onto the heap. All fifty-eight Sander had numbered, all rived and ripped apart by children clawing over them in search of augments during the last day and night. Indignation and rage festered at the center of Aden's spirit, pulsing around a wound two decades old—hate that had never died after Maleck came home like this after being broken over and over by his stars-damned brothers.

He wanted them dead.

Aden took up the flint, struck a cloth-wrapped torch to light, and met Ariadne's eyes. She nodded, but even then, hesitation deadened his arm.

They deserved better. They all should've been celebrating Chancellor

Salvotor's conviction still, after everything Ariadne, her sister Saychelle, and Aden himself gave up to see it done. And yet they found war and death instead; all that sacrifice had not brought peace, just another sword.

Blinking against the mist in his eyes, Aden tossed the torch onto the pyre. That was all it took: a kiss of flame, and their dead friends became an offering. Ariadne drew one of her sabers, stabbed it into the soil, and knelt before it, hands to her thighs, head bowed. Her lips moved in soundless prayers.

They had done this so many times in the last three months—too many pyres, too many dead. But each occasion was his honor, his privilege, his penance to stand watch over the horizon while Ariadne said the *visnpresta's* prayers for the fallen: for their Names to be remembered, their lives to be inscribed in the True God's memory, their families to be guarded and their love to live on. For them to somehow find Cenowyn, not Nimmus, now that the Second Death claimed them.

With those thoughts crowding close among the stone slopes where they'dp all nearly lost their lives the day before, Aden laid a hand to the four-point compass pendant hanging over his heart. Not for the first time during this sacred ritual, he thought of his father.

Kristoff Lionsbane had been nothing less than a giant, a legend, a hero in Aden's eyes for all his childhood; then he was presumed dead, his legacy twisted to one of betrayal and defamation of the Courts so no one would ever dare look too closely at what truly became of him when he disappeared and Tribune Marcel rose to replace him. For nearly twenty years, he'd rotted in the pits of Kalt Hasa while his orphaned son gathered guilt and scars beyond tally. And then, with freedom so close, he chose a noble death buried under the mountain, saving Thorne, Cistine, Quill, and Tatiana.

There'd been no one to say these prayers over Kristoff's passing as there'd been at his *valenar* Natalya's; no one to remember his Name or bless his life. Even when his death was feigned at the beginning of his interment, no one came to say a prayer with Aden, or Maleck, who was like Kristoff's second son.

Slowly, Aden drew his saber and pushed it deep into the cold ground.

Ariadne twisted her head when he knelt beside her. "What is it?"

"I'd like to say a prayer." His voice was raspier than he'd expected. "For my father."

Ariadne's brow creased. She took his hand. "For Kristoff."

In the cold quiet of the empty Chasm, they whispered prayers caught up into the smoke, a sacred offering to the gods. Though Aden himself never gave more than fleeting thought to the divine beings who'd granted them augments, who watched over the affairs of men with keen but distant eyes, somehow it eased the stitch in his chest to echo Ariadne's words. It unsnarled another piece of the knot that sat in place of his heart ever since Cistine gave him his father's necklace and sealed, once and for all, every doubt of his fate.

"I can see why you do this every time," he said when the fire began to wane, and he and Ariadne climbed stiffly to their feet. "There's consolation in the offering."

"Because it's the right thing to do." Ariadne swung up her blade and slid her palm along its flat side, wiping away sod and snow. "I can't fight for these people anymore now that they're gone, but I can give them a *visnpresta's* sendoff to whatever end they face. So I'll give them all I have— my blade in life, my words in death." She sheathed her saber with a sharp *click*. "I think that's the balance I've sought all these years."

Aden smiled. "I'm glad you found it."

She flashed up a hand suddenly, turning north. "Did you hear that?"

The smile dried with his tone. "The sound of your inability to graciously take a compliment?"

A sudden scream like shearing bone ripped through the Chasm, and a pair of shadows peeled off the high walls at the end and shot toward them with broad, sharp wingstrokes.

They were not natural figures, no great birds of prey or predators of mountain or sky—Aden knew it the moment he laid eyes on them. Too sleek, too dark, too cumbersome, they moved not like beast or man, but a stitched-together mosaic of the two. Their flight was unsteady, their frames lanky and heavy, and their faces, annealing into shape against white clouds and snow-heavy skies...

His stomach caved at the wrongness, a misshapen form of what might've once been a young man plastered against the hook of an eagle's mandible and a raptor's beady eyes.

The beak parted and a scream ripped from the creature, half-deafening Aden and sending him rocking back on his heels in revulsion. Ariadne shouted, "What in the *stars* are those?"

Then the shrieking, vicious creatures were upon them.

CHAPTER
TWELVE

FOR JUST ONE morning, Asheila Kovar wanted to rest. To forget the war and her nightmares and the perpetual feeling of ice under her fingernails, like she might wake up any day on the augmented tundra and realize she'd dreamed the last twenty years; that she was still twelve years old and fighting *against* Valgard, not for them.

She'd gone back to that place so many times awake and asleep over the last three months, sometimes the present blurred and her drowsy memories of Prince Cyril and Lord Rion were clearer than the uneasy faces of the warriors in the camp. Some mornings when she woke, it took more than a few moments for the visions of snow and blood and an augur boy with dead eyes to fade away.

Last night was one of those nights, fire joining the ice in her visions, the smoke of a burning city with sealed gates and flagrant walls scalding her nostrils, blood dripping between her fingers. When she woke, she laid there under the weight of Maleck's arm and wrestled alone with the new fear of her princess wielding two augments at once.

Maleck was up long before dawn as well, the nightmares in his gaze dancing with hers, so they came down to the communal bathing spring accessible only by a steep path—or more swiftly and safely by dragon's back. And now, hours later, there was no denying it: Maleck Darkwind took the longest baths of any man Ashe had ever met. She herself was washed, blood scrubbed from both their sets of armor, and dressed again while he was still tucked behind the hot spring rocks. She even took time to riffle through his pockets, looking for that journal he always carried and blocked from her view whenever he sketched in it. But he'd left it in the tent this morning, stashed away like he expected her to snoop.

Thwarted, she sprawled on rocks warmed by the water and her dragon's breath, and all she wanted was to sleep again. But every time she closed her eyes, her vision flashed gold; instead of lying on her back on the pebbly shore, she watched fish winnow beneath the sun-gilded water.

Cursing, she lurched upright at last. "Bres, do you mind?"

The dragon flicked her a bored glance. "What have I done to irritate your delicate nerves today?"

Ashe rubbed her temples with her thumb and forefinger. "That...that *thing* keeps happening. Where your vision cleaves into mine." It had happened twice during the battle in Jazva Chasm; the first time had kept them grounded, the pain and dizziness in Ashe's head too great for her to risk being on his back. The second had been just before that augur's lightning seared his scales and knocked him from the sky.

In battles before that one, it had happened almost too often to count.

"I have no control over it, *Ilyanak*. Its power lies within the bond branded on your palm." Bresnyar stooped his muzzle toward her hand, mercifully free of her tight gloves for once. "Wingmaidens are taught from childhood how to align and sever the bond to their dragon's mind at will."

"And you know I don't have any of that training."

"True. But I can't cut your end of the bond. I'm not forcing you to watch me fish, you know."

Groaning, Ashe flopped back on the shore. "Then stop fishing."

She watched through Bresnyar's eyes as he returned his focus to the river's surface. "Do you wish to eat tonight or not?"

"I'm not going to survive that long if I don't catch more than a few hours of sleep."

A flicker like gold lightning dancing across her eyelids, and then she saw herself, splayed on her back, arms tucked behind her head, armor drenched in morning dew. Dark circles ringed her eyes and fresh cuts marred her skin from yesterday's fight. There was blood in her hair she'd missed washing off, blending with the reddish shade of the locks and flaking into her armored scarf. Through Bresnyar's vision, she watched her own hand slide from under her head and chafe that well-worn cloth—a gift from Maleck at a time when she'd felt so far beyond redemption.

Bresnyar settled beside her, his great head on the shore, blowing steam to warm Ashe's body. "You miss the way things were before."

She let her hand fall and her eyes slide open; pain bored into her skull, then abated when her sight became her own again, the gold of Bresnyar's vision floating away. "I miss not having a gods-forsaken war hanging over our heads."

"Life was simpler then wasn't it? Mad kings, poisons and spies, angry friends, dances with one's own specters..."

Ashe swatted his snout. "You know what I mean."

He chuckled, a warm sound like coals turning in a deep forge. "These lines are fortunate to have you. Few have fought in harsh winters before. Fewer still won those battles. The insight you bring is valuable."

"If that were true, we'd be winning." Ashe left her hand on his nose, the gods-forged Wingmaiden rune on her palm pressed to his opalescent scales when she rolled over to face him. "Did you smell Pippet at all in the Chasm?"

Bresnyar's lips peeled back from his teeth. "These Bloodwights and their people, they all smell the same, *Ilyanak*. Wild and ancient and strange. Like Maleck."

His name swung into her like a punch to the side of the head, and she slammed her eyes shut against the knowledge that they were so similar, Maleck and the brothers he despised...the men he fought to bring down like they were his mistake to make right.

She glimpsed herself through Bresnyar's vision again: pain twisting her features, her hand curled into a fist between his nostrils. Blinking her eyes open, she lurched to her feet. "Get up. We need to train."

He stretched to his clawed feet and shook all over. "Steel against fire?"

"Mind to mind." Ashe faced him, arms akimbo. "Teach me how to control the...the cleaving."

Bresnyar's bony brow arched. "Is that what we're calling it now?"

She rolled her eyes. "Just show me."

"It cannot be shown, but it can be taught." He took two steps back from her. "The Wingmaiden must learn focus at all times, to meld her sight with her dragon's or banish its gaze when needed."

Ashe spread her feet and curled her hands twice. "I can do this."

"Then I will show you what I see. Force away my sight...if you can."

Before Ashe could muster a retort, her vision exploded in golden shards, senses roaring with not just sight, but sound and sensation: the weight of Bresnyar's scales laid over her body like armor, the sight of his face before hers, then hers before him, the cacophony of birdsong and the moan of the wind, the whisper of fish flirting in the water—

She slammed to her knees, grabbing her head as pain dug jagged claws into her skull. Bresnyar snarled and withdrew, the barbs of his sight peeling out until the ground swam back into focus before Ashe's watering eyes.

"God's bones," she rasped between gritted teeth, "it shouldn't be this difficult! I mastered the sword when I was *twelve*!"

"And Ileria mastered this at nine, and the sword at seventeen," Bresnyar said. "It's not a question of talent, simply of roots."

Ashe climbed slowly back up, every muscle tight. "Again."

"*Ilyanak.* I hurt you."

"I don't care. If I keep cleaving during battle, one of these days I'll get us killed. *We* need this. Two wings moving together. Help me, Bres."

He grimaced, dipping his head. "Brace yourself."

Ashe dug her heels in and set her weight forward. "I'm ready."

They both knew she wasn't. But it was better than sitting on the shore, thinking of this war; better than thinking of Cistine wielding two augments, of Pippet out in the wilds somewhere, of all the things they couldn't fix today.

They practiced for nearly a half-hour, with little success, before the sound of sloshing drew her attention from her dragon. On her feet still—but barely—Ashe twisted toward the cluster of rocks where Maleck had retreated to bathe. For all the time he took, he looked no better than when he'd disappeared around the bend. The circles under his eyes were no lesser, and as for the rest of him...

"Your hair looks disgusting," Ashe remarked. "Did you even wash?"

He simply stared at her, disheveled and dripping, body scar-marked and warrior braids hanging limp against his chest. Briefly, his gaze flicked to the bottle of rose oil in his hand—then lowered.

Ashe sighed. "Get back in there, you beautiful braided bastard."

Not even a smile, but he sank back until the water covered half the scar above his heart. With a parting stroke to Bresnyar's snout, Ashe slid onto the rock behind Maleck and poured a generous helping of oil onto her hands, working it into his scalp with deep, careful strokes, from his tense brow to the nape of his neck. With every pass of her fingers, he relaxed into her touch more and more, spreading his arms on the rock shelf and reclining to give her better access to his head.

"You're not going to believe what Tati said to me when I asked her why she even had this," Ashe said. "That she was happy to fight like a barbarian, but not to smell like one. *That* was her worry. But that's our Tatiana, I suppose." A low groan rumbled in Maleck's chest, and he leaned his head further back, slipping deeper into the water under her ministrations. Ashe lathered her hands again and tackled the thick mire of blood and sweat caked along his hairline. "Luckily for me, I won't have to worry about your stench driving me out of the tent tonight. Unless I wake up with my face in your armpit again."

His shallow snort barely rippled the water, but it was something. Ashe exerted gentle pressure on his temples, just enough to tilt his head back and give her leverage to his mouth. "There you are."

With her lips an inch from his, Maleck's eyes popped open. "You aren't wearing your gloves."

Ashe froze, leaning back to catch his worried gaze. "I don't keep them on while I *bathe*, Mal."

He surged out of the water, out from under her hands. "Put them on."

She glanced at Bresnyar. The dragon gave a shrug of his powerful shoulders. "Maleck—"

"*Please*, Asheila."

The crack in his voice picked at an equal wound along her heart. Ashe held up her palms. "All right. I'll go find them."

By the time she tugged on the padded leather gloves, Maleck was dressed again, all the trappings of a death-god strung across his body; yet he drooped like the last note of a dirge while he belted on his daggers and slid into his sword harness, every line of his body slanting into morbid memory. Gone was the man with whom she'd flirted in Astoria, the one who'd squared up to Rion Bartos. The months had aged him. Braggos had carved away at him. All the battles before and since took a chip, a cut, a fragment. Piece by piece, this war against his brothers was stealing him away from her.

Ashe met him at the shore, twisting her hands side to side to flash her gloves. "There. Better?"

Maleck took both her hands and brought them to his brow, a shaky breath going out of him. "You are my strength."

She might've argued that once; but seeing how bent he was now, how the weight of the war barreled over him night and day like a tide, she felt it. Felt how heavily he leaned into her, how moments like today were only stars in a dark vault, flickers of hope for what the world could be when this was over. *If* it was ever over.

She stepped nearer and slid her hand around the back of his neck, bringing her mouth up toward his to breathe life back into him, bring him back to her...and Bresnyar let out a low, throaty growl.

Ashe tensed, jerking back. In one smooth motion, Maleck drew Starfall and twisted it in hand, spinning up the shore toward the dragon. Bresnyar faced back toward the steep slope up from the spring. Toward the faraway camp.

"What is it?" Ashe demanded.

"Aden. Ariadne," Bresnyar said. "Their fear."

Maleck was already running for the path like his life depended on it.

CHAPTER THIRTEEN

Tatiana Dawnstar was finally asleep again, curled in the shelter of Quill's body and dreaming of her father's tinkering shop and Kadlin's prestigious offer of a place in *Heimli Nyfadengar*—and of a house in Blaykrone territory burned to ashes—when the screaming began.

For one traitorous moment after her eyes opened, her body still refused to move. She lay prone under the heavy press of Quill's arm tucked around her waist, nausea crashing through her body and cold sweats breaking along her limbs, and wondered what would happen if she just pretended to sleep through this latest crisis. If she pulled the threadbare blanket over her head and blended with the rock, let someone else manage it.

She hadn't wanted any of this. Not the cold, or the hunger, or the constant fear of the future. Not this stars-damned war. She'd been ready to hang up her swords and go to Blaykrone with Quill and Pippet, her father and Kadlin, to make a life as tinkers and students and Vassora. To have peace won by a decade of running in the wilds; to be *happy*. But fate didn't ask her what she wanted back then, and it wasn't asking now.

Quill's arm slid away, and he rolled upright, ignorant of the cold wind kissing his bare torso when he planted his hands on the rock and frowned through the hive of canvas rooms and corridors toward the edge of the rock. "What *now?*"

Then one woman's shout, louder than the rest: "*Chancellor Thorne!*"

Tatiana's wide eyes shot to Quill's, confirming this was not just another nightmare.

Ariadne.

Tatiana was on her feet in a heartbeat, nausea forgotten, shedding her last once-beautiful sleepshirt for the armor beneath. Quill yanked on his armor and banded on his metal fingers, the last invention Tatiana had and likely would ever make; then they ran, still shrugging on their weapons, all the way to the edge of the camp.

At the first sight of Aden and Ariadne through the crowd of gathered warriors baying for answers, Tatiana's stomach plummeted clean through her legs to the frozen rock, splashing bile up into her throat. There was no mistaking they'd faced a fight that ended badly; their armor was ripped along the sleeves, baring hints of the Atrasat inkings below, and blood striped their faces and necks. Aden held his side as if his ribs had given in; Ariadne favored one leg and bent double, gasping for breath.

Tatiana and Quill skidded to a halt beside them at the same moment Cistine arrived, windswept and pale, with Thorne on her heels. He went straight to his wounded warriors, a hand on each of their shoulders. "Are you all right?"

"We'll live," Aden panted. "We need to speak to you *alone.*"

Thorne straightened, turning to the crowd. "All of you, disband! Back to your posts!" The frightened onlookers dispersed at the Chancellor's order, but it took far too long. Tatiana's nerves sparked like stars blinking out of existence, setting her jittering in place so wildly Quill grabbed her arm to keep her still.

At last the final curious, concerned warrior was gone, and Tatiana and Cistine chorused, "*What happened?*"

"The Chasm was an ambush," Aden growled. "Something was lying in wait for us."

Thorne's icy eyes narrowed. "Some*thing?*"

Ariadne and Aden exchanged a look that set Tatiana's hair on end. It was searching, confirming between them what they saw—as if without reassurance, they might doubt it was real.

"It wasn't human," Ariadne said. "Nor was it a beast."

"Some blend of the two," Aden added. "I don't know how it was possible. But it flew, and it *spoke*."

"It wanted our augments." Ariadne's voice cracked. "Thorne, it sounded like a child."

Boots slid on rock, crashing to a halt. As one, the whole cabal looked toward the trailhead behind them. Maleck stood at the mouth of the path to the communal bathing pool below, still as a deer scenting a hunter. His sabers hung limp in his hands, eyes distended, nostrils flaring faintly with every breath. His gaze was frantic hazel light smoked with shadows.

He'd heard them. And whatever those words meant to him...

Ashe appeared at his back, heaving from the long run, eyes going at once to Aden and Ariadne. Worry ripped through her face at the blood on them, and she took a step forward, breathing Aden's name.

That same moment, Thorne launched into action. "Tatiana, Quill, see to their wounds. Maleck and Ashe, with me."

Cistine banded her arms tightly around herself and watched Thorne stride away. Maleck and Ashe turned to fall into step behind him, and as their ranks closed, purpose jolted through Tatiana like sobriety through a haze of mead. She took Ariadne's arm across her shoulders and nodded to Quill to do the same for Aden. "Let's get you to the medicos."

Cistine fell into step behind them, and no one spoke until Aden and Ariadne were seated on a pair of low cots between those wounded from the battle in the Chasm and those sick with infection inside the medico's tent.

"Are you sure you saw what you think you saw?" Tatiana asked while Quill snatched a pail of ice water and two thick cloths from a medico's hands. The man cursed after him—something about how those were in short supply after Braggos, and Quill had best be careful with them, or stars save him—and then her *valenar* returned, stormy-faced, and plunked the pail down between the cots.

Aden scooped up one of the rags, balled it tightly, and pressed it to his ribs. A low groan escaped through his gritted teeth. "I'm certain. Not even in my worst nightmares have I ever seen something so grotesque."

"You said it sounded like a child." Quill's voice was flat. "Was it Pippet?"

Ariadne flashed him a narrow look, pressing her own wadded cloth to her bruised hip. "She is not the only child suffering in this war, *Allet*."

"Was it *her*?"

"No," Aden replied firmly "Not her."

Quill sat back, and some of the fear broke in his gaze, letting a shard of horror through. "Children. With *wings*."

"And an eagle's beak." Ariadne shrugged helplessly when Tatiana scoffed. "I know *precisely* how it sounds, and yet..."

"We saw what we saw," Aden finished.

Cistine bent forward, hands cupped to her mouth. "What is *happening* in these mountains?"

"I don't know." Tatiana twisted to squint through the forest of canvas, her heart sinking further with every beat. "But I think I know how Thorne intends to find out."

Grim, choked silence descended, and she settled a hand on her queasy belly. She hated all the ways her friends were hurting, her kingdom was breaking, and she couldn't fix them. Not as a tinker. Not as a warrior. Not in any way.

Another medico wandered by, this time pausing to examine Aden's black-and-blue ribs and Ariadne's bleeding leg. He shook his head and shot them both tired smiles. "You'll live. After Braggos, this must feel no worse than a shallow cut, eh?"

Quill warned him off with a look, but it was too late. While he scampered away, Cistine rubbed her arms, looked around at them all. "What happened at Braggos? Why is everyone talking about it like a legend?"

So, she remembered that tiny blot of a city on the Valgardan map Tatiana taught to her as a frightened princess newly fallen into the north's cruel hands. She remembered, but she didn't *know*.

Aden's face was bloodless. Ariadne turned her head away, eyes falling shut. Quill tipped his hair shakily across his head. "That's...not a story you want to hear, Stranger."

"You should know me better than that by now."

"I know you better than most. And my word stands."

Cistine and Quill glared at one another, and of all the things she hated in the world right now, Tatiana hated that look most.

"It's somewhere none of us wants to go back to," she intervened. "And if you love us, *Yani*, you won't ask again."

That silenced Cistine, swift and sure. But that look in her eyes, equal parts cleverness and determination, kept Tatiana on edge. The court gossip was not yet satisfied; and stars help whoever she decided to wrestle that story from.

Tatiana only knew it could not be her; she had much different, much more terrifying things to worry about.

Judging by the marks on Aden and Ariadne, they all did.

CHAPTER FOURTEEN

A SMALL PATH curved around the stone hill in whose shadow the army had established its war camp. The dark stone windbreak with three free-flowing streams pouring down its face was ideal for keeping the warriors, oxen, and horses watered even on the coldest nights. Those streams, fed from some spring deep in the rock, created the only sound besides the plod of their feet when Thorne, Ashe, and Maleck ascended the trail, letting the camp fall away behind them.

Thorne didn't want to do this. Taking a knife to Maleck's chest would be kinder. But he had to know. This was what it meant to be Chancellor...to put the needs of the kingdom before the needs of one, even if that one was like a brother to him. Even if it meant danger for someone he loved. He'd learned that truth the hardest way imaginable.

Thorne's feet snagged on the rock. He braced one hand on his waist and rubbed his mouth with the other, but it wasn't enough to wipe the damning questions from his lips or keep the necessity at bay. Slowly, he turned to face Maleck and Ashe. "I need to ask you a question, *allet,* but it may take you to a place you hate."

Ashe grimaced, laying a hand on Maleck's back. He wavered, face paling, the scar down his right eye a striking ridge cleaved against his skin. "What is it?"

Thorne forced himself to hold that flighty gaze, to remember why he had to do this. "That creature Aden and Ariadne faced today, do you know what it was?"

Maleck stared at him, blinked sluggishly, and did not speak.

"They said they were like creatures and children," Thorne added when the silence lengthened. "Something stitched together of the two."

Maleck broke down without warning, his shoulder to the mountainside, and nearly slid to his knees before Ashe steadied him and Thorne gripped his collar and the side of his neck. He trembled, sucking down deep breaths like a drowning man—or one drinking in augments again the way his brothers forced him in Azkai Temple. His eyes were wide, dilated, gone deep into those horrific memories, slipping away from Ashe and Thorne.

"Darkwind, look at me!" Thorne shouted. "Stay with us! *Focus!*"

He didn't know how he kept his voice steady, how he managed not to panic himself with Maleck shaking between his hands and Ashe's like a fevered man, jaw tight, eyes bulging. But he made his voice and that Name an anchor, forcing his own fear at bay.

And Maleck latched onto that strength, his grip tight on Thorne's forearms, drawing himself hand-over-hand upward until he surfaced from the memories. His eyes fixed on Thorne's face, his fingers flexing in an iron grip around his vambraces, steadying himself while the violent shudders still wracked through his body. Ashe's arm slid around his chest from behind, gloved hand flat over his scarred heart, her chin descending on his shoulder, and she pressed her lips to the side of his neck.

Maleck's eyes fluttered shut. For several heartbeats, the only sound was the breath wheezing in and out of him. Thorne didn't ask again, simply clung to his friend while he went back to that dark place—slower and steadier this time—because Thorne had asked him to. The force of that loyalty knocked the breath from his chest.

At last, hoarse and soft, Maleck spoke: "When I was a boy, there were...rumors. The *visnprests* thought it might be possible to craft a new being altogether by breaking their acolytes' bodies and mending them with a beast's, also broken, using a healing augment as the thread between them."

Thorne's hand fell from Maleck's arm, utterly numb. "The healing and blood augments. That's the real reason they've been so desperate to find them."

Maleck's eyes opened, hazel dulled to pewter gray. "When I was still in Azkai, the notion was considered fanatical. Even my brothers would not dare it. The Order suspected it would require more than just healing augments ...*Gammalkraft* must be used to set the binding. And that went beyond what was known and permitted."

But those *visnprests* went on to use *Gammalkraft* in the ritual after the last war, working the oldest and most profound power over Cyril Novacek to forge the Key's power into his bloodline. There was little beyond their knowledge now—and little depth to which they would not stoop in pursuit of their ends, whatever those truly were.

"They called them Balmond," Maleck added. "The Forged. A killing force built of armored flesh and rage."

"And if we cut them down," Ashe whispered, "we're murdering Valgard's children."

"Can they be saved?" Thorne asked. "Separated and restored?"

Maleck held his gaze for a moment, then slowly shook his head.

The weight of this horror slid from Maleck's shoulders and onto Thorne's, bowing him lower. A headache rolled into place behind his eyes, and he turned away from his friends, peering into the gorge below where a river wended away, carving out its place in the world.

Nature. The balance, the order of things; it once made so much sense to him. But in this war against nine-foot creatures in skulled masks, vengeance-driven criminals, and now this—children blended with beasts, a slow and irrevocable death sentence—nothing made sense anymore. The world he knew was falling to pieces.

With his back to the hillside, Thorne collapsed on his haunches, legs cocked, elbows on his knees. He cradled his head, but that didn't stop the throbbing that shattered his skull into sharp, jagged fragments. With a soft scrape of sound, Maleck took one side of him, Ashe the other. Mirroring

Thorne's posture, but with arms linked around their knees, they stared over the open edge of the path and the lower hills of the Isetfells beyond.

"We're losing this war." Thorne spoke down toward the path. "It may take a miracle to keep the Bloodwights from winning it with those creatures."

Ashe flexed her hands, leather gloves creaking. "Not surprising. Think about your Courts' stories: a man chosen by the Wayfinders who risked his life to free Valgard from its oppressors. The willing warrior and the war have always been part of this story."

"I assume the warrior is me?" Thorne asked wryly.

"Actually, I'm terrified it's going to be Cistine."

Maleck's eyes cut to her, brow a slash of worry, but he didn't argue. Thorne wished he would.

For some time, they were silent, staring into the distance. Slowly the disgust and horror in Thorne's chest loosened its grip, and he could breathe again. Logic shouldered through the gap between a world he always understood and this new one full of abominations made from broken children and broken beasts.

He needed to act. To move. To lead.

Drawing in a long, deep breath, he lifted his head, and Ashe turned her attention to him. "What are you thinking?"

"That I need to speak to Bravis and Benedikt. These Balmond haven't been seen elsewhere in Valgard, or we would've heard of it by now, which means they must make their home in the mountains."

Ashe and Maleck exchanged another wide-eyed glance. "The stronghold," Maleck murmured. "You believe that's where they're being forged?"

Thorne nodded. "I'm finished asking for permission to do this. Prepare yourselves and rally the others. With or without the army's blessing, we're going into the mountains."

❧

"I don't like this, Thorne."

The words clattered in the war tent's dead quiet, and Thorne watched Bravis steadily. He'd prepared for this, for Benedikt to nod even before Bravis continued, "We must believe the impossible, the utmost corruption of every gift from the gods, if we're to speculate they're somehow weaving child and beast together. You realize how absurd that sounds?"

Thorne pondered for a moment—not the Chancellor's point, but how to navigate around it. It wasn't only Aden and Ariadne's word he was taking, it was Maleck's above all else, and he knew his friend was telling the truth. But he couldn't admit to that when he caught the sideways stares Maleck collected like new scars each day. It was as if the entire army expected him to burst into Bloodwight madness at any moment. In this war tent, his word counted less than anyone's.

Thorne's stubbornness would have to be enough.

"We've seen what becomes of Valgard when we ignore reports of this nature," he said, and Benedikt winced. "We knew about the Bloodwights' movements in Oadmark and did nothing until they stormed our gates. I don't think we can afford to ignore this threat the same way."

Bravis folded his arms. "And your solution is to go charging off into the mountains yourself? The lines between Courts may have broken down for the sake of efficiency, but that only holds so long as there are Chancellors to lead. We can't risk one of our own going into the Isetfells."

"And I won't send my cabal alone. But there's no one else I trust to go on this mission and live to report it." When neither of them spoke, Thorne braced one hand on the map table, taking the weight from his aching calves. "Let me make something clear: I'm not asking. I'm telling you we're going, and I'm leaving Sander in charge in my stead."

The frost in the air owed nothing to the vicious mountain winds tugging the canvas. Bravis and Benedikt exchanged a glance, and Benedikt said, "You sound very much like your father when you speak that way."

Thorne slammed his other hand down on the table so hard Bravis jerked back. "I'm not playing that game where you use his legacy to guilt me into doing things your way." Somehow, his voice managed not to shake, though his legs were not so obedient.

"He's right, Benedikt," Bravis sighed. "It's his reason we ought to appeal to, not his heritage. Thorne, listen to me, this is *madness*. Fighting this army on *our* terms, in the open, is the only way we've stayed alive."

"Stayed alive to what end? Look around you, we're losing! If these Balmond are unleashed into Valgard, it could be the killing blow we've dreaded. I intend to cut them off before it ever goes that far."

This silence was thicker, and far grimmer. Speculation roved between their faces, and Thorne wondered what drastic measure would be necessary if they tried to force him to stay. But to his relief, Bravis finally looked away. "When will you go?"

"Tomorrow," Thorne said. "I hope to return within a fortnight. If it's going to be much longer than that, Ashe and Bresnyar will bring word."

They exchanged a long glance, then Bravis waved a tired hand. "It's no Chancellor's right to command another. Go, then. But if you die, I won't hesitate to place Sander in your stead. Perhaps we're better off with his sense of self-preservation anyway."

"We'll soon find out."

"Thorne," Bravis added when he turned to go. "Stay a moment. Benedikt, give us the tent."

Skyygan's Chancellor shot them a curious look, but went. Scalp prickling with dread, Thorne folded his hands in the small of his back and watched Bravis's grave face.

"Hallvard saw you and the Princess on the battlefield at Jazva," Bravis said quietly. "Far more than a treaty, wouldn't you say?"

Thorne's calves twinged. "What we are—"

"*Selvenar?*" Bravis's mouth twitched at one corner. "I'm old, not blind. And it's not my place to say what intrigues another man. But if you're going off on dangerous missions with a woman you have affections for, I need your word first."

"I'm listening."

Bravis rounded the table and leaned against its edge, facing him. "You had us convinced with your logic of sending her away to protect the Key, but I don't want to hear anything like that ever again. If she goes along with you on this mission, she chooses to place her own life at risk. *You* fight for Valgard's future, not hers. I need to know we can trust that in your hands on this and every mission."

Thorne gritted his teeth, rocking on his heels at the blow of those words against his bruised spirit. "I give you my word, I'll do what's best for Valgard. That's why I'm here."

"Good." Bravis's face relaxed. "And good luck. I pray you're wrong about all of this, these creatures and this mountain stronghold, but if not..." He broke off, jaw working silently.

"I know. I pray I'm wrong, too."

Thorne slipped out, every step heavy from the war room to the usual fire where the cabal gathered to wait for him—every face solemn, every back stooped. Maleck did not even look up from sketching in his journal when Thorne lowered himself onto the log between Aden and Sander.

"What did they say?" Ariadne demanded.

A shiver of anticipation moved through Thorne's body, masking itself as a chill. "We plan now and leave tomorrow. We'll return to the Chasm and try to pick up a trail, track those Balmond to wherever they roost. Sander has the power of Kanslar Court in my absence."

The High Tribune nodded grimly. Ashe bent forward, drilling a piece of kindling into the stone, her eyes fixed on Thorne. "You want Bres to do the tracking?"

Thorne nodded. "Something tells me we'll have need of his fire as well when we find that stronghold."

Cistine cleared her throat. "There might be Bloodwights there... watching over the children and beasts."

Thorne's scalp prickled at her tone, bereft of fear but full of thought. "It's possible."

"What do we do if there are?"

"Run." Quill's voice was flat. "They're shielded with augments, too hard to kill. You see one, you get away as fast as you can. We all do."

Cistine scraped the toe of her boot through the cinders fanning around the firepit. "Or we could capture one."

The words pierced Thorne's chest like a blade. Aden sat taller, eyes narrow. The scratch of Maleck's pen halted.

"Capture one. Capture a *Bloodwight*," Tatiana echoed scathingly. "Have you lost your mind?"

"I just think it's worth finding out where they've been all this time, and why...whatever they're scheming." Fervor blazed in Cistine's eyes, brighter even than the flames. "Bravis and Benedikt may not think it's of any consequence, but *I* do."

And the Princess would not be denied her curiosity, not for anything; Thorne had learned that lesson long ago.

"Cistine." Ashe's voice was careful. "Think about this logically. You want to capture a *Bloodwight*? A creature we can't kill, that our weapons bounce off like stone. Even if we subdued it, we'd either have to keep it captive or release it eventually. We couldn't *end* this."

"We could experiment. Learn how to kill them by practicing on just one."

Quill dragged both hands down his face. "This is the worst idea you've *ever* had."

"Actually," Ariadne murmured, "I agree with her."

Thorne stared dumbstruck at his strategist, her eyes painted in long fingers of light when she leaned in, elbows braced on her thighs, hands loosely clasped.

"We've skirmished our way across our kingdom for three months," she said, "and what do we show for it now? Our advances, their advances, none of it does damage enough to coax the Bloodwights to the lines. If we were anywhere near success, they would show their faces. They're toying with us at best...or else letting us distract ourselves and run weary while they accomplish their ends elsewhere."

"And what ends are they accomplishing?" Cistine added. "We don't know where they are, what they *want*. To rule, yes, but what are the steps? Wars are won phase by phase—do we know which one we're even in?"

In the silence, Maleck's pen resumed its erratic scratching.

"If we captured one," Aden said at last, "how would you hold it?"

"Yager's hunters have *Svarkyst* chains. Tyve has poison to induce truth-telling," Ariadne mused. "We could send for Adeima, Maltadova, and Valdemar. Have them meet us here with their weapons and set the faces of all the Chancellors at once against the Bloodwights. Show them the power of the Courts united."

"And subduing it before we have those chains?" Thorne asked.

"Use a wind augment to knock it unconscious?" Cistine offered. "They're still men under those masks. They still have to breathe."

Thorne glanced at Maleck to confirm. He did not look up from his journal, but his chin jerked.

It was sound. Dangerous, brash, with almost a guarantee of something going horribly wrong—but sound, if the gods loved them and everything moved in their favor. "Sander?"

The High Tribune streaked a hand back through his dark curls. "I can prepare the camp to receive a prisoner. For all the good it will do."

"Your confidence is noted," Thorne said dryly. "Quill, send Faer to the southern lines. The rest of us will go, burn this stronghold to the ground, and capture a Bloodwight for interrogation if we can."

"Any other miracles Ariadne should be praying for, while we're already asking for too much?" Quill muttered.

"Pray that Pippet is there," Aden said, "so we can bring her home."

Silence descended, heavy and thick as snow clouds, broken only by the pop of the fire. Then Ashe rose, stretching. "Look at it this way: at least we have the advantage of surprise. They don't expect us to storm their stronghold or try to capture one of them, and we can use that." She tipped her head. "I'm going to bed. Mal?"

He shut the journal, stood without sparing any of them a glance, and followed her away. One by one the others left the fireside, muttering about the plan—this mad mission. Sander was slower to depart, pausing to clasp Thorne's shoulder. "I'll look after the lines. You parry the sword."

Thorne nodded mutely, keeping his gaze on Cistine across the fire. When Sander left, she said, "Do you think Yager and Tyve will come?"

Thorne propped his hands on the log and twisted his body slowly left, then right, releasing tension points from his back down through his hips and into his calves. "I trust Quill can write a letter suitably vague enough to tempt them up to the war camp without telling them precisely why."

Cistine's brow creased. "You don't trust this plan."

"I don't trust any plan that puts you directly in harm's way. And you will be, with a Bloodwight in our midst, subdued or not." He trailed a hand back through his hair. "All that aside, it's a good tactic."

His tongue refused to form words that exposed the darkness in his heart, the selfish reasons he would not stand in her way...not only because of all the times she'd warned him not to. If she knew his mind, she might despise it. Might despise *him*.

"Of course it's a decent tactic!" False cheer gilded Cistine's reply. "I've been reading an *awful* lot about wartime strategy."

Thorne dropped his hand and truly looked at her, in the light, for the first time since the battlefield. There was a new sharpness to her features, something shrewd besides the wisdom in her eyes. So utterly different from the frightened girl in the meadow he met all those months ago, crossing blades with him for her Warden's life. She'd come prepared this time; not a princess out of her depth, but a queen armed with knowledge and prepared for whatever blows life swung next.

He wished he could be like her, could catch his breath in this raging sea and feel for a moment like he wasn't drowning. She lived to disprove the assumptions about her, whereas he proved them all right. In every horrible way possible.

Cistine caught his stare, and a blush spread across her face again. "Why do you keep *looking* at me that way?"

He shrugged. "It's what men do when they're in love, I suppose."

She scooped up a handful of soot and hurled it at him across the fire. "Well, stop being in love for a moment, would you? It's distracting!"

"I'm afraid I can't. *You're* distracting."

She stuck out her tongue. "And *you're* impossible."

He laughed, but the sound was wrong. It *felt* wrong to laugh when he knew what was coming with the dawn. What his cabal would face because of him, the choices he'd made three months ago. Because of the woman sitting across from him at this fire.

What if he made the wrong choice again in the mountains? What if fate tempted him to think of her needs before his kingdom's, and he broke his word to Bravis—and to himself?

"Cistine," he said slowly, "I go on this mission as a Chancellor...not as a friend of Talheim or as your betrothed. I gave Bravis my word."

Solemnity softened her face. "I understand."

"And you believe we can endure that?"

"We have to." Her thumb swiped the opal band around her finger. "It's the only way to save our kingdoms."

CHAPTER FIFTEEN

MALECK COULD NOT be still.

Ashe watched him circle their corner of the tents, heart throbbing at the look in his eyes...the wild caginess of a Blood Hive creature, starved and chained, ready to snap free and run. Or kill.

"She doesn't know." The usual deep rumble of his voice cracked in veins of terror. "What they can do, what they *have* done..."

"She knows enough," Ashe said, though she hardly believed it herself. Anything to quiet the fear in his face—even a lie.

"They cannot be *subdued*." He paced another tight turn, fingers tearing back through his braids. "Even if we bring one this far, it will raze the war camp. It could take her, it could take any of us...Asheila, what if it takes *you?*"

"It's not going to. I'm not letting one of those things close enough to try."

"You don't understand how quick they are, how cunning. It could happen just like in all my dreams, their hands around your throat..." he jerked into another quick circle around the tent. "It won't be enough, *we* are not enough..."

Ashe stared at him walking laps on the rock over the pale track already worn by his boots, her despair giving way to frustration and helplessness. It was going to be another of these nights, then. She'd lost count of how many they had endured together since the war began: him, anxious, restless, terrified, and her, powerless to bring him comfort.

Or maybe it wasn't too late this time. Maybe she could settle him.

She hopped to her feet and stepped into his path. "Mal, stop. Look at me." She seized his shoulders when he made to barge past. "It *will* be enough. They're not taking me. They don't care about me at all, I'm just another face on the battlefield to them."

His head shook wildly and his hands spasmed, clenching against his thighs, around his elbows, then the sides of his neck.

Fine. If he wouldn't be distracted by reason, she would distract him some other way.

She stepped back from him a pace, started to remove her gloves, and Maleck's hands locked sharply around her wrists. "Not here."

She spanned a look at the empty canvas around them. "Mal, no one's coming, we're not going to—"

"I said *not here*, Asheila!" Raw aggression in his words—but beneath it, panic without end, a well he had not yet found the bottom of, always fresh horrors every inch he dug deeper. Every day this gods-damned war went on.

Cursing silently, Ashe wiggled her fingers in surrender. "All right. Will you at least lie down with me?"

He stared at her, dull eyes from a gaunt face, and when he neither agreed nor withdrew, she flipped her hands to take his wrists instead and drew him to the bedroll, where she sat and guided his head to rest on her knees. Flat on his back, he still didn't relax; his fingertips tapped the stone and his heels clicked erratically, jerking his bent knees like shaken hills.

"I can't," he said after a moment, every muscle coiling as if to leap up. "I can't sleep."

"Maleck, you *have* to." Laying a hand on his brow, Ashe held his head into her lap when he started to rise. "At least shut your eyes for a little while."

"Asheila—"

"You're sleeping one way or another. Am I knocking you unconscious or singing you a lullaby?"

A beat, and she wondered if he was truly contemplating it. Then his hand crawled up to hers, taking it from his brow, and he squeezed it so hard the bones ached in protest. She smoothed the braids back from his furrowed forehead, feeling out every deep groove in his permanent frown, every fear etching his face while she hummed under her breath the lullaby she sang to Cistine as a fussy infant, and Pippet, a small, angry knot of grief and rage traveling the deep woods together. She sang against the darkness, against her specters and his, all while his legs jerked and his hand tightened and loosened around hers, over and over—an anchor against whatever dark waves surged and crashed in his mind.

The world they'd built in winter seemed so far away. Wineskins on bridges in Darlaska's light, symphonies and stories, the mountain cleft where they first kissed...it all might as well have been a dream shared by two warriors who believed the war was finally behind them, not seeing the darkness on the horizon ahead.

A low, pained sound slid between Maleck's teeth, somewhere between a groan and a sob, and Ashe skimmed her hand down from his brow to his cheek. She curled over his head to kiss him, and even on his breath she tasted fear. Where power once hung, enticing as foreign spice and beguiling like shadowed treasure, there was now the pain of history, the uncertainty of the future. A terrible story bookended by his brothers, these gods-forsaken Bloodwights against whom not even Ashe's blade was enough.

She had no tangible comfort to offer. Nothing but her mouth against his every few moments and her hand stroking his face, until hours later the tremors finally eased. Not abated—they never fully went away, his dreams as restless as his waking—but at least he slept. At least he breathed more deeply.

Ashe continued her ministrations while her gaze trailed down the scarred and muscled length of him: the armor he never took off, his dagger Remany forever at his side, and the coat that served as a blanket and a shield most days, inlaid with the coarse hairs of some mountain wolf resilient to the cold. From the pocket by his hip, a square of leather peeked out.

Ashe had to remind herself to keep her hands moving, not to wake him as her intentions shifted from comfort to cunning.

He'd given that journal to her once, full of sketches of her own face, in case he died in a prison cell below Middleton's estate. But ever since the war's beginning, he hadn't let her touch it. When she asked to see it, it always disappeared into his pocket like a jewel filched by a thief.

Normally, Ashe was not as given to gossip as Cistine. A few healthy beatings at thirteen years old after raiding other Wardens' effects stripped the need to pilfer other people's belongings straight out of her.

But she was not a Warden anymore; and this was *Maleck*, her Maleck, keeping secrets from her.

Gingerly, she extracted her hand from his grip and waited, breath held. When he went on sleeping, twitching in dreams, she maneuvered her hand carefully into his pocket, slid the journal out, and flipped it open single-handed—past the drawing of herself in the dining hall at Middleton, past a rendering of all the cabal gathered together at Darlaska, past a sketch of Faer proudly preening, beady eye fixed on his artist.

Then she understood what Cistine had told her once about how sometimes it was better, saner, not to snoop.

Everything beyond that drawing of Faer was nightmarish, a gallery etched by demented hands. Dark sketches covered the pages, jagged halls and deep cellars with horrific faces surging up from their depths, broken figures limned in white and above them, always, the same six words over and over: *YOU WILL NOT SURVIVE THIS WAR.*

Ashe's breath snagged, and she looked down at Maleck; this man who sat beside her at every campfire, after every meal, and drew these things, wrote these words while his friends gathered around him, fighting a battle he'd already determined he would lose.

Rigor in her muscles made it almost impossible to slide gently from beneath him; but she let Maleck's head down carefully onto the bedroll, and he curled to the side, head on his arm, and went on sleeping while she stumbled up and shoved blindly through the alcoves of the tent, past brazier-lit warriors trying and failing to sleep, all of them still holding to light's last hopeful grain; most of them facing a battle outside, not within.

She found Aden tending the beacon fire, the brightest of them all, sheltered in a windbreak. All the Tribunes in this pocket of the front took shifts standing watch. Storming into the firelight, she hurled the journal into his lap. "It's worse than we thought."

"Good evening to you as well." He thumbed through the journal, levity draining from his face, mouth twisting tighter at every passing page. "Stars damn it. *This* is what he's been drawing all these months?"

Ashe nodded. "I need to take him. Get away from this war while we still can."

"He'll never consent to go."

"Why in God's name *not*?"

Aden snapped the journal shut and offered it back to her. "Because many of these creatures are his brothers, and he feels they're his responsibility to fight."

"Aden. Do you *see* what he's writing?" She circled the fire and snatched the book from him. "This is not about responsibility, it's his life hanging in the balance!"

"I'm aware of what it is and isn't. What would you have me do, force him? Do you really believe that's any kinder when it's the very thing his brothers did for years?"

Cursing, Ashe dragged her hands through her hair. "I don't know, but we have to do *something*. How did you help him before, after the last war?"

"That was far less my doing than it was my father's." Aden tweaked the compass pendant around his neck. "When he rescued Maleck and they traveled home from the lines together, some rapport forged between them. I never did fully understand it, but it pulled Maleck back to us whenever he slipped away."

"Well, he's slipping again, and I don't know how to stop it."

"You can't," Aden said with all his usual bluntness. "It's Maleck who must decide to fight, to come back from this place. We can stand with him, but we cannot fight that battle for him."

Staring down at the journal's well-loved face, Ashe forced out the words that haunted her every day while she watched her *selvenar* spiral deeper and deeper into despair. "What if he loses, Aden?"

No answer. When she raised her gaze, she glimpsed the anguish he tamped down for her sake, to be the person he thought she needed. "There's no sense dwelling on any possibility before we come to it. We focus on now, helping him however we can. I think leaving the war camp will be a good start. The ranks are so tense, it's enough to make the worst of any man."

It was a good attempt at comfort, but Ashe didn't feel comforted when she glimpsed the pain flickering behind his gritted jaw, how desperately he fought against the notion of Maleck giving up, losing the battle to keep his wits about him—just as she did.

Ashe squeezed his shoulder and walked away from the fire, into the shadows bordering the camp. She reached beneath her armored scarf as she went, perpetually smelling of charcoal and cedar from its previous owner, and withdrew the chain hanging heavy between her breasts.

"Bres," she said into the starstone, "meet me at the valley floor."

It still amazed her how this great golden dragon who goaded her to come face-to-face with her grief and guilt in the Calaluns somehow became the one she turned to most on nights like these. When despair and doubt came falling like a tide, Bresnyar was the bastion she leaned into; and she did lean into him when he met her near the pool, slumped against the warmth of his ribs on the rocky shore, face tilted toward the stars. He craned his head as well, and for a time, they had silence.

It was him, predictably, who broke it. "I smell the hopelessness on you again, *Ilyanak*."

He never told her what that name meant, just some Oadmarkaic word that made him grin every time she badgered him to translate. So she'd learned to let it go, like she did now, with a crooked shrug. "It's not about me this time. It's Mal."

"He worsens?"

She nodded mutely, running her knuckles along his opalescent scales.

"I did not realize," Bresnyar added after a time, "when I heard stories of the beast-slayer and rain-dancer of the Blood Hive, what capacity you held for love. And to fear for those you cherish most."

She snorted. "Love and fear put me in that place to begin with."

"Do you suppose it's the same for Maleck? That fear and love have built him a cage?"

Ashe pondered it, flexing her hands until her marked palm throbbed. "Maybe. He fears his brothers, knowing what they're capable of. And he's afraid because he loves all of us, and he knows what they would do if they knew that. If they took us like they took Pippet."

"Would he fight, do you suppose, if it came to it? Fight for you?"

Ashe swallowed back her immediate answer and considered the question deeply, though it made her feel heavy and grim. "I don't know. I'm not sure he has the fortitude left to face his brothers, even for us."

"Then will you fight in his stead? Be his left wing as you are mine?"

Ashe sank deeper against her dragon's ribcage. "As long as I have you at my back, Scales, I'll fight any battle they ask me to."

His muzzle nudged her side, steam blowing deep into her pores. "See how far we've come, you and I? If that isn't hope for the future, I don't know what is."

"You're going soft under all that armor, talking of hope." Ashe blew out her breath through rounded lips, gazing up the steep valley sides toward the distant mountains. Then she shrugged upright. "Let's practice cleaving."

Bresnyar sighed. "I truly wish you wouldn't call it that. It sounds so infantile."

"Oh, am I insulting your proud race?" Ashe rolled her eyes. "Limber up. We have work to do."

And perhaps because he sensed how much she needed to train, to be distracted, to do *something* useful when she could do so little to help the ones she loved, Bresnyar did not argue again.

∼∾∾

Ashe stumbled back into the tent an hour before sunrise, the horizon smoldering gray at her back, her eyes fighting to stay open and a headache thundering in her temples. Time had passed without her notice, practicing with Bresnyar; all she could think of now was the sweet relief of her bedroll.

But that relief was short-lived when she entered to find Maleck asleep still but restless, stirring beneath his cloak, fingers biting into the thin roll and scraping the stone below.

"No," he panted when she ducked inside. "No, not this, *please...*"

Weight crashed over her at his pitiful, torn voice. She knelt at his side and whispered his name.

He jolted but still didn't wake, face twisting with anguish. "Not this, not her, not her...take *anything*, I—just not *her!*"

Frowning, she reached for his shoulder. "Mal!"

His hand flashed up, snatching her wrist, and his eyes shot open, wild and unseeing. He surged up before she could react, flipping them, his free hand locking around her throat. "*You're not taking her!*"

His name whipped out of her, choked with panic, her throat already closing under his fist—

The tent flap snapped inward, and burly hands closed under Maleck's arms, ripping him off of her and flinging him against the tent post; the sharp impact woke him with a shout of pain, and he crumbled, gripping the back of his head.

Aden loomed between them, one hand raised to each, but his eyes on Maleck. "Are you awake? Look at us, say our names!"

"Aden," Maleck gasped, pushing himself up on one elbow. Ashe sat up with him, and his eyes widened in horror. "*Asheila.* You...I thought—"

Aden dropped his arms, shaking his head. "Stars damn it, *Allet,* you have to get this under control."

Maleck's eyes filled with agony, flicking between them. His gloved hand came to his mouth; then he whirled to his feet and left the tent, disappearing into the coming dawn.

Ashe groaned. "I have to go after him."

Aden offered his hand and helped her up. "Give him a moment. This is what he does when he hurts people."

"You say that like he does it all the time."

"Too often lately. I've seen the bruises from you wrestling him down after his nightmares."

She grimaced. "It's never on purpose."

"With a man of Maleck's size and strength, it doesn't have to be. Look at what happened to Quill's head." Aden brushed a thumb over the thin bruise already forming on her neck. "Maleck was the best acolyte they had. But that's not without its consequences now."

"I shouldn't have left last night," she cursed. "He needed me."

"What he needs is healing, and he'll never find it at long as he keeps looking back at them instead of at us." Aden's gaze followed her as she dropped Maleck's journal into the folds of his cloak. "You don't own his healing."

"Well, someone has to. And I'm not sure he has it in him anymore." She folded her arms, resisting the urge to brush the tender skin where her pulse leaped, fighting terror. "Do you still think I shouldn't take him out of here?"

"After this," Aden admitted quietly, "I'm not sure it's any safer if you two are alone."

CHAPTER SIXTEEN

TATIANA SHIVERED IN her fine coat lashed over battle armor, standing between Quill and Cistine in the heart of Jazva Chasm at bleak midmorning. Ahead, Ashe and Bresnyar scouted for a scent of the Balmond, moving as one, and Tatiana was content to leave the work to them. Even hours after waking up, she couldn't stop yawning. It was harder and harder to keep her eyes open these days, harder to slip away and do her business before Quill was conscious, and harder to resist the urge to wrap back up in the pelts and sleep for a few more minutes when he was still rousing, while illness and unease pummeled her guts.

She was not looking forward to this hike. Not in the least.

Quill nudged her. "I heard you leaving this morning. You sounded like you were gagging...are you all right?"

She grimaced. "More bad dreams. Mostly about Braggos."

Thank the stars, that was the one thing Quill wouldn't press into. He looked away, rubbing the back of his neck. "I have them, too."

Cistine traded her weight from foot to foot and tugged at the sleeves of the armor Tatiana had procured for her. It wasn't quite the right fit, the hems dangling well past her fingertips and midriff, but people raiding heaps of clothes stripped from the dead couldn't afford to be picky. "What if they don't find a scent to track?"

"Then we laze around and wait for another ambush." Ariadne slung an arm around Cistine's shoulders, her tone unconcerned, but the look she shot Aden was anything but.

Tatiana grimaced as well, peering around the empty battleground. Difficult to believe that only days ago, she'd crouched behind one of those slabs of rock kicked loose by an augur, letting Quill bandage a gaping wound on her shoulder; and he gave her that same look from when he found her in Braggos right before they went back-to-back on those nightmarish, bloody streets, ready to die together.

They hadn't, their lives owed to Sander, who'd snatched them from the jaws of Nimmus at the last moment. But they'd almost met their end again here in the Chasm, under the same din of clashing weapons and skirling augments...and it was different this time. She'd barely managed to bite her tongue then, to pick up her saber and fight instead of spending her last moments pouring out her heart to Quill.

She wondered how many miracles they had left between them before death found its mark.

She shuddered off the thought when Ashe and Bresnyar spun back to them, twin gleams in their eyes, Ashe's voice brimming with triumph. "We have something."

The cabal jogged to meet them, Thorne, Aden, and Maleck converging from their scattered patrol of the cliffsides. Ashe and Bresnyar bent over what seemed to be a strange glob of rock, its surface smooth all over except where the ends flapped. It took Tatiana a moment to realize it was a lump of flesh.

She slowed to a halt, bile surging up her throat and an ugly, wet retch sliding through her teeth. Quill halted beside her, eyes wide at the sound. "What was *that?*"

"Nothing. That's just not the sight I want to see first thing in the morning," she gagged.

Cistine stopped on Quill's other side. "What does it smell like, Bres?"

"Wrong." His nostrils flared, pupils such faint slits the fiery red-gold nearly eclipsed the black. "This is not natural flesh of beast or man."

"That much is certain," Aden muttered.

"You're sure it's from the Balmond?" Thorne asked.

"We did not wound them." Ariadne craned her head back to peer at the rocky ledges above. "But this was the cleft they ambushed us from. They might have tussled together before they attacked."

Cistine shuddered again. "If one scrap of their skin looks so awful, I can't imagine what the rest of them looks like."

"We'll know soon enough." Thorne hitched his satchel of provisions higher up his shoulder and turned to Ashe. "Fly on ahead and find spots to camp along the scent trail. We'll follow."

"Report every half-hour," Aden added, "so we know you're safe."

Ashe nodded curtly and swung onto Bresnyar's back. Her gaze lingered on Maleck, who stared at the dismembered flesh with remote, glassy eyes. "Be careful."

His silence jabbed at Tatiana's heart; she'd gotten so used to Maleck full of life ever since these Talheimics first darkened their doorstep, she never thought he'd go back to this place. Back to how he was after the last war.

With a swift, parting glance at Aden, Ashe squeezed her knees to Bresnyar's sides. The dragon flowed like water in a tight turn and shot toward the distant hills. The faint gleam of breaking daylight over the Chasm's sides caught his gold scales, paving a path like a falling star through the mountains, traveling northwest.

"That's our heading." Thorne started across the steep-sided cleft.

"Off into the Isetfells." Tatiana shot a look at Quill. "Just like old times, isn't it, Featherbrain?"

No reply, no clever joke about the first time they'd kissed, or the night they'd forged the *valenar* bond. That scar throbbed now like the pang in a wounded knee before a storm as Quill followed their Chancellor with unsmiling determination.

He and Maleck would be the death of her, if everything she was keeping bottled inside like ghostlight didn't do the trick first.

The cabal made a silent procession through Jazva Chasm and up into the foothills, and Tatiana couldn't help thinking of the last time they went on a trek like this, when Quill dragged them up into the Vaszaj Range to test Cistine's might with augments. As battered and bruised as they all were back then, that excursion had tasted of hope: Salvotor imprisoned, Thorne poised to take the Judgement Seat, all of them free.

Now the manacles were back, invisible bindings around wrist and ankle, head and heart. Absences festered like unhealed wounds: worry for Pippet, worry for the friends left in the war camp, and uncertainty about what lay ahead. They'd brought scant flagons; no healing, only a few of fire, lightning, and earth, and Cistine's ravaging darkness—and one wind augment, which Sander had stolen from stars-knew-where and passed to Thorne that morning with a grim nod.

A last resort so they could flee if something went awry.

Tatiana fell into step with Cistine, desperate to distract herself. "So. How was it really, being back in Talheim?"

"Stuffy and monotonous and *boring*," she said without hesitation, as if she'd been waiting for someone to ask. Ariadne shot her a wry smile. "Well, it *was*!"

Tatiana shook her head. "I think we did too good a work on you, if you prefer *this* to the comforts of home."

"It wasn't as comfortable as you'd think." Threading her thumb into her satchel's strap, Cistine shrugged. "There are some in my father's council who still don't believe I'm right for the throne. They've spent too many years doubting me, I think...they're setting their hopes on the man I'll marry, not who *I'll* be as Queen."

Thorne stiffened slightly. Aden said, "I imagine they won't be pleased to find their hopes thwarted by a Valgardan on the throne, then."

"That's just it. Even when they learned about the betrothal, I think they expected this war would solve that problem and open new prospects."

Thorne's eyes flashed to her, full of pain—not for himself, not for Talheim's hopes that this war would end him and any claim he had to kingship by the ring on Cistine's finger; but pain for her, that she'd endured their dismissal and their dreams that a man would rule in her stead. "I'm sorry we sent you away to that, *Logandir*. If we knew what waited for you in Talheim…"

"We thought everything would just go back to how it was if you went home," Tatiana added when Thorne tapered off.

Cistine offered a smile, small and sad. "How could it? *I'm* not how I was. And it takes more than three months of politicking at my father's table to convince them I'm not the cossetted girl they remember."

"You will convince them," Ariadne said. "In time."

That uneven smile broadened with gratitude. "I know I will. But in the meantime, there's work we can do here. And I'm better equipped for that than to put on a happy face in front of the nobles."

"Listen to that," Quill broke in suddenly. "Cistine Novacek, choosing war over politics. You're right, Tati…we trained her too well."

Cistine stuck out her tongue at him.

Tatiana guided the conversation as they climbed, away from somber matters and toward things Cistine enjoyed. They talked of the books she'd read in her absence and Astoria in the winter, of ration plans and reports from Mahasar's border, all while the landscape changed around them. Any discernible path crumbled away, and they wove between pine trees, the air spiced with sap. The snow deepened as well, drifts hugging their ankles, then their calves while they climbed. Infrequently, a shadow fell across them, and their hands floated to their weapons; but each time it proved to be Bresnyar, circling above and guiding them along the Balmond's invisible path.

By midday, Jazva Chasm was far gone at their backs. The terrain was silent, empty but for flickers of distant, tawny wildcats hunting on the clefts and ivory rams dotting the steepest hillsides. The cabal walked in a silent chain for some time, the clouds clearing above, the sky a deep blue and the sun nearly warm on their backs.

Tatiana tried not to wonder what she would be doing right now if the war never began. It was foolish to grieve what she'd never really had, but she was thinking of it anyway, like she had far too often since Braggos.

Right up until the moment the first snowball struck.

The slap of cold, wet pack on the back of her head sent her staggering forward with a yelp that brought the whole cabal to a halt, spinning toward her. She spun, too—toward Cistine, standing behind her with wide, innocent eyes, dusting the snow off her hands.

"What was *that?*" Tatiana brushed off her curls and flipped snow from her collar.

"According to Talheimic war theory, it constitutes an act of engagement." Grinning, Cistine bent double and gathered more snow, rolling it into a sphere between her palms. "As in, starting a fight?"

Tatiana stepped away from that glint in her eyes. Quill scowled. "You do realize we aren't here on reprieve. This is a war."

Cistine tucked her arms behind her back and flashed a mischievous grin. "It's about to be."

None of them saw the second snowball coming—it didn't fly from Cistine's hand. It came from Thorne on their right, and struck Quill straight in the mouth, whipping his head to the side. Laughter burst from Cistine's lips, and Quill whirled toward their Chancellor, thumbing the cold welt on his jaw. "You've got to be joking."

Cistine lobbed her second snowball at his head. His arm flashed up, turning it to powder before it struck, and his eyes snapped to her.

"All right," he growled, "if you want to start this."

The mountainside erupted into cries and torrents of flying ice as the cabal followed their Chancellor and their princess into a snow fight that set the trees shaking with threats—and, much to Tatiana's shock, with bursts of laughter. It was a training ground like all the times they'd unleashed their rage and fear on one another over the past decade—only they traded hard punches for wrestling matches now, a rock top for a wet mountain, and rather than shouts and snarls there was laughter, *real laughter*, freckling the air. A sound she hadn't heard in *months*.

Some of the weight peeled back from Tatiana's shoulders when she tackled Ariadne into a snow heap and shoved handfuls of powder down her coat; when she heard Quill's deep chuckles booming off the sheer rock while he chased Cistine, shrieking in mock-terror, toward Maleck—the only one not joining in the fun.

"Mal, protect me!" Cistine yelped, diving behind his height.

Quill slammed to a halt and backed away, palms up. "Oh no, that's not happening. I know my limits."

Maleck simply looked at him, no threat, no joy in his eyes. Quill's humor dimmed as well, hands falling at his sides.

Then Cistine yanked Maleck's collar back and dumped an entire handful of snow down his bare back.

The *sound* that came out of him, and the jig he danced trying to escape the cold, set tears of laughter flowing so freely Tatiana had to let Ariadne up. When Maleck finally halted his frigid dance, panting and shivering, there was something different in his face. A subtle shift, an ember burning in the depths of his eyes, settling on Cistine.

Tatiana blinked, wondering if she was imagining things—but that light lingered, and stoked when he advanced on the Princess.

"Oh, gods," Cistine held up both hands and backed away. "*Mercy!*"

"Too late for that." Quill cracked his knuckles, falling into step with Maleck. "Let's finish her, *Storfir.*"

Then they were after her, chasing her up the mountainside, her shrieks floating back on the wind. When that sound filled Tatiana's ears, it brought stillness—not sorrow, but something deeper. An understanding of what was happening right now.

This moment, this game, with these people. This was precisely what she would be doing if not for the war. And maybe—despite the perils, despite the threat to their kingdom, despite *everything*—she still could. She could seek glints of happiness like these if she dared. These, and...

She rested a hand on her stomach, a slow smile curling across her face.

She understood exactly why Cistine threw that first blow.

It was nightfall when they came upon Ashe and Bresnyar at last, settled into a small crevice between two cliffs, a fire built before them and a mountain goat's meat roasting over the flames. One look at them all—hair still dripping, armor soaked, faces red with cold, and mostly smiling—and Ashe's brows leaped. "What took you so long? Fall into a snowdrift...or ten?"

"We had to teach Cistine a lesson about respecting her mentors." Quill bumped her shoulder with his.

Cistine shoved him right back. "You're just sore I managed to shove your head into a snowbank. *Twice.*"

"It's not my fault you fight dirtier than you used to."

"You had a snow fight." Ashe's gaze leaped to Maleck. "Without me?"

He bobbed a small shrug. "Retribution was necessary."

"She dumped snow down his shirt," Thorne supplied, grinning widest of all. "It was a sight to behold."

"Perhaps it's for the best, Asheila," Bresnyar offered from behind her, his stretched-out body creating a windbreak between the canyon walls. "They do look awfully cold."

"Oh, I think they seem a bit too warm, actually." Ashe shot the dragon a smirk. "Don't you?"

She was the only one laughing when Bresnyar climbed to his feet, put his back to them, and kicked snow all over the cabal.

CHAPTER SEVENTEEN

IT WAS WELL after dark when Cistine dried out at last, stomach full and heart bursting with relief. Her snow game had been a risk, but she got what she wanted: the talk around the fire was far livelier tonight, and the cabal smiled at one another, and at *her*. The deadly pall they wore like a communal shroud peeled back with the late-evening clouds, ushering in laughter bright like the stars peering through the veil above.

For the first time since her return to the North, a sense of belonging swept over her. She stretched out next to the flames, her head on Quill's shoulder, and after a hesitant moment he circled an arm around her and grinned at Tatiana and Ariadne, arm-wrestling on a slab of fallen rock. "Want to make a bet, Mal?"

Across the fire, perched between Aden and Ashe, Maleck flicked a tired hint of a smile Quill's way; but deep thought, not humor, stormed his eyes, and they returned swiftly to the flames.

Cistine stifled a sigh. She was *mostly* successful, anyway.

Smirking, Aden lobbed his skewer into the flames. "Let's not forget the true loss of the day was Ashe missing Cistine's game."

"Oh, please," Ashe leaned around Maleck to scoff at him. "I don't need to see you breaking icicles out of your nostrils again."

Even Maleck snorted at that. Aden narrowed his eyes playfully. "Once, and *only* once."

"*Lobaesj!*" Tatiana cried triumphantly, smacking Ariadne's arm down and pointing to Aden. "*Lobaesj!*"

The others took up the Old Valgardan word in a chant, and Aden bared his teeth in a mock-snarl. "All right, *twice!*"

Cistine looked around at their grinning faces, bemused. "I don't get it."

They tapered off into silence. Quill shifted away, grimacing. Ashe swapped a glance with him. "It was just a joke that came out of a battle near the Ismalete on the way north."

"Can you tell me?"

"We couldn't even begin to explain it," Ariadne said sympathetically.

Because you weren't there. The unspoken words bored into Cistine's heart, reigniting her melancholy.

Thorne put an end to the awkward pause that followed, standing from his seat on the rocks. "We should rest. Plenty of walking ahead of us."

"Thank you for the *reminder,*" Tatiana whined as Ariadne slapped down her arm this time. "Who wants to play *koh, kendar, kest* for patrol?"

"I'm game." Ashe cast out her fist.

Thorne interrupted with a chuckle, "I'll take first watch. Aden takes second. Ariadne, third."

With a brush to the back of Cistine's head, he scooped up his sword harness and went to confer with Bresnyar, who would be taking watch at one end of the chasm all night, warning off any potential attackers with the sheer power of his body. The others paired off around the low-banking fire, and Cistine shivered when Quill stole his heat away to join Tatiana. In moments, it was only her and Aden left beside the fire.

She wasn't tired enough for sleep yet, still reliving the day's grueling trek interlaced with the humor of their snow fight and the return of her low mood now. It seemed Aden's thoughts strayed the same way; after several quiet minutes, he sat forward, prodding the flames higher. "It was good, what you did for them today."

A pleased flush warmed the bridge of her nose and cheeks. "I just want to help them remember who they are. Who *we* are." The words hung strange on her lips, and with a jolt she realized how foreign the concept of *we* had become.

Aden watched her through the flames for a moment. Then he said, "It's a pointless joke. Any time one of us tries to lie about something embarrassing that's happened since the war began, whoever catches it first gets the liar's share of rations from the next meal. Tatiana's been vicious about it these past two months."

"Oh," Cistine blinked. "So, *lobaesj*—"

"It isn't a pleasant word. But it makes the point."

"Of course." She tugged her hair slowly between her fingers. "Well, thank you for explaining it."

Shrugging, Aden prodded the fire again. "I know how it feels to be outside their jokes...and to not understand the struggles they've shared."

"Because of how long you were in Siralek?"

He shot her a dry look. "I see your penchant for curiosity remains unchanged." He tossed the stick into the flames. "I also haven't fought in all the same battles they have during this war."

"Tribune privileges?" she joked weakly.

"Something of that nature." Aden stood, removed his jacket, and flung it over her shoulders just like his father once had. And just like on that frigid mountainside, the heat and scent eased comfort into her aching bones. "Go get some sleep."

She smiled up at him. "Thank you, Aden."

He dipped his head and gathered his weapons, disappearing to take watch with Thorne, though his time hadn't come yet. Shivering at the added weight and cocooning warmth of his coat on top of hers, Cistine padded in the opposite direction to lie down.

Sleep still didn't come easily; she stared up at the stars wheeling overhead in slow, glorious streamers, her thoughts on her cabal—on their jokes and their new understanding of the world, and how it felt to be outside those things. She was still awake when a third of the night passed, punctuated by Thorne's arrival: the familiar, dragging gait of his weariness, the blow of his breath on the air. His weapons dropped to the ground, one by one. Then he fell beside her with a low groan.

Cistine rolled on her elbow. "Are you all right?"

"Sore. Exhausted." His voice was ragged. "I'm tired of this war, Cistine."

She didn't need to tell him they all were. He knew it. But of all of them, he was allowed to show it least. So she snuggled against his back instead, hips to hips, and draped her chin in the crook of his shoulder. "What do you need me to do?"

He reached back, fingers tangling in her hair. "Just stay like this. Stand watch."

Vision swimming, she nodded, tucking her chin more tightly into the dip between his neck and shoulder. They stayed that way long after his hand went slack with sleep; long after he drifted into dreams, she was still awake, her heart aching for him—for all of them.

As painful as it was to be outside their understanding, the burdens they carried were far worse. Three months of bloodshed knit them together in ways she couldn't fathom. They had new nightmares she would never share.

But if she could only make them laugh, and keep watch when they asked, she would do it. This princess was not finished giving hope; not when her Valgardan family needed her.

She would find her place among them again. No matter how long it took.

CHAPTER EIGHTEEN

NATURE WAS OUT of balance still. Even Ashe felt it by sunset their fifth day traveling. The passes were growing warmer, not chillier while they climbed; the snow melted so rapidly between one dawn and the next, a sound like rainfall followed them constantly from the sun's rising to its descent. Ashe's bladder twinged at the noise, but she welcomed the distraction from worry's gnawing grip on her chest.

Maleck was quieter than ever, taken with trembling at night and turned so deeply inward during the day, not even Ashe could rouse him. He barely spoke to her at all after his nightmare in the war camp. And the others carried a lingering air of determination, focused fiercely ahead, even if they occasionally bantered among themselves.

"You know, I never thought I'd miss Quill's obnoxious humor," she muttered to Bresnyar one day, "but here we are."

Here was another narrow pass, the kind where she preferred to pitch camp: defensible, windbroken, and suitably wide enough for her dragon to make himself comfortable blocking one end or the other. She leaned against his ribs now, warming herself after hours of scouting, while the others hunted and refilled their flasks at a nearby stream. Only Cistine remained, skinning a brace of hares Ariadne had trapped.

Ashe's chest constricted at the crestfallen look on her face. The last time she saw that look, Cistine was fighting with Julian.

She hadn't meant to leave her out of things, like their jokes. It just happened that way.

Warm breath spilled over her body as Bresnyar swung his head aside. "Go to her, before you jitter a hole into the ground."

She stopped tapping her foot. "If I do, I'll drag you down with me."

"For both our sakes, then. Go speak with Cistine."

"God's bones, what do I even say?" Ashe kicked a stone from the path. "This is just like when I came home from the last war. I couldn't hold a conversation with my parents anymore...they didn't know who I was, how I felt, the things I saw in this kingdom."

"If you have taught me anything, *Ilyanak*, it is that we need not share pain to share love. You and I come from separate pasts, yet we are one." His snout jabbed the backs of her knees. "*Speak to her.*"

"All right, all right, I'm going. Gilded lizard."

"Whining infant."

Ashe flashed him a rude gesture, then crossed the camp and knelt at Cistine's side. She scooped up one of the hares and began to skin it, keeping silent company for a time. Predictably, Cistine grew uncomfortable with it first. "Everyone's angry with me, aren't they?"

A lifelong instinct to protect this princess from pain twitched to life in Ashe's chest, but she quickly silenced it. This was not cossetted royalty sitting beside her anymore. "It's not anger," she said slowly. "Not that I can tell. They're just finding a way to relate to someone who wasn't here for the whole war and wants to be part of it now."

"Thorne thinks I should've stayed. That Talheim should've come to fight from the start."

Ashe measured her breaths, riding over the initial burst of outrage and indignation on behalf of a kingdom that was no longer hers to defend. "I'm not surprised."

Cistine's eyes swung to her, sparkling with unease. "Do you agree?"

"We did sign that treaty, Cistine. You of all people believe Talheim should be good for its word."

A harsh sigh burst from her lips, and her next skinning took a layer of meat as well. "The only thing I wanted was to keep Talheim from a war like this. Either I betray Valgard, or I betray us. How can I choose?"

"For now, you're doing everything you can." Ashe joined her cache to Cistine's and plunged the knife tip-first in a stubborn patch of snow, wiping it clean. "But patching things up with the others is a good start."

"I'm trying. I just feel like I'm not a part of this anymore. That they don't even want me."

"Well, try to see it their way. You left us."

"We voted!"

"I know. But you *left*. The war went on without you, *we* went on without you...no amount of love can change what we've seen while you were gone."

"You mean like Braggos?"

Pain twinged in the meat of Ashe's hand, and she tightened her grip around the knife. "Among other things."

"Well, *nothing* will change if no one will talk to me."

"I'm talking to you. And the others will, too. Just...give it time and keep reaching out to them, like when we first came to this kingdom." Ashe sheathed her knife and gripped Cistine's shoulder. "If it's any consolation, this is how war goes. It's messy and complicated, and I know you hate it. We all do. Just remember it's not about you...it's all of us."

Cistine offered a tremulous smile. "Well, I'm glad *you're* still speaking to me."

"That's because I'm selfish." Ashe offered a hand and tugged Cistine to her feet. "Besides you, my only choices are a sarcastic flying lizard and a man who's selectively mute."

Cistine laughed, a bright, rich sound Ashe realized just then how much she'd missed. "Maybe you're the problem, then."

"*You're* a problem." She squeezed the princess against her side. "But you're *my* problem, and one I'm happy to have for the rest of our lives."

And those, she prayed, would not be cut short by this hunt through the mountains.

Cistine seemed ignorant of her sudden melancholy, hugging Ashe back and then slipping off to the other side of the cleft where Aden and Quill returned with firewood. Ashe watched her go, chest still tight with emotion, heart heavy.

Rocks scattered, and Thorne dropped down beside Ashe from a ledge above where he'd taken watch. "Thank you for speaking with her."

She pocketed her hands and shrugged. "Never forget, she was mine long before she was yours."

"True." His gaze softened. "I haven't had the time to ask how you've felt, having her back with us."

"Glad and terrified." Ashe cocked a glance his way. "Whatever this is, you know she's not just here to fight, don't you? There's something else."

He sighed, raking a hand through his hair. "I know. I keep waiting for her to tell me, and I can see she wants to, but something holds her back."

"Have you asked?"

"I'm afraid to. There are some questions we know we don't want the answer to even before we speak them."

Like Maleck's journal. Her gaze darted across the cleft to where he and Tatiana had disappeared to refill the waterskins and had yet to return. "It's your choice. But one way or another, eventually you're going to find out why she's here."

"I know," he sighed. "One crisis at a time?"

Ashe bumped shoulders with him. "We should be so lucky, Brother."

CHAPTER NINETEEN

THE FULL MOON guarded Aden with a bright, watchful gaze while he guarded the camp in turn, arms folded, leaning against a tree at its edge. It was so unusually hot, he'd shed his cloak tonight, leaving just his armor and inkings kissed by moonlight while he lounged on the pine's strong body, surveying the shadows.

Not a flicker of aberrant movement or a breath of danger. Some part of him wished there would be; if they were truly drawing closer to an enemy stronghold, he expected more resistance than this. Scouts, spies, *mirothadt* lurking along the paths. The absence of any movement at all set his scalp prickling.

He nearly flinched at a rustle of undergrowth, but it came from behind, not ahead—from the small grove where they'd made camp. He relaxed at the familiar bearing and leaned more heavily into the trunk when Maleck joined him, draping himself against the tree's round edge so his shoulder barely knocked into Aden's. "Anything?"

"I've defended us from two hares since dusk fell."

"Mighty and bold."

"I'm certain the Bloodwights are trembling at my name."

A faint, amused snort; Aden's pulse kicked at the sound. Ever since that first day in the mountains, whether because of Cistine's antics or the absence of the army's communal fear, there were flickers of Maleck that felt like having his brother back. This was one of them, almost enough to distract him entirely from his duties.

"I'd like to talk," Maleck blurted out at last.

Relief gusted from Aden on a silent, long breath. "I'm listening."

"You know things have been...difficult. For me."

He flirted with disarming sarcasm, then gave up. "It's understandable. Not just your brothers, but being at war again. And the way Cistine reappeared."

Maleck swallowed audibly, gloved hands creaking into fists. "I can't even describe—"

"You don't have to."

"But I try to. The way it comes out of me is..." The rustle of a shaking head. "You've seen the journal."

Aden's shoulders gave forward, and he turned his head to catch the frame of Maleck's face in the full moonlight. "Ashe showed me."

"Did she make sense of it?"

"Which parts? The ones where you talk about dying in the war? Or the ones where you talk of the Bloodwights taking her?"

Maleck's flinch was audible, his armor scraping the pine's bark. "I fear that more than anything. More than losing myself, more than losing this war. If they take her because of me, because of what—"

"It will never happen," Aden cut in sharply. "Not even the Bloodwights are a match for that woman's rage. And if they broke past her guard, I'd be there."

"But if she fought distracted, if she fought for *me*, they would. They can use us against each other, *Allet*, like they used me against our family."

Aden grimaced at the memory of augment scars and scorched hair, of Quill's young screams.

"Do you fear me?" Maleck asked after a beat of quiet. "Because of what you saw in that journal? Because of what I did to Asheila?"

Aden gave his answer thought, his mind returning to the dark sketches Ashe had showed him in those feathered pages. It had been the greatest effort of the war so far not to show her how much those pictures disturbed him, the hideous echoes and grim, wild tracings so like the papers decorating Maleck's bedroom after the last war. The ones they finally burned together after their father vanished, presumed dead.

"I've never feared you. We both know I could destroy you in a fight." He waited for Maleck's cheek to tick before he added, "I fear *for* you. You're only as free as you let yourself be. Every time you focus on the Bloodwights and look for them in the shadows, you're choosing them over us."

Maleck slid a hand under his braids, scratching his neck. "It feels that way for me, as well."

Aden grimaced. "I just worry that there might be another Braggos someday, or worse, and you'll ruin yourself regretting all the things you didn't say or do. The people you didn't reach out to until it was too late."

"You know me well." A pause, heavy, and though Aden knew what was coming next, he couldn't quite brace for it. "You remember how I was, after *Aniya...*"

Aden shut his eyes against the memory of his mother choking on her own fluids, lungs ravaged by bloodcough. It took so many medicos that year after the war, first Tatiana's mother, then his. The memory that stood most starkly in his mind was how bright the room was the day of her death, and how Maleck had clung to her hand with both of his and wept for all the songs she never taught him and the conversations unspoken about healing and strengthening, finding their way back to the light.

"I know," he rasped. "I know what it did to you then. What it's doing to you now. What will happen if you don't make things right before we reach this stronghold."

Maleck's gaze landed on him sideways, full of deep thought. "You think I should speak to Cistine."

"And Ashe. If you don't, you're going to resent yourself later." He forced his eyes open, leaning deeply against the tree. "I know you're worried what comes of it if you let your guard down...whether the Bloodwights swoop in and take what's important if you show they matter to you. But you're forgetting the most important thing: *I'm here.*" He shot Maleck a smirk. "You can go on living. Let me fight the war for both of us. I'll protect you all."

"And while you do that, *Allet*, who fights for you?"

Aden shrugged. "The Hive Lord learned long ago to fight for himself."

Maleck hummed low in his throat, but didn't reply. For a time, they had silence apart from the confused chirp of insects and the unseasonable air stirring the thickets and undergrowth. Then Maleck's boots shifted. "I don't even know how to approach Cistine."

"The truth seems a decent place to start. People like her and Thorne swoon over blunt honesty and shed tears." He smiled at Maleck's ragged laughter. "Just speak with her, will you? She of all people isn't one to resent how you feel. Healing begins with being honest about the places where you're broken. Start there and find your way out together." He nudged Maleck's shoulder. "The same goes for Ashe."

"Indeed." Maleck was quiet again for a time, looking up at the stars; then he said, "I don't know if anyone's told you these last three months, but sometimes when you speak, you sound like Mira."

Aden shoved him aside by the back of his head. "I didn't ask for these insults."

"Nor do you have to. We're brothers. I give them for free." The flicker of humor died when they swapped smiles, and all at once Maleck was solemn again. "Having you at my back keeps my feet beneath me. I hope you know how much this cabal values you. How much *I* do."

But should they? Sometimes he felt unworthy of that gift of forgiveness—like at any moment, he would make the next wrong choice and prove their faith a mistake, just like a decade ago when he'd betrayed them for the memory of his father.

"I'll do whatever the gods ask me to keep you all safe," he grunted. "I haven't forgotten my oath."

"Nor have I. But I hope you know it travels both ways." Maleck straightened. "The Hive Lord may fight alone, but this cabal never does. I may not be the person you want at your back of late, but you'll always have me."

Throat tight, Aden shook his head. "There's no one else I trust there more."

With a last fleeting smile, Maleck vanished back into the shadows. In the distant camp, moments later, the purr of Ashe's sleepy voice welcomed him back.

Aden sighed and scrubbed a hand through his hair, scowling up at the stars. "If this is what you meant about them needing me, Mira, come take your task back. I'm tired of doing it for you. I'm not built for it."

The moon winked slyly down at him, offering no reply.

CHAPTER TWENTY

THE SPRINGLIKE FEELING strengthened the higher the cabal traveled; where the climes should have been frozen over, the air grew so warm they all sweated perpetually. But the gods still smiled on them, even if nature didn't; Ashe and Bresnyar found a trapper's cabin tucked away in a shallow valley deep in the mountains. It was a small abode, only one room with kitchen and cot and hearth, and abandoned for some time judging by the mustiness of its corners. The cabal built a fire and doled out rations, bantering about the woes of hardtack and waterskins, not commenting at all on how it felt like spring outside when a week ago they had a snow fight in what seemed like the firm grip of winter.

Cistine volunteered to go fishing, desperate for normalcy to interrupt the wrongness in the air; but sitting on the trapper's dilapidated dock offered no relief from the unbalanced world. The warmth forced her jacket from her shoulders within the first quarter-hour, and she sat on the moldering planks with legs crossed, holding a fishing pole forged of a long stick, a strong thread unraveled from her jacket seam, and one of a hundred confused worms she'd hopped over on her way down to the pond. She tried to enjoy the heat fanning her shoulders, the kiss of the setting sun on her neck, and to not to think of this as what it was.

Nazvaldolya.

She was alone nearly an hour with those thoughts and the stubborn fish flitting in the pond when the brush of a boot on damp wood near the shoreline jerked her upright, hand falling to her augment pouch, body twisting. She relaxed, but not entirely, when Maleck padded down the dock to join her, hands thrust in his pockets, head slightly sunk.

A reprimand was coming, she could feel it; a hard word readied for how she'd antagonized him during the snow fight. He didn't want to be bothered—didn't want anything to do with her at all. He'd made that perfectly clear ever since her return to Valgard.

But she couldn't bear the silence from him anymore; her protector, her friend she'd seen far too little of since her imprisonment in Kalt Hasa. He'd gone into a foreign kingdom of former enemies, to imprisonment, nearly to his death for her people, and she barely caught her breath enough to thank him before danger ripped them apart. And the way he'd looked at her, *flinched* from her touch after the battle in the Chasm...

That snow fight had been more for him than anyone; she had to try, just once more, to know if he still loved her. But he'd avoided her ever since that day, gaze turned in on himself, hardly looking her way.

It was answer enough. She didn't need him to come tell her so.

Yet here he was.

Her feelings in a knot, Cistine turned back to the pond and the fishing rod, bracing her heart and mind against the talk she knew was coming. Already, tears budded in her eyes.

Maleck halted beside her, the shadow of his body cast across hers. "Hello, *Logandir*."

"Hello, Maleck."

His braids rustled with the tilt of his chin. "May I sit?"

She scooted to one side, and he lowered himself on the dock, armor creaking. They were quiet for some time, watching the fish ripple in the still waters, a coy dance around Cistine's worm. But she no longer cared for fresh fish tonight; all that mattered was the silent man beside her and how much it ached that there was such distance between them. She never thought she'd grow to fear solitude with Maleck Darkwind again, but here they were.

He broke the silence at last, fingers deliberately shifting the hems of his gloves. "I have been...avoiding you. Since your return."

It shouldn't have hurt like it did; he was only confirming what she already knew. Yet the words still rived, turning her answer ragged. "I know. I mean, I've noticed."

Again, a quiet, thoughtful pause. "The moment you came down on the Chasm's edge, I knew what you'd trained for while you were away. I felt it that night in Stornhaz as well, before you left us."

She blinked at him. "You knew about the two augments?"

His eyes brushed over her, reading a story written in the lines of her frame—a tale no one else could fathom. "You...carry a sense about you. I've known it since our first encounter on the Vingete Vey. I understand now that because of what I suffered as an acolyte, I have a heightened sense of your power as the Key. I can taste the heat on the air when you walk past me."

"Oh." Her body pulsed with shock. "I had no idea."

"I've grown used to it as we've been together. But when you came back after so many months, things were...different. What you've done, how you've trained, heightens that sensation around you. Your entire body is limned in light I cannot see, but I feel it. You burn like a falling star."

No wonder he flinched from her touch. Hands that glowed that way, reaching out to him, were never meant to love...only to harm. "Mal, of course. Of *course* you should be avoiding me. I'm sorry, I didn't think—if you want to leave, right now—"

His heavy hand rested on her hair. "Peace, *Logandir.*"

Cistine stilled, eyes burning. She didn't realize how much she'd missed his casual, comforting touches until now, knowing *why* he kept himself from her. It took all her strength not to lean into his hand.

"You are not to blame for this," Maleck went on. "If you were dangerous the way my senses tell me, the others would share my reserve. Yet for all that I *feel* you clearly, they *see* you clearly. My gaze has been clouded since you returned." His hand slid down her hair to rest on her shoulder, and his eyes turned across the glittering expanse of the pond. "It has been clouded for longer than that."

A rogue tear escaped Cistine's control, threading down her cheek. "You're not to blame, either. It's the Bloodwights, what they did to you—"

"They're not worth discussing." His tone was firm, but not sharp. "Ever since we entered these mountains, it's occurred to me how I bring them to battle and to every moment between. I give them quarter in spaces they do not belong. In this cabal, with Asheila, and...with you."

Desperate hope knocked Cistine's heart against her ribs. "What are you going to do, then?"

A deep, long breath rolled through him, echoing on the valley walls. "I'm not certain of every step. But I do know it starts by forcing them out of this space between us. By telling you that from now on, even if I seem to take myself away...I will come back, Cistine. I give you my word."

Her breath rushed out in relief. "That's all I'm asking for. On your time and your terms, Mal. I don't want to lose you."

A half-smile dug into his cheek. "Nor I you." This time his arm came around her shoulders, slow and careful as if he expected it to burn; after a tense moment, he squeezed her against his side. "Welcome home, *Logandir*."

She grinned. "I'm glad to be here, Darkwind." And she meant it. Sore as she was from climbing these mountains, and frightened of what lay ahead with the Bloodwights, particularly in capturing one...for the first time in three months she was precisely where she ought to be.

Maleck released her, bending forward to peer over the edge of the dock. "You've drowned your worm."

She growled through gritted teeth and shook the pole. "I don't know what I'm doing wrong! Apparently these fish are too plump and happy to bother with being caught!"

"Do you have a hook?"

She stared at him, then glanced at her pole, the string tightly knotted around the limp worm. "I just...I thought once they bit the worm, I flicked my arm and they..."

Visions of fish sailing through the air onto the dock perished at

Maleck's crooked smile. "Shall I teach you to fish the way Kristoff taught me?"

"Please!"

"On your feet, then."

She hopped up and handed the pole to him; he set it carefully aside. Then in one deft movement, he scooped her up by the knees and shoulders and pitched her into the pond.

Cistine had no time to yell in shock, barely a second to catch her breath before she plunged under the water, fish scattering in every direction. Her boots skidded on the silty bottom and she surged up to the surface, gasping with rage, yanking her soaked hair from her eyes. "I'm going to *strangle* you, Maleck Darkwind!"

But then she stopped, chest-deep in the water, blinking in shock. Because Maleck, bent double with hands on his knees, was *laughing*.

She'd forgotten how much she loved that sound; how much it meant to her before she began to take it for granted, before all this madness ensued.

Spreading her feet and folding her arms under the choppy water, she mock-glared. "Are you finished?"

He thumbed his eyes, still chuckling. "That was for the snow fight."

"Fair." Cistine stretched out her hand. "Help me?"

He lifted her easily up from the water onto the dock. The moment her boots touched the planks, she tucked her weight, swept his ankles, and planted her knee in his stomach, flipping him over and into the pond.

"Now I can see why you laughed!" she chortled when he surfaced, braids spilling like black serpents around his head. "Are you done being ridiculous?"

Lips twitching, he shook his braids back. "I give you my word."

Something bobbed in the water behind him, a sleek black square, and Cistine yelped, "Mal, your journal!"

She knelt and stretched out for it, but he raised a hand to stall her. His eyes tracked the book as it floated off across the pond, a mess of waterlogged pages. "Leave it."

She snatched her gaze from the ruined book to his face, to the conflict of emotions there—melancholy and desperation giving way moment by moment to relief. When he swiveled back to her, his gaze was clear.

"Join me. This time, I *will* teach you to fish."

And because it was Maleck—and she would take any moment, even just one more, where he was smiling at her like a brother rather than avoiding her like an enemy—Cistine jumped back into the water.

They returned to the cabin still dripping, carrying a few fish apiece, late-day shadows twisting around their ankles in the short grass. Maleck would've done better than her at catching fish with his bare hands—he had the stillness and patience she lacked—but a small catch was something, at least. And they were both smiling, which was something even greater.

They entered the cabin to warmth and banter, Quill and Tatiana tending their weapons, Aden and Ashe sparring off to one side of the room, Ariadne and Thorne consulting a map by the fire. His eyes went straight to Cistine, and his brows leaped at the muddy, damp state of her.

She made a face. "Maleck threw me in the pond."

Aden thrust Ashe chest-first against the wall, one arm pinned behind her back, and cast Maleck a knowing look. "Fishing lessons?"

Tatiana bobbed her head sagely. "Ah, the sacred ritual."

"I still remember my first time," Quill reminisced.

"As do I, but I don't recall Kristoff being as soaked as the rest of us by the end of it," Thorne said mildly.

Maleck relieved Cistine of her fish and brought them all to the fire. "Well. None of us were the Wild Heart of Fire."

Ashe wriggled loose of Aden's hold, casting a long, cautious look between Maleck and Cistine. She offered her friend a smile in return, hoping that in silence to respect Maleck's privacy, she could still convey that things were slowly getting better.

With a shake of her head, Ashe joined Maleck fileting the fish, and Aden beckoned Ariadne to spar instead. Cistine joined Quill and Tatiana, the latter tinkering with Cistine's broken gauntlet and greeting her with a tilt of the chin; Quill looked up from polishing his sabers, eyes flicking to the hearth where Maleck and Ashe laughed at some private joke. "What happened out there, Stranger?"

Cistine shrugged. "He just wanted to speak with me. Why?"

"I don't know. He seems...lighter."

Happiness bubbled in Cistine, bright as summer sunlight, as Maleck touched the back of Ashe's head, fleeting and tender. "Well, I'm glad. This may be war, but we don't have to be miserable all the time. What's the point of winning if we lose all our joy along the way?"

Tatiana stiffened, her gaze flicking to Cistine with a glimmer like hope.

"That's easier said than done," Quill grunted. "They still have my sister. And they still have us by the throat."

Cistine's happiness wilted as she watched his face, once so full of brazen joy, now dark with a scowl when he returned to his weapons.

She'd helped Maleck today, but there was still plenty of suffering in this cabal. So much sometimes, she felt like it would drown her long before she found a way out of it.

CHAPTER TWENTY-ONE

GRATEFUL THOUGH CISTINE was that Ashe and Maleck now made space for her at every campfire, the others remained reserved. There was something Tatiana wasn't telling her, a secret bursting behind those clever amber eyes, but no amount of prodding spooled it from her. Though Ariadne was a beacon of warmth, her focus drew away from the cabal day by day, burrowing deeper into the maps she and Thorne checked every dawn and dusk. Quill and Aden were often together when the cabal pitched camp, stealing off to hunt or fish, moving with an easy camaraderie that spoke of their years of friendship—and perhaps of the burden they shared, the loss of Pippet more tangible between them than anyone else.

Cistine tried not to feel like an intruder on all these things when she returned from gathering wood one evening to find a fire already blazing in the shallow, high-mouthed cave Bresnyar had scented among the rocks, and the cabal sparring in its light; all except Tatiana, who lounged cross-legged under the discarded cloak from Thorne's armor and studied their map.

She halted at the cave mouth, arms seizing tight around the bundle of kindling while she watched them. This pattern was unfamiliar to her, nothing Quill ever taught her on the rock top; the fluid movements, the ducks and dodges, the way they traded weapons like augments in deft flings and sharp snatches, even making room for Ashe. In just three months, they'd found a way to fight that adapted her to their ranks, but Cistine couldn't see a place to leap into it.

She set the firewood down, and Tatiana raised her head, eyes wide. "That was quick."

"I've gotten better at quartering sticks, I suppose." She dusted off her hands. "Should I...*can* I join them?"

Tatiana's jaw flickered. "It's...well, they'd have to adjust their patterns. It's just what we do now. How we fight."

Of course it was. Slowly, she sank down beside Tatiana, limbs heavy. "Can I at least sit here, or is that an adjustment, too?"

Tatiana didn't rise to the bitter bait in her words. She sat up straight, fingers drumming on the map. "Let me guess. You're feeling guilty and unpopular, so you came to the one person who usually goes against the grain of how everyone else feels."

A dull smile tugged across Cistine's face. "Am I that obvious?"

"Only to anyone who's known you longer than a minute." Tatiana folded up the map. "I don't blame you, though. I wouldn't want me mad at me, either."

"Are you?" Her voice dropped. "Angry with me?"

Tatiana looked her up and down with an arched brow. "You really don't take well to being the outlier, do you?"

Cistine blew out a cloudy breath. "It's...new for me. And no, I'm not really fond of the feeling."

"Ha! Welcome to my battlefield, *Yani*. Sometimes if you sit with being an interloper long enough, it stops bothering you. Or, if you're sober long enough, you realize which parts you own and which parts you don't."

"You mean like the part where I walked away and betrayed the treaty *I* fought for?"

"Right, like that." Tatiana caught her by the chin. "And then there's the part where these *allotoks* all voted for you to go, so they don't really have any right to be bitter you went. And they should be working harder to include you."

"Then what do I *do*?"

"What you always have. Elbow your way into the middle of things. Make Quill train you. Get back in shape."

"I *am* in shape!"

"I mean this shape." Tatiana gestured to the others, where Quill smacked Maleck on the backside and vaulted out of reach, smirking. "The way things are now."

Cistine rubbed her chilly arms. "Why aren't *you* sparring with them?"

Just like that, the secret was back in Tatiana's eyes, snuffing out her sharp humor. "Oh, you know me. I'd just make them all look bad." She jerked her head. "Why don't you skin those ermines before we all die of hunger?"

The sparring dwindled once the smell of cooking meat filled the cave. The others drifted to refill waterskins and take watch, while Ariadne and Thorne huddled at the fireside, map spread before them, heads bent in deep conversation. The fierce scowl on Thorne's face and the hard tilt of Ariadne's brows set Cistine on edge; when Ariadne rose to accept her portion from Aden, Thorne stayed at the fire, thumb grazing his lower lip in slow, thoughtful strokes, gaze still trained on the map.

Cistine slid to the ground behind him and banded her arms around his middle, tucking her chin over his shoulder. "Hello, you. What are you doing?"

"Narrowing the circle of possibilities." Thorne traced his finger along the map of the Isetfells. "We turned our course today further north than west. According to Bresnyar, the scent is growing stronger. Layered."

Cistine frowned. "Then we're close?"

"Close is relative, given a dragon's sense of smell. We could have days further to go." He tapped a clot of mountains along the map. "But this. This gives me pause."

"Why?" It all looked the same to Cistine, another gray angle of rock on a map full of them.

"Ariadne's family roots are here in Spoek, and her grandparents told stories of ancient border feuds between Oadmark and Valgard. According to the legends, there was a place called Selv Torfjel—"

"The Heart of the Mountain?"

Thorne nodded, his stubble scraping her cheek. "A road into the deep. It connected all the mountains through a web of tunnels, across the Isetfells and down through the Vaszaj Range. Oadmark and Valgard warred for control of it in the times of the Elder Kings. According to the story, to control the heart of the mountain was a path to conquest. You could move men beneath a kingdom without ever being seen or heard."

Cistine bit her lips together, a needling thought pushing through: shadowy cavern halls, hewn rock, a pair of blue eyes flashing beside her in the dark. "Do you think that's where the stronghold is? In Selv Torfjel?"

Thorne tipped his head slowly side to side. "There's still plenty of territory between here and where it was rumored to be, if its existence is even anything more than legend. But we'll check the map every night—and pray we're wrong."

Cistine shivered, and Thorne rolled the map, tucked it into his satchel, and pressed his arm across both of hers, binding her touch closer to his middle. She stiffened when her fingertips grazed a ridged knot across his abdomen. It almost felt like—

Thorne released her abruptly, climbing to his feet. "Are you hungry?"

"I suppose so," she said slowly. "Thorne..."

But he was already gone, slipping in among the others at the back of the cave, leaving her with an unspoken question on her lips and her fingertips trembling with the memory of his new and unfamiliar scar.

CHAPTER TWENTY-TWO

AFTER DAYS OF travel, never certain if they would wake to warmth or chill, the passes growing more treacherous and the predators more vicious while they climbed, there was no sense denying it any longer.

The Balmond's trail led straight to Selv Torfjel.

It was a somber dawn when they admitted it at last, huddled around Ariadne's map just before breaking camp. Whispers of long-ago stories riddled the wind while they looked from the map to one another's solemn faces. Aden's skin prickled with wary instinct, the sense that something great and terrible lay ahead.

A siege within mountain tunnels, rather than at the gates of a fortress—preferable, perhaps, to some. But when he looked at Thorne and Cistine's pallor, at Ashe's scowl, when he felt the dull scrape of the pulse in his own veins, he knew: they four were disadvantaged in dark halls built like catacombs, like mountain halls where memories lurked in every shadow. But if they didn't do this, Bravis and Benedikt might disregard the matter of the Balmond, leaving their flank exposed.

And that was what Aden hated most: that they had no choice. All day long as they trudged through new, deep snowdrifts, the memory of his father's warning rang in tune with his steps...few things were more dangerous than being forced into a decision.

On and up they went, every stride heavier, every moment more fraught than the last. At midday, they entered the shadow of the mountain.

Flat on his stomach on the shale slope, Thorne on one side, Ashe on the other, Aden peered over the jagged lip toward the face of Selv Torfjel.

There was something not right about it; something foul in the sharp maw that led into blackness, the supposed beginning to all passes through all mountains in the North. Mountains could not breathe, could not bear ill intentions, but if it was possible, this one would. Malignancy roamed its bones from cloud-wrapped peak to roots plunged deep in the crevices of shadow far below.

Thorne braced his forearms on the slope and ducked his head, glittering blue eyes fixed on the mountain. "That's our way in."

"It seems too obvious," Ashe muttered. "No guards, no watch, nothing."

"If they're buried deeply enough, they may not think they need it. Or they may assume only fools and lost travelers would find this place."

They weren't wrong, Aden thought, but he kept quiet.

A shower of rocks scattered, and Cistine, Tatiana, and Quill slid down the hillside to their left, panting and winded, a gleam of triumph in their eyes.

"There's another entrance," Cistine announced. "Through a waterfall feeding the river."

"You're sure?" Ashe demanded.

Wedging herself between Ashe and Aden, Tatiana nodded. "We saw one of those...those *things* slipping inside right when we arrived."

Aden's neck flushed. He wasn't eager to face those creatures again—not just for the nauseating grotesqueness of them, but because they'd so thoroughly bested him and Ariadne. Not a single blow landed by his swords or hers, both fleeing like cowards into the hills, bleeding and beaten.

A great legacy, indeed.

He shook off the thought to find Thorne already speaking again. "—

better than announcing ourselves at the front gate."

"If we use that entrance, Bres can watch this one," Ashe offered. "As a last defense, if anything goes wrong, he'll create enough havoc to distract even a Bloodwight."

Thorne skimmed his thumb along his lower lip, and with a deft nod, crawled backward from the ledge. The others followed him—all but Quill. Beside him, Aden lingered, waiting. He'd known Quill most of his life, knew his silence as well as his outbursts and which to fear more. This turbulent quiet with which he stared down the mouth of the mountain was the most dangerous of all.

"Quill," Aden prompted.

"Pip might be down there."

His voice was soft, level, but the anguish that undercut it set Aden's chest throbbing. "We can't do this again. We won't make this another Braggos."

"I'm trying not to think of it like that, either. But we were so stars-damned close back then, and now..." he trailed off, knocking his fist slowly on his thigh. "What if she's in there?"

Aden swallowed and forced out the words he'd struggled with ever since they left the war camp, each time the thought of Pippet crowded in his mind. "Then you search for her. I can't."

Quill's eyes turned to him, steel-sharp. "Why not? You know what happened wasn't your fault. We *had* to go look for her."

He shook his head. "I can't go down that road with you again. My place is at Thorne's side."

Quill's shoulders sagged slightly. "Right. Whatever you say, Tribune."

His cold, pointed tone haunted Aden all the way back down the trail and across the miles to the camp they'd left Ariadne and Maleck to pitch. Bresnyar assisted, ripping great pines up by the roots and breaking them into firewood, shelters, and spears. Additional weapons, just in case. There was game as well, already sizzling over the fire, and Aden's stomach rumbled at the smell. He fought back a groan of resignation when Thorne forewent the meal and retrieved the map, yet again unrolled it, and turned it over face-down beside the fire. They all gathered around him while he started to sketch.

"Two entrances: one above the falls, one at the mountain face." He gestured to Bresnyar. "Will you stand watch at the mouth?"

"Consider it done."

Thorne swiveled to Ashe. "I want us to lead separate parties. You, Quill, Maleck, and Tatiana search for the children and free as many as you can. Cistine, Ariadne, Aden, and I will cluster the Balmond and any *mirothadt* in one place and use an earth augment to bury them."

"Efficient," Ariadne said. "Just as long as we aren't buried, too."

"I'll do it. We'll be all right," Cistine said, and no one questioned her optimism—or her control over the augment that would bring about the Balmond's end.

"And that Bloodwight?" Ashe asked. Beside her, Maleck stiffened, then shook his head sharply.

"Once the Balmond and *mirothadt* are dealt with, Aden and I will subdue it." Thorne's eyes danced from Cistine to Maleck, clear and sharp. "I don't want the pair of you anywhere nearby. Understood?"

Maleck nodded, relief stark in his gaze. Cistine was much slower to agree, jaw ticking.

"We have one wind augment," Thorne said. "We use it to subdue the Bloodwight, and once we're outside, to move that *bandayo* back to the war camp. If for any reason that fails, Bresnyar takes him and then returns for us. Agreed?" Silent nods and somber looks passed around the fire. Thorne rolled the map and tucked it into his satchel again, eyes traveling from face to face. "I have no doubt we'll succeed tomorrow. This cabal is capable of anything when we raise our blades as one. This is just another Black Coast, another wagon raid, another siege. We *will* triumph."

"Well said," Aden murmured.

Thorne clapped a hand on Quill's knee at his right and pushed himself to his feet. "Let's eat."

They broke down the skewers and did as he said, forming a loose circle around the fire. It was growing cold again—seasonably so, for once, as if the world foretold their success and began to right itself. There was chatter tonight, and just enough laughter that if Aden closed his eyes he could almost imagine they were in his home in Stornhaz again, a secret Court made of ambitions and dreams of a better future, gathered together to eat and share visions in a place of safety.

He wondered what became of that house he spent weeks rebuilding, aided and accompanied by Mira; if the Bloodwights laid waste to it when they took the city; if the hewn door and refurbished halls once more fell to ruin.

He tried to tell himself it didn't matter...it was the people who made a home, and most of them were gathered around this fire. But it still prodded at the hole in his chest, made him ache for a different world for all of them.

Silence stole in with the early dusk, and one by one they tossed their skewers into the flames and watched them burn. The pause settled across them, heavy and absolute, full of thoughts of what tomorrow would bring. Dreams of the best and worst chased around Aden's mind the same as theirs.

It was Cistine, predictably, who broke the pause, leaping up suddenly and stepping into Quill's path, blocking his sight of the fire. "Teach me how to spar like you all learned during the war."

He groaned and patted his stomach. "Not tonight, Stranger."

Lips pursed in a pout, she planted her hands on her hips and bent at the waist. "Don't tell me you're afraid I've *outgrown* your training?"

Quill gazed up at her through hooded eyes. Then, quick as a gust of wind, he spun on his knees and swept her legs out from under her, knocking her flat on her seat in the dirt. Tatiana burst out laughing, and Cistine grinned, palming the hard ground and springing back up. Quill rose to meet her, and for the first time in months, Aden watched them dance.

It had always fascinated him when he watched these two spar in Kanslar's training hall; the intrinsic bond between teacher and student was like none other. But he knew the way it sang in the spirit, had felt it when his father trained him, and when he helped train the cabal. And with Pippet, whenever she mastered another hold break, another punch, another kicking style—

That was pure pride, that look in Quill's eyes when he and Cistine swirled around the fire, doling out the distress of the last few months and the worries of tomorrow into each other's bodies. The others half-watched, the conversation reviving again; Tatiana pulled out Cistine's ruined gauntlet, and even Thorne engaged Maleck in discussion about map sketching, his gaze flicking occasionally to the grappling pair, a smile cocking the left side of his mouth whenever Cistine slid a blow past Quill's defenses.

"Someone's kept you on your toes," Quill chuckled when she pounded his ribs.

"Just a bag full of sand! Apparently, that's all the mentor I needed."

"*Oh,* that's a blow below the belt."

"Do you mean like this one?" Cistine spun, jamming her foot toward his groin, and Quill caught her leg and thrust her back, skidding and rolling into Ashe and Ariadne. They pushed the Princess back out with a laugh, and she was up, darting toward Quill, who slapped his palms together and held them out, ready for her jabs.

They went on grappling while the night darkened, while conversation rose, until only Aden was paying attention anymore; seeing them through the embers, but also seeing the children this cabal once were. Back then, they came to him so often for moments like this, to pour out their distress, to lift the weight of fear and expectations from their shoulders.

So much had changed since then; they'd learned to rely on one another more than him. Even when he came back from the Hive, that shadow of who he was and what he became still lingered. The man whose home they entered on Darlaska was not the man they saw with them in this war. Moments like these could shatter so quickly. In a heartbeat, everything could change.

No sooner had he thought it than he saw it happen, like a dark omen spreading across the camp.

The playful light in Quill's eyes was the first to gutter and shift; then the rhythm of his blows, switching subtly from light brushes to hard jabs. He came in quicker, harder, no longer keeping to his usual patterns but slicing into Cistine's. Ducking and spinning and ramming like a blade, he did his best to shatter her poise and dismantle her guard by any means—even dirty blows. Cistine's form changed to match his, a frown digging between her brows. She quickened her hits, blocked swifter, stepped faster. But for all her strength and training she was not yet Quill's equal. He clearly knew it, too, and every time they'd sparred before, he'd let Cistine fall graciously, made her failure a teaching moment.

This was not like that. There was no mercy, no gentleness when he caught her next punch, yanked her around and slammed her to the ground with her arm twisted behind her back. Her pained yelp told Aden just how little Quill was holding back tonight.

The conversations halted and the smile slipped from Thorne's face. He sat up, frowning.

"Quill, you're hurting me," Cistine panted. "Let go."

"Not until you prove to me you can save your own life," he growled. "If they're this close tomorrow, you're already captured. You're at their mercy if they try to take you, and we might not be there, do you understand me? Now get loose."

She wiggled against his hold and cursed. "I can't!"

"Break the *stars-damned* hold, Cistine!"

"Quill." Thorne got to his feet. "Enough."

Quill's head snapped toward him. "Stop coddling her!"

"No. *You* stop. She should never have to tell you twice." Thorne laid a hand on Quill's shoulder, the other on his elbow. "Let her go, or I dislocate it."

Tension choked the campsite. The cabal watched with wide eyes, rigid as Quill and Thorne held each other's gazes—a silent duel. Aden knew he ought to intervene, but he couldn't. They were both right. And both wrong.

Then in one powerful surge, Quill was up, snapping free of Thorne's grip and releasing Cistine. His gaze slanted away when Thorne offered a hand and helped Cistine up. She rotated her shoulder in its socket and shot Quill a glare of such reproach, Aden's guts writhed in embarrassment on his behalf.

Sliding a hand beneath the dulled pale sheaf of his hair, Quill flipped it across his skull and looked away from her. "Sorry, Stranger."

"Forgiven," she said after a beat. "Do you need to keep going?"

Quill shook his head and stalked away into the darkness, pulling a cinnamon stick from his pocket as he went. The smell trailed after him until shadows swallowed his form, and Tatiana sighed. "Are you hurt, *Yani*?"

"I'm fine." Cistine stared after Quill, her gaze more wounded than her shoulder seemed to be.

Aden's scalp prickled. He twisted his head and found Ariadne staring at him across the fire; when their eyes met, she jerked her chin in the direction Quill had vanished. Her intention couldn't have been clearer if she shouted at him.

But what could he do? He'd already proven he couldn't bring Pippet back; he couldn't protect Cistine from a Bloodwight if it came down to it. He couldn't mend any of this. Nor was he the right man to offer spine and heart to this cabal, when his proved so weak in the past.

He'd left, chasing his own desires. He'd abandoned them when they needed him most...and worse, he'd pulled Quill down that road with him.

Quill needed better than him. A better mentor, a better friend, a better pair of shoulders to help carry the load.

To his relief, Maleck stood at last, trailing after Quill into the darkness. That was good; they'd learned to lean on one another while he was in the Blood Hive.

Better that than relying on him to bear them up—and waiting for him to break again.

CHAPTER
TWENTY-THREE

TRY AS SHE might, Ashe couldn't sleep. The tension rattling their small camp bore down deep into her spirit, raking a heart that already leaped and pounded at the thought of what tomorrow would bring. Killing the Balmond, capturing a Bloodwight, freeing children—it was utter madness. But if Pippet was here, she might be back in their arms by the following sundown. If they slaughtered the Balmond, perhaps they would finally land the crippling blow they'd dreamed of since before Braggos.

But for both those things to happen, luck needed to be on their side. These days, that was rarer than a good night's sleep.

Really, she couldn't blame Quill for his outburst tonight. She despised it and would've offered to dislocate his shoulder herself had Thorne not intervened, but she still understood. The same volatility banded her muscles, keeping her wide awake long after the others began to snore. Skeins of light danced across her eyes when she tried to shut them, and all at once she was peering toward Selv Torfjel, and beyond it, to the wide mountain ranges. To the north, toward Oadmark.

Apparently, she was not the only one sleepless tonight.

She sat up and brought the starstone to her mouth. "Meet me at the trailhead."

Another glint across her vision as Bresnyar turned away from the distant horizon of his old home. Then she was herself again, rising to her feet, stealing away from the dead fire to the edge of the camp by moonlight alone.

Off to her left, shadows rippled. "That lasted longer than I expected."

Ashe's boots stuck to the cold ground, her heart sinking. She'd thought he was finally asleep for once. "Are you watching me, Mal?"

"Asheila, I would never impress myself on you that way." Maleck was darkness separating from darkness, joining her at the fringe of the camp. "Would you and Bresnyar care for company?"

She studied him, his shoulders locked and spine straight, gaze clear. Though the intent in his stare made her think it was all a bit forced—his focus riveted on her to avoid looking at whatever shadows climbed at his flanks these days—he *was* offering. Which was more than he'd tried in weeks, especially since that last morning in the war camp. So she nodded.

They didn't go far; Ashe couldn't bear to leave Cistine and the others undefended so close to Selv Torfjel. They found old game trails to climb, a switchback through the nearby mountains, and walked beneath the canopy of stars. Bresnyar ambled along behind them, his breath warming their backs, and the runemark on Ashe's palm pulsed with contentment—and melancholy.

"I owe you an apology," Maleck said after a time of silence. "The way I reacted with you when you woke me in the war camp..."

"It's already forgotten, Mal."

"Not by me." His hand flicked down to take hers, thumb gliding along her palm, over the mark and up to her wrist, where he tugged the glove on more tightly. "I treated you no better than Jad in that moment. I beg your forgiveness."

"I forgave you the second it happened." She let him release her hand, though her heart ached. "We all have nightmares."

"Yes, but not all of us lose control."

"And some of us do. We deal with it as it comes."

Maleck sighed that way he always did when she was being stubborn and he didn't feel like arguing. Head tilted up, he regarded the stars. "To think, we believed life was complicated when we slept above that symphony hall. We truly thought we knew what danger was."

"We were fools. I can't believe how much I took peace for granted, especially after the trial." She booted a thick rock from her path. "If we'd just *expected* Salvotor to have a contingency, maybe we would've protected Pippet better. Maybe we would've prevented the siege altogether. We could still be in the city, drinking wine and fighting at our leisure, not driven out like thieves."

Maleck squinted ahead. "I sometimes consider what I would've done differently if I knew that feast would be our last quiet moment. I doubt I appreciated it enough."

"No one ever expects a moment to be the last of its kind," Bresnyar interjected. "When Ileria and I flew from Ujurak that fateful day, I had no impression it would be the final time we took to the skies together. If I *had* known..."

Dazzles of gold flitted across Ashe's vision, and for a moment she saw, not Bresnyar's sight, but his memory: a plump black-haired girl dancing toward him, swords on her back and a flower crown in her hair, eager light flaring in her eyes. The runemark glinted on her palm like stardust where she trailed it from his snout to his back, her weight sliding between his shoulderblades—

"Asheila?"

She'd stopped walking. The heaviness between her shoulders was Maleck's hand. Breath shuddering, she reached back blindly until she encountered Bresnyar's muzzle. His grief rolled through her, sharp as her own—sharp as every day she'd watched Maleck slip away from her, that she'd mourned Julian's death, that she'd feared for her kingdom and her princess and her own place in the world.

I'm sorry, Scales. She knew he couldn't hear the thought, but she couldn't gather her voice to speak it, either.

Maleck's hand trailed down to the small of her back and up again. "Are you all right?"

"It's the cleaving." She dropped her palm from Bresnyar's snout and pried her eyes open again. "I've been training every day while we fly, but I still can't control it."

Maleck tilted his head while they resumed their journey along the trail. "Why is that, do you suppose?"

Ashe shrugged. "Apparently, I'm not good at letting go of things. That includes power over my sight."

"You, Asheila Kovar, struggling with surrender?"

She kicked his haunch. "Oh, be quiet."

Maleck's laughter plumed the air, filling Ashe's chest with warmth. She'd almost forgotten what that sound did to her, but ever since they'd left the somber war camp, he'd been like this: armor cracking, darkness peeling away bit by bit. She'd been cautious at first, afraid to believe it, afraid to press into him too deeply in case the shields rose around him again; but here he was, and tonight he seemed like his old self. Like they could've simply been Warden and warrior walking Astoria's streets again, climbing up to the symphony hall's hidden balcony, hearts knitted together by music and light.

She'd missed this. Had missed *him* in ways past saying. She didn't know whether to thank Thorne's mission or Cistine's return for it, but whatever the cause for his easier smiles and laughter, she'd never stop being grateful.

"What frightens you about the cleaving?" Maleck asked after a time, jerking her from her thoughts.

"Nothing. You know me." Ashe stuffed her hands in her pockets and shrugged her shoulders up to cover her wind-nipped ears. "Fearless is my name."

"Asheila..."

"Not being in control."

The words leaped from her like a swift kick, and they froze on the path, staring at one another. The admission took something out of her, made her feel lighter for a moment—then heavier, now that it was a spoken piece of the world.

His gaze softened. "Once again, we aren't so different."

She managed a half-smile in return. "I think it's always about control with me. What happened in Siralek, everything that changed afterward between Cistine and me, with you and me when we went to Talheim..." she shrugged her elbows out from her sides. "I don't like when I can't shape the outcome myself. Whether it's in your hands or Cistine's, or Bresnyar's sight...it never feels right to me."

Maleck said nothing, his silence offering a refuge for her secrets to hide in while they resumed walking.

"Did I ever tell you why I wanted to become a Warden?" she asked, and Maleck shook his head. "I was so small the first time my parents fought about me. I remember lying awake in my bed hearing my father lay out his plan for how I'd inherit his side of the family business, and my mother screaming at him that I was going to marry a good man from a good family and sell the shop so I could take care of them in their later years." The words tasted like turned confections on her tongue, rot-sweet and nauseating. "I decided right then I would become something neither of them could control: a girl who could fight for herself. If they tried to drag me off to an arranged marriage or chain me to the shop, I'd make sure I could fight back. I was going to become like the Wardens I saw marching King Ivan's family around the city. They seemed like they'd mastered their own fate."

"Little wonder control of your life is so important to you."

A prickle of guilt slid through her chest. "I know it's nothing like what you suffered as a child—"

"I'm not the only one allowed a painful past." Maleck glanced at her, shame bright in his hazel eyes. "I understand how my behavior these last months has added to your pain. How it's something you could not help, could not control, and that's shaken you. Shaken your faith in me."

"I wouldn't say that."

"Nor do you need to. I can see it in your eyes."

Ashe grimaced. "You do seem steadier these days."

Maleck answered, not at once, "I've been doing quite a bit of thinking since we left the war camp, about how I've allowed fear to be my guide since Stornhaz fell. Even without my brothers before me, I see them every waking hour." He stared ahead into the distance, jaw clenching. "But there are other things before me. People I should protect, and cherish, and treat well. And it occurs to me now that while I've lived for so long in fear of losing what I have, particularly since Braggos...I'm losing time anyway."

Ashe bumped shoulders with him. "You haven't lost me, Darkwind."

His gaze softened at his Name. "But I could. If by simply not paying you the consideration you deserve."

"Unlike Quill, I don't wither and die without attention."

"That changes nothing of what you *deserve*." She rolled her eyes, but didn't press the issue. "That first day in the mountains, when Cistine began her snow war...I didn't understand it at first. How she and Thorne could make games and laugh when Pippet is gone and all this sorrow and fear hang above us. But the more I ponder it, the clearer it becomes...it is precisely because of those things that our happiness matters. There is still much to gain in this life...all that has not been stolen by war. And if I forget the good around me, my brothers have already won. They've enslaved me again. And that is a victory I cannot abide."

His eyes slid to her sidelong, a small dimple carving his cheek.

"I let my journal go at the trapper's nest," he added. "It's finished. No more dwelling on the dark pits of the past."

Ashe sighed. "How long have you known?"

"I knew the moment you took it from the tent, but I could find no words to broach the subject. It must have terrified you, what you saw in its pages. How I behaved when you returned." He spanned his hands in a broad shrug. "Ah, but I'm forgetting, you are fearless."

Snorting quietly, she extended her hand. "I won't lie, I've missed this. It's supposed to be the other way around...you, breaking through every wall *I* throw up between us. It's been lonely on this side of things."

His fingers twined with hers, glove to glove, sturdy and strong. "I'm sorry to have kept you waiting."

Ashe squeezed his hand, scar tissue rubbing against the wool—a stark reminder of what she was, what she became before this war, and during it. And what she hoped would come after. "Stay with me from now on."

He squeezed back. "I give you my word. Whatever else I am, whatever I become, I am yours. I will never forget that, Asheila."

They rounded a bend in the path and halted in Selv Torfjel's shadow. It seemed anywhere they went in this stretch of the Isetfells, they always circled back around to the darkness it cast.

Ashe's stomach plummeted. "This is going to be a different battle. Not what we're used to. I have to keep Cistine safe in there, whatever the cost."

"And I have no doubt you will." A smile wreathed Maleck's voice. "After all, fearless is your name."

Ashe squeezed his hand, then let go to tug at the tips of her gloves. "May I?"

His eyes flickered uneasily at the test, the question, but after a moment of silent tension, his head bobbed. Ashe peeled the gloves off, stuffed them in her pocket, and laid one hand on his face, the other on Bresnyar's snout.

"Remember. No matter what comes tomorrow, it's still us," she said. "Three as one, until the stars burn out."

"Until the stars burn out," they echoed in unison the words first spoken after Braggos, in a starlit meadow with the world shrunk to just the three of them. Now, just as then, they sent a ripple down Ashe's spine and pooled heat in her core.

Bresnyar withdrew first, a wry look on his face. "I know that scent well. Send for me when you're ready to return."

With a surge of his wings, he lunged off the path and down toward the river below to hunt, leaving Maleck and Ashe alone, staring at one another.

She moved first, took his face in her hands and pushed him back against the craggy cliffside, and kissed him with all her might; to welcome him home, and to show him she truly was not afraid to stand in any darkness, as long as he stood beside her.

Even the darkness of Selv Torfjel.

CHAPTER
TWENTY-FOUR

WHEN THE KNIFE plunged into his stomach, Thorne stopped breathing.

His world turned to a long, lightless, agonized scream. Lances of pain bolted through his legs, deadening them, and his arms flexed and spasmed, too heavy to lift. A face loomed above him, shimmering like disturbed water through the tears in his eyes—bald, then bearded, Devitrius, then his father—

I've waited so long for this. She said I could have you, after what you did to us. You put us in Nimmus...now you can travel there yourself!

The pain crescendoed, dragging that last breath out of him in a roar that broke the blood vessels in his eyes, tore his throat, and sent him arching against the manacles of ice around his wrists and ankles, the augments that set his Atrasat inkings on fire.

The knife laid him open from hip to hip and dug in.

Thorne surged upright to the sound of a muffled shout, already halfway to the edge of the small camp before he registered the sound came from him; but he couldn't stop, couldn't let them see when he broke down. And it was close, bile already scorching his throat, shocky sweat spattering his limbs. He staggered down the trail, but didn't make it far. Barely out of sight from the others, he crashed down on his knees and emptied himself across the stone.

Somehow he was surprised it was vomit, not blood. He could still feel the knife exploring his guts, finding the most painful places to lay into him, a deliberate hunt meant to make him feel powerless, helpless, and weak.

He'd vomited then, too, had cursed and screamed and begged for his life like a coward, like a boy taking the belt from his father again. But he hadn't cared in that moment how cowardly he was; he only wanted to return to the fight, to be in the arms of his cabal when the Undertaker took him.

Violent shudders raced through him and sickness surged up his throat again, buckling him down toward the ground.

A gentle hand slid around his waist, another covering his clammy brow. The scent of jasmine and mint wrapped around him, and Cistine's voice breathed in the darkness, "Thorne, it's all right, I'm here...shh. Don't fight it, you'll feel better after."

He heaved up what was left of his dinner, and she held him, her touch steady, her voice calmer even than the times she'd comforted him after his nightmares in Stornhaz. Her hand traced slow circles on his back, and the other swept his hair away from his cheeks and mouth. Her knuckles tapped his spine—five deliberate beats.

You are not alone here.

He gritted his teeth around a sound that fought to escape, somewhere between a panting growl and tears. She leaned her weight into his ribs and held him until the shaking eased and the nausea ebbed, her fingers floating just above the new scar between his hips. Then her lips touched the back of his shoulder, her fingers still winding loosely through his hair. "It's all right. It's all right."

A desperate part of him wanted to believe that, and her touch almost made it possible. He pushed himself up straight on his knees and clamped his eyes shut; the host of stars spun over his head, a teetering white-and-black whirlpool threatening to suck him down. Sickness throbbed in his limbs again. "What are you doing out here?"

"I heard you wake up. It sounded like a nightmare." Her grip tightened around his middle. "Do you want to tell me about it?"

"I can't."

She was silent for a time, and he focused on breathing deeply, the wind teasing his skin, the bemused chirp of insects dying as the cold returned.

"It was Braggos, wasn't it?"

Thorne's eyes leaped open and he twisted to look down at her. She met his gaze frankly, hands never slowing on his back, but her look warned him against lying, breaking his promise to be honest with her in all things.

Thorne swallowed, and it raked like shards of glass. "Yes."

Her fingertips trembled faintly against his spine, coaxing up his protectiveness so sharply it murdered his own fear. Everything in the moon-licked pass popped vividly: ghostplant light low by the cliff base, shadows dancing on sculpted rock walls, firelight glowing back up the path where someone had stoked it to life again. And Cistine, crouched beside him, hickory hair stirred by the breeze, green eyes bright and wise and full of worry.

He touched a hand to her jaw. "It's nothing. It's behind us."

She pulled back, shaking her head. "It's not behind *me*. I don't even know what happened, I just know the whole cabal freezes at the mention of that place. How can I help any of you if I don't even know what specters you're dancing with?"

Of course that was why she wondered...because she was scheming and plotting how to heal the wounds ripped through the middle of their cabal; and without Braggos, she lacked the greatest power in her arsenal. But he didn't know if he could arm her with it. How to bring her with him to that place, into his nightmares...to the brink of his own death.

"Thorne?" Cistine murmured. "*Please.*"

Don't shut me out of your grief, she'd begged him after Baba Kallah's death. Being removed from the pain, locked out even for her own protection, sang to her own specters and reminded her of more than a decade spent believing she wasn't worthy to be told the truth or welcomed in, to share the burden.

Thorne tossed a prayer to the gods and pushed himself upright, reaching out to her. "Walk with me?"

She gripped his hand. Together they slipped deeper into the shadows, into starlight's embrace. The sounds of night closed around them: the gentle brush of wind, the insects singing, an animal foraging in the distance. Along the spine of the mountains embracing the narrow valley, a flicker of gold hardened into view, then vanished: Bresnyar, keeping watch among the crags, hunting prey.

Cistine didn't challenge the silence. There was trust in the tightness of her hand, the way it squeezed his in four beats, over and over. Through the bright tether of her touch, the reminder in that silent signal, Thorne unraveled the words from deep in that place he'd locked them away so he could keep fighting.

"We'd been at war for two months," he said hoarsely. "Fanning out the lines, then regrouping. The strategy seemed to be working...we routed the *mirothadt* from much of the southern half of Valgard. Morale was high, our prospects seemed strong. So when our scouts brought word of an enemy presence near the city of Braggos, it had all the signs of an easy victory. Perhaps even a blade stabbed to the heart of their forces.

"But it was a trap. They let us push them back that far, baiting and reeling us into a slaughter." A tremor passed through his voice, and he swallowed it with effort. "All those forces we thought we drove out were waiting for us around Braggos—all and then some. They shut us into the city with augments and steel, and the massacre began."

Flames painted his memory. Screams echoed in his ears. A waltz of shadow and lightning, broken earth and sculpted ice, and bodies falling before his eyes—friend and foe alike.

"None of us had ever seen a battle like it," he rasped. "Not even against the Middle Kingdom. Of the thousand who entered the city, fifty escaped. Of those fifty, only half survived their wounds."

Pain lanced through his calves, and he halted, reaching down to rub the back of his leg. Cistine stepped into his path, never letting go of his hand. "You were hurt?"

"The entire cabal was." His voice cracked. "I nearly lost them all in one stroke. A single battle. And I..."

The strength deserted him, and he sank down again, eyes shut against the memory of scorch and smoke on his face, the hot and humid triage tent afterward and how he'd finally gotten up against the medico's orders and staggered cot to cot, searching for the others, desperate to know his mistakes hadn't been their end.

Cistine came down with him, her hand hovering over his middle. Her frown told clearly she'd felt it when she embraced him—and she knew what it was. "Show me."

Grimacing, Thorne rolled up his shirt.

She caught her breath sharply, eyes blowing wide at the sight of the newest scar across his abdomen. How precise it was—a clean, methodical cut. He knew by the furious twist to her face that she recognized the mark of *Svarkyst* steel—and not an errant slice during the heat of combat, one amidst a flurry of mindless blows. They'd taken their time laying him open, a memory that still made him feel powerless, worse than any time his father had whipped him.

"Who?" The word rattled out of her lips, taut with rage.

"I don't know. His face is a blur. But I suspect he was once part of Sillakove, a man my father threw into the Hive for associating with me. Perhaps he endured Siralek by distancing himself from Nimea's Tumult."

An enemy who'd bided his time for a decade and took the opportunity on the battlefield to exact vengeance—that thought still unnerved him. He'd pinned Thorne down with augment shackles and *gutted* him, meticulously, ruthlessly, while his cabal fought and fell without him.

"Tell me he's dead." Thorne had never heard such viciousness in Cistine's voice, had never seen her look so ready to kill.

"Aden found us." Aden, who should not have been there, who Thorne hadn't seen for weeks before Braggos. When his cousin's face had swam into focus above him, bone-white with dread, voice chanting to *hold on, hold on, Mavbrat,* he'd thought he was already at the Sable Gates. That Aden and Quill had died on their self-proclaimed mission to find Pippet, their reunion finding them at the threshold of Nimmus. "He ran that fighter through and saved my life. His last healing augment...for me." The anguish wormed into his voice, underscoring the regret, the waste of that when those augments were already so few and precious. That one, they'd kept in reserve just to save Pippet.

It had saved him instead—and perhaps damned her.

Cistine splayed both hands on his toned abdomen, her thumbs brushing the scar's brown edges. That it *had* scarred despite the healing augment told a tale of its own: how quickly he'd nearly bled out. How close he came to death even with Aden's intervention. "I'm sorry I wasn't there. Thorne, I'm so *sorry*."

He took her chin in his hand, tilting her head until her glassy eyes met his. "I may regret that I sent you away, but I will *never* regret sparing you Braggos."

She blinked rapidly, and a tear escaped down the round of her cheek. "We were supposed to do this together. Find peace *together*. If I'd finished things quicker in Talheim, if I came back sooner—"

"You would've alit on Braggos's wall, glorious and mighty like you did on that mountaintop, and broken the Bloodwights' forces right then." Thorne tucked his sleeve over his knuckles and cleaned the tears from her cheek. "And you would've watched me die, because I would never have let Aden carry me off any battlefield you stayed on."

A shaky breath rattled through her parted lips, and her hands slid from his scar and took his shirt instead, covering the reminder of his pain and shame. "Just tell me how I can *help*."

"Be here. Be with us. Make the cabal laugh and smile and spar with you. Make them *remember* there was a life we loved before Braggos, and we can have it again." He set his brow to hers, and she leaned all her weight against him. "When they look at one another, they see darkness—they see other warriors who fought in this Nimmus. But you're a light from beyond black shores, Wildheart...you're a beacon. You guide us home."

She nodded, and the breath drew into her again, deeper and fuller this time. He heard it bearing down deep in her lungs, fortifying her resolve. There was no doubt she would be the light and leading for their cabal; the strength at his side that shored up his own when his ruling failed. His perfect equal in every way.

Gods, he'd missed her.

Cistine gestured to her leg. "Lie down." He did, resting his head in her lap, and her fingers smoothed through his hair in rhythmic strokes. "I'm sorry all of you faced that, and I'm sorry I wasn't there to play the part in it I should have. It's true, Talheim didn't keep its oaths. It turns out I have just as much of a tendency for cowardice as my grandfather. Except, instead of starting fights, I run from them."

Thorne frowned up at the silhouette of her head above him. "Cistine..."

She cupped her hand gently over his mouth. "I can't go back and change the choices I made when Stornhaz fell. But I'm here now, and I *am* putting Valgard first. I'm putting *you* first. No more battles like Braggos, and no more running away. I'll walk into any fight to keep that promise. Whatever it takes."

Hair tucked back, she bent low to press her lips to his forehead. He squeezed his eyes shut and held on to that feeling, precious and half-forgotten during their months apart. "And *I'm* sorry I put the weight of solving this on your shoulders. This was our fight to face together. I have no right to blame you for my poor choices. *You* came back...it was I who didn't have the courage to cross the Dreadline and find you."

Cistine's laugh was light and faraway as the cold stars. "So we're both young, and new to all this, and we're learning. We'll do better next time."

Reconciliation—forgiveness, even—should have tasted nothing but sweet. Yet with the danger looming on the horizon, the reminder of this war's cruelty etched in his body, into his dreams, and knowing what awaited in that dark mountain at dawn...

Unease clamped tight around Thorne's heart and would not let go.

THE SPECTER

OF

BLOOD AND SNOW

CHAPTER
TWENTY-FIVE

THE ROAR OF the falls reminded Cistine of the Nior River and Hellidom, of her garden at the Den and all the wonderful and terrible things that had happened there; and it reminded her to be thankful for Quill's training, as much as her heart still ached from their sparring session the night before, while she vaulted just beneath him up the slippery stone wall toward the cave mouth. On every side, the cabal climbed, black stains on blacker rock in the predawn gloom. Bresnyar had carried them down into the crevice under a veil of clouds and left with a parting growl, nostrils flaring, gazing up at the mountainside. "There's something strange in this place. A scent. Familiar."

"Pippet?" Quill had asked hoarsely.

Bresnyar slowly swept his muzzle side to side. "No. From before. I can't quite place it, but I *know* it."

Cistine was torn between hope it was a Bloodwight, and fear that there might be something worse—some other enemy lying in wait ahead.

She tried not to think of anything but the next handhold while she followed Quill's steady ascension up the slick mountain. Aden climbed below her, offering the comfort that if she fell, there were hands to catch her; and on Selv Torfjel's far side, the sun began to rise, painting the sky in fingers bright as fire and ribbons dark as blood.

Quill grunted suddenly, and with a leap and a heave, gripped the sheer ledge and flipped himself inside the cavern. He reached back for Cistine, pulled her up with him, and steadied her with a hand to her shoulder beside the waterfall's roaring edge.

"I'm sorry," he said, barely louder than the torrent's roar, before Aden picked his way up to join them, "about last night. I'm just...this isn't easy for me. What we're doing today, what we might find...what could find *us*, what it could do to you—"

Cistine squeezed his hand against her arm. "I know, Quill."

His eyes searched hers, haunted and desperate. "To Nimmus with Thorne's plan. If they find you, if they're coming after you, you get to Bresnyar and you *run*. We'll be right behind you, Stranger."

An odd shiver pierced her armor, shoving deep. "I would *never* leave all of you behind again. I gave you my word."

Quill shook his head but said nothing more. They parted at Aden's arrival, turning as one to face into the cave while the others crawled inside with them. It was utter blackness; no mineral deposits, no ghostlight to cut the gloom...as if the creatures they came to hunt needed no help to find their way, living and breathing the dark, uninhibited by it.

The cabal's first disadvantage.

The last inside the cave, Ariadne doled out ghostplants from her pockets; they broke them, tucking the glowing excretions gingerly in their fists. Splashes of red, gold, and pale blue limned their faces as Thorne brushed through their midst to take the lead. "Keep your eyes sharp for branching tunnels, and stay silent. Stay *close*."

Moving as one, they struck off into the darkness.

Cistine's heart thundered, a sound she was certain echoed through the whole mountain. The blackness, only thinly cut by the low light held close to their bodies, might've couched any predator, any creature—even the ghastly ones they were here to kill.

What if the Bloodwights were here, too, and they sensed the augments she carried? Sensed *her*?

We deal with challenges as they arise. Mira's voice wedged into her mind.

Worrying only makes us live the problem twice.

Ashe's elbow brushed Cistine's ribs, jolting her from her thoughts. With a chin nod, she gestured to the cave's arched ceiling.

It was not entirely dark anymore. Pale strands of glowworms, a light ultramarine, flickered into view when the cabal walked beneath them. They woke in ribbons and rows, garlands of ethereal light like the fingers of the gods pointing the way, a twisting, natural ribbon through the dark. And that color—

Cistine's gaze leaped to Thorne just as his descended from the roof to find hers. He smiled, small but genuine, and her pulse stuttered for other reasons entirely.

The river flowing through the mountain seemed to go on forever, and Cistine's legs tingled from the constant tread of boots on rock by the time they reached the tunnel's end. A broad lake spanned the cavern ahead, fed by another waterfall gushing from the rock itself, and here there was a watch: two augurs posted at the poolside, deep in conversation, utterly unaware of the warriors creeping into their stronghold.

At a nod from Thorne, Quill and Tatiana shot forward like arrows, slamming the *mirothadt* off their feet and snapping their necks in a single congruous motion, swift and practiced as a dance. Relieving them of their augments and dropping the bodies into the riverhead, they beckoned the others out.

To Cistine's relief, one of the flagons Quill tossed her was a healing augment. Gods willing, they wouldn't need it, but she felt better with it in her pouch.

The second corridor they entered was wider, and they stole along it in pairs, Cistine beside Ashe, tension vibrating off her friend with every silent step. A faint scrape of metal on metal told her Ashe was fingering the starstone—just in case.

They emerged at last onto a ledge, and at once Maleck gripped the back of Cistine's neck and forced her to her knees.

They were perilously high, clinging to a narrow lip of stone above the hive-like inner cavern full of hewn paths and stone alcoves wrapping the circular walls; forge-hammers banged, *mirothadt* shouted to one another, and somewhere in the distance creatures howled and screamed. The sound raised the hair on Cistine's neck, and she pressed closer to Maleck's side.

"Children." Tatiana nodded to the left side of the cavern where a stream of small, wasted bodies, some masked and some not, filed in and out of a corridor mouth.

Quill's fingers scraped the rock beneath him. "Pip is here."

"That's your mark," Thorne spoke to Ashe. "Wait for us to bury the Balmond and use the distraction to herd together as many children as you can."

"If they won't come quietly..." Quill flashed a new wind flagon. "There's always this."

Thorne grimaced, but said nothing. They all knew it would be impossible for Ashe, Maleck, Tatiana, and Quill to carry a heap of unconscious children away. But there was no telling Quill that.

The atavistic wailing reached a fever pitch, eliciting curses from several of the *mirothadt*, and Thorne half-rose to his knees. "It's time."

The cabal bumped fists and separated, Maleck with a kiss to the top of Cistine's head. She sent a silent prayer on his heels for his strength to hold in this small Nimmus ruled by his brothers, then followed Thorne, Ariadne, and Aden in a slow creep along the cavern's upper ledge.

"Plenty of tunnels here," Aden muttered. "Countless places to find a Bloodwight, not to mention the Balmond."

"I'll know when a Bloodwight is near," Cistine replied.

For a moment, they moved in utter silence. Then Ariadne drew ahead, cutting the side of her hand against Thorne's chest. "Wait here."

She turned up her hood and sauntered down the path. A terrified hiss pricked the backs of Cistine's teeth, her jaw leaping wide, but Thorne wrapped a hand around her mouth and gave the smallest shake of his head.

For minutes, they crouched against the curved cavern wall, unseen by the forces below. Sweat puddled in the small of Cistine's back and dappled her forehead; the small forges heated the whole cavern like a furnace, the steam fighting to escape from tiny vents broken open in the roof. With every second, her mind spun fresh horrors, scenarios where Ariadne was caught and the entire mission collapsed around them in blood and fire.

Something grazed her attention, a cruel talon raking her mind. Then it was gone, withdrawing at the sound of guttural laughter and an answering giggle, vaguely familiar but not, higher-pitched than Cistine ever thought it could possibly be. Her mouth popped open in shock when Ariadne rounded the bend of the stone trail, a man's arm slung around her shoulders, the wineskin in his hand reeking and his sloppy smile and yellowed teeth at Ariadne's earlobe telling precisely what he thought was waiting for them in solitude ahead.

Aden ripped forward like a drawn blade, taking the augur off his feet and away from Ariadne, slamming him against the wall. In the same fluid motion, she spun on heel and slammed her boot into the man's sternum; his eyes rolled up and he crumbled at her feet, either stricken or heart-stopped, wine pouring away like blood back down the path.

Ariadne scrubbed the saliva from her ear and turned to face them. "The Balmond are kept in a separate cavern...it seems their masters don't trust them except to track and return."

Cistine blinked at her, then at the man.

"What?" Ariadne smiled faintly. "Did you think I could be so close to Tatiana for a decade and not learn a few flirting tricks?"

Thorne shook his head in wonder. "You may be the most dangerous woman in all the kingdoms, Lightfall."

Ariadne's eyes glowed like a wildcat's at her Name. "I do what I must."

"Do you know which tunnel?" Aden's voice was ragged, fists still flexing furiously.

Ariadne measured him with a long look, then nodded. "They aren't shy to inform the newest recruits. I can lead us there."

Cistine stripped off her armored scarf and bound it around Thorne's hair, hiding the distinguishable silver threads. Then she towed up his hood for good measure and kissed his temple. "What are we waiting for?"

Cloaked in their armor to blend with the *mirothadt* below, they descended the path. Cistine's heart clenched like a fist at every augur who passed them, wondering if this or that one might've fought at Braggos, might've dealt a wound to her friends, might've killed someone she'd brushed shoulders with at feasts, in training, in the streets of Stornhaz. But Ariadne led them with head high and shoulders back, utterly in command. No one gave her a second glance when she made as if she belonged here. She ruled every inch of space she took up in this cavern.

So Cistine imitated her posture and bearing and imperious stare, letting none of the gazes that *did* flit toward them doubt that she was *mirothadt* and she belonged here, on a mission from the same Nimmus-cursed power that held them all in check.

At last, Ariadne turned them aside into a long, damp, empty hall, and Cistine breathed more easily.

"The Balmond's hovel lies at the end." Ariadne gestured ahead in the blackness. "Well-guarded, he said, but nothing the four of us can't manage."

Satisfaction spiked in Cistine—then perished against a pulse in her chest. The familiar call slid into her mind, dragging her feet to a halt.

Come. Come and see.

"Cistine?" Thorne took several steps up the corridor, but paused when she didn't follow.

The power of the gods whispered to her, lighting the way brighter than any ghostplant or glowworm's light. There were branching rooms here, niches all but utterly disguised in the shadows along the walls. And through one of them...

Cistine beckoned with a roll of her hand and jogged down the hall.

That call drew her like a beacon, spoke to the craving deep in her chest, the desperation to outfit the cabal with more than just steel. And some part of her, desperate, frightened and *selfish*, knew the more flagons Valgard's army had, the less was required of her. The longer she could delay what she truly came to this mountain in search of—what none of them knew she was looking for.

Silent curiosity burned from Thorne, Aden, and Ariadne, but they didn't dare raise their voices to ask what she was doing; they simply followed her down the path until she halted before another nondescript gap in the wall. The call pounded her skull, sharper and more violent than the clanging forge-hammers in the outer cavern, and she ducked through the narrow slit into an empty war room.

It looked so like the Chancellors' meeting place in the camp: maps laid out on a stone table, dim ghostlamps faintly illuminating their aged faces, and a stock of weapons along the walls—polearms, axes, daggers and swords...and augments. A full satchel on the stone table.

Cistine stepped forward, head and chest aching with the call, and Ariadne snagged her elbow. "No. I don't like this."

Thorne moved as well, not to the satchel, but to the maps. He spread his hands on the stone. "Come and see this."

Only Aden moved forward. Cistine tugged a step to follow, but Ariadne towed her back in an iron grip. Gritting her teeth, she watched the cousins bend over the maps, surveying the dark rings of *mirothadt* forces; the enemy's battle plans.

"Look at this." Thorne tapped the northwest corner of the map. "They've assembled a legion at the edge of the Isetfells. But *why*? What's out there that's drawn their eyes?"

"Could that be where all the Bloodwights are?" Ariadne asked.

"Possibly. Aden?"

He didn't speak, his fingertips tracing the markings of enemy locations across the map, north and south. His throat bobbed, and a deep frown sliced his brow.

"*Aden,*" Thorne repeated sharply.

"I know this pattern. This formation...the strategy. Even the handwriting. But I can't remember where it—"

All the sound rushed from Cistine's ears. Her heart stopped—then started again.

Something arrived with a brush of wind against her back. A choking, suffocating feeling of darkness permeated the war room, soaking the walls in decay, turning her stomach to a writhing heap of revulsion.

Her shout had no words, but it brought Thorne and Aden spinning from the table, sabers drawn, just as Ariadne jerked Cistine in a pivot to face the figure who blocked the seam in the stone—their only escape.

His unnatural height, his raspy chuckle, his beaked bird mask angled toward them, somehow seeming to sneer—all unmistakable.

"Hello, Key."

That sickening voice, echoing from a memory of unnatural storms and a lightless pit and cruel white eyes...

Vandred.

CHAPTER
TWENTY-SIX

TATIANA DESPISED EVERY inch of this place: the cold that reminded her of Oadmark, the darkness that reminded her of Kalt Hasa. Most of all, she hated being near these children, even with the height of the path separating her from them; it all floated up to her anyway, the hair-raising wrongness of either their masked faces or those blank, unfeeling stares, and the *hunger* that lurked beneath the void while their lithe bodies passed in and out of the tunnel mouth below.

She was no stranger to hunger; she'd grown up in the derelict quarter of Stornhaz knowing plenty of people who went to bed with empty bellies. But the raging need in these children's eyes, the desperate, darting glances, shivering limbs, and twitching fingers playing out a silent song against their armored thighs wherever they went...this was different.

Like addiction. Like craving more mead when the last drop was gone.

It awakened a long-forgotten nightmare of Maleck before the last war, a smiling boy consumed by that same hunger, hollowing out his cheeks and eyes until he better resembled a corpse. And the night he'd left them, when Tatiana had woken on her bedroll in Kristoff and Natalya's dining room to hear Quill sobbing in agony, and Aden screaming to his mother for help, the smell of scorched hair and blood filling the house...

She silenced that thought with a vicious shake of her head and leaned her weight slightly into Quill; he perched beside her, wrapped in shadows, his eyes following the stream of children through the cavern and into the hollow below. "Any ideas, Featherbrain?"

He skimmed his thumb along his lower lip. "We could try to pass as guards escorting them in."

On Quill's other side, gripping the rock like an anchor in a raging sea, Maleck shook his head too sharply, almost jerkily. "Children are watched closely, always by the same caretakers. They'll raise the alarm at once if we try to relieve their shift."

Ashe squeezed his shoulder. "Is there anything else we should know?"

Maleck wiped a shaking arm across his forehead and shrugged.

"Maybe it's not a question of blending in," Tatiana offered. "I don't think these children care who's guarding them. It's the guards themselves we have to worry about, and that's just a matter of being the quickest people in the room."

She looked at Quill; despite his distraction and the tremors of tension gripping his body, they'd still moved together as one in that lake cavern, their understanding of each other's patterns as flawless as ever. If they could move through that tunnel quickly enough...

"All right," Ashe said. "Mal and I will cover our faces and start herding the children. The pair of you, use some of that wind augment. Get down the tunnel as fast as you can, dispatch the guards, and take their place. Then we wait for Thorne's signal."

"It's a risk," Maleck warned. "If the shift change comes while we stand watch—"

"It's worth it." Quill drew the wind flagon from his pouch. "Ready, Saddlebags?"

Tatiana rocked her shoulders loose and offered her hand to him. He uncorked the flagon and poured a kernel of godlike power into the cradle of her fingers, then into his, and passed the rest of the augment to Ashe. Tatiana focused on the energy building in her palm with a hair-raising chill, licking at the Atrasat inkings below her armor, coursing along the stiff lines of her body.

She breathed it in, drew up the mouthguard of her armor, and shot a parting nod to Ashe and Maleck.

Then she and Quill were gone.

It never ceased to tie her stomach in knots, the swiftness of motion under duress of a wind augment. In half a step, they were off the ledge; then tearing down the hall past the children coming and going; then they were before the guards, six men and two women stationed at the broad mouth of a dim cave beyond.

Tatiana slammed her hand into the wall, slowing her momentum, and sent the rest of the augment ahead of her, blasting half the guards off their feet into the cave. Quill was on the others in a heartbeat, silent and lethal, chopping throats, breaking limbs, and cutting between them like a blade.

Tatiana's marks were swifter to recover; one woman drew her sabers, one man a crossbow, and the other woman ran for a bell set into the wall.

Not an augment among them. Tatiana didn't have to guess why.

She sent her last gust of wind to rip the breath out of the fleeing woman's lungs; then she drew her blades and met the other two in a quick, vicious duel, steel streaking and bolts flying. Experience had taught Tatiana to fear those dark-fletched arrows more than the sabers; she kept one eye on the man while she danced with his companion, driving them both deeper and deeper into the oblong room.

They were an even match. Too even. Frustration sang in Tatiana's fists when she and her opponents lunged, blocked, parried, broke apart and came together again and again. She needed to end this before the man's arrows found his mark, before the pain erupted in her shoulder again, or worse, in her middle.

Then Quill was there without warning, shooting from the tunnel mouth like an arrow himself, and his sabers came down on the man's wrists. His hands—and the weapon in them—severed to the floor, and Quill silenced his scream with a cut across the throat. He hurled a bead of wind to her, and Tatiana flung it into the woman's chest, blasting her against the wall. In one deft cut, she removed her head.

Silence. Even the tap of children's feet along the stone went quiet.

Slowly, Tatiana straightened, sheathed her blades, and turned.

A whole cavern of masks and emaciated faces angled toward them. Rows of children, coming and going, all stopped and stared.

Every hair on Tatiana's body stood on end.

"Get back to your duties!" Quill's shout made her jump, that cruel bark nothing like his usual accented swagger or the gentleness with which he addressed most children. But it did the trick; slowly, they revolved away.

All but one. One, in a whole sea of swaying bodies, who did not move.

Tatiana's heart separated from the rest of her and began a long, perilous drop through her body, down toward the icy stone to which her boots, abruptly, were moored.

A bird's skull hid her face, making it impossible to know if she had the same angular features and wide, dark eyes, the same mischievous tilt to her brows as Quill. But the black-and-brown mottling of her limp, tangled, overgrown hair, and the way she cocked her head like a curious raven and stood on the tips of her toes while she studied them, as if ready to cartwheel, or duel, or dance...Tatiana would know that posture anywhere.

Her lips trembled, but could not form the word. Quill's did. "Pippet?"

She didn't react like she knew the name, like she knew *them*. Her lean body quivered and held fast when Quill sheathed his blades, bared his palms, and eased forward one step, then stopped and waited.

She didn't flee. Didn't come to him.

Another step. "Pip. It's me. I know you remember me."

Her head gave an unnatural, harsh tilt back the other way, like a dog reckoning strange notes in a song. Then her beaked face turned toward the other children still flowing around her, a thin trickle of bodies separating her from Quill.

"That's right." Quill's tone gentled now, so desperately anguished it filled Tatiana's eyes with tears. "Look at me, Hatchling. I'm not here for them, I'm not here for anyone or anything but you. I'm taking you home with me. All right?"

He was almost close enough to touch her, and she tucked her hands behind her back and retreated a pace, shoulders curving in, like she feared he'd hit her.

Quill froze, fingers extended, heartbreak crashing through his face. Slowly, like a penitent man before a god, he sank to his knees. "I'm...I'm not going to hurt you, Pip." A thin crack seamed his voice. "We're going to get you out of here. Back home, back to Faer."

Again, that odd tilt of her head.

"Him, I know you want to see." Breathless laughter shook from Quill's chest. "He misses you, and you're not going to believe this...he'll tell you that himself. Cistine taught him to speak."

Pippet's shoulders stiffened at the Princess's name. Unease slithered through Tatiana's guts. "Quill."

He ignored her, reaching out again. This time Pippet didn't pull away, didn't flinch at all when he gripped the mask's beak and tilted it up to bare her face. Tatiana's heart fluttered from its resting place in the very pits of her, then wilted again.

It *was* Pippet, but in a nightmarish state; haggard and sallow, just like the rest of them. That same cruel desire burned in the punched-in sockets of her eyes like coals in the heart of a dying fire.

Quill's breath audibly stopped. "Stars damn it, Pip."

Still no recognition at her name. The sharpening of her gaze wasn't familiarity or relief or joy, but that primal hunger honing into a fixed point.

Fixed on *Quill.*

Right then, Tatiana realized what she'd sensed, what Quill was still holding in the threads of his armor, ready to use in a heartbeat.

But he wasn't seeing. Wasn't *thinking.*

Pippet was not cowering from him, her hands behind her back that way. Too late, Tatiana spotted the deadly glint of a knife she slipped from her waistband and swung in the same mortal backhand Aden had taught them all as children—all the way down the line to his youngest student.

Sense fled. Reason and logic perished. There was only the three of them—Pippet, Quill, and Tatiana—and there was that *Svarkyst* dagger in Pippet's hand aiming for Quill's jugular.

Time ground to a near-halt, stretching out heartbeat by heartbeat as

Tatiana lunged. She could summon no breath to shout. No warning came to her lips, to her mind.

Pippet, Quill, her, and the knife. Her *valenar's* neck, fully exposed to his sister's killing blow.

Tatiana slammed shoulder-first into Quill, hurling him to the floor.

The blade went into her instead.

Armored threads severed under the lightless ore. Then the skin underneath gave way.

She hit the floor, still silent, but she shouldn't *be* silent because the knife was in her, it was *in her,* and when she started to move, steel scraped her hipbone. From *inside.*

"*Tati?*" Quill's voice shattered through four octaves, cracking on every one, and his limbs slapped the stone as he scrambled to her side, yanking her onto her back, his hands on her neck, her shoulders, then at her side, slipping off of her armor—slipping in all the blood.

"Oh, no," Quill's voice dropped, harshened, all the strength gone at once. "No, no, *no!* What did you do, stars *damn it, Pip, what in Nimmus did you do?*"

Pain flared through Tatiana at his bellowing, at his touch, a slow burn at first, then brighter and hotter, shooting tines like lightning through every nerve, and stars, burning *stars* it was like she'd been set alight without inkings, without armor, with *nothing* between her and the pain. It traveled through her hip, down into her abdomen, and lower. Too low.

"Damn," she gasped, "damn, damn, *damn...*"

Not this. Not this. Not this.

The world was a whirlpool of color and sound, her limbs dead, numb, detached from her, ears ringing with screams. *Pippet* was screaming, a long, drawn-out wail, body bent into the sound while she backed away from them, raising the alarm.

Summoning her masters. Summoning their doom.

Boots skidded on rock, Ashe cursed, Maleck shouted, and with a flirt of color Pippet was gone, fleeing from them—her work already done.

"*What in God's name happened?*" Ashe shouted.

Maleck's hand descended on Tatiana's brow, the other grazing the knife, and when it wobbled within her she heaved, bile surging from her mouth, and started to choke. Quill pulled her upright so she could breathe, propping her against his chest, his heart racing like it would fail at any second, breaths staggering in out of him. "It was Pip, she was—I thought she knew me, I thought she *recognized* me, she..."

He trailed off, and dimly Tatiana knew he'd realized the truth. Pippet *had* recognized them. It was why she'd raised the alarm.

Cold metal grazed her face; Quill, taking her chin in his three-fingered hand. "Saddlebags! *Look at me*, don't close your eyes. Don't you leave me, Tatiana! *Do you hear me?*"

Her eyes were too heavy to open. The world slipped away from her, but she reached for Quill.

She had to tell him. Now, right *now*, before it was too late, before he did something, *they* did something that would break her, break this fragile thing inside her that she'd begun to see as happiness ever since their first day traveling into the mountains.

"Quill," she heaved, "I'm—there's a—"

She couldn't find the words, couldn't *remember* them, or how to tell him. In her memory, in her mind, everything glowed like an aurora and burned like the first and last kiss.

Then she was gone.

CHAPTER TWENTY-SEVEN

GET CISTINE OUT.

The words were a mantra in Thorne's head amounting to no plan, no strategy amid the dull clap of the Bloodwight's gloved hands from the war room's narrow doorway.

He was such a stars-damned fool. Of course this was a trap. Battle plans and augments left where they could find them, where *Cistine* could sense them...he never should've let them enter this room with only one way out.

"My brothers tell me the Key cannot resist the call," the Bloodwight chuckled. "It seems they were right."

"I'm surprised they tell you anything." The steel in Cistine's voice surprised Thorne. "First they leave you to rot in Detlyse Halet for twenty years, now they leave you behind to nanny stolen children? No love lost between brothers, I suppose."

Beside Thorne, Aden's fingers creaked audibly around the grip of his sabers. *Vandred.* Subtle but pointed, she was telling them who this was.

The Bloodwight was quiet for a beat. "Speaking of brothers," he purred at last, "where is Maleck?"

With a shout, Aden lunged. Thorne ducked around him and reached for Cistine and Ariadne, to sweep them behind him and what little of a shield his body provided. He met a wall of wind instead, slamming into him like a battering ram to the chest. For a moment he was weightless; then he struck the wall and came down hard, his leg twisting beneath him. Bone snapped. Heat shot up into his core and his vision went dark for a flash, just long enough for the Bloodwight to intercept Aden's attack. His cousin's pained shout and the crack of bone on rock stirred Thorne; he dragged his head up, blinking the shadows from his eyes.

Aden lay in a crumpled heap against the war table, blood seeping from the back of his head. Ariadne pushed Cistine toward Thorne, an arm across her chest, her hand to her own saber. Cistine's fingers were at her hips, tense, not drawing her weapons yet.

"You're far too predictable, Key." Vandred lurched up from the gap in the wall, gliding toward them. "One hint of the unnatural, and you came straight to us. We didn't even have to seek you out when we felt you cross through the storm."

Thorne groaned, pressing his hands into the rock, searching for balance. Pain thrummed from his left leg, and he didn't dare look at it. All that mattered was getting to Cistine...even if he had to crawl.

But his *selvenar* was not retreating from Vandred anymore. Nor was Ariadne, as if a silent thread of thought joined them.

Cistine's head sank slightly. "Who says you didn't come to *me?*"

Vandred chuckled. "Honestly, do you—?"

Flagons shattered, wind and rock exploded, and in one deft movement Cistine blasted the gap in the stone wide and tore the air from Vandred's lungs, piling him in a heap half-buried among the rocks. She barked Ariadne's name, cast what remained of the wind augment to her, and left her to bind Vandred with its power; then she whirled on Aden, healing white light already spreading across her palms.

Thorne's tongue cleaved to the roof of his mouth in shock, his addled mind working to understand the grim finality of what just occurred. Words failed him until Cistine moved away from Aden, still unconscious, and brought her glowing hands to his leg. White fire ripped through his veins when she moved it, shifting the broken bones, and he bit into his own arm to stifle the yell that jammed against his teeth.

In moments, the healing augment did its work; but pain still wrapped his calf, and he struggled when Cistine towed him upright, bracing his back to the wall. Finally he gasped, "The earth augment."

"I know, but I didn't have a choice." Desperation burned in her eyes. "I had to bury him, or he would've buried *us*."

But they couldn't bring down the Balmond's cavern now. They couldn't complete their mission.

"Cistine, take Aden." Ariadne heaved Vandred's arm across her shoulders, grimacing at his weight and height. "I've got this one."

And Thorne, with pain pulsing in every heartbeat from his leg, up his back, into his head, could do nothing but snatch up the augment pouch from the table, draw his swords, and follow them—Cistine supporting Aden, Ariadne dragging Vandred—back to the cavern.

They found it in chaos.

Someone had raised the alarm, turning Selv Torfjel into a writhing knot of frantic activity. Augurs converged, flagons cracked, steel shrieked from sheaths. In the heave of bodies ahead, Maleck and Ashe dueled their way free, Starfall and Stormfury singing, Odvaya cleaving through bone and sinew like butter. Behind them, Quill; and in his arms—

Horror dumped through Thorne, heavy as a snow sheet, at the sight of Tatiana; at the *state* of her, armor ripped, blood pouring down her side.

Ariadne hurled Vandred to the stone floor at the mouth of the tunnel and bolted to meet them, weapons drawn, covering Quill's way. He ducked past her and slid to his knees on the stone next to Cistine, cradling Tatiana against his chest, eyes wide and wilder than Thorne had ever seen. "Cistine, I'm begging you, please, that healing augment—"

"I used it." Horror deadened her voice. "Quill, I *just* used it..."

His arms spasmed around Tatiana and he shouted, spittle flying from his lips and tears streaking down his cheeks, *"You have to have something!"*

"All right, all right, just...let me see!" She laid her hands over Tatiana's side and closed her eyes, brow scrunching, a feeble strand of light playing between her fingertips. Quill rocked on his knees and held Tatiana to him, one hand pressing her head over his chest, his gaze fixed on Cistine like she might be his salvation—or his doom. Thorne stood over them, pulse kicking, prayer after prayer passing in and out of thought while his focus snapped back and forth between Quill, Cistine, and Tatiana, and Ariadne, Ashe, and Maleck fighting for their lives against the converging *mirothadt*.

It was all going to Nimmus, and he'd brought them here, straight into Bloodwight hands; arrogant, desperate to prove his theory, to stanch this bleeding wound in the mountains before it killed them all. Instead he'd led his cabal into a slaughter...just like Braggos all over again.

Cistine's breath rushed out and she slumped so sharply Quill could only catch her with their heads pressed together. She leaned against him, panting. "That's all there is, I don't have anything else. She needs a medico."

"I know. I know, stars damn it—"

"Thorne!" Maleck's voice lashed through the tumult; they were falling back, step by step, and soon they would be trapped in this cave mouth between the Balmond and the *mirothadt*, with Vandred at their feet.

And then, with a mighty groan like the bones of the kingdom itself snapping, the far wall of Selv Torfjel burst inward, boulders the size of a man spraying in every direction, crushing *mirothadt,* even flattening children. Ashe bellowed in heartbreak, but there was nothing that could be done for them when Bresnyar plunged into the cavern, fire spraying, carving a wide whip of flame in a shield around the cabal.

The moment the dragon's talons touched the rock, Ariadne heaved Vandred onto his back, then slid on behind him. Quill passed Tatiana up to her, every movement careful yet still eliciting dying moans from deep in her throat that shredded Thorne's heart. In one deft leap Quill was on the dragon's back as well, taking his *valenar* in his arms again.

Bresnyar grunted at the weight of four on his back, flanks heaving, the fire struggling out of him toward the *mirothadt*. Thorne's eyes shot to Ashe, crouched beside Aden, feeling his pulse, her hand on his shoulder while he lay delirious. Her gaze held his, and he knew.

Thorne offered a hand to Cistine. "You're next, *Logandir*."

She swung up ahead of Quill and yanked her head desperately. "Give Aden to us!"

"Bres." Ashe's voice was steady. "You can't carry any more and make it to the war camp in time for Tatiana. You have to go *now*."

"No!" the dragon bellowed. "Never without you!"

Augmented lightning speared through the cavern, knocking chunks of stone from the roof. Maleck's shoulder rammed Thorne's, shoving him aside, but to their left there was a pained shout cut too short.

"*Asheila!*" Maleck whirled back and fell to his knees beside her limp body, blood branching across her nose and down her cheek from a gash across her brow. He took her face in his hands and shouted her name again, voice lost under a concussive burst of thunder, more lightning slamming the stone apart. Debris clipped Thorne's shoulder and brought him down to one knee, gripping his armor where the pain radiated out, and Cistine's scream echoed louder than the thunder. Louder than anything.

Thorne looked into her terrified eyes and made his choice. Not for himself. Not for her. But what Valgard needed most.

"Bresnyar, you heard your Wingmaiden! *Go!*" Thorne hurled the augment pouch up to Cistine, and she caught it by instinct even while she sobbed his name; Bresnyar roared with fury, but the next bolt of lightning nearly seared his eyes. Cursing in every tongue, the dragon whipped around in a tight turn and streaked down the mouth of Selv Torfjel.

For the rest of his life—however little of it remained—Thorne would never forget the sound of Cistine screaming for him while Bresnyar carried her away.

But he could not think of her. They had moments before the dragonfire faded, and then they were all dead. He ripped Cistine's scarf from his hair and tossed it to Maleck to bind Ashe's brow. Then he bent and slung Aden's arm across his shoulders, heaving his cousin up and staggering toward the base of the path up to the falls—their only hope for escape.

Bresnyar's fire, that final gift, bought them precious seconds—enough that they were halfway up the stone slope before the *mirothadt* broke through. They ducked into the tunnel at the top, leading the enemy away into the mountain.

But it was borrowed time, every step; Maleck flagged under Ashe's weight, and Thorne under Aden's. They had no healing augments, no triage, no weapons but their swords, and nothing awaited them through the tunnels but a river and a plunge into the waters beyond. With every staggering stride, Thorne felt death pressing closer, the Undertaker's scythe ready to cut him at the knees.

He hadn't said goodbye to the others. Not even to Cistine. And unlike Jazva Chasm, when death seemed a noble relief, he ached to live this time. He craved survival so desperately it inspired a panic like none he'd ever knowm.

And it would still not be enough.

The tunnel blurred before his eyes and his leg throbbed in bursts, the knitted bone showing signs of its trauma. They reached the broad pool, and Thorne stumbled to a halt, shoulder catching and dragging against the wall. "Mal. We make our stand here."

Maleck slowed, his arms tightening around Ashe. He peered down at her pallid face, the blood stark against her blue eyelids. "Not like this," he mumbled, "not to them."

"*Maleck.*"

"I swore to give her better, to stay with her, this—this was not what I promised—"

Shouts resonated along the tunnel, the echo of steel clattering, the enemy closing in. Thorne settled Aden on the basin rim and grabbed Maleck by the shoulder, yanking him around. "Darkwind, I need you with me! I need your blades!"

But Maleck's eyes had gone vacant, full of horror, his head shaking violently at the realization of death so near. He bowed down to his knees, a moan ratcheting deep in his throat, body seizing with violent tremors. He dropped back into his panic so quickly Thorne couldn't reach him.

He cursed and whirled, drawing his sabers and spinning them to loosen his wrists. If Maleck would not fight beside him, then he would do what he could to give him and Ashe one last moment together before they saw the Sable Gates or Cenowyn.

Stars, let it be Cenowyn.

Lightning and fire crackled in the tunnel, streaking silhouettes of Hive warriors and prisoners and children, fighters all, barreling toward them.

Two sabers or four, it would not be enough.

Fear closed Thorne's throat, but he dug in his heels and braced, let it wash over and through and out of him with the breath that fell from his chest. He did not look away. He did not blink. He retained nothing for himself but a calm, murderous power he'd only felt once before: the day Vassoran guards cornered him in the Izten Torkat and tried to step past him to reach Cistine. The day he felt like a death-god, merciless and mighty and unstoppable.

He would be that again, one last time.

Footsteps pounded the stone, closing in on them. It took Thorne a second too long to realize they were not just coming from ahead, but from behind.

Black armor flashed like a *Svarkyst* blade, winnowing past on his right, sliding between Thorne and the approaching hoard with a furious bellow. Fire ignited with a slam of hands against the tunnel walls, streaking in gouts and dripping ribbons down the stone; its heat sent the *mirothadt* reeling despite their armor, and as the flames mustered and roared, the man who commanded them snapped around on heel.

For one heartbeat, his gaze held Thorne's. One heartbeat, and Thorne knew he was already standing among the ranks of the dead in Nimmus.

Then those gray eyes speared past him, and the man shouted at Maleck, "*Afiyam*, I need you to get on your feet!"

Maleck's head shot up, jaw tumbling open and eyes blown wide, as Kristoff Lionsbane took a knee and bore Aden up across his shoulders like a grainsack, straightened without a hitch in his stride, and kicked his boot along the stone behind him, shooting a last arc of flame down the tunnel to hold the enemy at bay.

"Thorne! Maleck!" he roared. "*Move your feet!*"

Maleck surged up with Ashe clutched to his chest again, Thorne sheathed his blades with a deft twist, and they followed Kristoff at a dead run through the tunnel on blind faith. Above them, the glowworms curled back up, cringing away from the desolation that flowed beneath them at the same barreling pace as the water and wind. Step by step, darkness suffused the cavern's roof.

The roaring river nearly masked the sounds of pursuit, but when lightning spurted after them, blowing out the rock wall to their left, Thorne knew the *mirothadt* were closing in again.

"Both of you, on me!" Kristoff shouted—and with all his might, he leaped into the river.

Thorne did not pause to question. If this was already death, what did it matter?

So he and Maleck took a running jump as one, plunging into the water.

CHAPTER TWENTY-EIGHT

CISTINE'S TEARS DID not stop all the way back to the war camp; nor could she keep from looking over her shoulder, even when Selv Torfjel was lost to the horizon.

The world blurred around them as Bresnyar taxed both his hearts to their limit, hurtling across the miles. The moment the war camp came into view, Quill cursed with relief, clutching Tatiana tighter against him. Bresnyar's feet hadn't quite touched the path and the warrior was already down, hitting the stone with knees bent and breaking like a madman for the tents, shouting for help. Cistine dismounted, gathered herself to bolt after him—then hesitated.

Duty before despair.

She turned back, helping Ariadne slide Vandred from Bresnyar's back. They dragged him up the path and met a wall of wide-eyed warriors waiting, stirred by Quill's passing like a violent wind. Some recoiled, some leaned in, others offered up prayers to the gods and curses to the stars while the two women hauled the deadweight Bloodwight into the tents.

"That's far enough."

Bravis's brittle voice boomed through the canvas alcoves as he stalked to meet them with a handful of Tribunes in tow. Cistine nodded to Eskil, the sturdy and quiet man who'd overseen Salvotor's trial, then turned her eyes back to Bravis. There was hate in his face as he beheld Vandred slumped between them, like he would slit the creature's throat in a heartbeat—if only he could.

"We still need him alive," she heard herself saying, though the words were too queenly and calm for the screaming in her spirit, the girl's fracturing heart within the woman's heaving chest. *Bravis.*

The Chancellor jolted, shaking his head, and looked at her. "The other Chancellors have arrived. We'll take this one, bind it outside the camp. Tell Thorne to join us once he's seen to his warriors."

Cistine had not mustered an ounce of truth for him before he was gone, his Tribunes taking up Vandred between them now, weaving sharply through the stunned, muttering camp.

"Would you go with them and keep watch?" Cistine murmured to Ariadne. "I know Bravis means well, but I still trust this cabal's eyes better than anyone's."

"Consider it done." Ariadne brushed shoulders with her and slid into the crowd like an ink stain, lost in moments on Bravis's heels.

Cistine retreated to the top of the path where Bresnyar crouched, elbows jutting, head to the ground while his sides labored. She rested her hand on his muzzle as she'd seen Ashe do while they traveled. "Thank you. For everything."

"It was...my duty." There was nothing in his gaze but desperation burning brighter than the fire in his gullet—a desperation Cistine shared.

She could leap onto his back right now and burn across the sky, straight back to Selv Torfjel, to find Thorne and the others. But Bresnyar was exhausted, the skin of his nostrils a bright, bloody red; if he flew again as he'd flown them here, he would plunge from the sky, and that would serve no one.

"Rest," she murmured. "We'll look for them soon, but for now, you need to recover your strength."

"I suppose I have little choice." The dragon swiveled his head away from her, looking back the way they came. "I smelled her blood. Before we escaped, it filled that cave. If she is not cared for..."

"Maleck knows battlefield triage." If he even had time to bind it, if he hadn't broken down the moment they were gone, if he wasn't overcome along with the rest of them—but she silenced those thoughts with a shake of her head. "Thorne will lead them out. In the meantime, take care of yourself. And keep one nostril on that Bloodwight."

His brow crinkled. "I don't like the smell of them. It's worse than rot. Living, festering, forever ripping itself apart and repairing. Like a dead thing that won't keep to its tomb. Unnatural."

Cistine swallowed. "I know."

"Ah! Princess, there you are!" Sander's voice knifed the cold air, and Cistine's heart sank. With a last touch to Bresnyar's sinewy neck, she faced Kanslar's High Tribune ducking from under the tents, a grin on his face. "I see the mission was successful—" he broke off at the sight of her, shaking and alone, and his wide eyes swept the path behind her as if at any moment, his Chancellor would appear. "Where *is* Thorne?"

Cistine shook her head. "He stayed behind. With Maleck, Aden, and Ashe."

Sander towed his curls back from his brow. "I see." Awkward silence hung between them for a moment. Then, "I can delay the Chancellors. Give you a few minutes longer to prepare a report."

She could manage no more than a limp smile. "Thank you, Sander."

The High Tribune took her shoulders and ducked his head to catch her eyes. "Now, see here...I've known Thorne a bit longer than you, hm? Ten years in the wilderness could not destroy him. His father could not destroy him. As long as there's a fight to be had, he will not give up. So we'll just have to manage this mess with the Bloodwight until his return."

Cistine nodded and drew in a shallow breath. "Tell the Chancellors I'll be there shortly."

Sander gave her a knowing look and a nod, and with a last squeeze of her shoulders, they parted ways: him to entertain the Chancellors, and her to the quiet pocket of the tents where she and Thorne stayed that first night. Somehow, she held her composure until the thick canvas veil slid into place behind her; somehow, for every pair of eyes that found her walking through the tents, she managed a dip of the head, an encouraging flicker of a smile that felt nailed on, ripping her mouth at the corners.

Finally, she was alone. Then Cistine wrapped one arm around the tent post and sagged into it, knees giving out, her other hand muffling the sobs that heaved out of her like retching. In the darkness behind her squeezed-shut eyes, she saw it over and over again—that cavern, Aden unconscious, Ashe's eyes full of resignation, Maleck's voice breaking around Ashe's name. And Thorne, the way he looked at her before he ordered Bresnyar to go.

She'd already broken her promise. Already left him on a battlefield without her to guard his back.

She choked out fear and gulped in deep breaths, beating down the sharper angles of pain that jabbed through her chest until all that remained was a dull twinge. Then she pressed a hand to her middle and focused on how she breathed—in through her nose, out through her mouth, the way Mira had taught her.

She had to control it. Like Baba Kallah told her once, the princess could mourn safely here, but when she rose from this place, she must rise a queen.

In solitude, Cistine wrestled with her pain and panic until they submitted, until she could think and see and breathe past them. Then she straightened up from the tent post, blowing air out through her rounded lips, rolling her shoulders back and raising her chin high.

Spine straight and head erect, she went to meet the Chancellors.

They were waiting at the war table, and the moment she stepped under those steepled folds, she decided she was fed up with rooms like these and everything that took place in them. Her ears rang with the snap of Thorne's broken leg and the crack of Aden's head on the stone table in Selv Torfjel when she stepped inside the warm circle and greeted the Chancellors. Bravis and Benedikt, though grim, radiated a fresh vigor at the turning tide. Valdemar, scowling as ever, did not even look up from the maps; only Maltadova and Adeima seemed happy to see her, both stepping forward to grip her hands and kiss her cheeks.

"Bravis informed us of your return." Maltadova laid a hand to his chest and lowered his gaze. "Valgard is grateful for Talheim's aid."

"And we are grateful for *you*." Adeima didn't look away from Cistine's eyes, one ruler to another—though such was a secret still in this tent, as far as Cistine knew. But no one questioned her presence, perhaps because she and Maltadova were already so rarely apart; and the double-ended spear and twin swords harnessed across her back left no doubt of her place in the war. "For what you have given and what you risk. We will not forget that this is a personal sacrifice."

Cistine forced a smile. "That's what allies do."

Adeima smiled in turn, and as one they all three stepped up to the war table. Maltadova rested a hand in the small of his *valenar's* back and braced his other arm on the table. "When do we interrogate the creature?"

"Tomorrow," Bravis said. "No sense wasting time. I would've liked to wait for Thorne. However..." His gaze trailed off to the left, and only then did Cistine realize Sander was there, half-masked in shadows, reclining against the tent post. Brow drawn, he stared down at the maps.

"I'm prepared to speak in his stead on this important occasion." He shot a glance toward Cistine, words conveyed through that pointed stare: *until he returns to us.* "Still. Let's give it one full day, for pity's sake."

The Chancellors exchanged heavy glances. Valdemar said, "The longer we give the poison to take effect, the more pliant he'll be."

"Do it," Bravis said, "but keep watch on him at all times."

It was a narrow window within which Cistine could work her own intentions, but narrow was better than none. "There's something else you should all know...something we saw inside the mountain. May I?" At Bravis's nod, she spread her fingers along the map, following the lines to the northwest. "Some of the enemy forces are stationed in the upper range...it might even be where the Bloodwights themselves have been these past few months."

Doing gods-knew-what. She didn't want to wonder.

"You're certain of this?" Valdemar's first words to her, ringing with suspicion...appropriate and predictable.

"We saw on their own war maps where their people are gathered."

"Could it have been staged?" Benedikt asked. "A trick to make you *believe* their focus was elsewhere?"

Cistine's mouth leaped open in protest, but no words slid past her lips. Vandred *had* tempted them to that room, to the augments—and all to trap her, by his own admission. What was to say the maps, too, were not a trick?

Nothing. There was nothing to suggest that but a low, incessant tug in her chest, almost like the call but fainter. Not yet fully formed.

"It's too great a risk," Bravis said, firmly but not unkindly, when Cistine offered no rebuttal. "We will not send our warriors into another ambush."

Thorne was not the only Chancellor still carrying shadows in his eyes from the siege in Braggos. For their sake, she bit her tongue. That was not a wound that needed prodding, not today; especially when she might need their support in other matters before long. "You're right. I'm just eager to deal them as harsh a blow as they've dealt us."

"All in good time. We'll have the answers we need soon enough." Bravis straightened. "In the meantime, we'd like to know exactly what happened in that mountain."

Of course they would; one of their own had gone missing, the line of succession knocked off-balance. She'd learned early on in her readings on war strategy how imperative it was to defend leaders for the sake of perpetuity and moral.

Keep the leaders alive, and the cause survived. Thorne's absence was a blow. Even with Sander here, they all felt it.

So Cistine told them everything, despite the pain that lumped in her throat. She laid out every step, withholding only the call that had beckoned her to that war room and knocked the mission awry. Foolish of her. Despite how she'd grown, how she broke and healed herself over and over to become stronger, there was still that weak vein in her armor where augmentation was concerned, where the call and curiosity collided.

The notion hollowed her voice and bent her body, hands to the table, by the end of the telling. The Chancellors were quiet for a time, looking at the maps, looking at each other.

Bravis broke the silence first. "Thorne was right. There was a stars-damned stronghold."

"It was a hornet's nest," Cistine murmured, "and I'm worried we only kicked it today."

"You did what you could with what resources you had," Maltadova said. "It was a task for a hundred warriors, not eight."

Bravis shot him a scathing look. "The northern front is my charge, and thus far we've held the enemy relatively at bay. Remember that."

"That's twice you've seen a Chancellor fall in an attack like this," Valdemar argued. "The *same* Chancellor, no less."

"I am not Thorne's keeper. He's his own man—too much of one sometimes."

"Let's not forget," Sander cut in sharply, "that Thorne is not among us today because he saw his people out before himself. I've not seen *your* faces on a single battlefield since this stars-forsaken war began, but I've fought beside him on every one. Meanwhile, you're all content to sit on your pretty asses and watch your warriors die."

Benedikt scowled. "Well, now *your* pretty ass can join ours, because you are leader in Thorne's stead and we cannot afford to lose you, too."

"I would, quite frankly, rather die."

"You're not dying," Cistine snapped. "No one is, and that includes Thorne. *When* he comes back, he'll make his own choices about which battlefields to take, like he always has." They all gave her the same look, with varying levels of sympathy and reproach. Groaning, she kneaded her temples. "I'm going to the medico's tent. Send word if you need me."

No one stopped her, though Adeima gave a parting nod and Sander bent his shoulder to bump hers when she ducked past him. She would have to spend some time thinking about this subtle yet profound shift in how he spoke about Thorne, and how they moved around each other. Perhaps it had begun on Darlaska, the night Thorne marshalled his forces to protect the High Tribunes and save Mira, Sander's *valenar*; perhaps it was the war, the bleeding and bloodletting on the battlefield together. But for the first time, the two men truly reminded her of Chancellor and High Tribune as they ought to be, united and of one mind, stroking like oars in tandem thrusting the ship of their kingdom's wellbeing forward.

It was difficult to feel elation about that when so much else was breaking down around them.

Out of sight of the war tent, Cistine broke into a jog, then a sprint, weaving between posts and fires and clusters of warriors until the cots grew more populace and the scent of herbs wreathed the air. She found drapes in the canvas like the one around Thorne's sleeping spot, cordoning off spaces along the rock where the sick and wounded lay. There were fewer rolled up now than when she'd come here with Aden, Ariadne, Quill, and Tatiana after the ambush in Jazva Chasm; how many had fallen ill of the elements while the cabal scaled the mountains?

"Over here, Stranger."

Cistine whirled left toward that voice and spotted Quill by the stippled thatch of his hair. He sat on an overturned crate, head in his hands beside a wall of canvas. Dragging her heels, she sat on the crate beside him. "Where's Tati? What did the medicos say?"

Quill slanted his head toward the drape. "They're still working. There's a *complication* with fixing this, that's all they'll tell me."

Agony ravaged his eyes, and his mouth wobbled close to weeping. Cistine's heart fissured once again with that desperate need to piece the bleeding cabal back together, but all she could do was press her shoulder to his. "It's Tati, Quill. *Our* Tati. She's going to be all right."

"But she almost wasn't." Elbows propped on his knees, he rubbed his face. "Because of me. Because I couldn't get through to Pip and I didn't know when to stop."

"Any of us would've done the same."

"But I'm the one whose *valenar* is lying in a medico tent, because *I* let my guard down." He pinched the bridge of his nose, eyes twisted shut. "I didn't think she'd do it. I didn't want to believe she was that far gone."

Cistine took his free hand and squeezed it with all her might, until he looked at her. "We are going to save Pippet, Quill. I'll do whatever it takes."

His eyes cleared some as they held hers, his cheek ticking slightly. "Missed that hopeless optimism."

A brush of feathers on the wind, and Faer glided in through the tents, settling on Quill's shoulder. "*Quill, Quill, Quill...*"

He scoffed quietly under his breath. "At least I'll always have this bag of feathers." Stroking Faer's back, he set his eyes on Cistine's face. "The medicos said the healing augment saved Tati's life. Even though we had to leave the knife in, whatever you healed inside her, it's the reason she didn't die on the flight back."

Relief melted some of the icy dread from her core. "I'm just glad there was enough left."

Quill scoffed quietly, shaking his head. "All this time climbing through the mountains, I was worried about what you were going to do in there, what you had up your sleeve that would turn this whole mission on its side. But it turns out I'm the one who sent everything to Nimmus in a knapsack. Funny how things go, isn't it?"

Frowning, she squeezed his hand again. "Don't think like that."

He turned his gaze to the dark canvas separating him from his *valenar*. "I don't think I can take losing one more thing. First Pip, then you, and now this. If Tati dies, or if we lose Thorne and the others..."

Cistine didn't have the heart to tell him that with Vandred here, things were poised to change again. If she had her way, everything would.

But he didn't need that burden today; so she simply laid her head on his shoulder and sat with him through the long hours while day tumbled down toward an early dusk...while they waited for word from beyond the veil if Tatiana would survive.

CHAPTER TWENTY-NINE

*D*O YOU EVER *think of legacy, Aden?*

The hoarse whisper, full of sand and satisfaction, churned in the shadows. Aden lay with his eyes closed, trying to shut it out, imagining himself anywhere but here—in this cruel bed, under these soft, claiming hands.

What is a legacy?

He thought he knew: a girl with mottled dark hair and bright eyes and a missing tooth lost late; a girl whose lanky arms helped put the pieces of him back together that never made sense before. Legacy was hard blows and soft embraces and flowers woven into his beard.

Legacy was lost. Just like him.

A legacy, I suppose, is the sum of all we are. Don't you think, Aden? It's where we've been, who we are, and where we'll go. You and I are forging a legacy together every time you come to my bed. And what would your legacy be without this place, without me? Liar. Betrayer of the Judgement Seat. Enemy of the Courts. I'm saving you, Aden. Who are you when you're not in my arms?

The thin crescent slices of Deja fingernails turned to the stroke of a lash against his back.

My name is Aden, son of the Lion, son of the Storm. I will not break.

I will not break.

I will not—

With a grunt, Aden opened his eyes.

It was dark. Cold. Catacomb walls arched over his head and the coarse threads of his bed cradled him from below. He knew the dim flicker of ghostlight on the walls, knew precisely where he was.

He squeezed his eyes shut.

My name is Aden, son of the Lion, son of the Storm. I will not break.

How long since he'd chanted those words to himself in the dark? Since the first time Deja took him, perhaps—or the second? Whenever he became too ashamed to whisper the halves of his parents' Names to himself in the cold solitude of the Hive Lord's chamber, unworthy of carrying those sacred words with him to Deja's bed and back.

He'd become strong enough to stand without them, but now, back in this place, back in this *Nimmus*...

Something cold and damp pressed to his scalp, and a familiar voice murmured, "Take your time."

Thorne. Thorne couldn't be here, in the Hive with him—

No. Not the Hive. Selv Torfjel.

The sensation of Deja's nails on his back faded, replaced by the battle maps, the Bloodwight, the brush of Thorne's arm against his side in a silent command. Rushing the creature had been an invitation for injury or worse, but to steal a few seconds for his cousin to reach Cistine and Ariadne, to pull them to safety—

That was the last thing he remembered. And now this cave, the thin folds of silver ghostlight fingering the walls, and his cousin crouched beside him, pressing a soaked cloth to his skull.

"Welcome back." Thorne's tone was warm, but the dance of secret fears in his eyes was enough to prod Aden closer to sense.

"What happened?" he mumbled, tongue stiff and heavy, slurring the words.

"The Bloodwight polished his table with your skull." A poor attempt at humor, but it explained why all his thoughts felt like stars pulsing just out of reach. "Cistine healed both of us, but I had to send them away.

Tati...Tati was dying."

That woke him entirely, sharper than a kick to the ribs. He pried his eyes fully open, though even the gentle ghostlight bored pain into his temples, and focused on Thorne's frame silhouetted in a chilly glow: silver hair spilling across his brow, blue eyes dark like wounds in his hollow face. "Who else is with us?"

"Maleck. Ashe." Thorne fell suddenly, deeply silent and reached around to press the cloth to the back of Aden's head again, where everything felt rigid and hot, not quite fully healed. But that wound wasn't enough to account for Thorne's averted gaze.

Aden gripped Thorne by the inside of his elbow and thrust his arm away. "If Cistine healed me, why are you looking at me like I might collapse any second?"

Thorne's bearded throat lurched in a hard swallow. Panic lanced through Aden at the silence, and he planted his hands on the rock and pushed himself upright, his whole torso throbbing like he'd rammed into a wall, not just been knocked head-first against a table.

I will not break. Whatever this is, I will not break.

"*Mavbrat*," he growled. "Tell me—"

The words died on his lips. For the first time, he got the full measure of where they were: the deep recesses of a cave slicked with ghostlight, the plants growing naturally through cracks in the floor and roof, broken open by hand and foot. Pelts and small casks lined the walls: weapons, bandages, supplies. Outside, the Ismalete River gushed between canyon walls, its headwaters fed by deep reservoirs in other mountains like Selv Torfjel. There were three figures at the cave mouth, illumined by the waning daylight.

Three. Not two.

Maleck, propped against the round wall, knees cocked, head braced forward with primal focus; Ashe, her back to his chest, head tucked in the crook of his shoulder, utterly unconscious and braced by his grip, her forehead turned toward the light. And the man kneeling at their feet, stitching her brow with nimble, practiced strokes.

Breath surged into Aden's nostrils, and he shut his eyes.

He was nine years old, too short still for his feet to graze the ornate rug beneath the dining table, so his heels kicked the wooden crossbar instead. Fingers curled around the underside of the seat, he stared at Maleck's troubled face, eyes detached, focused anywhere but on the gash in his upper arm and the needle flashing in and out of it like a quicksilver fish, knitting the torn halves together.

"Which of you boys wants to tell me how this happened?"

A swift glance between them.

"I fell," Maleck mumbled.

"I pushed him."

"Hmmm. Is that what happened? Or did you take the corner too sharply at the top of the stairs and run into that nail poking out of the wall, which I warned you about sixteen times this week?"

Another guilty look.

"You don't fix a mistake by lying about it. Honesty first in this house. Understood?"

"Understood," the boys chorused.

"Are you going to tell *Aniya*?" Aden mumbled after a beat.

A quiet snort, followed by the snip of thread. "Luckily for both of you, your mother's taught me enough about stitching that I don't think we need to worry her about this."

Maleck's focus flicked from his sutured arm to Aden, and they shared a relieved smile.

Gray eyes flashed with humor, missing nothing of that look. "Now. Let's see about fixing that nail."

Thread severed, its whisper bringing Aden back from that day in his childhood home to this cave, a gateway joining life and death together...and to the man resting a hand on Ashe's soiled hair.

"That should do it. As I said, I don't feel a skull fracture, but watch her just in case. You know the signs." He set aside suture and needle, dipped his hands in a bowl of water beside him, and called over his shoulder, "Thorne?"

"He's awake." Thorne regarded Aden warily, a silent question in his eyes. For the first time in his life, Aden couldn't read that look. Nothing made sense about this, not one damned thing, because Deja and the Blood Hive were somehow a dream, a hallucination on the verge of waking, a memory worth forgetting; but *this* one was supposed to make sense, because Thorne *spoke* to this vision.

Garbed in dark armor, silver-streaked hair cut short like a man readied for war, this hallucination lingered on his heels for a moment, looking across the river. Then he straightened slowly and turned into the ghostlight, toward Aden.

For the first time in twenty years, he beheld his father's face.

Little had changed about it; more chiseled, his stubble graying, his brow carrying more creases. But his crooked smile was the same, and his eyes softened the way they always did when he said, "Hello, *Afiyam*."

Aden shot to his feet, staggering wildly, and Thorne rose before him, putting out a hand to steady him. He struck it away, keeping his gaze fixed on this impossible being, a shadow guttering in the last gasps of daylight.

Kristoff's brow furrowed with worry, and that, too, was familiar. He stepped deeper into the cave, into the darkness, toward him. Aden flicked up a hand, palm out—warning the specter back. "Nimmus or Cenowyn."

Kristoff froze. "What?"

"Nimmus. Or. Cenowyn," Aden enunciated every word with all the steel he could forge. "Which one is this? So I know which direction to crawl, up or down, to fight the gods for doing this to me again."

His voice cracked when the word rolled out of him. Kristoff's gaze gentled, and that was unbearable, unforgivable—another line crossed. "Aden."

"No. I am *finished*. I've fought their war, I've prayed until I had no breath left for words, and this is how they repay the sacrifice? They can't keep giving you back and taking you again! I don't...I don't have enough pieces of me left to give the next time you go."

And there it was, his weakness laid bare. What did it matter, if this was death?

He pivoted, striding away from his father's specter into the welcoming embrace of gloom at the back of the cave, yanking his hands down his cheeks and telling himself to wake up, to focus, to come back to life enough that this unlikely shadow would disappear.

"It's not Nimmus," Kristoff called after him. "If it was, you would see the Sable Gates."

"Fine," he spat back. "Cenowyn, then."

"Not there. You know why."

Maleck's voice cut after him, quiet but certain. "Not without Natalya."

Aden froze, his mother's name settling over his shoulders, bringing every inch of the cave into sharp relief. Bringing an impossible, unspeakable truth to clarity.

Heels sticking to the stone, he wavered in place, dug his fingers into the damp rock, and held on with all his might. If he turned back now, and the collision of day and dark, light and shadow consumed Kristoff—if once again that perilous hope he felt when he'd betrayed Sillakove Court to Salvotor, or when he stood on the balcony of Keltei Temple and spoke to Cistine of Kalt Hasa, was ripped from his hands, taking another fragment of the beating heart from his chest—

Son of the Lion, son of the Storm. I will not break.

True or not, real or not, even if this was all just a passing shadow on the brink of oblivion, he could prove that much; he could do as he did in Siralek and face hope's dying light, show them all he would not bow.

So he gathered his wits, steeled his resolve, and faced them: Maleck holding Ashe to his chest, Thorne on his feet, bearing more heavily to one side, tensed as if to intervene if Aden collapsed or attacked; and Kristoff, no less tangible than a moment ago, body loose and hands turned out at his sides, inviting whatever Aden hurled at him next.

A blow. A curse. An accusation. All the potentials roiled up in him and died swiftly, a tempest with the wind yanked out of it; and then he was simply nauseous and unsteady, unsure if that was the lingering pain in his head or the shock coursing through his blood.

"Look at you," Kristoff chuckled hoarsely, breaking the strained silence. "I thought I told you to stop growing."

"And I begged you to come back. Every night for ten years."

Thorne's eyes widened. Aden hadn't dared tell him that—or anyone else, not even Maleck. And after Salvotor took that desperation, that weakness, and forged it into a weapon at the cabal's throats, he'd felt unworthy to plead anymore. Unworthy to pray. The gods couldn't love him that much. *This* much. Not after everything he did.

But here was his father, regarding him without loathing, without the hate and disgust he'd magined in the dark after that first night with Deja. There was only compassion in his gaze, as familiar as Aden's own heartbeat, when Kristoff stepped toward him. "Would you believe me if I said I heard you? That loving you and Maleck kept me alive in Kalt Hasa—that even when hurling myself from the heights seemed a better fate, it was *your* face that drew me back from that edge?"

Breath heaved in and out of Aden's chest, too shallow and quick, bright glimmers popping before his eyes. "Stars damn it, Mal was right. I *did* inherit my flare for dramatic speeches from you."

He broke down, the weight crashing over him all at once, and his father's hands snared his collar and brought him gently to the floor—strong. Sturdy. *Real.*

Then their arms were around one another, great shudders rocking through them both, and a moment later Maleck slid to his knees on the rock beside them and embraced them. Kristoff scoffed with husky laughter and gripped the backs of their heads, fingers careful of the wound on Aden's scalp as he pressed his forehead to both of theirs. "My boys. *My boys.*"

Between his father's grip and Maleck's, Aden shattered at last. He wept like a child. But for the first time in more than a decade, that did not feel like failure; it felt like the last of what he was burning up in fire so that something better, something stronger, could be reborn.

It was some time before they all composed themselves enough to build a fire. Thorne set about it first, giving Aden, Maleck, and Kristoff a wide berth to gather their wits again. When Aden did at last, he couldn't believe how easily breathing came, or how much less hopeless everything felt. Perhaps that was still a child's ignorance, the feeling that his father could turn the tides of the world and the war with a single hand. But he'd believed it at fifteen, enduring Maleck's absence and the fear of Talheim's conquest by that steady faith; he would not forsake it now when it kept his feet beneath him.

He and Thorne built the fire up, and Kristoff retrieved cured meat from one of the casks while Maleck returned to the cave mouth and knelt beside Ashe, stroking the hair from her brow. "How long before she wakes?"

"Any time now, I expect," Kristoff said. "It was a glancing blow. Head wounds always look more gruesome than they are."

Aden shot his father a wry look. That was the same assurance Natalya had given Quill, and then his father Corvus, when Maleck dealt *him* a glancing blow by an augment, shocking half his hair pure white.

"What if she's bleeding into her skull?" Maleck fretted. "If her mind is damaged—"

"I doubt we'd notice the difference," Aden said, and Kristoff popped him soundly on the back of the head.

"I *heard* that."

Relief almost sent Aden back to his knees at that groggy retort. "Have you been listening all this time for the right moment to say your piece?"

"If I was, I wouldn't have waited this long. I'm sure you've said at least sixteen ridiculous things I could've had your ass for in the past five minutes." Groaning, Ashe pushed herself onto her back, squinting up at Maleck when he bent over her, hands planted on either side of her head. "Hello, you beautiful, braided bastard."

He pressed a kiss to her mouth, muffling the last two words; Kristoff arched a brow, but said nothing.

Ashe groaned when Maleck pulled back, and swept her brow with one hand, wincing when her fingers encountered the bandage there. "Who hit me, and did one of you kill them?"

"You can rest easy. We taught that shard of rock a lesson it won't soon forget," Aden deadpanned.

Ashe shot him the sort of unamused look that had goaded him countless times to a sparring of wits in Siralek. "Did Bres get the others out?"

Maleck nodded, then peered at the sliver of sky visibly through the cavern's jagged maw. "They must be back to the war camp by now."

"Thank the gods." Ashe sat up gingerly, steadying herself with a hand on Maleck's shoulder and squinting past him deeper into the cave. "Am I delusional, or is there a man standing next to Aden who looks suspiciously like him?"

"Is that what *all* of you hallucinate? Well-dressed older men?" Kristoff teased.

"Mass hysteria is an ugly thing." Thorne put out his hand. "Give me that food, would you, *Nahdar*? I'm famished."

Maleck pulled Ashe to her feet and walked hand-in-hand with her to the fire. Aden bumped her shoulder in passing, and she hit his ribs in return—a question asked and an answer given in a language of sand and blood few knew but them.

"Now that she's awake, let me introduce you properly to Asheila Kovar, rain-dancer, beast-slayer, and tide-turner." Maleck flashed a smile at Ashe. "Asheila, this is Kristoff, my f—" He broke off midword, rubbing the back of his neck and casting his gaze askance.

"I'm Maleck's father," Kristoff finished without hesitation, offering his hand, smile full of warm mischief.

Ashe's eyes narrowed slightly, but she shook his hand. "Quite the pair of sons."

"You have no idea." Kristoff tilted his head slightly. "Kovar. I understand that's a Talheimic family name."

Ashe's hand slid from his, tension threading the line of her shoulders. "Is that going to be a problem?"

Maleck stiffened, but Kristoff didn't bristle at the challenge in her voice; he merely searched her face. "I had the unique privilege of unlikely encounters with Talheimics during the last war, the same as Maleck. In fact, as I recall, he owes his escape from the lines to a young girl-Warden with hair colored very much like yours."

Aden blinked, looking between Ashe and Maleck, whose hands tightened in their entwinement. He had heard that story only in passing, a jumbled retelling from Maleck, but it never occurred to him to wonder if the stars could align that much. If the gods' plans truly went that far.

"Talheim is no enemy of mine." Kristoff added, and gestured to the fire. "Let's sit."

They did, distributing the meat Thorne warmed over it, and the swell of emotion in Aden's throat made swallowing nearly impossible when he looked at these faces gathered together.

All of this—Ashe meeting his father, even—was something he'd never entertained even in his wildest wonderings of what the world could be if things had gone differently. To be in it now, his broken family knitted back together, was a gift—a beacon of hope in the heart of war.

"How did you find us?" he asked when Kristoff's eyes settled on him.

"Purely by accident." He separated his meat into respectable portions—a Tribune's decorum still trained into him—and spoke between bites. "I've been watching that waterfall cave for more than a fortnight now, trying to plot my way inside. Imagine my surprise when my usual morning patrol found eight people, some *quite* familiar, scaling the cliffs."

Thorne frowned. "Why were you watching it?"

"More importantly," Maleck added, "why have you been here and not with us?"

"Perhaps I should start at the beginning." Kristoff lowered the bite he'd brought to his mouth. "When Kalt Hasa collapsed, only two of us escaped—Dain and I. We traveled north...I should say *he* traveled, and dragged me on a wooden plank behind him all the way. I dreamed I saw the Sable Gates more times than I could count. But when we could go no further, the gods sent us aid from Oadmark: a tribe living near the border took us in and drew us back from death's brink."

Aden swallowed the stab of indignation that first rose at Maleck's pointed question. He could not begrudge his father a slow recovery from near-death.

"It took longer than I expected for our strength to return." Kristoff's mouth cocked in a wicked smile. "Long enough for Dain to fall in love with the woman who tended his wounds. If I had to measure our time in that encampment by bright-eyed declarations of devotion from that boy's lips...too stars-damned long."

"We wouldn't know anything about bright-eyed declarations, would we?" Ashe dug an elbow into Maleck's ribs, and his cheeks reddened.

"But then you came back to Valgard," Thorne pressed.

Kristoff smiled, though his gaze remained grim. "Unlike Dain, I lacked for distractions. When I spoke to the village elders, it became clear they'd crossed paths with old enemies of ours. Some I personally owe a painful death for what they've done to my family."

Maleck's gaze lurched up from the flames and held his.

"A few months ago, things changed," Kristoff went on. "Movement all throughout the north, ripples of power I hadn't felt in twenty years. I'd been tracking the Bloodwights' movements through Oadmark for weeks when they began their descent into Valgard. I told Dain to stay, took what rations I could, and picked up my weapons again."

An errant shiver played down the notches of Aden's spine.

"I began my hunt in Oadmark, starting where the Bloodwights themselves set out and making my way south. All paths led to that mountain—Selv Torfjel. So I laid down my roots here and started scouting for a way in." Kristoff's eyes shadowed, reflecting the fire. "The things I've heard from inside that mountain...what has emerged from it over time...I wish I could forget."

Aden grimaced. "As do I."

His father's gaze jumped to him. "You've seen them?"

He nodded. "The Balmond. Children and beasts hemmed together by augmentation and *Gammalkraft*."

Kristoff swore more colorfully than Aden had ever heard. "I knew the old Order was vile, but *that*—stars, we should've cut them down when we had the chance."

"What's done is done," Thorne said. "What can you tell us about the Bloodwights, *Nahdar*? Anything that will turn the tide?"

"Numbers?" Ashe added hopefully.

Kristoff peeled a piece of kindling from the fire and scraped inarticulate, sooty shapes along the stone. "It's impossible to tell how much they've grown their ranks, but I can tell you this: not all the blood you shed in this war is Valgardan."

It took a moment for it to sink in; then Aden groaned deep in his throat, and Thorne's voice cracked with outrage: "*Oadmarkaics* are fighting for the Bloodwights?"

"The village that cared for us tried to put a stop to it, but the people are frightened. Many went to war to spare their children the same fate. Others are convinced the Bloodwights are young gods, and when a god tells you to go to war..."

Silence, apart from the hiss and pop of the fire.

"What about the wing legions?" There was a strange tilt in Ashe's voice, thoughtfulness in how she balanced her elbows on her knees, stacked her fists, and rested her chin on them, watching Kristoff. "The Wingmaidens and dragons in the north."

"There's no sign they've turned. Only the tribes so far."

"That's something," Aden muttered.

"Speaking of the dragons," Thorne addressed Ashe, "we need to summon Bresnyar and return to the war camp."

"*Bresnyar?*" Kristoff's eyes widened. "He's still with you after all this time?"

Maleck smiled. "He is Asheila's, and she is his."

Ashe shrugged modestly. "He chose me as his left wing. Or the gods did, we never really settled on whose fault that was."

"Wingmaiden *and* warrior," Kristoff mused. "A woman of many talents...and a tide-turner indeed."

There was something in the look that passed between them Aden couldn't define. It seemed impossible they shared a mind about anything, having just met, nothing but stories to one another before now; but still his scalp prickled at that long, thoughtful stare.

"Ashe," Thorne prompted, breaking the moment, "summon him."

"Not yet," Kristoff interjected. "We rest the night here. I want to keep watch on that mountain and ensure nothing is stirring after your foray inside."

"He's right," Aden agreed. "We struck the enemy a blow today, but we didn't fulfill our mission. If anything, we're worse off: you were right about the stronghold, Thorne. About what lies inside that mountain."

"It's what *isn't* in the mountain anymore that concerns me." Unease glinted in Thorne's eyes.

"Asheila and Aden need the night at least to recover," Maleck argued. "As does your leg."

Thorne scowled, tugging a hand back through his hair. "We put it to a vote. Maleck votes we stay, clearly. Ashe?"

She slid the starstone along its chain, grimacing. "Much as I hate to agree with him on this, I feel like the world's burliest giant is waltzing across my skull in steel-toed boots. Just...give me one night to rest."

Thorne's shoulders bowed. "*Nahdar?*"

"You heard me."

Thorne's gaze turned to Aden. "And you?"

Aden gritted his teeth and shrugged.

A long silence. Then Thorne pushed himself to his feet. "Tomorrow, first thing."

He walked into the back of the cave, and Ashe sighed, bending her head into her hands. Maleck rubbed her spine, worry scripted deep in the lines of his face. Kristoff stood and slung on his sword harness. "I'm going to take watch. Aden?"

"Right behind you." He clapped Maleck on the shoulder, kissed the top of Ashe's head—eliciting a growl that reassured him she was not too wounded to heal, despite how short the reprieve—then followed his father from the cave.

His father. It was so impossible that this was all happening. Yet here they were, and he hadn't woken from any sort of concussed dream.

"How's your head?" Kristoff called above the ceaseless roar of the Ismalete, its echoes cradled in the high gorge walls.

"Not too sore to keep up with you, old man."

Chuckling, Kristoff led him up a narrow game trail from the canyon floor, hardly more than a paler strip of rock where many cloven feet had trod. They traveled more a mile, looping the backside of the jagged mountain and following the river's eroding path, before Selv Torfjel came into view again. It was perilously silent, as if the day's chaos had never befallen it; the only sounds came from the river and the waterfall gushing from that cave mouth above. Measuring the height with his eyes, Aden saw it was the gods' mercy they'd survived the plunge at all.

"It's quiet," Kristoff observed after a moment. "Like any other night."

Aden cast him a sideways glance, trying to read his face... so familiar yet such an anomaly now, like a vision half-remembered from a lucid dream. "That disturbs you."

"When you break a man's arm, you expect him to scream. Silence becomes the enemy." Kristoff settled his back to the mountain, hands in his pockets, not even his boot tips grazed by the moonlight peeking around the curved stone. "Speaking of silence. When you were a boy, you know, Natalya and I never worried you were too loud. We never tried to silence you in public places the way Rakel and Salvotor did to Thorne. You found your voice early on and learned to use it well."

Scoffing, Aden reclined beside him. "Some might disagree on the latter."

Kristoff shook his head. "It was your silence we learned to fear. When we could hear you, we knew precisely what you were thinking, what you were doing. When the house was quiet, we started to pray." Aden wished he had a clever retort to that. The silence while he searched for one seemed to make his father's point. "You were quiet when Thorne asked you to vote."

Pocketing his hands as well, Aden shrugged. "It was one against three. My vote wouldn't have changed the outcome."

"A voice is meant for more than tipping the balance. People deserve to know where you stand."

"This wasn't a tribunal, *Athar*."

Kristoff's mouth quirked up at the affectionate Old Valgardan title for one's father. "True. But you *are* one of his Tribunes, aren't you?"

"How could you possibly know that?"

"Aden, Thorne has been declaring his intentions to have you in the Courts beside him since he was old enough to stop lisping the words. It was only a matter of time. And as such, your vote should count for double."

"Yes, I'm his Tribune. I'm also blood. Family. And with the history between us..."

Kristoff frowned. "What history?"

Grimacing, Aden looked away. When he blinked, cold grazed his face and fire leaped behind his eyes. Braggos burned and Thorne's blood covered his hands. "I've made mistakes. I'm not the boy I was when you left."

"Nor I the man who went away." Kristoff knocked shoulders with him. "It's a different world, a different Chancellor. A better one, if we win this war."

A better Chancellor. A better future. How many times in the last three months had he and Sander toasted to that over watchfires while the others slept? But to hear his father tell it, his silence left the sole burden of bringing about that future, and aiding that Chancellor, to Sander.

Aden pulled at the back of his neck and peered up at Selv Torfjel again. "Thorne would be better off with you as his Tribune."

"My time has risen and set. Now is the age of young men like you, a new generation of Chancellors and those who help carry their burden. It's you he needs, Aden. He always has."

"And I would serve him and die for him. But I don't think I can help him rule."

There. He'd finally said it. The words that had hounded him ever since the night of the siege when he lost Pippet and Thorne didn't bring him to the meeting of Chancellors and Tribunes; the notion that drove him to reckless feats and finally, finally, that stars-damned night. "You don't know what I've done. Why I don't deserve his favor."

"*Afiyam*, you just described grace in its entirety. Of course you don't deserve it. I don't deserve to be alive after twenty years rotting in a mountain prison while my boys suffered, parentless and adrift. But the gods chose otherwise, and here I am, maybe for no other reason but to tell you Thorne *needs* you. Not just your agreement, certainly not your silence. He needs the cousin who knocked sense into him when they were boys, the one who had his back at all times."

Crossing his arms, Aden rested his head against the stone. "I'll think about it."

"That's all I ask for." Kristoff mirrored his posture, and together they watched Selv Torfjel breathe shallowly in the dark. When the minutes ticked by with no end to their silent vigil, Aden began to hope, beyond any desperate longing ever entertained in ten years, that this would not be taken from him after all.

"I still can't believe you're real." The gruff words escaped him without warning. "After all this time, after *everything* we went through—"

"I know." Kristoff's voice was quiet. "I'm sorry I didn't come looking for you the moment I crossed back into Valgard. I should've said to Nimmus with duty, but—"

"You wouldn't be Kristoff Lionsbane if you did."

A smile curved one side of his mouth. "In truth, some part of me feared you'd be furious when you laid eyes on me. That you'd resent me for being gone all this time."

"Some part of me wanted to be," Aden admitted. "But it wasn't your choice to go. And I've lived my life in the shadow of far too many goodbyes lately. I won't take another second for granted, even if I wake up in Selv Torfjel any moment, concussed and delusional."

"I can at least promise that won't happen." Kristoff shifted and rolled the hinge of his neck. "This old body is far too stiff from jumping into that river to be someone else's dream." They shared a laugh the way they used to when they caught each other creeping into the kitchen for cake at unreasonable hours of the night. Then Kristoff cleared his throat. "Do you want to tell me about them? The goodbyes and the mistakes?"

Aden sucked in a hard, deep breath, his gut twinging. "It's a long story."

"We have all night. And *you* have my full attention."

That was grace, Aden decided; that was the uttermost gift. Because he deserved absolutely none of this...but here his father was, back from the Undertaker's own hands, offering the council Aden had craved and suffered without for twenty years.

He cleared his throat. "I abandoned Thorne when he needed me most." Kristoff offered no argument or comfort, merely a silence Aden barreled headlong into, the words pouring from him like a torrent. "There was a girl...Quill's sister, only twelve years old. The Bloodwights have her."

Now Kristoff swore, low and vicious, and Aden could only imagine he was remembering Maleck at that age, stolen and half-turned by the same creatures. "You and she are close?"

Heat pricked Aden's eyes. "She's family." Though even that was too weak a word for what Pippet meant to him. "I've spent this whole war searching for her, hunting her whenever Thorne could spare me. Over a month ago, I thought I finally found her."

Another bleak span like Jazva Chasm, another battlefield they'd returned to in search of flagons from the dead; only that time they'd found not those winged abominations, but the children peeling over the corpses. And among their ranks, one with black-and-brown hair and a birdlike mask who fled when Aden cried her name across the devastated warground.

"We had another mission ahead of us," he rasped, "but I didn't hesitate. *Quill* and I didn't hesitate."

You're sure it was her you saw?

I would stake my life on it.

Then this hunt is mine. Let's go. We're getting her back.

"Thorne let you go?" Kristoff asked.

"He practically drove us from the camp. Him and Tatiana both." Their departure was all a whirlwind, a series of hesitations and insistence; the next battle was meant to be a tide-turner, but an easy one. They had a thousand, they wouldn't want for two even if one was a Kanslar Tribune. "Thorne was confident, Tatiana desperate. They all but begged us to go. We just...*I* just wanted to bring her home."

He dashed his arm across his burning face.

"Quill and I were halfway through the Sotefold when we stumbled onto the enemy reinforcements and realized it was a trap." The words emerged raw, barely louder than a breath. "The ranks in Braggos were nothing compared to the ambush waiting to enclose them. Thorne expected a siege. He was walking into a massacre."

Even now his lungs remembered ripping themselves apart in the reckless sprint back toward that tide-turning city; his muscles relived the ache of thundering through the forest, heedless, abandoning the pursuit of the fleeing Pippet for the imminent death stalking the rest of their family.

"We were too late." His voice stuck in his throat. "They had wind augments, we didn't. By the time we reached Braggos, they'd locked Thorne's forces inside and the slaughter began."

"How did you get to them?"

"We clawed our way over the wall." The deafening echo of dying screams raked his ears. "I've never seen a battle like it, not even in Siralek. I barely found Thorne in time."

Spectral blood dewed his palms, his cousin's pained, perishing breaths filling his ears, his last healing augment given up in penance for what he'd failed to prevent. The healing augment Thorne had passed to him when he went to find Pippet, urging him to use it if he must, to wean her—to save her.

"Ten years," he muttered, "you would think I learned my lesson. But it seems I'm still the same man chasing vague hopes of redeeming what's lost, abandoning his cabal to face the consequences."

"This was not only your choice," Kristoff said. "Thorne and Tatiana asked you to go. Quill went with you."

"And because he was with me, there was one less scout on the wall to spot the ambush."

"Not your fault."

"It is my fault!" Aden burst out. "As a Tribune, I could've told Quill to stay. No lives needed to be risked but mine. If anything, I've proven I'm no leader. We didn't even rescue Pippet, after *everything*—"

"Your cousin *lives* because of you." Kristoff's voice slashed across his, halting his angry tirade like a fuming boy again. "Even if you were there for the whole battle, you couldn't save everyone. That is not your duty, Aden. A Tribune's place is to advise and obey his Chancellor. And your Chancellor told you to go."

"Then we were both wrong."

A sad smile curled Kristoff's mouth. "If only he had a Tribune who would argue when he's wrong and give an honest opinion, then."

Aden's mouth dropped open, then slammed shut again.

"There will never be a perfect Tribune," Kristoff added gently. "*You* will never be a perfect man. But you help no one if you remain silent forever. Learn. Grow. Move forward. Thorne still needs you."

"Even if I wasn't there when he needed me in Braggos?" Aden scoffed.

Kristoff gripped his shoulder and shook him. "You were there when he needed you *most*. The only question that matters now is, will you be there when they need you again?"

CHAPTER THIRTY

IN HER DREAMS, Cistine walked stone halls scripted in ancient runes, blood and breath pounding in her ears, the world a heartbeat away from collapsing around her.

A gentle touch grazed the small of her back, and blue eyes like the heart of flame flared in the dark.

I'm right here, Wildheart.

A jolt of uneasy laughter woke her, sitting with knees pulled to her chest against the tent post in Thorne's alcove. For a moment she was frozen, hands gripping her thighs, watching the black filaments of a shadowy catacomb anneal into the endless gray blotches of the war camp. At a fire nearby, that same warrior laughed again, a forced sound waved desperately like a standard in the face of fear.

She hadn't meant to fall asleep, just to shut her eyes for a moment and rehearse her plan. But with darkness slithering down the mountainside, there was no more room left to plot. Only to act.

Cistine stood and shed the augment pouch taken from Selv Torfjel, tucking it away underneath Thorne's belongings. She'd already tallied the stock and found it lacking in anything curative, but rations were rations. What the Bloodwights saw as bait, she considered a prize far too valuable to bring along on this venture.

Strapping on a saber stolen from the communal armory, she towed up her hood and hurried through the maze of canvas tents out toward the trailhead leading up the mountain where, according to Sander, the Bloodwight was bound. Few looked her way in passing; few expected a princess to creep off in armor and weapons to accost their unlikely prisoner. She might've feared what they made of it once, but there was no concern for appearances in war. With the fate of all the kingdoms in the balance, her focus crystallized, and through it she saw the world differently. This was the sort of action that books of war theory and history called brash but necessary—the kind that shaped victory, if all went to plan.

But she should've known it would not go that way for her.

"I was wondering when you would finally play your hand."

Just beyond the trail's mouth, Cistine froze at that familiar voice, its cadence equal parts exasperation and appreciation. Slowly, she turned back to face Ariadne, the warrior peeling herself up from the curve of the mountain where she'd reclined, masked in utter shadow. Cistine hadn't spotted even a flicker of her presence in passing, not a glint of her eyes or a sway of her inky hair.

She sagged. "How long have you known?"

"Since you first suggested capturing a Bloodwight. The others are too distracted, but I see you, *Logandir*, and you are not the same girl who went away three months ago." Ariadne halted before her, arms crossed, studying her face with head cocked. "You didn't only come back to fight. You came prepared."

Cistine raised her shoulders stiffly. "Like you all taught me."

"I am *fairly* certain we didn't teach you to take powerful prisoners or to creep off and see them in the dark."

Fidgeting with the finger-loops of her armor, she glanced up the trail. She'd spent the better part of the long afternoon marking who was on watch, seeking ways around the layers of guards on Vandred. Her window was narrowing with every second she wasted. "Ari, I have to do this."

"I know you believe that. But I do not appreciate being used as a weapon to get your way, knowing you're keeping something from us."

Shame pricked Cistine's cheeks, reeling her focus fully back to her friend. "I'm sorry. I *was* telling the truth, that I think we need to interrogate him. That knowing more about the Bloodwight ranks and strategies could be just what we need."

Ariadne tilted her head. "But you have a question of your own to ask." She nodded mutely.

After a fraught silence, Ariadne's arms fell from their cross. "There's a hind pass to reach the rock where he's bound. I managed to secure a position on guard there thanks to Sander. The watch shifts in a quarter-hour, but there's going to be some confusion in who takes the next one." A wicked smile curved her lips. "It should take another fifteen minutes or so to untangle the misinformation of who goes where. In the meantime, I'll be on guard further down the trail. For a bit, it will be just the three of us."

Gratitude made it difficult to swallow. "Thank you, Ari."

Ariadne swatted her toward the mountainside—the mouth of the hind trail where she'd leaned and waited for Cistine to sneak by, guarding the entrance. "Less talking, more walking. Leave the guards to me."

"You're not going to flirt with *them*, are you?" Cistine tossed over her shoulder.

"Please, *Logandir*, I do have a broader repertoire than that."

Laughing under her breath, giddy with nerves, Cistine started the long climb up the hind trail.

Any humor faded by the time she finished the rugged, winding ascent and emerged onto the broad span of rock where the Chancellors had bound Vandred. It was a black abyss filigreed in moonlight, the Bloodwight himself a splash of dark against dark. They'd laced him to an upright spear of stone not only with *Svarkyst* chains, but armored manacles as well—elements of the world to keep him in check. He hung in folds of steel and scales, chin to his chest, mask still fixed in place.

She couldn't blame the Chancellors for leaving it on. She'd heard the rumors in the camp all day about the disfigured countenance of the Bloodwights, their skin scarred by the power searing through them, twin to the markings on Maleck's chest. It didn't bear seeing.

She waited for any ruffle of motion down the main trail, but heard and saw nothing. Ariadne's plan must be working, but even so, she had no time to spare. Silent, she stole across the broad rock to Vandred's side and crouched before him, reaching to shake him awake—then hesitating.

Come, his body sang to her. *Come and see.*

Slowly, with only the tips of her fingers, she brushed his armored robe. It helped carry some of the burden of that power, but beneath it...

She twitched his collar aside and laid a hand on his bare shoulder.

The sensation that rocked through her was some vile, terrible blending of the call and the ruination of *Nazvaldolya*, setting her back on her heels, teeth gritted against the feeling like a lightning jolt. Vandred's entire frame hummed beneath her hand, wrapped in a hive of power, an energy current; she could almost *see* the augments that poisoned and corrupted him, the threads like a webwork of scarlet acid guttering over his body.

The Key's power moved of its own accord, the court gossip's curiosity in tandem with it, reaching out to strum the threads of the most prolific augment that drugged Vandred into ecstasy. Her mind supplied a name for that taste. *Blood augment.*

And another. *Fire.*

And another. *Healing.*

Four. Five. *Six* augments at once. She teased those threads, her power tugging at them and feeling them out like a weaver's tapestry—all that power, layer upon layer, an armored shell of its own making. It was no wonder the *Aeoprast* had survived her attack in Stornhaz; no wonder Salvotor hadn't been able to wound him. These Bloodwights, with so much power singing around them, were even better-defended than Kanslar's former Chancellor with dragon scales under his skin.

Unbreakable. Unstoppable.

Vandred gasped awake, a retching heave that sent Cistine scrambling back, blade out, her muffled shriek blending into his. The Bloodwight choked and shuddered like a man surfacing from a nightmare, and Cistine kept wide distance from him, saber drawn and angled, heart pounding.

But Vandred did not snap loose. He recovered his breath in deep gulps and yanked against the chains, thrashing left and right in their indelible grip before falling eerily still, like an animal realizing its struggles only tightened the net further. "What is this?"

Under the soft viciousness of that voice was something Cistine hadn't thought Bloodwights capable of feeling: *fear*.

Of course he was afraid. Two decades he'd spent locked away in the dark; now he was chained again, the unyielding stone at his back not any different from the cell walls in Detlyse Halet. He wore the mask of a creature, but he had the soul of a man still tucked away somewhere, sharing the same terrors as Cistine herself after her long imprisonment in Kalt Hasa.

"What *is* this?" Vandred repeated when she kept silent, studying him. "Who's there? Who *are* you?"

She blinked, then frowned as he wormed against his restraints again. She'd forgotten he was blind.

It was no wonder his brothers left him in Selv Torfjel. For their own interests, perhaps, so that his inhibitions would not slow their plans; or maybe they still had some mercy to spare for their own and left Vandred where he was comfortable, where he could navigate through the same halls over and over, learning his way through a world without sight.

When she didn't speak, he stilled, head tilted like a dog scenting the air. "Ah. There you are, *Key*."

She tensed, hand tightening on her blade.

"Release me at *once*," Vandred snarled, the fear in his tone covered up by cruelty now, "and I will ensure you a painless death on the Doors."

"You know I'm not going to do that." She took a knee again, keeping distance between them. "We're going to have a conversation, you and I."

"You may find me less talkative now than when you crawled into Detlyse Halet."

"And *you* may find that with the herbs coursing through your veins, you have no choice in the matter."

A long silence, with malignance fuming from below his crooked mask, all but daring her to ask her questions and see what consequences came of them. That might have sent her cowering before, but she'd spent three months preparing for this moment. These questions.

She started with the easiest, testing his pliancy. "Can the storm be broken?"

It was a long moment before Vandred answered, "Yes."

"How?"

"Cleave it."

Cistine frowned. "With what?"

"You already know."

He truly thought she did, or else he wouldn't say it now. She mulled the thought for a moment. "Augments?"

"Well, look at you."

The words stirred an old, long-buried panic. Since he couldn't see her regardless, she let herself turn away, shutting her eyes and drawing in a deep breath of the chilly air, envisioning the beauty of Darlaska over the cold, dark rock of a mountain hall.

Augments to cut the Dreadline. She would have to consider the particulars later; for now, they had no flagons to spare for the task, none to waste. Not until she knew the full truth, the real reason she'd brought this creature here in chains.

"Is it possible for a Key to open the Doors without giving their life?"

Speaking it felt surreal, finally giving voice to the question she'd wrestled with alone in her dark room night after night, knowing how greatly outmatched Valgard was now that the Bloodwights held Stornhaz...and all its augments.

Vandred chuckled, the faintest lilt to the sound—surprise thinly hidden. "Is this desperation? Do you hope to bargain for your life from us?"

"I'm not bargaining *anything* from your kind. Answer the question, *bandayo.*"

Vandred was silent for so long, it seemed he might've fallen unconscious again. But he swallowed audibly at last, choking against the Tyve poison's compulsion. "Not without the proper tools."

Her pulse kicked in her wrists and temples. "What are they?"

"Augments."

"*Which* augments?"

"Not ones you'll find easy to come by in this war."

Cistine set her teeth in a grimace. "*Which ones?*"

"Ones you don't have."

He was crafty, this Bloodwight. But if she gave the poison longer to take effect, his clever wordplay would fade. She just needed time.

"Is this what you hope for?" Vandred hissed. "To bleed just enough to save them, to hand the augments back to Valgard without giving your life? What would your father think of that, I wonder? What of *Meszaros* of Cerne Mosiar?"

"I don't need their approval to make my plans." But doubt jerked her heart, and Vandred chuckled as if he heard it stumble in its beat.

"Such a little coward," he said. "If you think this will save them, why waste a moment searching for ways to ensure your own survival? Is your life truly more important than every one that will be lost while you hunt for these answers? Was it worth the ones you left behind in the mountain?"

Rage blistered in Cistine's fingertips. "That's what you want, isn't it? For me to die on a Door right now, so you and your brothers can descend on it like vultures on carrion."

"Do you really see this ending any other way?"

A vicious smile jerked across Cistine's lips. "You don't have the first inkling of what I see."

Vandred was silent again, wariness in his pause—a predator sensing that its prey was perhaps not as weak as it first assumed.

"I'm not desperate enough to be pushed onto a Door." Cistine straightened, dusting gravel from her palms. "But I am grateful. You've been *extremely* helpful, Vandred."

She turned away, and only then did he speak—low and hoarse, his tone swirling like dark music. "Whatever contingencies you dream up, whatever plans you make, this only ends one way."

Cistine froze.

Icy mountain wind stirred her hair, awakening specters in the silence, pain dancing across the rock between her and Vandred—across the plains of her memory. A red-ripped sky, the grip of Julian's spectral hand around hers, the sense of world-ending doom filling every inch of her.

Either you stand alone, or you fall together.

Slowly, she swiveled back. "Do you know what that means?"

The smile was back in Vandred's voice. "It means you cannot outrun sacrifice. You do not walk away from war with everything you ever wanted…that's not how any of this works. I'm prepared to die for my cause, and until you're ready to do the same, you will never best me."

Her fists flexed at her sides. "Bold words from a man chained to a rock."

"Better boldness than cowardice, hm?"

She stormed back to him, planted her hands on the stone on either side of his head, and slammed her knee into his groin so hard he doubled over in his bonds, gagging. Then she left him hanging there, hacking and coughing, and descended the trail to join Ariadne.

She stood posted in the middle of the trail, blades out, watching for the next rotation to arrive. She didn't turn at Cistine's approach, only said, "Did you get what you came for?"

Cistine sighed. "Enough to know I'm looking into the right things. But not enough to know what those things are."

She halted beside Ariadne, her friend's eyes settling on her sidelong. "And what could the Key possibly be seeking from a Bloodwight that she would lie to her friends to keep hidden?"

Cistine was saved from having to answer by the next shift of guards arriving at the base of the trail, keeping the secret locked safely inside her.

CHAPTER THIRTY-ONE

ALONE IN THE firelight, Ashe slowly unraveled the bandage around her head and peered down at her reflection in the dish of water trapped between her knees.

It really wasn't so bad. Kristoff had done clean work suturing it, and while her brain still pounded the inside of her skull like escape would be preferable, at least her wits were coming back; enough that she recognized just how fortunate they were that Aden's father had found them and they all escaped Selv Torfjel with their lives.

All their lives, she hoped. The odds hadn't looked good with her last glimpse of Tatiana.

She shut her eyes against the memory of her friend's torn armor, but she couldn't escape the echoes that came with that vision, worse with every throb of her head: Pippet's ghastly shrieks summoning the enemy, forcing the cabal to separate yet again; the moment her eyes had met her young prodigy's and found no recognition, only hate and hunger.

She could've grabbed the girl; could've chased her down, tackled her, and dragged her out with them. But the betrayal, the fury bludgeoning her heart, and the panic at the sight of Tatiana with so much blood on her and knowing *Pippet* did that, turning every lesson Ashe and Aden ever taught her against them...

She had made a choice in that moment, to let the girl go while she helped Maleck steady Tatiana's wound enough to move her. She wondered what that made her; what it meant for their hope of saving Pippet's life. If it was even possible anymore.

A tear tracked down her cheek, and she scrubbed it hastily away.

Boots swished on stone, and Ashe didn't bother to turn when Maleck crouched behind her, his hand on her shoulder. "Odvaya is cleaned and polished, ready for the next skirmish."

She let out her breath in relief. She'd wanted to do the task herself, but her head ached too badly. "Thank you."

"I've taken stock of Kristoff's weapons as well. Three augments, a handful of Oadmarkaic blades all stone and antler-made, and a sword."

Ashe shot him a dry look over her shoulder, though moving her head hurt. "You've been keeping busy. Trying not to hover over me?"

His cheek feathered, but the smile didn't quite form. In silence, his hands began to work kinks and knots from her back, unraveling the tension from their fall into the river and the battle beforehand. Swallowing a groan at the pleasure of having her hurts seen to, Ashe turned back to the water dish and dabbed her cut, cleaning the bloody whorls around it.

"I owe everyone an apology," Maleck said at last, "but I do not know how to say it."

"For what?"

"The way I was in that mountain...when I saw you injured, when the enemy closed rank, I lost myself again." His fingers were steady at their work, so the shakiness found its way into his voice instead. "I saw death or worse for us all, and rather than picking up my blades, I left Thorne to face our foes alone. I went back to that dark place you and Cistine have worked so tirelessly to pull me from."

"No one blames you for that, Mal."

"I do." His hands took her shoulders firmly, and he pressed his forehead into her hair. Warm breath ghosted down the nape of Ashe's neck, raising gooseflesh all along her arms. "I thought I moved past this into a better place, an understanding of myself. I rid myself of my sketches, I went into that mountain prepared to fight...but I'm still the same man I was. The man who buckles before his brothers, who returns to Azkai's halls at the first prod of memory. What if that man is all I ever become?"

"Well, then he's loved. But he's *not* all you are, Maleck, he's just all you can see right now. And that's all right. You can't just *decide* your past doesn't affect you anymore. I'm still shedding Talheim's prejudices, you know that...but you don't think I'm worth any less while I'm still broken."

"But you did not abandon your Chancellor while you retreated down the paths to your past."

"No, you're right. I was so *useful* back in Talheim when I let Jad goad me into fighting you, and when Kashar had me captive in that cave, and when I stayed in the mountains with Bres while you rotted under Middleton..."

Maleck pulled back. "Whenever I hesitate, my cabal is harmed. I will not make that mistake again."

A chill raked down Ashe's back. "You have no idea how much I hate when you say things like that. It usually ends with you bleeding."

Maleck took her chin and turned her toward him. "Protecting my family is all that matters. If I bleed, I bleed."

"*No*," Ashe snarled, and his eyes widened. "No more bleeding. Do you hear me, Darkwind? We've bled enough."

After a long moment, his startled gaze softened. He pressed a kiss to the edge of her sutures and the hot, tender skin around them. "I hear you, *Mereszar*."

Ashe grimaced, pulling back. "Oh, wonderful. Another name I don't know the meaning to. Are you and Bresnyar consorting now? Trying to see who can confuse me the most before I lose my mind?"

Maleck chuckled, drawing her away from the fire with one deft tug, landing her between his sprawled legs. She settled against him, head propped under his chin, her back to his chest; his arms wound around her waist, tugging her close until there wasn't a breath of cold mountain air between them. Together they gazed through the cave mouth to the moon-silvered river, the stone walls ringed in the same pale glow.

After a time, Ashe gave up trying to search for a meaning to that Old Valgardan word buried in her head; the language had never intrigued her the way it did Cistine. "It must be strange, having Kristoff back from the dead."

"More than I can say," Maleck admitted. "I put little stock into omens, but I can't help seeing this as one."

"How do you mean?"

His shoulders bobbed in a shrug, tightening his grip around her. "In the last war, Kristoff appeared to me just like this, a specter of blood and snow. He helped me find my way back, not only to Stornhaz, but to myself. I don't believe he ever saw Talheim as the true enemy...I never saw him fight any Warden but one."

Rion. It was inevitable—*Meszaros*, the Butcher, had hunted Maleck across the swamps and southern tundra; and if Kristoff came for Maleck back then, no doubt he'd crossed Rion.

"His foe was never Talheim," Maleck went on quietly, "but my brothers. Where the Chancellors saw their knowledge and daring as an asset to win the war, Kristoff saw them and us as we truly were. He came to the front lines not to fight Valgard's war, but to bring me home." His ribs and chest lifted in a slow, deep breath, and he let it out in a sigh that brushed her ear. "And now here we are in the middle of the same battle, and he appears again, that same specter come to stand with us against the true enemy."

Ashe chafed the starstone on its chain, her mind drifting back to their conversation about Oadmark, the tribes serving out of fear or reverence; and that look Kristoff sent her when he learned she was a Wingmaiden, when she asked about the legions Bresnyar was once part of.

It all set something stirring in her mind...something she couldn't look deeply into just yet, with her head still a hive of hurts and their cabal pulled apart.

"Well, I'm glad he's here," she said. "Judging by what we saw in that mountain today, we're going to need all the help we can find."

CHAPTER THIRTY-TWO

THE MOMENT TATIANA woke, she knew.

She was in the medico's tent, the heavy weight of a blanket wrapped around her, a gaping emptiness in her chest and pain flaring dully between her hipbones. With her eyes still closed, she listened to the murmurs—not from the ailing or the medicos, but from Quill. Both his hands clutched one of hers, a dip in the cot where he leaned his elbows on it, brow pressed to their joined fingers.

"—and if it's burned down, or if some *mirothadt bandayos* have been living in it all this time, we'll rebuild it." His voice was hoarse, as if he'd rambled at her bedside for hours. "Chase them out, cut a few throats if we have to. Then we do the repairs. Mort can help, he's handy with a hammer when he's not bashing his thumbs to pieces...it just needs to be done by winter. You know how Blaykrone winters can be."

He was talking about their house, the one he'd deeded to her for Darlaska—a night and a dream that seemed so far away now, part of some other woman's life. She could barely remember what she'd envisioned back then, the first thaw giving way to spring, her and Quill and Pippet all sharing that home together.

The vision perished now, winking out like a dying star, leaving just a trace of another dream that had blended into it after Braggos—one she'd told no one else about. One where it wasn't just the three of them anymore.

Now...now she wasn't certain it was any more than just the two of them, just her and Quill against the world again. She tried to make that all right, tried to shift and pummel her mind into accepting a future like that...just her and the man gripping her hand. Just Dawnstar and Nightwing, the beginning and the end. She tried to tell herself that was all that mattered.

The void gaping in her middle wouldn't let her believe it anymore. Not when, for just a flicker, it had become something more.

She must've tensed at that thought, perhaps let out a sound too soft to hear over her own pounding heart, because all at once Quill was up, letting go of her hand with one of his so he could smooth the curls from her brow. "Tati. Are you with me?"

"Most of me." She meant it as a joke, but her voice cracked around the truth buried under it.

Quill's breath gusted out in relief, and he pressed his lips to her brow so fiercely she could feel the twist in his features, knew without looking how his eyes had slammed shut hard enough that his whole face scrunched. "Thank the *stars*."

She forced her heavy eyelids up, a churn of herbs still eddying in her veins, and Quill leaned back to study her. There was no mistaking the redness in his eyes, the thin crust around his nostrils; he'd been here, weeping and sleepless, for hours. Now he stared at her the same way he'd looked at the first sunrise after she'd let him out of Detlyse Halet, like she was the most precious and stunning thing he'd ever seen.

As if she hadn't ruined their whole future in that mountain.

"How long?" Those were the only words she could form between staggered, painful breaths, but as always, Quill understood.

"Half the day and all night. It's almost dawn again." His fingers flexed on her shoulder. "You weren't answering me even with Cistine's healing augment doing its work, and after whatever that stars-forsaken *complication* was, I thought...Nimmus' *teeth*, Tati. If this is how you felt when we were in Oadmark together, I don't know how you didn't lose your mind."

"Who says I didn't?"

"Hilarious." His hand returned to her brow, smoothing the tacky ringlets from her eyes, and for some absurd reason that simple motion made her want to cry. "I'm sorry. I should've moved faster, I should've been watching for the knife. I just didn't want to believe she—"

"I can't." The words burst harshly from Tatiana's lips. "I can't do this right now, Quill." One pain was enough. If she thought of Pippet too, she would come completely undone.

"I hear you," he said after a beat. "Tell me what you need."

"Soup." She had no appetite, but it was the first thing that came to mind; something that would force him to leave the tent so she could speak to the medicos in private and hear the answer to the question raging inside her, once and for all. Then she could lay to rest the ember of hope that this pain was merely from the wound above her hip, and not deeper; not so much a soul-wound as just one of the flesh.

Quill hopped to his feet, dashing his arm against his eyes. "Whatever you want, Saddlebags."

She waited for the familiar cadence of his steps to fade. Then she slowly sat herself up, looking left and right at the medicos straggling between the canvas folds. Though there were more drapes lowered and more coughs riding the wind, they were far less busy now because there were far less wounded here than ill. Most from Jazva Chasm had either healed or died.

Tatiana felt like she stood with a foot in each.

"Excuse me?" she croaked, and one of the medicos turned. "Can you find Visalie?"

The man nodded and hurried off; in moments, a familiar face ducked into the cordoned-off corner of the tent, pretty, amber-skinned, and green-eyed—the girl from Erdotre territory who'd stitched her wounds after Braggos; and afterward, when the battlefield carnage became too much for her, when the nightmares started, she was the one Tatiana went to again.

Back then, just like now, she needed Visalie to confirm what she already knew.

"You shouldn't be sitting up just yet," the medico warned, sidling between tent posts to her cot and taking Tatiana's shoulder firmly. "You're full of sutures and enough herbs to put a carthorse on its knees. Lie back."

Tatiana gripped the girl's wrist. "Is it over?"

Visalie's fingers spasmed, but she held Tatiana's gaze steadily, sorrow flickering in the depths of her eyes. "I'm sorry."

She knew, but even so, she was not prepared for all the weight that crashed into her, the agony and the emptiness, and the cruel, unbelievable *relief* all braided up together, choking off her breath. Through clenched molars, voice shaking, she whispered, "Did you tell him?"

Visalie slowly wagged her head. "I'm bound by oath. I can tell Quill absolutely nothing without your consent but that you're not going to die."

She blinked away tears and managed the jerkiest nod of her life. "I'll do it, when there's time, I just...not yet. Not now."

Visalie helped her lie down again, and Tatiana rolled over with her back to the girl, clutching the limp pillow in sharply-flexing fingers, grasping for something that was no more. That perhaps was never meant to be. She hadn't intended for any of this to happen and hadn't realized how desperately she wanted it until it was gone.

"You're going to be all right." Visalie stroked her hair. "I saw to it. There's no hint of infection, no further complications. And maybe, after the war..."

"Maybe," she rasped. "Thank you for everything, Visalie." It was the only dismissal she could manage without screaming like a hawk and breaking the girl's wrist just to be free of her touch, to stop her from speaking useless consolations and well-rehearsed platitudes.

After a moment, Visalie's feet tapped quietly away. Tatiana curled up tightly, shielded her ravaged middle, hid her face in her pillow, and wept until her whole body ached; until it felt like she'd tear every suture that held her together with the force of her sobs; until she couldn't breathe or see or think or hear.

It was because she couldn't hear over her own hacking tears that she didn't realize Quill was there until his weight shifted the cot. He settled in behind her, wrapped his body around hers, and pulled her back against his chest; his arm circled her front, pinning her elbows to her body, and his face rested in her hair, breaths giving a cadence for her to match, to keep from hyperventilating and vomiting all over the bed.

He didn't speak; perhaps he sensed, through that wondrous and unfathomable bond that hsd long lived between them, that the pain she suffered now went deeper than any words could touch.

Safe in his arms but not sheltered from the grief, Tatiana buried her forehead against his wrist and shattered to pieces.

CHAPTER THIRTY-THREE

WARM AIR NUZZLED through Thorne's collar when he gave up sleeping and mounted the path to join his uncle, the first licks of the wind promising another unseasonable day even before dawn. Aden had returned from watch half an hour ago, the impact of his body falling in a heap beside Maleck and Ashe the final end of Thorne's fruitless attempts to rest.

It was a relief to escape the cave, where he'd stared at the roof for most of the night, listening to Maleck and Ashe talk about anything and everything, then listening to his own heartbeat; all while worrying about the war camp, about the Bloodwight they'd captured...about Cistine.

Better to be in Kristoff's presence where he was posted against the mountainside, watching Selv Torfjel with a thoughtful crease to his brow. Thorne reclined beside him, offering a flask of water and a bag of dried fruit. "Do you ever sleep?"

"Kalt Hasa trained it out of me." He accepted the rations with a grateful half-smile. "I dozed here and there while Aden was on watch."

"You must be elated to see him again. Both of them."

"More than words can say." Voice husky, Kristoff swigged from the flask while Thorne watched the mountain; it broke up from the ground like bone through a wound, angular and unsightly, and he wasn't certain he imagined how it seemed to roil with malicious intent. "Aden told me what became of Salvotor. How are you?"

Thorne folded his arms and shrugged. "Better than I thought I would be. The war helps, as absurd as that sounds. I have no time to look for a deadman's shadow when I'm chasing living ones."

"Fair enough." Kristoff handed back the flask. "What of Rakel?"

Thorne couldn't begrudge Kristoff's concern for his sister, Thorne's own traitorous mother, a love that lingered even though her betrayal put him in Kalt Hasa. It was the same with Aden, whom Thorne had never stopped loving even after they left Stornhaz, when he could hardly look his cousin in the eye. "Last we heard, she and Devitrius bent the knee to the Bloodwights."

Kristoff palmed his hair, wincing. "Ah, Kel."

The endearment gave Thorne pause. No one had called his mother that since Kristoff disappeared twenty years ago. "You know she feels no remorse. She helped Salvotor escape and capture Quill's sister." The mere thought of Pippet made his chest ache, a haunted memory of her tearstained face and hands reaching toward him landing like a blow straight over the heart.

"I know that. And I know she must face justice for it. But love is a foolish thing, it has no sense of self-preservation. I'll love my sister until the day I die, even if I'm the one who puts a blade in her chest. I'd be wiser if I didn't care, but I can't make it so."

"I know something of what that's like." Thorne tapped his fingertips restlessly against his elbows, keeping his gaze fixed on the mountain.

"When you sent Cistine back to Talheim, you mean?"

Aden really had told him everything. And that was good...Thorne wasn't certain he could relive that cruel day yet without being choked for words. "Things would be easier if I hadn't given my heart away to a woman who's always going to leave. But I think I'm beginning to realize love isn't about keeping the heart safe. It's about setting it free."

Kristoff clapped him on the shoulder. "Speaking from experience, freedom is the only way to be truly alive. I'd rather be dangerously free than safely confined."

Thorne cuffed his back in turn. "You don't know how glad I am you survived that Nimmus-pit, *Nahdar*."

"And I you. You've grown so much since then, Thorne. I see a Chancellor before me—a man coming into his own. What you've done for this kingdom, even the way you led your people into that mountain—"

"For all the good it did." Thorne's good mood vanished. "The Balmond still live. All we know is where the Bloodwights may be gathered. Or not."

Kristoff frowned. "Gathered?"

"They haven't been seen since the war began. Not even near Stornhaz, according to our scouts."

"That's news to me." One arm crossing his middle, Kristoff stroked his lower lip with his thumb. "What did you learn in there?"

"That unless their maps were another part of the trap, they're gathered in the northwestern Isetfells. My hope is Cistine will learn the truth of that from the one we captured." He paused. "*Nahdar?*"

Kristoff's tan face soured sickly white. "What do you mean you *captured* it, Thorne?"

"Exactly what I said. Cistine rendered it unconscious with a wind augment, and she and the others returned it to the war camp." The hair on the nape of his neck prickled at Kristoff's horrified stare. "What is it?"

"Thorne, it's a stars-forsaken *Bloodwight*. Its body is full of augments, do you really believe chains and fetters can hold it?"

He ground his molars, biting down against a surge of the same fear he'd wrestled with all night. "If it had broken free, if it was *possible*, we would know by now."

"Unless *this* is the trap. Unless it wanted to be taken."

"*Why?* What advantage would that pose?"

"The *Key* captured it, Thorne! She brought it straight to the heart of the Valgardan war camp—the one place the enemy hasn't been able to find and ransack yet!"

The war camp. Where all the Chancellors now convened.

Like a chuckle, like some dark god laughing at the terrifying realization, Selv Torfjel gave a great, heaving groan.

Thorne and Kristoff swung toward it as one, hands going to their weapons for no reason that mattered. Sabers alone were nothing against what came pouring from the stronghold's gaping front maw.

Mirothadt streamed through the gaping void rendered wide by Bresnyar's passing the day before, some carried by winged Balmond, others borne along by wind augments; dozens, then hundreds of them, a tide spilling like blood from an open wound. And behind them, rising up from the mountain to crown its upper peaks in shadow and storm—

Thorne did not need Cistine's intrinsic sense to know what that wicked presence was, the feeling of rot and decay seething out ahead of them.

The Bloodwights had returned. And now they rose, forging a maelstrom of wind and lightning and darkness, moving toward the war camp.

Toward *Cistine*.

"We have to go!" Thorne bellowed. "If Ashe summons—"

"No time. I have a wind augment. That will be enough." Kristoff gripped his shoulder and spun him away from Selv Torfjel. "Go, Thorne! *Run!*"

They broke down the path at a dead sprint, storms and wingbeats and cruel cries erupting across the mountainside behind them.

CHAPTER THIRTY-FOUR

TATIANA HAD NO desire to drag herself from the medico's cot when morning light slithered through the canvas. There was no real distraction waiting for her; she knew it the moment she woke.

The first thought that struck her was how she'd lost her satchel in that mountain. Everything she was tinkering with, her distractions, all the creations she was dreaming of...fitting that it all ended there.

She ached for the numb void of sleep, and she might've given over to it if Quill sitting up and pulling on his boots wasn't the thing that had woken her. Instead, she propped herself on her elbow and half-turned to face him, blinking her stinging, swollen eyes until his mismatched hair came clearly into view. "Where are you going?"

"The Chancellors just brought that Bloodwight to the war tent. Interrogation."

The Bloodwight who'd ruled Selv Torfjel, where Pippet was kept, corrupted, blade in hand, and that blade went into her and ruined *everything*—

Tatiana flung the blanket back, grimacing at the twinge of sutures through her middle, and sat up. "I'm coming."

Quill's booted foot fell to the floor, his gaze raking over her. "I'm not sure you should be moving yet, Saddlebags."

"If I break your nose, maybe you'll feel differently."

He sighed. "Just...go slow, all right?"

She didn't have any other choice. Everything ached, and her face throbbed like she'd gotten into a brawl with a hefty drunkard over cheating at cards. It took her entirely too long to drag on her armor, and in the end Quill helped her lace up her boots; bending was the worst, every contortion sending fresh lances of pain through her core.

He took her hand at last and helped her up, worry eclipsing even the fury always burning so bright in his eyes these days. "Tati. You're sure about this?"

She really wasn't now that she was on her feet, the world swirling around her and nausea swooping through her stomach. But it was better than lying on this cot and crying alone. "I'm sure. Let's go, Featherbrain."

She did not let him release her hand the entire walk through the camp to the war tent. Ariadne waited for them beyond the lowered canvas drapes, her gaze going straight to Tatiana. First surprise, then compassion twisted her features, and for an absurd second Tatiana was certain she'd somehow guessed—maybe the True God himself had told her.

But Ariadne said nothing, only swept Tatiana into an embrace so tight it awakened new points of pain throughout her body and fit all the broken pieces together again at the same time; so maybe she could survive this encounter and return to the medico cot without coming undone.

"Did they start without us?" Quill asked when the women drew apart.

"Hardly." Ariadne jerked her head. "Inside, quickly."

They were the last ones to enter, the Chancellors and Sander and Cistine already gathered, and at Bravis's nod Ariadne tugged the canvas fully into place, sealing off the war tent. Cistine offered a quick, shaky smile to Tatiana, haunches still planted against the map table and arms folded in a way that managed to look both defensive and furious at once. Her eyes were fixed on the Bloodwight who lay fettered on the floor under a spiderweb of *Svarkyst* chains.

Tatiana had never hated anything so much in her life. Until this moment, she hadn't even realized she was capable of holding so much rage in her body, like she'd found a place to store it inside the hole this creature and his corrupted ranks had ripped into her.

"Is the poison working?" Cistine demanded, though something in her tone pricked Tatiana's ears. There was none of the usual curiosity there, as if she already knew the answer.

Chancellor Valdemar kicked the creature onto its back. "Do you have a name?"

The maskless Bloodwight rolled toward them, and Tatiana stared down at it, repulsed. The havoc of abused augmentation stretched across its face, distorting the skin like the leprosy cases in her mother's old medico books. Lesions ate into the upper lip halfway to the eyelid, exposing the bone of the sinus cavity beneath. Its lips were chapped and flattened to the skull, almost nonexistent, and it was hairless—no eyelashes, no brows. There was little left of its nose either, just a crooked, formless lump in the center of its face, with nostrils forward-facing and distended like a serpent's.

This was the living warning of why augments ought not to be trifled or experimented with. Tatiana fought not to shudder as the creature gazed at them with half-dead, drugged eyes in skull-deep sockets.

"Name?" Valdemar barked.

"Vandred," the creature rasped.

"He's telling the truth," Cistine said. "He was a prisoner in Detlyse Halet under that name."

"Do you know where you're being held?" Maltadova asked.

Vandred's teeth jutted through the gaps of his ruined mouth. "*No.*"

Sander scoffed appreciatively from where he reclined against the table beside Cistine. Maltadova knelt before the Bloodwight, resting his wrists on his bent legs and clasping his fist gently in his opposite hand. "Tell us why you are here."

"Because you captured me."

"No. Why are you *here*," Adeima stepped forward, hand to her blade, guarding her *valenar's* back, "in Valgard. For what purpose have you come and built an army of our criminals? Our *children*?"

Tatiana rested her hand in the small of Quill's back and felt him shudder just as she did—if for different reasons.

"We have come in conquest for the new age." Vandred's voice scraped from his ravaged throat. "It is our duty to clear the path before the *Aeoprast* and the return of augments to our land. Soon Valgard will run fertile with the power of the old gods again. Then we will enslave them as well."

Stunned silence descended for a beat; Tatiana wasn't the only one struggling to make sense of those heretical words.

"You speak madness." Rage, disbelief, and indignation rattled Ariadne's voice on behalf of the gods she loved. "You profane the True God and his vassals."

"He is not my god. He is nothing more than a relic of bygone times when man did not know his own strength, when he was forced to rely on Wayfinders and *Gammalkraft* to guide him. But that time is ending. When the gods poured out their power on us, the elect seized it and learned just the beginning of how they could harness its full potential. A new age is coming now, with new gods...and the augments will lead us there."

"The augments are just a tool," Valdemar snapped, "sealed behind the Doors. They can do *nothing* for you."

Vandred was quiet for so long, Tatiana had to resist the urge to glance at Cistine.

"And this is why the people of Valgard will serve us, as you now serve the old gods. You are too small-minded to know any better," Vandred said at last. "Augments were not created to serve man, but man to serve the knowledge of augmentation...and we are the chosen vessels to carry that knowledge. If that means we bring into submission those who now serve other masters, then so be it. Slaves of one kingdom become slaves to another in conquest...that has always been the way of war. And we will bring the truth of augments not just to one kingdom, but to all."

"Talheim?" Cistine snarled.

"And Oadmark, and Mahasar. In the north, it has already begun. We will gather your men and women for our army and we will give your children the greatest honor of all: to become vessels for the might of augmentation's progress. By them, we will discover new horizons of worship and application."

"You mean the Balmond," Quill rasped.

Vandred's tongue, slit down the middle into a near-perfect fork, grazed his lipless mouth.

"What are these Balmond?" Adeima demanded, and Tatiana shot a furious glance at Bravis. Clearly he hadn't taken Thorne's concerns into consideration enough to tell the other Chancellors about their true mission in Selv Torfjel.

Vandred took it upon himself to answer. "They are *our* children. Our new race, created in our image."

"A new race?" Benedikt scoffed. "That isn't *possible*."

"We have learned the way. It was all that separated us from the gods: the power to create something new." Vandred's broken teeth bared in a fanatic smile. "But we have forged the Balmond. We *are* gods now. Only one step remains before we march against the old ones and cast them down."

Cistine straightened from the table's edge. "What step?"

"To grasp the power that will end the war in a single blow. The power of the old gods."

A stiff, frigid breeze traced the canvas flaps, and Tatiana stopped breathing.

"Impossible," Valdemar said. "You don't even have the Key."

"What if I told you that there is not just one Key? And that the Keys were not objects, but people?"

Quill and Ariadne both fell suddenly, threateningly still. Tatiana felt like the rock had cracked open under her feet. Shallow breaths hissed in and out of her open mouth, her gaze fixed on this creature, hands aching to go around its throat, to choke the life out of it.

"I would say that you're lying to distract us," Valdemar murmured.

"I may be keen to distract you, but I am not lying. Thanks to your vile poison, I cannot."

"How would a *person* open the Doors?" Adeima demanded. "With the touch of a hand?"

"With their blood."

"That's enough." Quill stepped forward, drawing every eye to him. "How do you intend to end this war in one blow?"

"I do not. My brothers do."

"*How?*"

"Why don't you ask them yourself?"

A soft, agonized huff escaped Cistine, and Tatiana whirled to face her. Her arms dropped from their cross, her horrified gaze shooting up to the canvas above, its folds bowing inward under a new, harsher breeze. "Oh, gods, they're *here.*"

Vandred chuckled softly. "I did warn you I was distracting you."

The tent burst into flame.

CHAPTER THIRTY-FIVE

ASHE HAD BARELY a second to wake up and fathom what Kristoff and Thorne were shouting about when they barreled into the cave. Before she even fully comprehended this was not a nightmare, Aden took a portion of the wind augment from his father's hand and seized her and Maleck by their shoulders. Then the miles were blurring by, the world in conflict between new daylight and unnatural darkness screaming on their heels, and no matter how swiftly the power of the gods moved them, they couldn't escape the *mirothadt* horde or the Bloodwights themselves all descending on the war camp. Coming for Cistine.

That was what Thorne had shouted. That was what they were moving with godlike speed to intercept now.

As sparingly as Ashe had used augments during this war, even she knew when theirs started to gutter. The mountains sharpened from a smoky blur to jagged granite teeth below, and they dropped too far, too fast, Ashe's stomach vacating its place and soaring out of her mouth with a scream. They struck down on a rocky shelf in a copse of trees, tucking and rolling at the last moment to slow their descent, and the pain in Ashe's brow revived to a thumping, dull ache when she came up on her knees. To her left, Thorne lurched into a dead sprint for a trail down from the shelf, toward the bathing pool below and the opposite side of the steep gully. Through the evergreens, across the span, Ashe saw fire and heard her dragon's mighty cry.

The war camp was already burning.

She staggered up, fear and anger unspooling in her core, bringing a false strength to her limbs that would utterly wind her after. But for now, there was no after; there was only the smoldering camp and the space from here to there, to *Cistine*—

The world went from day to darkness in a single heartbeat, black as a moonless night. Ashe had no time even to catch her breath before the dark augment poured over the mountaintops and slammed into them. Blinded by the power Cistine called ravaging darkness, Ashe flung out her hands, reaching for anything to anchor herself. Screams of panic echoed from the distant war camp as the storm and shadows speared toward them.

And then, light.

Bright and milky, it flared to Ashe's left, a sizzling golden shell wrapped around Kristoff's body. Brow creased in concentration, he wrapped the light tighter and tighter, forging a glistering ward against the dark; then he sent it out, fracturing the black tide and forcing it back inch by inch.

A second flare to the right: Aden was beside Kristoff, wreathed in fire, the flagrant glow rising to meet his father's. Without a word, they locked light and flame like a shield, and the darkness broke and scattered against it enough so that Ashe could find Maleck's broad silhouette and leap to his side, winding her fingers around his. He was shaking so terribly she didn't fathom how he kept his feet beneath him, knowing what lurked out there in the darkness. She could barely stand, herself.

But they would face this battle like they had every one before it in this war: together, on their feet, weapons ready.

The void cracked suddenly around them, and daylight spilled across their bodies. Aden had turned, put his back to Kristoff's, and opened a narrow channel to the trees. A way out for Ashe and Maleck.

"Get through!" he roared, fire flickering, shadows pounding at his flames. Ashe skimmed her hand along his side and surged through the gap, making only six strides before she realized no footsteps echoed in pursuit.

She whirled back and found Maleck halted at the tunnel's mouth. He looked at her, then back again—to his shaking friend and to Kristoff, his shoulders to his son's, facing the coming tide.

Maleck's voice carried, low and steady. "Close the tunnel, Aden."

Ashe snarled under her breath, ripping Odvaya from its sheath, readying to step back through the fiery gap and close ranks, to fight beside them—beside *him*.

"Asheila. Stop."

She froze at that soft command carrying above the bellowing darkness, the crackle of flames. Maleck was no longer trembling; he faced her from the other side of those shadows, and that *look* in his eyes—

"You must go. Get Cistine out of these mountains. I'll find you after."

"Mal—" she began.

"Our princess is in your hands now." He stepped back. "Protect her."

He and Aden exchanged a glance. A dip of their heads.

"*Maleck!*" Ashe roared his name as the fire winked out and darkness crashed down, blasting her back on her heels far from the encasing dome of shadows. From him and Aden. From his *brothers*.

Ashe coiled up to fling herself forward, to use what little knowledge she had of augments to break through again. Even if it tore the armor from her body, the flesh from her bones, she had to reach them. Every nerve in her body sang with the need—but Maleck's words rang in her head.

Cistine. Those bastards were here for *her*. If Ashe and Bresnyar got her out, away from the war camp, then the Bloodwights would scatter. The quickest way to end all of this was to do as Maleck had said and honor his choice.

Gripping Odvaya and swearing at the sky, Ashe turned and ran toward the edge of the cleft. She didn't bother speaking into the starstone; instead she fought with all her mind to cleave and trusted Bresnyar to hear her shout.

Her vision traced in gold whorls, then cleared again. Her dragon bellowed, and the guttural crack of his flames sent a trace of power singing through her chest. She broke the cover of the trees, ran straight to the edge of the gully, and leaped with all her might.

Bresnyar was already there, rolling into place beneath her so her knees caught around the ridge of his spine. He righted himself with a snap of his tail, and she steadied her weight against him. "Angle low, Bres."

He tucked his wings and swooped along the gully floor, wingtips skimming the surface of the pond, spearing straight toward the black-clad figure still running toward the path up from the gulch.

Ashe shouted his name, and Thorne checked his stride, looking back. Arm out, she nudged Bresnyar with her knee; fluid as molten gold, the dragon rolled once more to the side, and Thorne slammed to halt, reaching up. Ashe caught him, shoulder screaming as it wrenched in its socket, and heaved him up before her. He cast her a grim nod of thanks and drew his sabers, ready for the inevitable slaughter.

Ashe shut out her fear for Maleck, Aden, and Kristoff, the pain still echoing in her head, even her worry for her own life. That would all come later, when Cistine was safe.

Together she and Thorne lunged from Bresnyar's back and landed at the trailhead, the tide of *mirothadt* and Valgardan warriors breaking and clashing across the stone. A spate of augurs turned on them and the dragon behind them, his jaws parted, a shield at their backs.

"Let's find our princess," Ashe growled.

Thorne's chin sank a bare inch. "Right behind you."

Furious cries searing their throats, they lunged into combat.

CHAPTER
THIRTY-SIX

CISTINE'S WORLD WAS an inferno. Strong arms surrounded her, and for a moment she was back on the trail of the Izten Torkat, carts exploding before her, Thorne's body a shield, a sanctuary. Then her head started to clear, and she smelled embers and the hot scorch of lightning, her body pulsing with the tension of augments straddling the wind.

Weight eased from above her with a gasp of breath, then a curse next to her ear—*Sander*. He was smothering her, protecting her from the collapsing tents. The scratchy weight of the canvas pressed over their bodies, so hot and near it felt like being burned alive. Panicked, Cistine arched her weight, and Sander slid off completely. Together they clawed through the canvas swaddle and out into the fiery dreamscape of Nimmus itself.

Around them, the war camp was in chaos. The *mirothadt* fell from the sky, carried and dropped by twisted, uncoordinated beings, ghastly and unnatural things that had no place in this world—yet here they were. Vandred's so-called children, creatures of winged shadow, plunged toward Valgard's warriors, talons leading, maws gaping, and shredded through their reinforced armor like silk. Every claw sharp as *Svarkyst* steel, every tooth its own spear tip, they quartered Valgard's strongest with ruthless precision.

A howl surged in Cistine's throat, and she struggled to her feet, Sander beside her, the others rising around them: Adeima, Valdemar, Bravis and

Benedikt, Ariadne and Quill and Tatiana—

And Vandred.

Unshackled, darkness writhing around him, standing over eight feet tall and every inch of that humming with power, he turned his unmasked face to Cistine with filmy, void eyes, and somehow still saw her.

More than that, she saw *him*. Everything he'd given her the night before, every moment he'd seemed under their control—a lie. He'd broken those chains without effort. And now he thrust his hands into the wreckage of the war camp and pulled out Maltadova by his throat.

Tatiana buckled, a hand to her mouth. All the other Chancellors moved as one with Quill and Ariadne in the lead, hands to their weapons, shooting forward—then stopping when Vandred's fist tightened and a choked cry spilled from Maltadova's bleeding mouth.

Cistine's breaths whipped from her chest in quick, shallow pants. She had her augments, her saber, a dagger, and if only she could draw a single flagon without catching Vandred's attention—

If only she could unleash more than one without dooming herself to these desperate Chancellors.

But suddenly her life mattered less, her own mortality a flickering inconvenience while the world burned around them and Maltadova, kicking weakly, hung in Vandred's grip, his death so much nearer than hers.

"Did you truly believe you were safe," Vandred snarled, "that you could bind us? Subdue us? You cannot overcome a god. It's time you fathomed just how far beneath us you truly are...what we can do to your mortal flesh."

His grip tightened around Maltadova's throat, wrenching a gasp from him, his eyes flying wide. Cistine jerked open her augment pouch, fingers singing between one flagon and the next, wind, fire, whatever would both spare the Chancellor in his torn armor and bring Vandred down in a single blow—

Maltadova cried out in earnest when Vandred's grip tightened again, a sound so broken it cracked Cistine's heart as well

"*Enough!*" Adeima shouted, the word pitching and rising again with rage and anguish.

It was only a moment Vandred froze—in shock, perhaps in curiosity that someone he considered less even than the Chancellors themselves would dare speak to him. Only a moment, but to Cistine it seemed like a lifetime. Long enough for her to take both augments in her hands; long enough for Maltadova to raise his eyes to find his *valenar's*.

Cracked, bloodsoaked lips stuttered to form words. "I love—"

Vandred ripped out his throat.

The Chancellors and the cabal recoiled; Cistine's scream and Adeima's lashed out in tandem to the surge of power from the Key's hands, her fire blasting into Vandred's chest, blowing Maltadova from his grip a second too late. The Bloodwight tumbled head-over-heels into the canvas, and Cistine flattened him down with her flames. Through vision stained with tears, she watched Adeima crawl to her *valenar's* body and gather him into her lap, clutching his head to her chest, his gored throat spewing blood against her armor.

And Vandred laughed while Cistine held him down. The only reason he hadn't broken free yet was that he was *enjoying* this spectacle; she couldn't pin him forever. So Quill and Ariadne sprang on the Bloodwight; but that only steepened Cistine's panic when they were so close, hanging off that creature's fatal hands.

"Help me!" she shouted, but the other Chancellors did not move. They stared at Maltadova's corpse, weapons dipping, eyes vacant with shock.

"That!" Vandred cried, and they all flinched. "That is how simply we can kill your Chancellors!"

"He was not Chancellor."

At Adeima's trembling, furious hiss, the wind itself dropped.

"*He was not Chancellor!*" She raised her head, gaze shooting toward the Bloodwight, her whole frame shaking with world-ending fury. "*I* am." She lowered Maltadova into the canvas and towered up to her full height, hands drifting to the knives at her sides. "I am *Chancelloress* Adeima of Yager Court. You killed *my valenar*, beneath *my* stars, in the time of *my* Hunters."

Her blades whispered from their sheaths.

"This kill is mine."

Daggers flashed, and in the same instant she struck, Vandred broke Cistine's cage around his arms and legs, hurled Quill and Ariadne away with a burst of power, and shot upright, his own fire slashing in a whip toward the Chancelloress.

It met a scythe of wind, slamming him back down and cracking his head against the stone so hard he went limp for an instant.

Cistine lowered her hand, flame and wind dancing together between her fingers. For a heartbeat, she held Adeima's stunned gaze, felt the other Chancellors staring at her in wonder...then in dawning comprehension as they knitted Talheim's role in this war and her actions with Vandred's taunts about a human Key.

She'd just sealed her own fate.

So she did the only thing she could think of: she wrapped her wind and fire around Vandred and ripped them both from the mountain, the cabal's screams of shock and fury lost to the roar of her power.

They didn't make it far—barely to the span of rock where Vandred had played at being imprisoned—before he returned to his senses enough to fight her. He writhed in the augment's grip, his power storming, his voice slicing through the frigid air in a venomous, hateful shout.

There was a swift *yank*, a burst of energy fighting against her hold, and all at once they were falling from the fist of the wind, crashing down on the rock and rolling. Something cracked inside Cistine at the impact, pain arcing through her ribs, and she screamed and coiled up around the heavy stone of pain ricocheting down her chest—then rolled away from a gout of fire slapping the rock where she lay.

Blood dribbled from her lips when she grabbed the stone where they'd bound Vandred and staggered up to face him. He regarded her with hate in that twisted countenance. "Do you really think you saved them, Key? I will flay the flesh from each of their bodies, and I will do it slowly because of you. I will *enjoy* it."

She didn't bother with taunts or retorts; if she spoke, she'd start sobbing at the pain. Instead she sent out the fire, twin cords whizzing toward Vandred's sides. He broke them with his own wind and snapped out a fist, manacles of the breeze seizing Cistine by her wrists and ankles. With a single jerk, he brought her to him, her struggles feeble against the pain crashing through her broken ribs, her fire flashing and falling again and again.

Body-to-body with him, she entered the cage of his embrace, and there it struck her—that same sense from the night before, the hive of augments even more tangible with this much of her body touching his. The web of intersecting threads brushed against her, a contrast of lightning and wind, the scarlet threads of a blood augment.

Her mouth watered against her will, coveting that power; her arms flexed weakly in the iron bands of his might.

The breeze began to rise around them, quickening, preparing to launch them away to his brothers, even to one of the Doors.

She couldn't let it happen. So she latched onto that sense of power with all her might, and through the dizziness of agony, through the taste of blood in her mouth, she started to cut those cords.

Not just the wind, but the fire, and the blood augment, the ice and lightning. It was no different from snipping threads in a stitching project, except she navigated by feeling rather than sight, like that day in the Vaszaj Range when she'd followed a fire augment deep into herself. She pushed her power into every crevice where she felt Vandred's cords dangling, and seized control.

Finally, she *pulled.*

The power slid out of Vandred's body and into hers. Not given up willingly—she *took* it, stole it from him and carried it deep into herself where he could not reach.

The Bloodwight hissed and wheezed, his body stiffening, contorting around hers, the shackles of wind loosening from her wrists. "What—how are you—that is *enough,* stop it this *instant!*"

Cistine did not. Not even when his talons pierced through her armor and into her back. Not even when her body went to war against itself, that blood augment struggling to fill her veins again while her life dripped from her mouth, her back, her nose and eyes.

She was dying. She would die alone on this rock top with him if she did not let go. But she couldn't, not while Vandred still had weapons to spare against her friends. Against the Courts. Against *her*.

Whatever it takes, she'd promised Thorne. For Valgard. For them all.

The power singing to her from Vandred's body crescendoed into a shriek of many calls in her head. She had only moments at best before she lost consciousness. Before it was *done*.

Vandred roared and hurled her back against the rock. Her head cracked its edge and her body went numb, ears thundering. That roar went on and gained volume, turning familiar—

Cistine hit the ground knees-first, then slumped to her side, and this time she did not rise. Through the cascade of hair clogging her eyes and mouth, she watched an armored figure, a vision, a death-god, hurtling across the rock; and she saw Vandred broken down before her, limp and swaying on his knees, bleeding from every orifice. His white eyes were twin stars burning out to nothing, his face hollow, empty. No more power pulsed from his body, because, somehow, she'd managed to steal all his augments.

And now she gave them up, pushing her arm weakly forward and hurling a blow of shadow and fire, lightning and ice, and every other gods-given power she'd taken from him.

Vandred broke, bones shattering audibly throughout his body, at the same moment twin sabers connected with his neck. His head sailed one way, his body the other; and as Death and Slaughter spun toward her, shouting her name, Cistine convulsed once, a final, frail struggle against the darkness.

She felt Thorne's hands on her face, then nothing more.

CHAPTER THIRTY-SEVEN

RAVAGING DARKNESS SWALLOWED Aden on every side like a humid night without stars or moon. He skidded with the buffeting dark, trees breaking around him under duress of a different augment—wind, perhaps, or lightning—but he could see none of it as the violet dome of shadows shut them in on every side.

His shoulder slammed into something solid, and a hand snared his arm: Maleck. He was shaking, but held fast when Kristoff enclosed him from the other side, his light the only thing that led them, a pillar and paladin in the shadows. In silent accord, they formed a line that drew the enemy's eye from the Key and straight to them.

A flicker of movement perforated the darkness ahead, annealing into a towering figure, skulled with branching antlers, its height nearly nine feet and its gaunt body brimming with power. Kristoff breathed, "The *Aeoprast*."

All around them, augmented fires ignited, drops like flagrant rain singing down through the darkness. Wherever they struck, Bloodwights appeared, barring the way to escape. They did not track after Thorne and Ashe or pass on to the war camp to find the Key.

There was something more at play here.

Kristoff and Maleck turned, placing their backs inward against Aden's while more and more Bloodwights alighted around them, their gruesome hoop interring the men in a cage of power. The air turned to soup, bubbling with augmented energy. Fury scorched Aden's throat, and he gripped his swords with all his might, gaze fixed on the creature called the *Aeoprast* when it stepped forward, closing the circle completely. Trapping them within.

"Hello, Mal." The creature's voice was the demented twist of shadows whispering to a wanderer at night. "It's good to see you after all these years. I wondered if they executed you after the last war."

A tremble passed through Maleck's stiff arm pressed against Aden's. "Why have you come?"

"Isn't it obvious?"

"For the Key," Aden spat.

"The wise wolf does not waste energy tracking wounded prey," the *Aeoprast* said, and Maleck's breath hitched to silence. "The Key is not the only weapon we need." His skulled face angled toward Maleck. "We came back for you, *Allet*. For our reunion."

Three Bloodwights stepped forward with eerie symmetry and peeled up their masks. Maleck buckled, nearly slumping to his knees, and Aden wavered as well. He knew these faces only dimly; he'd met them more than twenty years ago, when Maleck brought them along on a reprieve to Stornhaz from Azkai Temple.

Olaf, Gisli, and Svan—acolytes from the former Order.

"No." Maleck's voice cracked. "Why are you here? I thought the recruits were new to their fold. Criminals. *Children*."

"They brought us back." Gisli's voice quivered with lust. "Us, and the others from the old Order. They made us what we were crafted to become, *Allet*. We were never meant to blend with this world, this kingdom. Haven't you *felt* that these last twenty years? We no longer want, we no longer feel bereft. They brought us home, made us *whole* again, just like we were before the last war. They could make you whole, too."

"We escaped," Maleck hissed. "We *escaped* that life, and now you willingly return to it? To *them*? Why didn't you *write* to me if things were so terrible? Why did no one tell me you were being pursued?"

"Because no one cares what becomes of the former acolytes," the

Aeoprast scoffed. "Perhaps the Chancellors were glad to see someone scoop up these poor, addled creatures and carry them away from sight. They certainly never trusted any of you. They're happier when you're gone. It's time to put an end to your loneliness and come back where you belong." He stretched out one hand and curved a finger. "It's time you came *home*."

Hate and fury coiled in Aden's chest. They were here for Maleck again just like they'd dragged him from his bed above the symphony house in Stornhaz as a child and carried him off to be their prisoner. Their experiment. Their acolyte.

Never again. Aden had sworn that oath twenty years ago while he kept Maleck company in the dark of their adjoining bedrooms, nothing but sincere words and brotherhood and his arm around Maleck's shoulders to chase the nightmares away. *I'll never let them touch you. I promise, Allet. They'll have to kill me first.*

But it was not Aden who moved now; it was Kristoff, brushing forward and sweeping an arm across Maleck's front. "You will not take him again."

Even with that mask fixed in place, the creature's eyes tangibly narrowed, his anger evident in the subtle, vicious shift to his tone. "I remember you. The Tribune who voted to have our Order disbanded and hung. It was your house Maleck ran away to whenever his weakness reared."

"He has always been stronger than all of you put together."

"As if you know him. You do not share his mind and heart. You aren't his true family."

"I am his *father*." Kristoff spun his sword-hand once, loosening his wrist. "And I will die before I let you lay a hand on him again."

A gentle wind sifted the grass beneath their feet. "So. It's going to be a fight, is it?"

"You're stars-damned *right* it is," Aden growled, stepping up to his father's side, barring the way to Maleck.

"So be it."

The wind dropped, then lashed out.

Aden thrust his father and Maleck aside and threw himself below the cut of the deadly gale; the Bloodwights behind them captured the *Aeoprast's* wind and dissolved with it, flirting through the dark dome like shadows shifting by the curve of daylight. Aden and Kristoff lunged into combat side-by-side, their own armor soaking up and sizzling with whatever augments still trailed on the air. Maleck cleaved through blades of ice and fire with Starfall and Stormfury, ducking and rolling beneath Olaf, Svan, and Gisli's joint strikes. They hammered against him like this battle was personal—as if they held Maleck somehow responsible for their many years of suffering, deprived of augments.

Aden dodged through the Bloodwight ranks, seeking a path to escape. They had to get Maleck out of this forest, away from the *Aeoprast*, before the Bloodwights found a way to subdue him. Before he disappeared again.

Thwarted by darkness on every side, he cursed and changed tack, lunging into the fray beside Maleck; he took Olaf and Gisli's attention and left Svan for him.

But even with the might of the Hive Lord's training behind his blows, Aden could not crack their defenses. Augments forged a steel shell around their bodies, turning their flesh to adamant. Every slice glanced off; flame and ice shrieked alternately along his blades. He could not cut through, could not land a single blow that mattered.

At Aden's shout, he and Maleck whirled and ducked around one another, trading opponents, and Aden forged what little of the fire augment he had left into a spear, hurling it at Svan's head; even that did not pierce his guard. Shadow broke fire, and they were back to dueling.

It was a losing fight. They had to run, and pray Ashe and Thorne had gotten Cistine out already. This distraction would not last any longer. Aden had just one augment left: his father's last fire flagon, enough to punch through the shadows as he'd done for Ashe and let them flee.

He reached into pocket, yanked out the flagon—and a pained shout, cruelly familiar, jerked his attention to the left.

His father had hewn through all resistance straight to the *Aeoprast*, but their duel was already over, the flash of sabers and light in Kristoff's armor not nearly enough against this creature's ageless power. It caught him in a fist of darkness and flung him against a tree, the shadow augment's vicious fingers seizing his arm at the elbow and slowly turning his blade back on him. In seconds, it would pierce his armor; then the augments would flood in, destroying his body, because he did not wear the inkings the cabal did. Nothing but his armor and a last trickle of light in his threads defended him from death.

Aden shouted to his father and hurled the flagon toward him, drawing the *Aeoprast's* attention for just a heartbeat. Then he spun and yanked Maleck from the path of Gisli's next blow, a whip of lightning that cracked the ground open in a brutal maw.

"Get to *Athar!*" he roared in Maleck's ear. "Get out of here, I'll hold the line!"

Maleck's gaze shot past Aden, a cry of warning and fury bursting from his lips. Kristoff's light had severed the manacle of shadow around his arm, and he dropped and dove for the fire flagon—then lost his grip on it when the *Aeoprast's* own flames caught him square in the stomach and dashed him back against the tree.

Bone snapped. Kristoff dropped among the roots and lay in a heap, retching. The world stopped moving at that sound, and Aden with it.

Maleck roared Kristoff's name like something inside him had broken, too, and the ice of shock and horror shattered from around Aden's limbs. He ripped forward, lunged toward his father—and slammed to the edge of a tether Svan had flung out while he stood frozen, watching this terrible, endless moment unfold. A noose of power tightened around Aden's throat, hurling him to his knees, choking and writhing. Maleck shot past him, wounded and staggering, but he almost made it to Kristoff's side before an oppressive, eye-watering energy hurtled from Olaf's hand and slammed him to his chest, pinning him to the ground as well.

With his arm outstretched, he could almost touch Kristoff's hand.

Panic sealed Aden's throat when the *Aeoprast* stalked forward to stand over Kristoff, kicking his saber toward him. "Look at your pitiful sons, Tribune. Do you hear them crying your name? Do you still want to play this game?"

Panting, spitting blood, Kristoff struggled to rise, then broke down again. Cruel laughter burst from the Bloodwights on every side, and Aden's thoughts became a cacophony. He could not do this, could not have his father back for one *night* only to watch him butchered by the Order he'd helped drive out to protect their kingdom, to save *Maleck*. He was not strong enough, not sane enough to watch him die again.

"I'm waiting, Tribune," the *Aeoprast* deadpanned. "If Maleck is your family, why won't you fight for him?"

Under the heap of Olaf's wind still holding him down, Maleck struggled to raise his head and slowly swiveled it until he met Aden's eyes, his face full of anguish and heartbreak and a terrible, mortal resignation.

Aden knew that look. Knew Maleck's mind like his own.

"No," he breathed.

Maleck's fingers inched forward, closing around the fire flagon.

Aden cursed, struggling to rise, hissing, "Maleck. *Maleck, don't!*"

"Bloodsinger," Maleck said, and at the sound of his Name, Aden stopped fighting. "Forgive me."

"No—"

"I love you, *Allet*."

"*No!*"

Maleck broke the flagon against his armor.

Aden couldn't fight the drawn-out roar of heartbroken fury hurtling out of him, the same word again and again, *no, no, no, no!*, carried forward until his voice cracked and lost all strength while fire soaked up the wind and grew to a heaving column of flame.

The noose broke from around Aden's throat and Svan lunged to confront Maleck. Choking and gasping down on his knees, all Aden could do was watch his brother, a fire-wrapped warrior, twist on heel and slam a blow into Svan's chest so hard it blasted him away through the trees, knocking his augments and his mask away. Then he morphed into a blur of battle, a death-god carving through the Bloodwights with sweeps and scythes of flame. They fell back, cackling as their brother fought back at last, bringing down the youngest acolytes of which he was always most powerful. He ripped the augment pouch from Olaf, and another flagon sailed through the air, smashing into Kristoff, breaking on his armor. The warm white glow of healing poured over his body, and he arched and gasped, rolling to his knees, stricken eyes fixed on the unholy sight before them. On Maleck, wreathed in both fire and shadow now, battling his way through the ranks of the Bloodwights like a specter of Nimmus.

They didn't fight back. They were taunting him, drawing him in, forcing him to snatch up and smash more augments, more, and *more*—

He sent two of his brothers shattering backward through the forest at last, the stench of charred flesh and singed hair suffocating the wind. The rest broke rank at that and fled, leaving Maleck and the *Aeoprast* dueling with whips of fire like swords. They cleaved into one another, armor and robes sparking and dancing with flame, and in that moment Aden saw the boy who'd left them twenty years ago—the augur, the acolyte, heedless of danger and grim as the Undertaker.

The *Aeoprast* fell back, loosing a wild burst of triumphant laughter. "You made this almost too easy, Maleck. Come. Let's feed you."

Aden's blood ran cold, and he staggered to his feet, shouting Maleck's name; his words were lost in the torrent of the *Aeoprast's* wind augment. In a blink, he vanished—but his wind remained around Maleck, who faced away from them, the fire low against his body, watching the way the *Aeoprast* went. He did not move.

"Maleck." Aden took a step toward him, and Kristoff snagged him under the arm.

"Don't—*don't*, Aden." His voice was low, anguished. "This was what they wanted. They made him choose it for himself, just like last time. There's no turning back."

"No!" Aden roared. "Let me go, stars damn it, I can still reach him!"

"You can't, not now. He's not himself anymore."

In the breath it took Aden to summon a retort, Maleck pivoted toward them—and he saw it was true. This was not his brother, it was a creature wearing his countenance, blood spattered across his cheeks, his gaze brimming with a desperate, wild hunger Aden had never seen before...not even in Maleck's acolyte days. There was no love or recognition in his face, his cheeks sunken with a need beyond reason—a thirst for the augments around them.

Maleck flung out his arms, and the ravaging darkness screamed toward him, soaking into his armor like a cloak, and blinding daylight struck Aden's face so hard he twisted his head away for an instant. When he looked back, Maleck had shed his saber harness and dagger belt, snatching up a fallen augment pouch instead.

Aden snarled, wrenching forward again. "Maleck! *Don't.*"

His head swiveled back toward them, empty eyes resting on Aden's face. All that remained in that stare was want and rage, dismissing them when he sensed they carried no more power.

They were nothing to him now.

A wind augment shattered. In the turn of a moment, just like his brothers, Maleck was gone—leaving only his sabers and a cruel breeze behind.

CHAPTER
THIRTY-EIGHT

THE MOMENT CISTINE was in his arms, Thorne did not stop moving.

On every side, the war camp was a tumult, warriors and *mirothadt* and Balmond locked in battle. Dragonfire spewed across the dark rock; augments stormed the air. But there was no sight of the Bloodwights yet; somehow, Aden, Maleck, and Kristoff held them at bay.

Thorne would fall to his knees and thank them later. Right now, it was all he could do to clutch Cistine's limp body to his chest, blink the blood from his eyes, and keep running. Corpses blockaded his path, his people and theirs all the same in death, a grisly echo of Braggos that knocked on the doors of his head and heart, the glassy eyes and gaping jaws vowing he'd see them again tonight when his own eyes shut. If he could even bring them to.

All for later. Right now, he had to get Cistine out of this camp before someone else saw Vandred's body and realized what she'd done. What he could barely comprehend himself.

Fire erupted overhead, a streaming garland of heat that sent Thorne ducking back with a curse. Flaming shards of stone rained from the mountain face, and he slipped into cover for a moment, balancing in a crouch on his heels and settling Cistine in his lap. He brushed the hair from her face and gripped her chin, studying her closed eyes, her mouth ajar, and the *blood*...so much blood. He'd almost lost his stomach at the first glimpse of her around the bend in that path, the Bloodwight's claws sunk into her body, scarlet pumping mercilessly not just through her armor, but from her lips, her nose, and her eyes.

And the *power* in her. He was no great augur, but even he had sensed the prism of augments around her body, a torrent and a storm. And he knew where those augments came from, but it was still impossible to comprehend what had happened in that short span of time she and Vandred were alone together after he saw Key and Bloodwight vanish up the path in a blast of wind.

The concussion from an earth augment rocked him forward almost to his knees, and he gritted his teeth. He needed to keep moving; the others could not wait for him forever where he'd sent them in retreat, Quill carrying his still-healing *valenar*, Ariadne and Sander guarding their backs.

If they'd even made it that far.

He banished that thought and staggered up, seizing Cistine closer to his chest. "We're almost there, Wildheart."

Urgency possessed him at the faint stir of breath from her parted lips, and he stepped from around the shelter of rock, gathering himself to run.

A blade touched his throat from behind. He froze, steel licking delicately at his leaping pulse.

"The Princess. I see now what she is."

Adeima.

Thorne's arms tightened around Cistine. He dared not move any more than that when the Chancelloress circled around his side, blade still at his neck. Dark tear tracks carved her umber skin, more silvering her eyes. Blood frosted her knuckles, saturated her armor, and crusted her chin. He'd passed her in battle, so many men screaming when they fell before her merciless blades, but now that he saw her closely, there was too much blood. Something had happened.

"I should have suspected the night Stornhaz fell, when you sent her away to her kingdom," Adeima added. "Protecting the Key."

The strength in Thorne's knees gave way. Only one word escaped his clenched teeth: "Please."

Adeima studied Cistine with grief-stricken eyes. "Bravis and the others will want to spill her blood on the nearest Door and replenish our flagons."

"Adeima, I beg you..."

"A Chancellor does not beg."

"For her, I will. I *do*."

Adeima's gaze turned from Cistine's face to him, and unbelievably, softened. "I saw what she did. For us. For Maltadova...my Flamewalker. Even though it was not enough, I saw her."

Maltadova's Name, given so freely, sent anguish twisting in Thorne's stomach. The loyal *valenar* of Yager Court defended each other's Names and true titles by life and death; for Adeima to speak her beloved's now could mean only one fate. "Adeima, I'm sorry."

"We are all sorry today." Yet with every word, her gaze cleared. "But it was she who tried. When the others recoiled, she stepped forward for *my selvenar,* even knowing they would all see."

Frustrated fondness racked through Thorne's chest. It was such a Cistine choice to make—to weigh the fate of kingdoms in the balance and still decide that in the moment, love and loyalty mattered most.

"Spill her blood, and we will have more augments. But the power that lies within her, that is a strength none of us possess. It may be enough to win this war if she learns to wield it." Adeima stepped nearer, blade tightening at Thorne's neck. "Swear to me you will train her, you will see her come into that might for our kingdom's salvation, and it will be as if we never saw one another here."

"I swear it." There was no lie in him. What he'd witnessed in his Wildheart today... "I see it, too."

Adeima let her arm fall. "Carry her to safety. Bravis and the others will hunt you, so do not show your faces again until she is ready to stand with that power in hand and fight for her own life before the Courts."

Mutely, Thorne nodded.

"When you have need of the Hunters, we will answer the call," Adeima added. "We keep our vows. And we stand with the Starchasers."

The jolt of his Name unwittingly spoken had not finished racing up Thorne's back when Adeima blended into the shadows, her parting words drifting back to him.

"For Maltadova. For us all."

Lightning flashed and thunder boomed, a many-layered echo against the mountains driving Thorne into motion again. He broke cover, tearing through puddles of fallen canvas and broken tent poles, through flaming heaps of matter and shredded corpses toward the edge of the rock and the bathing pool far below.

He was accosted yet again at the trailhead, not by an enemy, but by a burned, soot-covered, wild-eyed Sander. The High Tribune paused hacking down *mirothadt* to gesture Thorne over with a wild wave of his arm. "The others are below! They wait for you, Chancellor!"

"Not Chancellor anymore." Thorne slid to a halt next to him. "Not with the powerful enemies we made today."

Sander's dark brows tweaked. "How many more of those can you afford?"

"We're about to find out." Thorne nudged shoulders with him. "Kanslar Court is in your hands now. You lead them. Keep them alive."

Pain lit in that tawny gaze, though not resentment for the title. Of all his Tribunes, Sander had always most respected what it meant to lead. "Where will you go?"

"Somewhere we can heal and plan."

The High Tribune's gaze dropped to Cistine's ashen, inert face; then he twisted suddenly, slamming his blade backhand into an augur racing toward them, the thoughtful peak in his brows turning to one of hard will. "Mira is in Holmlond. If you go to her, she will help you concoct a strategy."

"Thank you."

"Don't thank *me*, I'm just helping you clean up your mess so I can go back to the Tribunal where I belong."

"Then take my last order to heart: survive what's coming, and I'll return with reinforcements at our back. Enough to win this war."

"Why didn't you say so in the first place!" Sander shoved him toward the trail. "And what are you waiting for?"

Thorne cast a last look at the carnage behind him, the battle he ached to save his people from. But he was only a man, and he was not enough, not alone; not without a plan and the right people to execute it.

So he went, the screams deadening as the valley walls rose around him. At the bottom of the trail, the cabal clustered around Bresnyar: Tatiana hanging from Quill with one arm around his shoulders to steady herself, Ashe and Ariadne with weapons out, facing the path. But Ashe's eyes turned again and again to the opposite side of the gulch where the wind augment had dropped them at their arrival.

Ariadne spotted them first, eyes widening. "Is she alive?"

Too breathless for words, Thorne nodded when he reached them. Quill cursed with relief and pressed his hand and a kiss to Cistine's brow, then whistled Faer up from his shoulder and helped Tatiana onto Bresnyar's back. The others leaped on, one after another, and Thorne felt the weight descending on the dragon's spine the moment he contacted the bone. And he still had three more to carry away from this mountain and across the others.

Grimacing, Thorne clung to Cistine while Bresnyar fumbled to rise, wings stroking the scorched air and lifting them up to the cleft. Timeless evergreens were smashed to kindling, decay ravaging the grass blue and black, the rock sundered in places and still smoking in others like a small army had gone to war in a dim echo of what raged behind them across the valley.

The instant Bresnyar settled in the furrows between the trees, Ashe lunged from his back and sprinted into the devastation, Odvaya already drawn. Thorne surrendered Cistine to Ariadne's arms and leaped after her, hitting the ground in a wild run to meet the two men trudging toward them.

Two. Not three.

Thorne's feet slowed along with his pulse, something strange and heavy squeezing his lungs, his guts, his heart. He recognized Aden first, matted and bloodied, wearing Starfall and Stormfury strapped across his back, the beloved sabers Maleck would never part from unless...

Ashe did not slow until she was abreast of Aden and Kristoff. Panting, she skidded to a halt. "We need to leave, *right now*. Where's Mal?" She looked left and right, expectation clear in her posture and tone. Then confusion settled in, her head cocking when her gaze did not find him emerging between the broken trees or rounding the ruins of shattered earth where they'd fought the Bloodwights.

Aden watched her with raw eyes. "Ashe."

She took several paces back from him, eyes still sweeping the cleft. "Maleck? Maleck, we need to *go*! Get out here!" A beat, in which only the stirrings of battle far away gave answer. "Maleck, gods *damn* it, *answer me!*"

Thorne's knees buckled, and he gripped one of the few standing trees as grief's cold fingers wrapped his heart and ripped it straight from his chest; his heart, the *cabal's* heart, that strong and ever-beating presence that was Maleck Darkwind.

Gone. Gone. *Gone.*

"Ashe, look at me." Aden's voice was low, hoarse, but still a command.

She rounded on him, spitting, "*What?*"

"I'm sorry." The pain in the words sent Thorne sinking sideways against the tree. "I'm sorry, I tried to protect him. I lost him."

"You're saying that you...you just *lost* my...my *selvenar*." Ashe's head snapped into a full tilt, a small, cold, disbelieving smile jerking her lips. "You *lost Maleck?*"

"He gave himself over to them," Kristoff interceded, his voice far calmer than his son's but his eyes stroked with the same agony. "To protect us."

"Gave himself over to—"

"He has become a Bloodwight."

The silence deafened.

Thorne was a spirit detached from his body, drifting upward on the teasing fingers of the icy wind that squeezed the back of his neck, and the mindless urge possessed him to shout for Maleck as loud as Ashe did, to cry out his Name on the wind, to summon him back as he had from battles, from breaking, from his own memories so many times.

But if he called, there would be no answer now; if Maleck had not already come when *Ashe* yelled for him like her heart was breaking, then it was true. His brother, his friend, his strong right arm was gone. And Thorne *felt* the pain of that like a limb truly ripped away, the agony sending him sliding down the tree all the way to his knees.

Aden reached out a hand to Ashe, and she jerked her body away at an angle, shaking her head. "No. He was getting better, he was walking out of that place. *Away* from them!"

"He didn't want this," Aden said. "He was afraid, I saw it in his eyes. But he took it into himself to save us."

Maleck's name escaped Thorne with what little breath he had left.

Ashe hurled a punch straight into Aden's face, the sudden, harsh *crack* of knuckles on bone splitting across the cleft, and he took it without flinching. Then he took the next blow, and the next, landing so quickly Thorne barely tracked them. "You let them *take him,* you *gods-damned* bastard, you were supposed to watch out for each other, you *knew* how bad things were, you knew this could happen and you *let him go, gods damn it, Aden!*"

A hand caught Ashe's wrist, strong as iron, and she half-twisted toward Kristoff, roaring in fury. The iciness in his eyes stopped her anger quicker than anything Thorne had ever seen, quicker even than speaking a warrior's Name. "That is *enough.* Yours is not the only heart that loves him or the only one that breaks. And you *do not* hit my son in front of me."

Ashe's gaze snapped back to Aden, who'd done nothing to defend himself, and now bled freely from the mouth and nose. She stared at him for a long moment; then, snarling under her breath, she tore free of Kristoff's hold and stalked away into the trees. Aden's gaze trailed after her to the gaps between the gnarled trunks where the rest of the cabal, one-by-one, emerged. Tatiana, in the lead, stumbled to a halt at the sight of Kristoff. Her hands cupped her mouth, amber eyes wide and bright, and she whispered his name.

"You're *alive?*" Quill barked, keeping one hand around her waist and yanking the other through his hair. "*Again?*"

Kristoff strode to them, catching first Tatiana, then Quill in a swift embrace. Then he was at Ariadne's side, his hand on Cistine's forehead. "We haven't had the pleasure," he said to Ariadne, "but I have some experience with healing. May I?"

Her gaze flicked to Thorne in a silent question, and he managed a nod.

"What happened to your face?" Quill said to Aden. "Where's Mal?"

"He lives." Aden's voice was thick with blood, and he spat on the grass. "He's become a Bloodwight."

A beat of silence while the report struggled to soak into all their minds, to make sense. Horror turned Tatiana's features waxen. Ariadne's eyes widened and her jaw gaped with shallow breaths. Quill's face became a corpse's, rid of all emotion.

"No." The air soured with that single word, all his shock and rage contained within it. "No, this isn't happening. Not now, not with...the lines, what happened in that mountain to Tati, with *Pip*, and now this? Now they took *Maleck,* too? We've already lost too *stars-damned* much!"

He swung on heel and punched the nearest tree so hard Thorne both heard and *felt* his bones rattle.

"I'm not letting him get away from us," he snarled, spinning back on them. "We have to find him. Which way, Aden? *Which stars-damned way?*"

Quill's desperation jolted Thorne back to clarity. Maleck was gone, Ashe and Quill unraveling, Aden carrying the weight of the guilt within himself, and Cistine badly hurt. His cabal needed him to pull his wits together, to *lead.* So he gripped his own grief and anguish and stuffed them down in the deep pits of himself. He could mourn and fear for Maleck later; now he had to stand without his friend's wisdom and support, something he hadn't done in more than a decade.

He strode to his uncle's side, cuffing him on the shoulder. "We need to put distance between us and the army. Is she well enough to travel?"

Kristoff nodded, stroking the hair from Cistine's brow.

"How much distance?" Aden demanded. "How bad is it?"

"Bad." Thorne looked around at his cabal, all wounded, all in varying degrees of shock, and gave them the only order he had left. "We run."

CHAPTER THIRTY-NINE

CISTINE WOKE TO a cacophony of pain in her limbs and the warmth of someone's cloak wrapped around her.

For a time, she lay curled on her side, feeling out her surroundings with trepidation: a cage of high-vaulted trees stirring above her, warm ground beneath her—not cold stone. Either the weather's moody patterns had swung once again to heat, or they were no longer in the upper passes of the Isetfells. She listened to the wind sighing among the branches, training her ears for whispers of combat and hearing none. All was peaceful, the quiet broken only by scuffles of nature and a gentle, faraway grinding that reminded her of Citadel kitchens and houses of healing.

A mortar and pestle. Herbs being flaked.

Slowly, carefully, she wiggled her fingers and toes, then stretched her limbs. Each one was a lead weight strapped to her body, and it took far too much effort just to roll over and see something other than the span between the trees; and that was not in her best interest anyway. Dizziness cracked the side of her head like an errant punch so hard her eyes clamped shut again to stop the world spinning. To her everlasting humiliation, she couldn't stop the moan that burst from her lips, either.

The grinding stopped. "Lie still. You lost quite a bit of blood."

Cistine's breath caught. That *voice*...

Her eyes popped open, and this time she didn't care that the world swirled like a feverdream. All she cared about was the man perched on an overturned tree nearby, watching over her just as he had to the best of his might in Kalt Hasa.

"*Kristoff?*" she whimpered.

A small smile graced his lips. "I've missed that face."

Too weak and shaky to rise, she stretched out her hand. He set aside the mortar and pestle and came to her, taking a knee swiftly, and she flung her arms around his neck. He smelled and felt exactly how she remembered: stone and earth, solid and steady. She cried into his collar with relief, and with horror at what she was beginning to remember: the battle in the war camp. Maltadova. What she had done to Vandred; what he did to *her*.

Kristoff held her until the hysteria abated; only when she loosened her grip did he do the same, keeping one hand on her shoulder when she wobbled.

"How—*how* are you here?" she gasped, wiping her arm against her running nose.

"Oadmarkaic medicine and the grace of the gods." He swept his armored cloak from her lap and tossed it around her back instead. "Before you ask, it's been two days since the battle. We're in the Sotefold Forest now. The others are on patrol."

"Even Thorne?"

Kristoff snorted quietly. "I had to put my boot up his backside to force him away from you, but yes, even him. I see the pair of you haven't let what began in that pantry go to waste."

Heat pulsed in the base of her skull, and she quickly changed the subject. "Where have you *been* all this time?"

He held up a finger and whistled; Faer descended from the treetops above them, and with another whistle Kristoff sent him to round up the others. Then he turned back to her. "If you don't mind a long tale, I'll tell it while I build us a fire."

She nodded mutely, banding his cloak tight at her throat while she listened to his story of frozen mountain treks and foreign villages, and how he came to learn of the Bloodwights and the war. Soaking in the sound of his voice was a bastion against the darkness of all the other lives lost in the battle. So many friends, so many allies...she didn't even know how many had survived, or what those who did would think of her now.

Her secret would spread. Benedikt and Valdemar especially would never keep quiet about this. The Chancellors *and* the Bloodwights would be hunting her now.

Gods help her. Everything had gone so *wrong*.

Undergrowth crackled almost in tandem with the end of Kristoff's tale, bringing her to his night in the mountain cave with Aden, Thorne, Ashe, and Maleck, and her heart leaped at the shadows materializing between the trees. Thorne reached her first, far more composed than she'd expected, crossing the camp on quick but steady feet. He sank to his knees to brush a kiss against her temple, his hand on her back, and that was where she felt the fragility in how he held himself together.

He was the cabal's leader once more, the man of the wilds bred and built for survival; but that mask was thin, already showing cracks in its face, his eyes damp when he pulled back to meet hers. She kissed his jaw, six swift pecks to tell him she saw, and she was proud of how he held himself together for them.

With a bump of his brow to her ear, he was up again, helping Kristoff with the fire, taking a brace of hares from Quill and freeing his hands so he could come to Cistine next, squeezing her shoulder. "You scared the skin off our backs, Stranger. Don't ever do that again."

Wild laughter burst from her lips. She wasn't certain he knew precisely what she had done—if she herself even knew.

The others fanned out around the small camp, all dull-eyed, pale, and haggard. And when the seconds ticked by, leaving their ranks bereft by one, it became horrifyingly clear: there was a warrior who would not emerge from those shadowed trees.

Cistine cleared her throat against a swell of panic, bitter and metallic and more potent than anything she'd felt since her first session with Mira. "Where...where is Maleck?"

Quill's hand spasmed, sinking away from her shoulder. Across the camp, perched on the log beside Kristoff, Faer croaked his name like he *knew*.

The cloak dropped from around Cistine when the feeling left her fingers, then her entire body, rushing out from her head like a terrible spill of ice into her stomach, hips, and legs. Vicious shivers clawed from the back of her neck down her spine, and dizziness whirled through her again, vomit surging in her throat.

If he was gone, if he'd been cut down—if her mentor, her friend, her *Darkwind* was *dead* because of the enemy she'd brought into the camp, she would never forgive herself. She might not even get up from this forest floor.

"No," she breathed, tears thickening her voice. "No, *please*, Thorne, *please* tell me he's not—"

"He isn't dead."

"He might as well be." Ashe spoke down toward the ground where she crouched, ruthlessly skinning a hare, taking off as much flesh as fur. "Knowing him, he wishes he was."

"Ashe," Ariadne said gently, "that helps no one. And you're ruining that meat."

She hurled down her knife and rocked back on her heels. "Not that I was hungry to begin with."

The shakes would not stop rattling Cistine's body. "What happened? Where is he?"

No one seemed inclined to speak—least of all Aden, who stopped skinning his portion as well and simply sat on his heels, staring into the fire.

"Augments," Kristoff said at last. "He used them to save our lives. And it...completed what they began in him two decades ago. Consumed him. He's addicted now. He's like one of them."

Every word was a separate blow slinging into Cistine's heart, raising memory after memory in the fissures left behind: a dark bridge in Jovadalsa, the lights of Darlaska, the dock near the trapper's cabin in the Isetfells. All those times Maleck had told her of his near-fate at his brothers' hands, what he feared most to become.

The future he'd fled since childhood, catching up with him at last.

Ashe popped to her feet and walked away, disappearing into the trees. Cistine pushed her boots into the dirt, struggling to rise, desperate to follow her, but Aden motioned her back with a cut of his hand. "Let her go to her dragon. He's the only one who's consoled her these past two days."

As usual, he knew Ashe's mind better than almost anyone; the sound of wingbeats soon broke the quiet, traveling north. Once they'd faded, Cistine whispered, "They're going to look for him?"

Thorne nodded. "It hasn't done any good yet. But she tries."

And she would keep trying until they found a better plan. Because it was Ashe, and she needed *some* sort of motion, some purpose to keep her head above the waves of grief. In that way, they were like sisters.

Cistine wrapped her arms around her knees and pressed her forehead to them while the others prepared the meal in silence. Tatiana came to sit beside her, a faint odor of sweat and grime about her body—something Cistine had never known her to allow before. But near-death often changed one's priorities; she remembered that all too well.

Sniffing back tears, she spread Kristoff's cloak around them both. "I'm so glad you're all right."

A soft, damp snort was the only reply at first. Then Tatiana muttered, "I lost your cuff blade in that stars-damned mountain."

"I don't care," Cistine said fiercely. "You're the only thing that matters."

Tatiana sucked in a heavy breath and wrapped her arm around Cistine's shoulders, and they pressed closer together under the warm folds, watching night's hold tighten through the trees.

It was truly dark when they gathered around the fire to eat, picking listlessly over rations seasoned with the contents of Kristoff's mortar and pestle. Cistine only ate because of the looks they gave her when she didn't, and because a last sliver of logic reminded her that after what had happened with Vandred, she needed to recover her strength for the next battle—which could happen at any time.

After the war camp, that thought terrified her more than ever before.

"Thorne," she said when he gave up on his ration at last and sat back, arms loosely linking his knees, "what happened in the mountains?"

His eyes met hers across the fire. "A question for a question?" Even knowing what he would ask, and how much it terrified her, she nodded. Thorne's shoulders lifted and sank. "We think Vandred allowed us to take him. He wanted to be brought to the camp so they could strike us from within. The Balmond must've followed the sense of him straight to us."

"Because they wanted to kill the Chancellors?"

"And leave the army scattered, lacking true leadership," Ariadne agreed.

"I was such a *fool*," Cistine groaned. "I thought we could *capture* a Bloodwight? Hold him captive? What in God's name was I *thinking?*"

"That you could turn the tide," Quill said gruffly, offering his dinner to Faer. "No one holds that against you. We all went along with it—we were *all* desperate."

"And that was their weapon at our necks," Aden muttered.

"It's my turn." Just a hint of teasing flavored Thorne's tone, then vanished when the question emerged. "Tell us about the rock top, *Logandir.*"

She separated her ration into strips and fed herself one by one, biding time to think. "I don't know. I just...oh, how do I even *say* this? I know it isn't possible!"

"Neither was wielding two augments at once," Tatiana said. "But then there were the Bloodwights, and then there was *you.*"

Cistine finished her food and set aside the leaf she'd used as a plate. Kneading her temples, she stared into the fire. "I think I...I pulled the augments from Vandred. Stole them, or cut them out, somehow."

Silence pressed over their small camp, unique in its tension, as if at any moment someone would leap up and storm away like Ashe had, or start shouting. But when Thorne spoke, his voice was calm, careful. "That was how it looked to me."

She blinked. "You saw it happen?"

"Not all of it. But Vandred wanted to escape you, and he couldn't. Whatever you were doing to him, he was trapped—and too surprised to fight back." He shrugged. "If you say you were severing his augments and stealing them for yourself, I believe you."

"I agree," Kristoff said. "The potential in your power is endless because we know nothing of its limits. For now, we can assume everything impossible is now possible. Even likely."

She shot him a grateful half-smile. In those terms, she felt less like a gruesome aberration of nature, like *Nazvaldolya* given shape.

"What happened to that Bloodwight *bandayo* when you took his augments?" Quill asked.

"Thorne decapitated him."

Another silence, thick and heavy, as every eye swiveled to their leader.

"*We* couldn't wound them," Aden said, "in our battle on that ledge. Their augments deflected our blows."

"But if I can take their augments like I took Vandred's..." Cistine began, excitement flickering in her chest.

"That's not a solution," Ariadne said. "There is only one of you, and there are *many* Bloodwights. I cannot foresee a battle where you do this over and over."

"She's right." Fresh worry brightened Thorne's gaze. "It nearly killed you this time."

Cistine shuddered. "I know. If not for the blood augment I pulled from Vandred..."

Death. Everywhere she turned, it flashed its teeth her way.

"But we can't disregard the potential advantage, either," Kristoff warned. "You don't let a blade dull because it can't win the battle alone."

"True," Thorne agreed. "It's a skill worth sharpening, if we can."

"I'll think about how to do that," Cistine said, and the subject dropped. Thorne nudged his portion to her with his foot, and she took it gratefully; now that she'd started eating, she found herself ravenous. "Are the Bloodwights stalking us now?

She strove for calm, but her tone wavered, and Thorne's attention speared back to her over the flames. "Ashe and Bresnyar haven't seen a trace of them on patrol. It seems they've retreated to wherever in Nimmus they've been hiding all this time."

Cistine frowned. "Vandred mentioned something about that, but I don't know what it means."

"Right, that remark about ending the war in a single blow," Quill grunted. "That's a problem worth solving."

"Whatever their focus, the *Aeoprast* doesn't seem to believe there's a need to hunt you yet, Cistine," Kristoff added in a tone oddly piercing. "He suggested you're already on a path that will lead you to him."

Gooseflesh pebbled Cistine's skin when she met his sharp gray eyes. She would have to go carefully from now on, and not make mention of the thoughts tumbling in her head until she was absolutely certain it could be done right, without giving the enemy some advantage. "Well, I'm not going to him just yet. What's our plan, Thorne?"

He leaned forward into the light. "Sander recommended hiding in Holmlond, where Mira's retreated. From there...I don't know yet. But I will if you all give me time to think."

"Time is what we need," Kristoff said. "We've been dealt many blows in short order."

Cistine nodded vigorously. Selfish, perhaps, to agree when so much of the kingdom suffered around them, but her heart leaped at the thought of seeing Mira.

"I want to be clear about what this is," Thorne warned. "It's the last time we'll be able to show our faces anywhere. The Chancellors know what Cistine is. Adeima warned me they would hunt her...hunt us all. They want the Doors opened, and the Talheimic line of succession won't matter to them given what's at stake."

"So much for alliances," Tatiana muttered.

"An enduring alliance has no merit in a kingdom reduced to bone and ash," Ariadne pointed out.

She was simply being factual, but the words still stung. Cistine had done this to herself for nothing. She'd been too slow to save Maltadova anyway, and now they were all being hunted because of her. Her heart grieved, but her mind already rushed ahead, searching for a way to solve the issue and stop the bleeding.

While she pondered, the cabal broke apart; Tatiana went to lie down in the fallen tree's shadow, Ariadne, Kristoff, and Aden to take patrol around the camp. Quill whistled Faer up into the trees to keep watch, then followed Tatiana, taking her shoulder and murmuring in her ear. Cistine studied them a moment, her heart aching at the way Quill's fingers hovered over Tatiana's wounded middle and she brushed him away, shaking her head.

Her scalp prickled. Thorne remained at the fire, looking across it at her, something lurking in his troubled gaze that drew her focus fully back to him. "What is it?"

He blew out a long breath. "The only reason we walked away from that war camp with our lives was that I swore to Adeima I'd train you in your power. She believes you can do more to help win this war alive than with your blood shed on the Doors...and I agree."

She mustered a small smile. "Not just because you're in love with me?"

"That's only half the reason." He paused, then amended, "Possibly slightly more than half. However..."

That reluctant smile grew. "Go on."

Thorne shifted himself around the fire to sit beside her, staring into the same shadowed pocket of forest beyond the flames. "Adeima is right. You have more power than any of us...more than we know what to do with. How many augments did you steal from Vandred? Three? Four?"

She licked her lips and swallowed, the spectral burn of that might still branded in bits and pieces of her body. "At least seven."

Thorne cursed in quiet awe. "*That*. That you can do this at all, and *how* you do it...Bravis, Benedikt, and Valdemar won't see why it matters. But I do. Baba Kallah told me once to pay attention to the things a clever woman can do that a Chancellor can't—and she was right. I'd rather have you and all your power at my back than Bravis, even with a well of augments at his feet."

Gratitude swirled in Cistine's core, forging gentle seas for her fears to float on. "I'm willing to train, especially if I'm the only one who can do these things. I have a duty to hone them."

Thorne opened his arm to her, and she leaned into his side, closing her eyes when his kiss to her head poured heat all the way through her chilled, aching body. "This kingdom owes you a debt more than it will ever repay. The other Chancellors might never say it now, but we're grateful for it."

"I try." She drew her bottom lip between her teeth. "I wish I'd been enough to save Maltadova."

"You weren't prepared for that fight. We'll make certain that isn't the case next time."

Her eyes fluttered open again, the toll of grief ringing through her so sharply her vision blurred. "Thorne, what are we going to do about Maleck?"

His hand tightened around her arm. "I don't know. I don't know what we *can* do. I've spent two days discussing it with Ariadne, but nothing has presented itself yet."

"We can't just leave him out there. He's going to hurt someone, or hurt *himself* to keep that from happening."

"I know. I can't even sleep, thinking about that," Thorne confessed. "But my first concern is getting all of us to Holmlond. Once we're safe within its walls, we can find a way through this."

Though her mind screamed to solve it all now, he was right. More than that, she trusted he would not neglect any one of those necessities. "You know," she mumbled, letting her eyes sway shut again, "with all this strategy and politicking, you would make a good king."

A chuckle rumbled through Thorne's side and into her ear. "Given all that's happened, I think even my own kingdom would disagree. But I appreciate your vote of confidence, *Logandir*."

"I mean it, Thorne. You would."

A beat. "Thank you."

His reply was more cautious, wondering now...just as she was wondering. Because if what Vandred had hinted about the things she could accomplish was indeed true, then Thorne being driven out of the Judgement Seat might not be the end of all hope.

In fact, it might become the providence of the gods.

THE MEMORY

OF

WIND AND
SHADOW

CHAPTER
FORTY

I T TOOK NEARLY a full week to reach Holmlond; Bresnyar could not fly swiftly while carrying so many, and between spurts of travel Tatiana was frequently sick, still mending from the wound dealt to her in Selv Torfjel. Everyone was mostly silent in the crossing, hearts bleeding with their common wound: the absence of Maleck. There was venom in Ashe's silence, heartbreak beyond reckoning in Aden's and Quill's. Though Cistine could hardly eat with the grief writhing in her middle, she still forced herself to keep the peace, to be present for the others.

Morning light on their sixth day of travel guided them to Holmlond on the wind's jagged spine, its fierce gusts ripping tears from Cistine's eyes when Bresnyar descended from the cloudbank. Her breath caught—first at the sight of the Agerios Sea, gray as a mynt coin and choppy beneath a coming storm, and then at the breadth of Holmlond arranged over the hills: a great fortress comprised mostly of high-walled, window-dotted towers, its breadth spread across the sable-shale crags where the Vaszaj Range married with the black basalt columns overlooking the sea.

"What *is* this place?" she murmured to Ariadne, perched ahead of her.

"A refuge very important to the *visnprest* Order." The wind fought to snatch her words away while Bresnyar descended in tight spirals down toward the black ground. "In ancient times, it was a temple, but ever since the war against Talheim it's been a place for the wounded and disabled to find peace."

"Because the kingdom no longer sees a use for them?"

"If it ever did."

They all dismounted the moment Bresnyar landed and stumbled, sinking down in a heap of exhaustion, wings draped unceremoniously across the rock. Ashe circled to his head and gripped it in her gloved hands, touching her brow to his. No words passed between the haggard Wingmaiden and her weary dragon, but for half an instant Bresnyar's slitted pupils flared, and Ashe jolted sharply, leaning back from him. They stared at one another, Ashe's face twisted in a scowl. Then she snapped around and strode up the long path toward the fortress's pike-barbed doors.

Cistine trailed a hand across Bresnyar's ribs. "Thank you for carrying us all this way."

"You can thank me by keeping both eyes on her." Bresnyar's gaze followed Ashe like an arrowhead. "That anger will consume her, I know. It once consumed me."

Worry pounded on Cistine's heart. "We'll do whatever we can."

The others fell in behind her on the long walk up to the doors, where they found Ashe had already greeted the guards—and started an argument.

"We don't let just anyone in here!" One of the Vassora snarled when Cistine and Thorne jogged up on Ashe's heels. "This isn't a gambling house, for stars' sakes!"

"I'm not asking." Ashe's voice was hoarse from days of disuse, and vicious enough that Cistine winced. "I'm coming inside, so you can either open the doors for me or I'll use your body as a battering ram and *make* them open."

"Ashe." Thorne's voice was the unsparing tone of a Chancellor, but the look she shot him gave no quarter, either. "Let me handle this." To the guard, he said, "My name is Chancellor Thorne of Kanslar Court. My people and I need food and shelter."

The man squinted at him. "How do we know you are who you claim to be?"

Ashe's mouth jumped open in a retort that would likely turn this whole exchange to blows and ruin their chances of any rest; then the creak of opening doors silenced them all with a mighty groan, ancient iron and blackest wood clattering apart, and a familiar, faintly-exasperated voice issued between their parted halves. "Oh, *stars*, Egram, how many men do you know who have *silver hair* before they've even seen their thirtieth year? Let the Chancellor and his retinue inside!"

Egram and his companion, grumbling, gripped the doors and helped swing them the rest of the way apart, framing a tawny-skinned, dark-haired woman between them, cardigan tightly banded around her body, her smile greeting them like the sun after a dark night.

"*Mira.*" Her name rolled from Cistine in a gasp of relief, and then their arms were around each other, tears and laughter spiraling out together.

"It's so good to see you! *All* of you," Mira added with a flirt of mischief in her voice, turning to embrace Thorne next. "Look at you, bloody and bruised as usual, and you *stink* like old fish..." She trailed off, hand sliding from his shoulder, wide eyes peering past him. "Well, either I'm in need of my *own* services, or Aden's father has risen from the dead. *Again?*"

"I see you fit right in with this lot." A tired twinkle stirring in his eyes, Kristoff stepped forward and offered his hand. "Mirassah, you've flourished. No surprise there."

"Ah, you always did have enough faith for ten men." Mira clasped his hand with a kind of imperious warmth that reminded Cistine of the Vassoran guard she once was, serving the elite in Stornhaz—men like Kristoff—before her unpredictable seizing fits ruined her dream.

When she released Kristoff's hand and stepped back, her gaze raked the cabal again, making silent tally of the heads and faces. Her mouth twisted faintly to one side. "Come inside, all of you. It's either freezing out there already, or it soon will be. This stars-forsaken weather..."

They trailed in, shedding old blood and mud on the beast-hide rug at the center of Holmlond's foremost tower while Egram and his man shut the doors behind them. The entry was warm, rustic the same way as the Den: dark stone wreathed in tapestries and skins, antler chandeliers burning in staggered rows from the high roof, and ghostlamps set into niches along the wraparound staircase framing the right wall. After weeks in war camps and the wilderness, the sight pacified some selfish, anxious longing in Cistine's heart. She'd missed being somewhere safer than the war-torn wilds.

"I see you all have a story to tell." Mira's tone was low and soothing, an appeal aimed toward skittishness, and Cistine's muscles responded to it as they always did: loosening through her shoulders and down to the aching small of her back. "Let's get you all bathed. I'll find Iri and Saychelle and have soup readied in the kitchens."

"We appreciate the hospitality," Thorne said. "We won't take advantage of it for long."

"You just can't wait to be away from me. Ever since I sprang that session on you before Darlaska..."

Thorne dragged a hand through his hair. "It isn't that."

"No, no, no need to worry for my feelings. *Somehow* I'll survive." With a long-suffering sigh and a roguish wink, Mira led them up the staircase to a mezzanine overlooking the foyer and into the corridor beyond it.

The stronghold's interior was like a small city built through the series of interlocking towers. The center of the first was hollow, the walls ribbed with shops and apartments, and the smooth circular center dotted with couches, tables, and seats where the inhabitants reclined, tending to small crafts. Amid the bright ghostlamps and dazzling silks, banners, and adornments strung across the tower from wall to wall, laughter echoed and chatter flowed freely. These were the first Valgardans Cistine saw not carrying the weight of the war on their shoulders, and a portion of her tired spirit envied them for it. She could only imagine how it felt for the others, embroiled in this battle for nearly a quarter of a year now.

Shaking off that melancholy, she hurried to fall into step with Mira. "Where does all the food and drink come from? Who takes care of these people?"

"Some things they buy," she said. "There are plenty who weave baskets or craft wares, and merches sell them for a decent profit. Others give to Holmlond charitably. And anyone who sends family here for care is required to pay a portion for their sustenance."

"I've seen Holmlond on every map of Valgard, but I never knew its purpose," Thorne said. "Why wasn't I told?"

"You can imagine it's not popular among the elites. Even I was ignorant of the care it offered until Iri asked me if my parents ever considered sending me here." Mira cast a saddened smile over her shoulder. "You're the first Chancellor to have ever set foot inside. It's no wonder Egram was so suspicious."

By the determination burning in his eyes, it was clear Thorne wanted to change that—not only for the sake of the people here, who could use far more support, but for the memory of his beloved grandmother with one leg ruined, a cruelty dealt by Salvotor to render her outcast by their kingdom.

Cistine took his hand, and he smiled gratefully.

Mira led them across a broad balcony around the first tower, into the second, then down a side hall that was notably cooler, drilling deep into the black hill itself. They emerged into a broad, dim cavern full of steaming pools, and Mira gestured with a sweep of her arm. "You have your pick of the baths. Leave your armor, I'll have it cleaned and mended. There will be fresh clothes when you come out."

"Thank you, Mira," Thorne said.

The others streamed past with mumbled gratitude and exhausted nods, only Ariadne pausing to wrap Mira in another hug before she stole away into the shadows. Feet sticking to the rock with exhaustion, Cistine made to follow them, but Mira caught her elbow. "Which of you should I speak to about Maleck?"

Cistine's heart lurched at his name, her shoulders bowing under the weight of loss and anguish. "Not me, Mira, I'm sorry."

"What have I told you about apologizing?" She thumbed a freckle of old blood from Cistine's chin. "Not Ashe, either, clearly."

"I think it should be Kristoff. He and Aden were there, but I think Aden is..."

"You don't need to tell me a thing about Aden." Mira squeezed her elbow gently. "Kristoff it is. Thank you for your council." With a kiss to

Cistine's head, Mira departed, summoning attendants with a song-sweet shout in the tower beyond.

Cistine tucked herself into a shadowy corner far from the rest of the cabal and disrobed rapidly. Her whole body stinging with cold, she slid into the water up to her nose and settled against the bottom of the pool. Curling into a ball, arms wrapped around her knees, she listened to silence.

There should've been banter. Quill and Tatiana in adjacent pools, slapping water at one another; Maleck and Ashe discussing things in warm and biting tones; Aden, Thorne, and Ariadne arguing menial matters. But she couldn't even hear them all breathing in the dark; just the swift tread of footfalls when the attendants took their armor, left them clothes, and gave them privacy again. The hollow silence echoed the pit in her chest into which she feared she'd never stop falling.

She shut her eyes and let the grief shudder through her, let her tears drip into the water and slide into that hole that refused to stop hurting.

The hole where Maleck should've been.

The baths revived them enough for supper, and enough to greet Iri, Saychelle, and two of Mira's companions without crumbling. Iri looked as wan and weary as Cistine felt, her black hair in tangles and eyes ringed with shadows, but her smile was genuine when she wrapped Ariadne in her arms for the second time that night. Saychelle, though still prim and poised as the day Cistine met her, beamed when she took a seat between her sister and Mira on the long bench at the dining table.

They were the only ones in the hall tonight, which seemed like Mira's doing. Seated across from her, Cistine watched her ladle soup into all the bowls and push them one by one to her friends. Her stomach growled, and Thorne snorted quietly. Cistine stuck her elbow into his side.

"So. How is Sander?" Mira asked, sliding a bowl to Thorne.

Hana, her lissome and pale guard, rolled her eyes. "Well, that took all of a minute."

"I let them bathe first, didn't I?" Mira swept the next bowl high when

Hana reached for it. "*No.* No soup for you after that little jab."

The next jab came from Kendar, a woman dark everywhere Hana was light, her hard poke to Mira's side coiling her up with an uncharacteristic shriek. The bowl dropped straight from her hand, and Hana caught it deftly, sliding onto the bench next to Ashe.

Chuckling, Thorne curled his arm around his own bowl and bent to blow on the soup. "Sander is everything a High Tribune ought to be. I'm fortunate to have him."

"I hope you're not telling *him* that, he's insufferably sure of himself as it is," Kendar complained.

"For once, he has every right to be," Aden admitted grudgingly. "His battlefield prowess is almost unmitigated for a man who's never fought a real battle in his life."

Mira, Hana, and Kendar swapped sharp smiles, and Mira said, "Well, when you hire twenty-six women to guard your *valenar,* and every one is proficient with a blade..."

"Let's just say we taught him a thing or two to help pass the time and burn his energy when Mira was unwell." Hana curled her fingers twice. "Pass the salt, would you, Cistine?"

"I'm insulted you think this soup needs perfecting." Mira ladled up the last bowl for herself and settled beside Saychelle. "So, I take it since you're all here, Sander is in charge of Kanslar's lines for the foreseeable future?"

Thorne froze with the spoon halfway to his mouth. Cistine's heart lurched heavily.

"We made enemies of the Courts," Ariadne admitted, "what we would and would not let them do."

"I don't blame you, given how unfair the laws of this land can be," Kendar said, "but you cannot run from the Courts forever. No one can."

"Do you have a plan?" Mira's eyes flicked between Thorne and Cistine.

"Not yet," Cistine said.

"It's being made," Thorne added.

Silence for a beat, apart from the scrape of spoons in bowls. Then Mira said, "Well, if there's anything I can do to help..."

"Not unless you can tell us why the Bloodwights are more fixated on the northwest corner of this kingdom than the war effort itself," Aden grunted.

"Or you could tell us how to *save* one of them," Ashe cut in.

"Save?" Iri echoed. "I'm afraid I don't understand."

"Let's pretend as if we do," Mira interjected graciously, her gentle eyes on Ashe. "You want to know if there would be a way to turn them from darkness back to light?"

A challenge edged Ashe's crooked shrug.

Saychelle tapped her spoon thoughtfully on the edge of her bowl. "It could be possible, I suppose. They're addicted to augments, of course, but any addiction *can* be conquered."

"I second that." Tatiana raised her spoon, and Quill nudged his body against hers, lips tugging up in a proud half-smile.

"The problem lies in whether they *want* to conquer it," Mira said. "No different from seeking help for ailments of the mind. Any man, Bloodwight or not, who is forced away from his substance of choice by others will return to it at the first opportunity."

"But they're too intoxicated to think clearly," Ashe snapped. "They don't *know* what they want with those gods-damned augments coursing through their bodies. If they knew better, they'd *choose* better. They did it before." Cistine's heart clenched at the pain in her voice.

"She has a point," Quill said. "When they have the augments, that's all they want."

Saychelle gestured to him with her spoon. "And therein lies the problem."

"To end the addiction, they have to want a different life," Iri agreed, "but to see the way forward, they must be sober-minded long enough to choose, and then to stay the course. And to convince a Bloodwight of that...I just don't see it being possible."

Ashe hurled her spoon into her bowl, scowling at them. "So you're saying there is *no* hope. None. What gods-damned help *are* you, then?"

Mira met her outburst with a steady gaze. "What we're saying is that under the proper circumstances, anything is possible. We cannot force the cure, but we can try to create the circumstances in which they choose it for themselves...and fight to be well."

"Wean them off, you mean?" Ariadne shook her head. "We've tried with some of the children, but we lack the time between battles and the spare augments to transition them."

"Most of them die." Quill dragged a hand through his hair. "The shock is just too much for their bodies. And no one has tried to deprive a full Bloodwight of its augments."

No one at all—except Cistine.

A trace of thought nudged her mind, then coiled back into shadow when Ashe shoved away from the bench and stood. "Where's your medico bay? I have some wounds I need to clean."

"I can help with that," Iri offered, rising as well.

"I'll do it myself." There was no compromise or gratitude in her voice.

Slowly, Iri took her seat again. Saychelle rattled off the directions, and Ashe left the dining tower, soup mostly untouched, her empty seat between Hana and Ariadne a gaping hole into which all the conversation toppled and met its end. Cistine ate half her portion with effort; the others hardly picked at theirs anymore.

"Is that how we plan to win this war now?" Hana asked at last. "We cannot defeat the Bloodwights, so we hope to turn them again and make them face justice as men?"

"Or rehabilitate them," Mira mused. "Though I'm not certain one woman is enough to manage them all—not even a woman with my talents."

A faint chuckle fluttered around the table, but Mira's eyes were on Cistine, and there was no humor in them at all.

Pulse drumming, she excused herself from the room.

Anxious energy did not carry her far; on the balconied path overlooking the tower's hollow middle, she stopped and bent, arms wrapped around herself, elbows on the railing, and watched the people moving below.

Such joy here; such light, despite the darkness encroaching their walls. The cabal had brought trouble into their midst for now, but soon they would be gone, and she and Thorne had both told the truth: there was no plan—yet. But there would be one, if she could sort out the tangle in her thoughts.

Feet padded on rock. "Wildheart."

She closed her eyes and breathed in that Name, the soothing calm of Thorne's voice and the touch of his hand to the small of her back.

"Tell me what you're thinking?" he asked.

Cistine skimmed her thumb along the betrothal ring at the base of her finger. "I don't even know how to say it."

He took her elbow and guided her around to face him, his hands rubbing her biceps in long, soothing strokes while she went on hugging her middle. "You know you don't have to guard your words with me."

Cistine bit her lips together. "Thorne, what if...what if what I did to Vandred is how we save Maleck?"

His hands stilled.

"I know what it did to *me*," she rambled, dropping her gaze to their feet, toes nearly touching with how close they stood, "and I saw what it did to *him*, how broken he was. Whether I struck him or not, whether you took his head off or not, maybe he would've died anyway. But you heard what Mira said. What if that's the only way we bring Maleck home?"

Thorne was deathly quiet, and when she dragged her gaze up to his face she found a blur of panic and desperation and pain in his gaze. "Cistine, we're playing with power we know nothing about...power that nearly took you away from us once. If not for the blood augment you stole from Vandred, you would have bled out on that rock. If Maleck doesn't have the same power you can draw out of him—"

"Vandred was trying to kill me in other ways, though."

"Even so. It's a risk."

"Then you're saying no?"

Thorne's gaze sharpened. He stepped nearer so that her back was pressed to the railing, and he braced his hands on it, sheltering her body in the shadow of his. "My duty is not to stand in your way, it's to clear you a path. If this is the course you want to take, we'll train for it. But we go carefully. I love Maleck, I would lay down my own life for his without question. But the same truth applies to him as to you and I: I can't place him before this kingdom."

The weight slumped her back. If it was Maleck or Valgard, if the way to save him sacrificed the entire Northern Kingdom's future, that was a choice they would have to make; a choice *she* would have to make, if saving him demanded her life. But for now, while there was still a trace of hope... "I want to try. I promised him on Darlaska, if anything happened to him, I wouldn't let him go."

Anguish edged Thorne's gaze again, but he merely slid his hand around her neck and brought her mouth to his. For a moment, he did nothing but kiss her, stealing the feeling from her fingers and curling her toes. When he released her, breathing hard, he rested his brow against hers. "I'm dreaming of a day this world stops finding new reasons to take us away from each other."

Cistine unfolded her arms to press both hands flat to the scar across his abdomen. "I'm not going anywhere, Starchaser."

But they both knew that was a promise contingent on hope. And even in this place of light and laughter, hope was a fragile, intangible thing, quickly lost to the shadows.

CHAPTER FORTY-ONE

HOLMLOND HAD NO training room, only a weapon's chamber, so Aden had to make do. The sack of old rice wasn't quite firm enough for his liking, but it was the only thing he could steal from the kitchens without incurring wrath from the cooks; and it did take his blows well, strung up from the wall of the small room where Holmlond's attendants directed him—thankfully without asking questions.

He pummeled the hours out against the threads, his body begging for another battle, for anything but this waiting, trapped here and knowing his brother was out there, suffering, sick with craving, and Aden couldn't do a stars-damned thing about it. Maybe none of them could.

Another dodge, another weave, another hit.

He'd seen that look in Thorne's eyes at dinner tonight, and after the war camp, and every day between. There was something he was running from within himself, and Aden could guess what it was.

Another bob, another blow.

Cistine. What she did to that Bloodwight changed everything. She'd made the enemy vulnerable, she could make them all that way if she tried...if she was willing to risk her own life to do it. Death by severing a Bloodwight's augments, or death bled out on the Doors to enrich the Valgardan armory. Either way, Thorne would lose her. *They* would lose her.

Another feint, another kick.

Everywhere this cabal turned, there was death and loss and suffering. And he couldn't stop it, couldn't shield them, wouldn't know where to begin even if it were possible for a traitor and a barely-competent Tribune to carry that burden.

Another punch, another jab. Another set of breaths joining his in the gloomy room.

"I see you haven't changed," Mira said from the doorway. "Beating your insecurities into something rather than facing them head-on."

Panting, Aden revolved to face her; she leaned against the stone archway, arms crossed, the hungry light of a former guard in her eyes—a look that told him she'd once faced her problems the same way.

"*Insecurities.*" Aden dropped onto the wooden bench shoved against the wall and unraveled the wrappings from his fists. "I see *you've* been speaking to my father."

"When did I ever need Kristoff's counsel to know his son was as stubborn as an unbroken ass?" Mira settled beside him. "Do you want to tell me more, or shall I begin guessing?"

Aden eyed her askance. "You know I hate when you do that."

"Then let's make this easier on us both, hm?"

Heaving a sigh, he inclined forward and stared at the rice sack. It shouldn't bother him that she'd spoken to Kristoff; she was likely trying to sort out why he wasn't vocal at dinner, trying to silence Ashe or find Maleck or counsel Thorne and Cistine. Any of it.

She matched his posture, forearms on her thighs, hands clasped between her knees. "Thorne would make quicker, better plans with your guidance."

"He would make worse mistakes more swiftly, you mean."

"Is that all you believe you have to offer? Mistakes and poor judgement?"

"I have a habit of that, if our sessions together in Stornhaz taught you anything." Aden ran a hand back through his hair. "My father told you the rest, I take it."

"You mean the bit where you and Quill ran off into the wilds to find Pippet while the others faced the worst siege in the war?"

Aden grunted quietly. "Every time Thorne asks for my opinion, I think of how badly I miscalculated the risks and rewards before Braggos, and I might do it again." He shook his head. "I abandoned duty and title to chase what mattered to *me,* just like I did ten years ago when I betrayed my Court to Salvotor. For that alone, I don't deserve to serve beside men like him. Not even men like Sander, insufferable as he is."

Mira was silent for a time. "What would make you worthy, do you think?"

He scoffed under his breath. "If I'd never left."

"Well, you did. And you betrayed them ten years ago, as well. You can't change the man you were, Aden. But you can change the man you are, and the man you will be from this moment on. Look at your cabal; they're carrying a weight too great to bear. It's breaking them...they need someone strong enough to shoulder that burden. Can *you* do it without breaking?"

My name is Aden. Son of the Lion, son of the Storm. "I think it's dangerous to try."

"Fine. Then don't begin with carrying all their burdens. Start with Ashe." She sat back, shaking her head. "That woman is one breath away from smashing this fortress apart just to make someone else hurt as badly as she does. I doubt she sees someone already is."

"*That* is a worse plan than telling Thorne what to do."

"Have you even tried?"

"To what *end,* Mira? She despises me. I lost the man she loves."

"But Maleck was not the only person she has." Mira laid a hand on his arm. "You remember what I told you the night Stornhaz burned? You are the one they need. The one *she* needs."

"They don't need the Tribune who broke his oath to his brother." He shook his head, a weak effort to dislodge the pain boring into his skull. "I swore I would never let them take him again. And I failed."

"No. You kept your word. Maleck chose to go, he wasn't taken. And I have no doubt he went because he knows what I know: that you are a good man, and you're here to pick up the pieces broken behind him. Now go and pick them up, or I'm going to hit you so hard you remember which of us trained to be Vassora and which was the pampered Tribune's son."

Aden's brow slid up. "Your methods are unconventional as always."

"Desperate cases require desperate measures." She shoved him with her whole weight. "Go find her."

Groaning, he lurched to his feet, casting a glare down at her. "Insufferable woman."

She planted her foot in his backside this time. "*Go*, I said!"

He went—and found that despite what lay ahead, despite the unease of what he would find, the stitch in his chest eased just a bit when he ducked from the shadows and back into Holmlond's light.

Mira always had that effect on him.

Ashe had not left the medico's room yet, nor was she doing anything to bandage her wounds...of which there were many, Aden saw when he slipped inside the brightly lit chamber. She had stripped down to her armored breastband and pants and sat cross-legged on one of the polished wooden tables at the center of the room, a spool of bandages half-unraveled in her lap. Scabbed cuts and grisly bruises splashed across her body from the battle in the war camp where she'd fought so desperately to reach her princess, to carry out the mission Maleck gave her.

If Aden had only told him to go with her, to not be so loyal for once in his stars-damned *life*...

He shook the thought away. It was not for Maleck that he'd come.

Ashe did not turn her gaze from the black stone wall when Aden announced himself with a cough. But if that silence was his punishment, so be it; he still wouldn't leave her sitting here, wounded and alone. This was not the Blood Hive anymore, and he was not the Hive Lord.

He stepped into her line of sight, jutting out his hand. "Let me."

She raised frigid eyes to him, the same cold fury cracking their depths as the day on the cleft when she'd beat his face bloody. The marks left by her knuckles and nails still twinged, worse now when she branded over them with that feral stare.

But Aden did not yield, curling his fingers twice. "You're welcome to hit me again if you wish. Unlike my father, I won't stop you. But let me help you first."

She didn't move, toward him or away, not even when he snatched up the bandages. Taking that for consent, he poured out a pitcher of water and carried a bowl and rags to the table. Beginning with the deepest cut—a scour along the back of her neck, just above where her collar ended—he went to work. It was a quiet task Aden's mother had taught him and Maleck and his father, a familiar one his hands settled effortlessly into. What surprised him was how much it soothed him to do it, to offer this small service; a way to put the pieces back together, like Mira said.

An insufferable, dangerous woman, indeed.

Ashe submitted to his triage like Blood Hive wounds, like tunneling into the dark catacombs of their own spirits in that place. Her frame shuddered when the cool water spilled over a bruise wrapping around her front and back just above her hip, and words came out with the shiver. "I'm sorry about your face."

Aden stilled. "If you're about to call it hideous—"

"For what I did to it."

Slowly, he resumed his work, moving on to a wound along the top of her arm and saying nothing.

"That's not who I am anymore," Ashe went on, so quietly the stone walls nearly swallowed her voice. "I'm not the woman you knew in the Blood Hive, the one who cut her way through every Valgardan in her path just because she was angry. That isn't *me*."

"I know that."

"But it's who I was with you again, back there. I'm sorry, I just...panicked." She curled her hands around the table's edge, bending her weight forward slightly. "When your father vanished, and you thought he died. Did it make you realize how *much* he meant to you?"

Aden squeezed out the rag's drippings, letting them run down her back while he gathered the bandages and soothing tinctures. "It did."

"Did that make you feel weak? Vulnerable?"

He uncapped the tincture and slathered it across her bruises, grimacing at her hiss of pain. "Like I would never be safe again." It was more than he'd ever told the cabal—more than he'd even told Mira. But if it would provide Ashe a sense of being seen, there was no end to what he would give.

She nodded slowly and didn't speak until he began to bandage her wounds, starting with the thick bruising across her middle. "I thought I was steady on my own, but I'm not. I'm steady with all of you. With Bres. I was steadier with Mal. Now it feels like I've been under a riptide for a week. Aden, I'm sick of not being able to breathe."

He tucked the bandage beneath her arm and squeezed her shoulder. "You should know by now you aren't alone in this, Ashe. You have not been alone for a single second since you set foot into the Blood Hive."

Hoarse laughter burst from her, hitting all the wrong notes. "Since the first time you knocked me on my ass, you mean."

Wrong as her tone was, it was still better than the silence hanging around her ever since they flew from the cleft, when her blows and glares and the quiet afterward made him feel like the same traitor who'd left Stornhaz on the cabal's heels. And this time he didn't even have Maleck to vouch for him.

He circled around her to bandage her arm, and this time she watched him without reproach.

"I know," she murmured, though he hadn't said anything. "I know you love him, too. If Kristoff hadn't been there, I'm sure you would've let Mal tear your throat out before you let him go. I was wrong to blame you."

His chest tightened. "Apology accepted."

A flicker of a smile teased her lips, there and gone again. "So, you're with me? Whatever comes?"

He raised his gaze to hers and found her eyes overbright, fixed hungrily on him, waiting for the oath that already branded his lips. "I won't leave your side until this over, whatever comes. I give you my word."

She drew in a shaky breath. "Good. I'm going to need someone at least as mad as I am to pull this through."

"You're planning something dangerous, I take it. To bring him back."

Leather creaked as she squeezed her knees, focus shifting back to the wall over his shoulder. "I'll do whatever it takes."

Aden sighed, finished binding the wound, and rocked back on his heels. "Still my greatest source of pain."

Laughter scalded her throat again, cold and croaky, and when she sagged he met her first with his shoulder, then with his arms. She clung to him in dry sorrow, a raging inferno of anguish and anger endlessly shaking. He held her and did not speak, letting himself be what Mira told him to be: the Tribune, the protector, the ward against the dark.

And somehow, in the dying ghostlight with Ashe leaning into him for strength, the impossible and unpredictable world made a bit more sense. The waves broke, and he began to see above them to what the world ought to be; and in a flicker of a moment, he saw his own place in it. Who they needed him to be.

Just this. Just the one who took care of them when the world came undone.

CHAPTER FORTY-TWO

DESPITE THE COLD, uncomfortable conditions, the entire cabal settled into a single room together at the night's end. Curled between Thorne's chest and Quill's back, Cistine stumbled through a pattern of waking and falling asleep long into the night, full of fretful dreams.

When a voice whispered her name, rousing her once more, she ignored it at first. But then she heard it again. And again.

"Cistine." Then, louder, *"Logandir."*

She rolled from under Thorne's hand tucked against her hip and found Mira's bright brown eyes watching her from the gloom at the cavern mouth. "What is it?"

"Come with me," Mira whispered. "Bring Ari with you."

The strategist roused at a fleeting touch to the arm, and together they stole from the room to join Mira on the broad path overlooking a now-empty tower, the couches vacant and ghostlights capped to gentle flickers. Yawning, Cistine rubbed her eyes. "This couldn't wait until morning?"

"As if any of us were sleeping well after the discussion at dinner." Mira beckoned with a tilt of her head and started down the broad balcony. "You told me I could help you if I knew where the Bloodwights were. Well, I just might have an idea."

Those words woke Cistine like a splash of icy water to the face. She swapped wide-eyed looks with Ariadne, and they darted to catch up to their friend, who snatched up a ghostlight to paint their way. By its blush radiance, they passed through a tunnel connecting two spires of Holmlond and entered a world snatched from a dream.

The library was ancient and hewn, reminiscent of Nygaten Temple before the Bloodwights had sacked it. Pillars and statues vaulted between sharp shelving squares, ghostplant sap smeared along every ledge to illumine the spines in a faint teal glow. The air hung heavy with dusty knowledge and the smell of old paper and ink, and Cistine's spirits rose so swiftly at the familiar sensations, tears warped her vision. "Holy gods..."

Ariadne whistled lowly, turning a full revolution on her heels. "There must be more than a thousand books here."

"Three thousand, seven hundred and fifteen, to be exact." Mira marched straight to the first square of shelves, stretched up on the tips of her toes to pull down a volume as thick around as her forearm, then beckoned Cistine and Ariadne to a cluster of seats in the center of a pillar ring. "I've spent a considerable amount of time perusing these shelves over the last three and a half months."

"Shocking," Ariadne deadpanned, and Mira kicked her ankle.

"It was your sister who first put the thought in my head, actually: what do the Bloodwights truly need to succeed? What would not just aid their cause, but guarantee its success?"

Cistine fought back a shudder. "Nothing, I hope."

Mira's eyes fixed on her across the low stone table between the seats, full of sympathy she didn't want; any form of pity coming from a woman of Mira's experience meant dire circumstances indeed. "Nothing they've found *yet*."

Ariadne folded her arms tight at her waist. "Explain."

"I spoke to Kristoff more after supper tonight, and given what he told me, I can understand your concern—the Bloodwights' focus ought to be along the fronts, yet they hide in the northwestern mountains. And why there? Nothing but snow and rock to speak of. No villages, even."

"Do you have an answer?"

"Possibly." Mira turned the book toward them, laying it open to one feather-edged page. "According to Iri's memory, when the former *visnprest* Order fled north, they didn't just raid the augment stores. They stole from the temple libraries as much as they could carry. Very specific books about ancient things, written in Old Valgardan, no less."

"They must've been learning to read it all this time," Cistine mused.

Mira nodded. "Which is precisely why, I think, it's taken them so long to act. They weren't only waiting for a Key, they were searching for something else."

Ariadne laid a hand on Cistine's back, bending to read the book over her shoulder. "Something in those mountains."

"Something that could end the war in one blow?" Cistine asked softly. Neither of them answered her question, so she bent forward to study the runic language of the book, a flicker of memory dancing in her mind like lightning, there and gone. She traced the map that took up one page, following the articulate black sweeps of an artist's touch—familiar, but not. "This map is different from the one Tatiana taught me."

"Because it's ancient," Mira said. "From the time of the very first Order, when the wells were newly mined. These are the ancient temples where *Gammalkraft* was practiced."

Cistine jerked her hand back, fingertips burning with the phantom memory of a blade grasped in her shaking hand. "Kalt Hasa."

Mira nodded. "Among others. Long ago, Detlyse Halet was one as well, a temple now turned to a prison. And there was another, would you like to guess where it is? I'll give you a hint: my *valenar* was quite fond of it for a time."

Ariadne's mouth coiled down in anger. "Siralek."

"Or Thalma Geris, as it was once called." Mira tapped the map. "The catacombs Sander, Aden, and Tatiana found underneath that Nimmus-pit didn't belong to an arena of bloody sport...those were temple vaults."

"And the Bloodwights sacked them both," Cistine said. "Not just to plunder criminals for their ranks."

Mira shook her head. "I've spent weeks poring over this book, and what

I've learned has been...enlightening. Much like finding an asp coiled in your boot."

Ariadne snorted quietly, the only lick of amusement in the shadow-hugged room. "Dare we ask what you found besides the asp?"

"I wish you wouldn't." But Mira carried on quietly, "There are...other augments, not like the ones we use. They're different. Stranger. And far, far stronger and more dangerous, according to this text."

Ariadne's hand tensed over Cistine's shoulder. "I've never heard of such a thing." *And I was once an acolyte.* The words hung unspoken, prodding like a dagger's tip against Cistine's racing heart.

"According to Saychelle, no one hears this legend until they take the vows of the Order, and then they're forbidden to speak of it to anyone."

"But she told you, of course."

Mira's lips twisted in a dry smile. "We know your sister, and we know these are desperate times." Her fingers brushed the book again. "Augments derived from what occurs naturally in the world...darkness and light, fire and ice, wind and water...those are endless. There will always be day and night, storms and seasons. But there are rarer things out there. Only a few wells produced augments that could heal the body and mind or restore blood, for example. And only one held powers like these."

"Like *what*?" Cistine demanded.

Mira tapped the cracked, ancient page again. "This one calls them the *Stor Sedam*, seven augments with no equal. The tales don't tell precisely what they do, but the implications are mastery over life and death, time and perception, foresight and fate, creation itself. Almost a weaving of *Gammalkraft* and augmentation, if you will." Her fingertip skimmed beneath a pattern of runes repeated across the page. "*Stoj. Haval. Sinn. Faravost. Skyjun. Izmeret. Nadzor.* They are the oldest and most powerful of all augments, and there is only one of each. The *visnprests* scattered them to keep anyone from finding all seven. A man like Salvotor could have controlled the fate of the world with these."

Ariadne sucked in a sharp breath through her nose, but it was from Cistine's lips that the words fell: "And you believe the Bloodwights are searching for them."

The quiet was tomb-like. Every vapor of hope shriveled up in the distressed dance of Mira's gaze. "I'm afraid so. As you said, Cistine, it's the blow to end the war. We don't know precisely what these augments are capable of, but they were dangerous enough to be hidden in nearly-unreachable places. The Bloodwights could whittle us down in time, but these augments could stomp out every war. The Bloodwights may even think them powerful enough to defeat the gods themselves."

"How do they even know of them?" Ariadne demanded.

"From what Saychelle tells me, there were only three tomes that ever spoke of the *Stor Sedam*. The Bloodwights have two. This one was stashed so deep in Holmlond it took me a month of searching every single day to find it."

Ariadne sank back in her chair, releasing Cistine's shoulder at last. "Then that's what they're doing at the ancient temples...first Detlyse Halet, then Siralek. They're searching for these augments."

Chills tumbled down Cistine's back so swiftly and violently her heart threatened to stop. "We can't let the Bloodwights find them."

For the first time that night, there was a smile in Mira's eyes. "Fortunately for us, we have something they don't: the book that matters."

Relief punched a breath from Cistine's chest that for once, the Key was not the answer. "Because of the map?"

"Precisely. According to rumor, the other books have tales, but no map. They may have deduced enough to search the ancient temples, but that doesn't tell them where within the temples these flagons are. Or in which temples, if that's where they truly are at all. There's some evidence to suggest a few were scattered elsewhere."

"Still," Ariadne said, "if they raze the temples, it matters little. Map or none, they'll pick through the wreckage until they find what they're searching for."

"Not if the flagons aren't in the wreckage."

Chills of a different kind raked Cistine's stomach as she studied Mira's mischievous face. "Underneath. They're hidden underneath?"

"The one in the northwest is, at least." Mira pointed to the map's uppermost corner. "If what I've read is true, Kosai Talis has vaults below where powerful artifacts were kept hidden, just like Thalma Geris. The text is vague, but I would bet what little wealth I still have that if you found a way into the vaults, you'd find one of the *Stor Sedam* inside."

Cistine writhed in her seat. "Then we have to go *now*."

"Peace, *Logandir*," Ariadne said, smoothing a hand through the air. "What we need is a plan. If we steal this augment from beneath their feet, the Bloodwights may turn to finding the next...or they may focus the full might of their fury on the army, on the rest of Valgard, and on *you*."

Cistine's hope guttered, banked, then flared again in a desperate pulse. "I might have a plan for that already."

Mira puffed with laughter. Ariadne's eyes narrowed. "Would this have anything to do with what you sought Vandred for?"

Ears heating, she nodded.

"Should I go wake the others?" Mira asked.

"No. Not yet. I'll tell you two first, and if you think it may be enough to turn the tide of the war, then I'll tell everyone else."

Mira settled back in her seat. "Our ears are yours."

Cistine twisted her betrothal ring around her finger and sent up a silent prayer to the gods for strength.

Then she told them her plan.

CHAPTER
FORTY-THREE

FRENETIC ENERGY HEMMED Cistine's body brighter than a lightning augment when she woke the cabal in the morning. Stiff and sore from sleeping on the stone, Thorne stumbled out to join her, Ariadne, and Mira on the balcony, leading the others in a yawning procession. One look at his *selvenar's* sweat-shined, eager face, and Thorne was wide awake. "What did we miss?"

"I'll tell you over breakfast." Cistine shoved the small of his back, turning him toward the dining hall.

It was crowded this morning, so they swiped up bowls of porridge and plates of bread and cheese before Mira led them to another tower stacked top to bottom with bridges and mezzanines, a frond-edged pool set at its center. They passed no one else on their way to the highest seating area, a crescent balcony jutting over the wide tower and glistening water far below. Once they'd settled—Kristoff, Quill, and Tatiana dragging seats over to the railing, Thorne cross-legged on a low table, the others choosing the floor— Cistine burst out, "I know where we need to go next."

Ashe's gaze shot straight to her. "To find Maleck."

"Before that. We have to go to a place called Kosai Talis...a temple of the old Order." She looked Thorne dead in the eyes. "It lies in the northwest Isetfells, almost as far as Oadmark."

Slowly, he let his spoon fall, the strength deserting his arm. "Tell us everything."

She wove the tale with a storyteller's enthusiasm, an impossible history of ancient vaults and hidden wells and augments called the *Stor Sedam*. By the end of it, no one was eating anymore; they all stared at her, slack-jawed and wide-eyed, and in the silence after she'd finished Aden profaned so colorfully that his father slapped him upside the head.

"That explains where those *bandayos* have been all this time." Quill fed a morsel of bread to Faer on his shoulder. "And it fits what Vandred told us. Why bother fighting battle after battle when you could find the weapon that ends all wars?"

"Do you know which augment is in that temple?" Aden demanded.

Cistine shook her head. "But does it matter? Any one of them would be devastating. That's why they were hidden in the first place."

"Well, what are we waiting for?" Quill unfolded his legs and braced to leap up. "We need to find that augment before they do."

"It's more complicated than that, I'm afraid," Ariadne said, and his muscles slowly uncoiled, slumping him back on his haunches. "The Bloodwights have kept their attention so far on one augment traced from stolen books. If we take that purpose from them, they may turn back to the lines, the army."

"To us," Mira added, "and to Cistine. She will once again become paramount to them...the Key back to the augments they still *can* obtain."

Thorne's breakfast curdled in his stomach, and he set aside his plate and bowl, sitting up straight to study Cistine's face across the circle. It was carefully calm, her gaze steady, her jaw firm. Not a trace of fear to be found. "I already expected their focus on me the moment I crossed the Dreadline," she said. "I won't lie, it's been a welcome reprieve having them look somewhere else. But it's not worth it if they're searching for something that could kill us all anyway."

"Then what's the plan?" Tatiana asked flatly.

"Get the augment. Find Maleck. And keep training. My hope is that by the time we reunite with the army, I'll be strong enough to do what I did to Vandred to all his brothers. Then we cut them down, one by one."

Only now was there a faint tremor in her words—the worry that it would not be enough. The fear that saving just one, even if it was Maleck, would be the end of her. The same panic from their conversation outside the dining hall the previous night surged in Thorne again, and again, he shoved it away. This was not about him; it was about what his kingdom needed, and the things Cistine wanted to do, the blows only she could land.

"Are we in agreement, then?" he asked, bringing their attention to himself and offering Cistine a moment to regain her composure. "To Kosai Talis first, then to tracking Maleck?"

Ashe rubbed her face with both hands. "I don't think we have a choice."

"She's right," Kristoff sighed. "We can't ignore the enemy's maneuvers."

"Keeping that augment out of their hands is our duty," Quill agreed. "And I for one can't pass on a chance to steal something from *them*."

Tatiana's face was dark with a rage that made Thorne's skin crawl. "*Agreed.*"

"The sooner the better," Ariadne agreed.

"Aden?" Mira prompted.

He reclined at Quill's right hand, leg cocked to his chest, wrist hanging from his knee. His eyes traced from Mira's expectant face and iron-edged smile to all the rest of them, one after another, and he swallowed. "No one else knows of this augment. Bravis and the others have never taken the Bloodwights' absence seriously. This cabal has always shouldered the burden of addressing the concerns and struggles the rest of Valgard ignores, like the stronghold in Selv Torfjel. So...I agree. We go. It's what we've always done."

Mira winked at him, and he shot her a playful scowl Thorne found impossible to decipher—and decided he didn't want to. It was enough to have his cousin's wisdom added to the conversation, a reminder of past and present that brought strength back to his own stiff limbs. He could do this. It was what he had always done, the very principles on which Sillakove Court was founded: addressing the wrongs that went unnoticed by the other Courts, forging a better world by the strength of their own backs, by the blood in their veins.

Fear faded. In its place, he saw only his warriors, all the good they'd ever done written in scars across their bodies, in exhausted eyes and strong faces gathered around him, still fighting despite the pain. "Tomorrow at dawn. We travel northwest."

Ashe pushed herself up. "I'll tell Bresnyar."

Cistine hopped up as well. "Tati, can I speak to you?"

Tatiana grimaced and shrugged, and they hurried away. The others broke up after them, Kristoff and Quill to gather supplies, Aden and Ariadne to plan their course through the mountains—leaving only Mira and Thorne, who found himself hunting desperately for an excuse to escape the penetrating look in her eyes.

"It must be exhausting," she said when he leaped up and stacked all the dishes, "having to carry the blame for every single terrible thing that happens in this war."

The brown knot of scar tissue across his middle gave a goading twinge, and he stabbed a spoon into a bowl harder than he should have. "I don't know what you mean."

"You like to assign blame because it helps you make sense of things. If every problem has a cause, it becomes rational, preventable in the future. And if you can't assign a purpose and reason to it, then you take it on yourself and make it your own fault."

Shaking his head, he scooped the plates under one arm, the bowls under the other, then halted when Mira rose with sinuous grace and stepped into his way.

"The trouble is, when you take on all the blame, you start to fight the war against yourself," she said. "*You* become the enemy to outsmart. And that is not a battle any man can win."

A deprecating smile yanked the corner of his mouth. "I seem to be losing them all anyway."

"Thorne, sometimes you are going to face enemies who are cleverer than you," Mira said gently. "They will outmaneuver and outwit you. You *will* walk into ambushes and traps, and you won't see what's coming until there's a knife at your neck. People will be hurt—friends and strangers alike. But that doesn't make *you* the enemy. You have enough battles to fight without fighting against yourself."

Emotion wedged in his throat. "If this is about Maleck..."

"It's about the look I've seen in your eyes since the moment you crossed our threshold. And it's about what your kingdom needs you to be. What *they* need you to be." She jerked her chin to the railed steps where the cabal had vanished, then carefully slid the bowls from under his arm. "You have to choose which war you can afford to fight: the one against yourself or the one against the Bloodwights. Because it *will* come down to one front or another where you can direct your attention. And the longer you focus on fighting yourself, the less you'll pay attention to what the enemy is doing."

Thorne cleared his throat. "Your past with the Vassora does you credit."

She checked his hip with hers. "You're also not the first Chancellor I've advised in matters like these."

"But I may be the first who sold his kingdom's safety for Talheim's."

Mira's gaze leaped to his face, and Thorne swallowed a curse. Why in the *stars* had he said that? To *Mira*, of all people?

"You can't tell me it wasn't a mistake," he added defensively.

"I'm not going to tell you one way or another," she said after a beat. "What I will say is this: you are *allowed* to make mistakes, Thorne. Yes, even great ones. You're allowed to fail on your way to becoming the Chancellor you were born to be. You're worth more than a tally of perfect decisions."

A faint prickle laced between the scars on his back, the memory of belts and backhands. "Tell that to my father and mother."

She tipped her head. "They made you believe mistakes were unforgivable."

"Not just them." Thorne shifted his grip on the plates. "There is a standard expected of a Chancellor when we take our oaths."

"Do you really believe Bravis, Valdemar, Benedikt, and Maltadova never made choices that wounded Valgard? Need I remind you that two fell prey to Salvotor's infiltration, and the others nearly gave way at the last moment? But I've never heard you call for their trial or disbarment. You should afford yourself the same grace."

Grief banded Thorne's chest at the thought of Maltadova. "What they've done doesn't excuse—"

"It excuses no one. But it reveals a very important truth if you're willing to see it."

"What truth?"

"That we are all imperfect, broken, hurting things, and we survive not by perfection, but by grace. The grace we give each other, the grace we give ourselves." She laid a hand on his arm. "Whatever debt you began when you sent Cistine away, I can see in your face how much you've paid for it, and what you're still willing to. It's a greater betrayal by far to rid this kingdom of a Chancellor who cares so deeply for its needs than to choose love over land in a moment of panic. It's time to let grace do its work so you can do *yours*, Thorne."

Dampness snaked against the side of his nose. "How do I forgive myself for that choice?"

"By making a different one now: choosing to look ahead, where to aim your blade. And going into Kosai Talis, I strongly advise you to point it at the true enemy."

A rush of fear clogged his throat. "You suspect another ambush?"

"Stars, no. I don't think the Bloodwights want Cistine anywhere near these augments. It's not *their* intentions I fear." Mira beckoned him across the first of the bridges back toward the dining hall, her gaze unusually grim. "It's the minds of the *visnprests* who hid the flagons to begin with. They obviously feared to unleash them, even for the sake of destroying them forever, so they buried them deep. And I'll tell you what my work has taught me: anything worth burying deep is also worth protecting. And the means by which they'll have protected this secret...well, I suspect you're all going to meet your match." Her eyes locked on his face now, full of wisdom and worry. "Cistine is going to need you focused and at your best if she's going to reach that augment before the Bloodwights do. And as for Valgard...we need you to help her do it, or all our lives may be forfeit in the end."

CHAPTER
FORTY-FOUR

TATIANA HAD DREADED this moment since she first woke in the medico tent and had avoided being alone in Cistine's presence for that very reason. But there was no way to deny her in front of the others without arousing suspicion, particularly from Quill; so here they were, standing outside a small booth giving away cinnamon pastries in the first tower's lower level, and amidst all the happy chatter and splendor, Tatiana had never felt so out of place. She wanted to rip the colored streamers off the walls, rend the banners and suffocate the ghostlamps. But it was absurd to want those things; the world had every right to go on being cheerful even if her heart was broken.

Still. She resented it.

"I have a request," Cistine said, taking the pastries from the booth keeper and handing one to Tatiana. She accepted it, though she'd barely touched her porridge that morning and still had no appetite. Visalie had warned her to replenish her fluids and nourish herself frequently with all the blood leaving her body, but it was difficult to summon any appetite. She wondered if she was cursed to remain in this blank fog, feeling her way blindly forward, every day for the rest of her life.

"Don't you want to know what it is?" Cistine prompted, and Tatiana realized she'd completely ignored the mention of any request in favor of staring at her pastry.

She shrugged. "Aren't you going to tell me anyway?"

If Cistine suspected anything was wrong, she gave no sign, and that irritated Tatiana, too. This girl, who she considered her closest friend in the world besides Ariadne, couldn't even see that she was gutted, her heart torn from her chest. She was too wrapped up in notions of her own destiny, of augments and battle and what would come next.

Tatiana struggled to silence her own raging thoughts while she followed Cistine to a pair of chairs in the tower's flagstone center. Cistine dropped into one and inclined toward Tatiana when she took the other. "I need you to write to your father."

Tatiana stilled, pastry halfway to her mouth, blind panic slicing through her middle. "What? *Why?*"

"Because we need all the help we can find now that the Chancellors know my secret. If Morten could rally *Heimli Nyfadengar*—"

"No. I'm not dragging him into this war."

"Tati, he may not have a choice. It might come down to fighting beside us or fighting without us if the Bloodwights have their way."

"I said *no*, Cistine!" Tatiana's voice cracked, fear pounding her skull at the thought of her absent-minded, noble, beloved *father* suffering the same fate as so many warriors, as Maltadova, as—

"Will you at least consider it?" Cistine begged. "Maybe he doesn't participate, then, but the rest of the guild can! They're some of the most brilliant people in Valgard, we could do so much with their help. If you could just *ask*—"

"I'm not writing to him! And if you go around my back to speak to him, I will never forgive you."

Cistine sat back, blinking wide-eyed. "Tati, I would *never* do that."

"No, you're just begging *me* to bring what's left of my family into this war," she seethed. "I don't see *your* people here, I don't see *your* father suiting up for battle, but since it's our people, our families, that's all right, isn't it? As if we have any less to lose!"

Hurt seared through Cistine's gaze. "I'm not keeping aid from Valgard.

I'm risking my whole kingdom's future to be here."

Tatiana knew that; but the hate and hurt she'd bottled within herself for the past week while they'd traveled, too weak to beat it out into Quill's hands and too ashamed and grieving to speak it to anyone else, burst from her in vicious verbal blows slung at the unsuspecting princess, and she couldn't seem to stop punching. "I know exactly what you're risking. The princess, the sole heir, always deciding the next battle we walk into." She stood, hurling the pastry into her empty chair. If she didn't leave now, this would turn to physical strikes, because the fire burning in her veins already raged nearly out of control. "Well, you're not deciding that for my family anymore. I'm not writing to my father, and that's the end of it."

She stalked blindly away toward the mouth of some other tunnel stretching into some other tower. Maybe that one would lead somewhere she could finally let out all the anger eating at her insides.

Predictably, infuriatingly, Cistine did not let it go.

"Tatiana! Don't walk away from me!" The princess stormed after her. "That's not how we handle things with each other!"

"That was before the war, *Princess*." Tatiana ducked into the tunnel, and Cistine was right behind her, the echo of their boots too loud, too sharp, echoing the drum of Tatiana's heart. "That was before *everything*!"

"Tati, I know how it looks when you're running. I know you're afraid!" Cistine's hand caught her elbow and yanked her around, and even in the ghostlit dimness she saw how the hurt had already morphed into rage just like hers. "If this is about what happened in Selv Torfjel, I understand, I understand *completely*—"

"No, you don't. You *can't*."

"Yes, I can! I was stabbed the same way in Kalt Hasa, don't you remember?"

"It's not the same, Cistine, it just *isn't*!"

"How is it any different? You were hurt, I was hurt, we were both healed, we both have scars from it—"

"I was *pregnant*!"

The shout boomed along the walls, vibrated into the ribbed rock before and behind them, and the darkness swallowed it. The first time she'd spoken those words to anyone. The first time she'd ever admitted it outside her own mind since Visalie told her what the vivid dreams, the illness at the battlefield gore, and the insatiable exhaustion all meant for her. For their future.

Cistine's eyes blew wide, and she fell back, a hand to her mouth, the horror in her gaze writhing in perfect tandem to Tatiana's. "You're—you were—?"

"Pregnant." The word emerged ragged this time, pushed out by her heaving breaths and churning stomach. "Since before Braggos. Eight weeks, maybe a bit less. The signs started early, the same as my mother with me. I learned right before you came back."

"Oh, *Tati*." Tears shook Cistine's voice, and Tatiana wanted to hit her for that more than anything. But she also wanted to say it all. She couldn't *stop* saying it, now that the words had begun.

"I was searching for a way to tell Quill, for the right time, but he's been so lost in the war and trying to find Pippet, I just kept waiting. And kept waiting." Now her vision blurred, and *her* voice rolled with unshed tears. "And then Selv Torfjel happened, and there was just too much damage, or too much strain on me, I don't know—"

"Did I do this?"

Tatiana blinked, vision clearing abruptly. "What?"

"When I healed you in the mountain, did I do something that made it...that made your body—should expecting mothers even use augments? Was the power too much?"

"Oh, Cistine, stars damn it. I don't *know*." Tatiana raked her curls back from her temples. "I don't know how any of it works. I just know it was over after, and now it's done. The bleeding's finally slowed, I'm not...I'm not a mother anymore."

There it was. The word she'd whispered to herself on dark nights when the dreams woke her, with Quill slumbering beside her in the war camp; the title that had begun to mean something once the shock faded, once she started to think of that house in Blaykrone with her and Quill and Pippet.

And a baby.

That hopeless dream, that vision of life beyond the war, taken from her. Shredded. And she deserved it.

"Do you know what the worst part is?" she whispered. "For an instant when the medico told me it was over, I was *relieved*. I'd been losing my mind for weeks, wondering how I was going to bring a child into this war-torn kingdom, how I was going to be a mother *and* a warrior, how I was supposed to protect this tiny life when I couldn't even protect Pippet, who already knew how to fight for herself. And when she told me it was gone...I felt a weight come off me." Ragged, disgusted laughter ripped her throat, and she rubbed her face with both hands. "What sort of stars-forsaken *creature* feels *relieved* their child is gone? But there I was, crying until I couldn't breathe, feeling all that grief...and feeling glad, too. So maybe I killed it with all my fear, wondering whether this was a blessing or a curse. I don't know, Cistine. Maybe hating everyone and feeling this distance from Quill ever since it happened is the punishment I deserve."

Cistine's fingers gripped her shoulders swiftly, vise-hard, and at their sharp flex Tatiana turned her eyes back to her friend's face. Her expression was steel and flame, full of certainty. "You are not a terrible person, Tati. It's natural for *anyone* to wonder what it would be like to raise a child during a war. I'm sure Julian's mother felt the same...if Rion had died here, how would she raise their son alone?"

"But she didn't have to. That's the difference."

"It's *no* different. You didn't do this just by wondering. You fought for that child to have a chance in a home without war, and the Bloodwights took that future away." Cistine shook her gently, earnestly. "Of course you feel relieved, because you don't have to face something that terrified you. But you're grieving, too. You're grieving because you *loved* that little life. Because you're a mother, like *my* mother is to my brothers even though they're gone. The loss doesn't change what you are. Nothing can take that away from you."

Tatiana spanned her hands helplessly—empty hands she'd begun to imagine cradling a small child, a perfect blend of her and Quill, at the end of nine fraught months. "I have nothing to show for it."

Cistine's thumb caught a tear that slid down Tatiana's cheek. "You have this."

A great, heaving sob wrenched through her at that, so vicious and abrupt it felt like her spine snapped, like all her ribs caved in. She sagged into Cistine's arms and wept, and the princess held her, stroked her hair, and whispered words of comfort and compassion that Tatiana couldn't fathom yet—and didn't have to. Someone *finally* knew. It was not her secret shame and despair alone to carry.

She didn't know how long she sobbed, how long Cistine held her before she ran out of breath, before she was able to swallow and heave in air and finally make sense of the things Cistine was whispering between kisses pressed to her temple and shoulder.

"You can survive this," Cistine murmured. "You're the strongest person I know, and you've climbed out of darkness before. You're going to do it again, and you're going to turn all this pain into strength. Make it your weapon."

"I don't know *how*," Tatiana choked.

Cistine's fingers trailed through her matted ringlets. "By fighting for the future your child would've had. For *all* the children this war has made sacrifices of. You'll go to battle for them, and for the other babies you and Quill will have someday, so they can grow up safe."

Tatiana had no answer for that, only another sob that pushed through her in a gentler wave this time, rocking her on her feet but not breaking her bones with its passing.

"I know there are going to be other children," Cistine added softly, "but that doesn't make this one any less important. It doesn't make it hurt less. I'm so sorry, Tatiana. I'm *sorry*."

She believed that with all her heart. Of all the cabal, it was Cistine— sister to two miscarried brothers, daughter to a mother and father of three with only one they could ever embrace—who understood the vastness of this grief. The sheer magnitude of it. "*I'm* sorry. I shouldn't have said what I did...I *know* you're not offering us up for a sacrifice, I just..."

"You can't write to Mort because you're not ready to tell him about this. But you don't want to lie to him, either." Tatiana nodded, the tear-soaked collar of her friend's pajamas scraping her brow. "It can wait. Everything I want can wait, Tati. All I care about right now is helping you. What can I do?"

Sniffing back what few tears had not escaped, Tatiana braced her hands on Cistine's biceps and rocked back from her. Even in the gloom, she caught the shine of tears on her face; her friend, as always, mourned and suffered with her. "I think I need to speak to Mira before we leave. I don't want to find my way back into a bottle of mead."

Cistine nodded. "Do you want me to go with you?"

"Is that even allowed?"

"You're going to find out Mira is exceptionally unconventional in all the best ways." She wrapped an arm around Tatiana's shoulders and steered her toward the light, and Tatiana hugged her waist in turn. With her weight leaning into Cistine, the journey was a bit easier to manage.

CHAPTER FORTY-FIVE

Holmlond's weapons chamber was rarely used by its guards, tucked away in the furthest tower; though dim and dusty, Ashe found it well-stocked when Mira pointed her there to prepare for their journey to Kosai Talis. The first level alone sported racks of daggers, stands of swords, polearms, axes, and bows—a plethora of weaponry as familiar to Ashe as old friends.

When she shut her eyes in the embrace of these sights and sensations—the cold air sighing through a chink in the mortar, the sharp tang of metal and the soothing aroma of polish tinging the air—her mind returned to the barracks in the Citadel, to the Wardens' haunts in Astoria.

But this was not Talheim. And home was far from her grasp now.

The angry, vicious haze had cleared some after her talk with Aden, but morbid determination clawed into the crevice it left behind. She would go on this mad mission with Cistine and watch over her, because protecting her was still as much a part of Ashe as her own blood and bones. But after, nothing would keep her from finding Maleck, whether the others were with her or not.

At least Aden would be.

Boots clacking on the cold stone floor, she went to the rack of offhand daggers recessed under the stairwell connecting the tower's five levels and took them down one by one, weighing them out before she chose one, dull but long, its brilliant scabbard and full tang a testament of fine make and quality. Snatching a satchel of tools from a hook on the end of the shelf, she wandered deeper into the tower.

She wasn't alone; the gentle chafe of whetstone against steel reached her ears just before she rounded a wedge of halberd racks and spotted Quill. He sat on the long bench between the stands with ankle propped on knee, a dagger in his hand, drawing the whetstone along the edge more carefully than she'd ever seen him move. There was a dangerous glow in his eyes, a furious spark waiting to be stoked into flame. Ashe had seen it every day since they'd fled Stornhaz, but now it burned stronger. She wondered if that was because he'd come so close to finding Pippet in Selv Torfjel, and instead of coming with them, she'd stuck a blade in Tatiana. Tried to stick it into *him*.

That beloved little face flashed through Ashe's mind, there and gone like a stroke of lightning and leaving an imprint just as bright when she blinked: her messy hair, her wicked smile, the light in her eyes, the strength of her embrace when Ashe came back from Talheim. That girl was her responsibility, like watching Maleck's back was her responsibility; and just the same as the man sitting on the bench before her, lost in the motion of caring for his weapons, Ashe had nothing but empty arms and anger raging in her chest to show for what was once hers.

She made her way down the row and lowered herself onto the bench facing the opposite way from Quill, drew the offhanded dagger, and began to sharpen it with the same long, steady strokes as him—matching their work to one another, matching their hurts the same.

The silence didn't last long. With Quill, it never did.

"Mal gave me this dagger," he said. "I don't even remember how old I was...fifteen? Sixteen, maybe? One of those birthdays my parents forgot."

"My parents usually forgot my birthdays, too." Ashe glanced at the fine weapon over her shoulder: intricate runes whorled into the steel, the handle made of sturdy, bronze-colored wood. "Does it have a name?"

"*Fjadar*." Quill turned it to the light, surveying its wicked edge. "It was my first weapon. It's been with me through every battle I've ever been in. Just like Mal."

Ashe studied the dagger in the low ghostlight glow. During this war, she'd seen countless battles where Maleck and Quill tossed it back and forth, cleaving through the *mirothadt* as cleanly as the rest of the army traded augments. From that first day she'd laid eyes on them on the Vingete Vey, they'd seemed invincible as long as they were together. But now...

"He's out there." Quill followed effortlessly along her silent spool of thought. "Hating himself, if there's enough of him left to feel anything. And you know what the worst part is? I didn't think twice before we left him with the rest of you in that stars-forsaken mountain. I just wanted to get Tati back to the war camp." He resumed sharpening his steel. "If he came with us instead of Ari, he'd still be here. He'd be all right."

Ashe exhaled her anger and brought in the quiet and calm with every breath, every stroke of her dagger on the whetstone. "Wherever he was, he would've fought beside this cabal. And that still would've put him in his brothers' path. They were there for him, Aden said...they were always going to find him."

And that was what she'd wrestled with for so many nights while she and Bresnyar searched the mountains fruitlessly for him; it was never about taking her to use against him, it was about taking *him* back. She'd loved and protected something she was doomed to lose. And after everything she did to fight for him, he'd walked into those shadows of his own volition to save his family.

In the end, he chose to bleed.

"So, they found him." Her blade slid off the stone. "Now we get him back."

Quill sheathed Fjadar and twisted toward her, their shoulders bumping. "It's going to be a fight, Shei." She rolled her eyes at the name only Quill ever got away with, a slip-up from some forgotten battlefield he'd never stopped teasing her about...and somewhere along the way, she forgot to keep hitting him when he used it. "Are you ready for it?"

"No." Of all people, he would understand that; because in the entire cabal besides Aden, he loved Maleck the most. And she couldn't say these things to Aden when he carried the guilt so heavily. "But the Bloodwights have never asked if people were ready for anything. They just take, and take, and take..." A slide of the whetstone punctuated each declaration, "until there's nothing left to give."

She paused, drawing a deep breath. This time it brought no calm.

"I hear you," Quill said. "No one ever asks us, do they? But we always end up fighting all their battles for them and losing what's important along the way. Baba Kallah. Julian. Helga. Kristoff for a while." His voice cracked. "And Pip. And now Maleck. I'm tired, Shei. Tired of seeing this cabal fall apart and always wondering if it's the last time."

"It won't be. We can't let it be." There was far too much at stake now: Cistine's training, the Chancellors on their heels, Maleck and Pippet lost to the wilds, and this reckless, mad mission to Kosai Talis. They had to have it in them—always one more storm, one more fight, one more escape and regroup. One more miracle to save the ones their empty hands were missing, to mend the holes in their hearts. To mend the world before the Bloodwights destroyed it.

Ashe flipped the whetstone case shut. "We'll get them back. Both of them. Whatever it takes, we bring them home."

Quill's eyes narrowed on her. "You're sure about that?"

"I'd stake my life on it."

"Good. So would I." He fished in the pouch at his hip, withdrew a glowing silver-blue flagon, and tossed it to her. Power hummed against Ashe's palm the moment the jar contacted, stirring old fears and new strengths she'd discovered during this war when wielding augments was not a choice, but a necessity.

She looked up sharply at him. "Where did you get this?"

"Poached a few from Kendar and Hana's private stash. I figured Sander wouldn't send his *valenar* and her guards off without some clout at their backs, and I was right."

"Is this for the raid in Kosai Talis?"

"That. But if seeing Pip in Selv Torfjel taught me anything, it's that the Bloodwights and their acolytes are drawn to that sort of power. They can sense it, and they'll come for it." His eyes met hers, and Ashe saw what daring, desperate attempt they were about to make. "It's always been you, you know that? Ever since he laid eyes on you on the Vey. If anyone can bring him back, it's you."

Ashe's hand flexed around the flagon, feeling the edges of that icy pulse. Then she tucked it into her armored pocket, close to her heart. "When the time is right, I'll use it."

"Good. And if it doesn't work for some stars-forsaken reason, *I'll* do it. Somewhere in this kingdom, there has to be something that wakes them up. That brings them back to us."

Hope fluttered in Ashe's chest, too flighty to be tamed. And maybe it shouldn't be; perhaps hope was the only thing that made this war worthwhile. The hope she'd felt that night before Selv Torfjel when Maleck acted like himself. The hope when Cistine came back to them, wreathed in power. The hope that came from putting one foot ahead of the other and realizing she was still alive despite all the despair that came against them. And as long as she lived, there was still a chance the world could be redeemed.

Clinging to hope with all her might, Ashe offered her fist to Quill. "Whatever it takes."

Smiling grimly, he knocked his knuckles against hers.

They reunited with the others in one of the centermost towers, where a high fire burned in a stone ring. Ashe's body hummed with the cool calm of weapons prepared, her body hanging with blades; Quill sauntered at her side, just as armed, just as focused and fierce. Between them, secret, stolen power lay dormant, waiting to be called.

If the others sensed it—if Cistine sensed the flagons they carried—it went unspoken. They all stared into the flames, hardly shifting when Quill slid into place beside Tatiana and Ashe beside Aden. Tatiana leaned her head on her *valenar's* shoulder, and he slipped an arm around her waist, drawing her close against him and kissing her hair.

The pause elongated, unbroken by even a hint of life or laughter from the adjacent towers. Ashe looked around the circle of solemn faces, taking note of downcast eyes and withdrawn features, and who was absent. "Where are Iri and Saychelle?"

Ariadne's gaze shot across the fire to Cistine, then flicked back to the flames. "On a mission from me. They're leaving Holmlond soon."

Ashe grimaced. "That doesn't seem wise. The Bloodwights were hunting the Order when we left Stornhaz."

"Yes. And the rest have gone into hiding." Secrets danced with the reflection of floating embers in Ariadne's dark eyes. "Saychelle and Iri are going to find them."

"Plenty of dangerous missions to go around." Mira's voice was chipper, but shadows stalked her face. Kendar and Hana were equally solemn at her sides.

"We'll be all right," Kristoff said with the same steady, indomitable faith as his sons. "This cabal is built strong."

Strong enough, Ashe hoped, to pull off this siege better than the last; and strong enough to reckon back what seemed beyond redemption.

CHAPTER
FORTY-SIX

THE CABAL DEPARTED Holmlond while darkness still hugged the world, a flurry of embraces in the foyer the only flair to their sendoff. Mira and Sander's trained wolf Vihar saw them off, his shaggy bulk leaned tight against Mira's hip. By his focused attention, it seemed one of Mira's fits must not be far off.

"Will you be all right?" Cistine asked when Mira's arms came around her last of all.

"Don't mind me. It's not the first time it's happened since we came here, nor will it be the last." Mira tugged her off a bit from the others, face graver than usual. "Cistine, listen to me. About this plan of yours...you should tell them as soon as possible. They all deserve to know, but especially Thorne."

Nervous energy sizzled across her scalp, too close to panic for her liking. "I *will* tell them, Mira. Soon. I promise."

Humming under her breath, Mira pressed a kiss to Cistine's brow. "I wish I could be there to see their faces when you do. Go carefully out there. I know I showed you the path, but I fear you having to walk it."

"We'll be fine." Cistine squeezed her friend one last time, hiding her face, and her fear, in the warmth of Mira's shoulder.

When they drew apart, Mira pressed a tooled leather pouch into her hands; power flickered from inside it, jouncing over her fingertips. "For Kosai Talis. And for your training after."

Cistine blinked, wide-eyed. "Mira, I can't—"

"You must." She nodded sharply. "It isn't much...two of earth, all we could spare. I wish we had healing augments, but those are in short supply everywhere."

Cistine swallowed, fists curling over the augment pouch, bringing it close to her chest. "I wish you did, too."

Mira cupped her cheek, eyes full of faith. "It will be enough. Go *carefully*. And know all our prayers and hopes go with you."

Then they were out in the cold of the Vaszaj Range, hurrying down the long path to meet Bresnyar where he waited on the black basalt, tail-tip twitching, wings folded back, eyes on the sky. It hung pregnant with clouds, a pale, thick stillness suffocating the mountains and rocking the deep cobalt sea. "Neither sound nor scent of the Balmond."

"Good." Ashe grazed her hand along the dragon's ribs, gripped his wing joint, and swung onto his back. "Let's go before that changes."

Cistine cast a last look back at Holmlond. She would miss the brief security of its strong towers and Mira's calming presence, her wisdom and counsel. And she would miss a world where she was not yet being hunted by the Courts as well as the Bloodwights. There was no place left for shelter or safety. They could not even risk returning to Holmlond once word of Cistine's nature began to spread.

This was truly farewell.

꩜

Kosai Talis was a distant suggestion on the map Mira had helped Tatiana memorize and trace, the sketching in the book itself far too important to risk bringing along near the Bloodwights. But the northern temple, at least, she'd captured perfectly, tucked away in the corner of the kingdom where the Vaszaj Range linked together with the Isetfells.

The journey took four days of intermittent flying, the air swarming colder and thicker, the winds churning relentlessly. Rime ice coated the trees on every cleft where they paused to rest; sleeping in snatches as travel permitted, Cistine woke forever cold, usually to Ashe or Thorne dusting snow off her shoulders to wake her.

The further north they flew, the more keenly aware she became of an insatiable pull within her chest. What began as a twitch of awareness the second day of flying was a steady thrum during the third. By the fourth, it was constant and keening, utterly unignorable.

Come. Find. Take.

Not like the call of base augments, not the whisper she'd spent most of her life ignoring. There was urgency to this summons, pulsing hotter with every mile they crossed until she could barely sleep for the unfamiliar call slamming like a second heartbeat against her breast. Almost as if the augment knew how near it was to falling into wicked hands.

On the fifth day, dawning clear and frigid, the cabal stirred from another bout of uneasy slumber to find Tatiana already awake, wrapped tight in Kristoff's armored cloak and studying the map by the sun's gaining light. Her sunken eyes met Cistine's across the small, dark crevice where they'd made camp, blocked from the wind by Bresnyar's bulk, and at that one look Cistine's nerves rattled like iron pots banging together.

"What's wrong?" she and Quill asked in unison.

Tatiana twirled the crudely-sketched map around on the frosted stone. "We're too close to fly anymore. If Mira's map was right, Kosai Talis is just over this ridge."

Kristoff and Thorne swapped grim glances, and Quill jammed a cinnamon stick between his teeth, rocking back on his heels. "Plan?"

"If I may," Aden offered, "Ariadne and I have plotted a strategy that should see us in and out of the mountain with minimal confrontation."

Thorne nodded. "By all means."

Aden took a knee beside Tatiana. "According to Mira's book, the risk doesn't lie just within the temple. The augment will be defended, but not by man or beast—and those are who we have to fear, current circumstances considered. It's a matter of reaching the vaults without being seen, without drawing their attention down to the depths."

"And once there," Ariadne crouched on Tatiana's other side, "remaining that way. Two could slip inside easier than eight."

"Thorne and me," Cistine said.

Aden nodded. "You'll enter by the sea. It's a long journey, but better than trying to creep over the mountains where the Bloodwights roost."

"And the rest of you?" Thorne asked.

"A layered defense," Ariadne said. "We divide our numbers with more strategy this time. Three rings to watch for Balmond and Bloodwight patrols. At the first hint of trouble, word travels to the others."

"Quill, Ariadne, and Tatiana will form the first ring of defense." Aden formed a tight circle with his finger close to the marking of Kosai Talis on the map. "My father and I will take the second. Ashe, Bresnyar..."

"Third," the Wingmaiden and her dragon chorused.

Aden hung his wrists from his knees. "If they catch wind of the vaults, we have three opportunities to slow them before they reach Cistine."

Slow them. Not stop them. Because given enough time, the Bloodwights would shred through their defenses no matter how well-layered. They would spread themselves thin not just to confuse the enemy, but to buy Cistine as much time to succeed as possible—even if not all of them survived.

Her heart keened in agony at the thought. Hoarsely, Thorne rasped, "Are we agreed? This is the strategy we take?"

The cabal all looked around at one another, brothers to sisters, fathers to sons. Cistine longed for them to say it wasn't—for Tatiana to dig in her heels and push back, for Ashe to scoff, for Kristoff to raise a counterpoint, for Quill to say he wasn't going to stand outside while she and Thorne went into danger alone. But one by one, they all nodded, sealing their fates for her sake, to buy her a chance in the vaults.

"If we don't get our hands on that flagon, the whole kingdom falls." Tatiana's glittering eyes held Cistine's, raked by the cool kiss of a pastel dawn. "There's no future in that."

"But I don't want a future without all of you in it," Cistine said. "So you stay alive. No matter what comes, *stay alive.*"

Aden took the map from Tatiana, and at her curt nod, fed it to their tiny fire. "I don't think any of us came here planning to do otherwise."

"Much as we love you, we're not looking for an excuse to fall on the next blade for you." Quill thumbed his nose and cast her a crooked, halfhearted smirk.

Cistine wanted desperately to believe them. But when she looked at Ashe, peering off toward the faraway horizon and grazing a hand over her pocket where an ice augment pulsed like a tiny, gentle heart, she wasn't so sure.

CHAPTER FORTY-SEVEN

I T WAS MORE than half a day's journey to the vault entrance, or so Tatiana claimed.

"Mira's map didn't give precise details," she said when she and Cistine hugged farewell. "Just follow your nose for trouble. I'm sure you'll find what you're looking for."

Cistine didn't deny it, which Thorne found both amusing and nerve-wracking. She hadn't told him yet, but he knew this strange augment called out to her; she'd rolled away from him frequently during the night to face northwest, a hand pressed to her heart like it fought to slide from her sternum and run toward some distant summons.

Some men shared their beloved's heart with another; some shared her with an ancient, godlike power.

He was glad to have the time alone together, however miserable the trek along the Black Coasts. This far north there was no shelter of columns or trees rising up from the shore, and the wind whipping off the sea stung like shards of ice. Thorne kept himself between it and Cistine, breaking the merciless breeze and chilly spray, and listened to her chatter nervously about the life she'd lived while they were apart: the state of her kingdom in the absence of Jad's threats, the endless meetings and politicking he found so foreign and fascinating.

She fell quiet after some time, hands trapped in her pockets, gaze searching the sky and sea for threats. "I'm sorry for going on and on about matters of royalty when you...I mean, when your title is..."

Pain twisted in Thorne's chest. He'd tried with all his might not to wonder what would become of his position in Kanslar Court after the war. Would the other Chancellors see his choices for what they were—sanity in the face of wartime desperation? Or would they convict him of treason and send him down the same road as his father?

"It will be what it will be," he said, as much for his consolation as Cistine's. "I need no title to accomplish what we came here to do, and that's what matters."

She halted so abruptly she stumbled, and Thorne threw out an arm across her front to catch her. Her fingers gripped his sleeve, twining deep, her gaze cast to the storming sea. "Thorne."

Following her stare, he saw nothing at first that ought to have drawn her eye. But after a moment the tide shifted, inhaling the whitecap away from the shoreline, and where the black cliffs slid into the water he spotted a strangely articulate slope: unremarkable even now, and he would not have noticed it at all had Cistine not spotted it first. But the riveting of her gaze on that rock told him everything.

"Not a natural landslide," he said.

She shook her head. "Earth augment. This must be where the old Order collapsed the tunnels."

Thorne wondered if she could sense some latent spark where the power had touched. Placing faith in that, he strode to the edge of the black cliff and crouched, peering down the slope; it was steep, the bottom smoothed and sealed by countless years of tide, but halfway up, the incline became jagged again, gaps winking between stone and basalt. "We'll have to climb down. It might take a day or more, but I think we can tunnel through."

Cistine knelt beside him, gripping the ledge, looking over the side at the sea. "Aden said they needed three to spread out their formation. We'll have plenty of time."

Chills chased one another down Thorne's back, leaping from divot to divot among his scars. They were really going into this place built to keep out common men, to bury a power so mighty none ought to wield it. And his Wildheart would be the one to lay hands on it.

Bitten with frantic energy, he straightened, shed his armored overcoat and the ration pack they'd brought from Holmlond, and offered his hand to Cistine. "Plenty of time, but none to waste. Let's go."

They toiled along the stone slope through what little daylight remained, digging a straight and careful hole through the landslide. Navigating the wave-slick rock was the most treacherous part, and Thorne kept one eye on Cistine, mindful of her balance as well as his own.

Their progress hardly felt like enough when they conceded it was too dark for safe work. They clambered out, not up, at Cistine's request, tucking onto a spit of shore alongside the rocks, facing the sea. Thorne built a driftwood fire, at little risk of being spotted with the waves ahead and the cliff at their backs, and Cistine laid out their rations. Neither of them spoke until the flames leaped to life, and Cistine shrieked with delight when the blue-green light stroked the angles of her face.

Thorne smirked. "I take it driftwood fires aren't customary in Talheim."

"No, but they ought to be!" Hands clapped to her cheeks, she stared into the flames. "Thorne, this is *beautiful*."

Dusting off his palms, he dropped onto the shore beside her. "The salt in the wood makes it burn this color. Pass me the jerky, would you?"

They shared the rations, watching the thin film of sunset's last light drain into the western horizon until all they knew of the world was teal flame and stars peeking through the shroud of fading storms above. Then Cistine bent forward, looking around him at the slope. "This would be so much easier if we used an earth augment to burrow through."

Thorne stopped chewing. "You have one?"

"I have two from Mira." She patted the augment pouch, a permanent fixture at her side. "Fire as well, and darkness and lightning left over from what I stole in Selv Torfjel. But I want to save them for when we train."

That was wise; they could dig through rock with their bare hands, but the training he'd promised would only come about with the power of the gods in their hands, and they had precious little of that. Propping himself forward, Thorne scrubbed a hand through his hair. "We may have to consider raiding an augment storehouse if it means the difference in your training."

Cistine's face twisted. "But there are so few to go around already."

"I know. But the only other choice is an enemy camp, and after this..." He let his gaze wander back to the cliffs—not only a doorway to these vaults of legend, but the opening of another door entirely into a world where everyone's focus truly was on capturing and killing his *selvenar*. "We'll want to stay as far from the Bloodwights as possible."

Cistine dragged her knees to her chest and laced her arms around her ankles. "I'll find a way to make do with these six, somehow."

Thorne watched her sidelong, her stubborn will written into the curves around her mouth, the groove in her brow. Seeing her by starlight never failed to make his heart clamor; it was always the same as that night beside the Nior River when he'd taught her the stars and glimpsed the woman she was beneath the dresses and jewels. The warrior princess built of a different strength, who'd ordered him out of her way if he wouldn't help her, who stood for her people when she had so much to lose, who teased him about being a child and looked on his kingdom's way of life with fascination rather than her ancestors' fear.

She caught him staring now, and with a shy half-smile she tucked her hair behind her ear. "What are you thinking about, Starchaser?"

His chest ached with love and worry. "That I'm fortunate to have earned the heart of Talheim's princess. And that I'm glad to go with you into this and every danger."

Cistine laughed. "It's a rare man who's *grateful* to chase his betrothed into peril. Most would try to stop her." Her thumb grazed the betrothal ring he'd given her on Darlaska. "Thorne...there's something I've been meaning to ask you."

His stomach gave an uneasy lurch for no reason he could name. "Then ask. You know I'll keep nothing from you."

She breathed out a shaky laugh, her thumb separating from the ring's black band, gaze fixed across the waves for several endless seconds. When she swiveled toward him at last, her eyes shimmered. "Will you tell me the story of Sillakove again?"

Not what she'd wanted to ask, clearly. But he could see how much the true question distressed her, setting her hands shaking and tightening her jaw, so he didn't press. He merely lifted his arm. "Come here."

She crawled across the rocks and settled into his side, head tucked against his chest, arms tight around his waist, holding onto him like he was the driftwood and she the sailor clinging for her life in the raging sea.

So he told her again the story of the first Starchaser and the Wayfinders—a tale Baba Kallah had read him until he'd learned it by heart. The waves took the words and washed them out into the depths, making them a part of the world, infinite and sundering in shadows.

Part of the world he and his Wildheart were fighting for.

CHAPTER FORTY-EIGHT

Cistine's dreams were uneasy again, full of shadow-ridden halls and an endless pulse of power waking her before the sun fully rose; but even then, she was already alone. She bolted upright at once, sleep forgotten, heart crashing like the nearby surf. "Thorne?"

"Up here."

His reply came with the sound of shifting rocks, and Cistine peeled her damp hair from her cheeks and mouth, squinting up the slope at him; he was already hard at work, and had been for some time, judging by his sweating shirtlessness. His many scars flickered in the early-morning glow, joined now by the thick braid of tissue along his middle and the six diagonal slices rendered across his chest, woven in among his Atrasat inkings. She could hardly remember when he was so reluctant to show her those wounds; there was no fear in him now while he bent and hefted another rock, chucking it off the crater they'd dug and casting it into the sea.

"Content to admire the view?" he teased. "Or did you plan to help?"

She stuck out her tongue, shed her jacket and rolled her sleeves, and leaped the narrow channel between shore and slope to put her hands to work alongside his.

They spent all that day and the next in bouts of work and rest, sharing waterskins and rations and talking when labor permitted, and somewhere during the second day Cistine decided she could be content with a lifetime of this. No thrones, no Judgement Seats, nothing but hard work during the day and Thorne's arms around her at night, his voice rumbling from the cavity of his chest beneath her ear, telling her stories until sleep swept her off like the tide.

But life had not asked her what she was content with; the call reminded her of that at dawn on the third day, when she and Thorne mounted the rock pile to gaze at the progress they'd made: a decent amount, but not enough. And they were out of time.

A glance found her frustration and hopelessness reflected in Thorne's eyes; arms cinched tightly, he stared at the stone heap as if by the power of his glare alone, he could pulverize the obstacle in their way. "We have no choice. Use it."

Breathing in the inevitability and breathing out defeat, Cistine retrieved one of the earth flagons Mira had gifted her. Just a bit would do; she would still have the rest for training and wouldn't have to raid an enemy camp or a friend's storehouse for more, she hoped. She *prayed*.

With that prayer still hanging on her lips, she uncorked the flagon and unleashed a thin thread of power into her hand.

It was strange how the augment brought both comfort and disquiet; how her nerves calmed yet hummed brighter, how her muscles loosened and leaped. Motioning Thorne back to the sturdier stretch of the slope, she mustered that small kernel of power for all it was worth, and *punched*.

Rock, sand, and basalt caved inward, the impact setting Cistine back on her heels so sharply Thorne lunged to catch her shoulders. Through the spindrift and spray, she squinted and searched.

She had not broken through. Cursing, she dealt out more of the augment and took another wild swing at the rock.

More cracked. More gave. Still more was required. In moments she was hitting mindlessly, like throwing rogue blows into Quill's palms or hitting the strung-up sandbag in the Warden's training hall. Blast after blast of power sent more of the slope crumbling, but never enough; more power wasted, sacrificed for a single step, as if she and her cabal hadn't sacrificed enough. As if Pippet wasn't gone, and Maleck, and Maltadova. As if she was not hunted, coming here to give up what little safety she retained to keep the balance from tipping irrevocably in the Bloodwights' favor.

You cannot outrun sacrifice. You do not walk away from war with everything you ever wanted…that's not how any of this works.

With a bellow of rage, Cistine shattered the flagon completely, brought her hands together, and slammed them against the bow where slope met cliffside; the impact rattled through her teeth, her head, her bones, and with a mighty crack the rest of the stone severed, bursting inward in a projectile spray.

She did not register the sound buried beneath the roar of breaking earth, the dull metal whine and grind of something manmade coming from within the hole, until Thorne shouted her name, gripped the back of her neck, and slung her down against the slope, his body shielding hers. A volley of spear-sized bolts, tar-black and dagger-headed, launched above them and streaked across the sea. From under Thorne's arm, she watched them go, a specter pain hurtling along her bloodpaths in tandem when they finished their arc and dropped one-by-one far out into the water.

To go such a distance, so straight and true…they would've slammed straight through her armor, through her body, and out the other side.

Panting, she wiggled from under Thorne's bulk, sitting up on her knees to stare into the black maw yawning before them and the shadowed outline of a turret bonded to the stone walls by thick silver wire, its mechanisms released by the falling stone. "I suppose that's as warm a welcome as we can expect in this place." She offered her shaking hand to Thorne and helped him up. "Thank you."

"My pleasure." He didn't look pleased in the least, staring ahead into the darkness. "I'd say we found the vaults."

He was right, proven not just by the trap that had awaited them but by the call crying along Cistine's bones. Her mouth felt full of sparks, tingling and buzzing, and she licked her lips. "There's no turning back now."

They crossed the wreckage of rock in two strides and dropped into the tunnel beyond, sidling past the empty turret. Cistine palmed her hair from her sweat-soaked brow, peering ahead where the darkness deepened, and Thorne's hand grazed the small of her back—a fleeting and gentle comfort. "I'm with you, Wildheart."

Chills cascaded down the back of her neck and across her arms, and she whipped her head toward him. "What did you say?"

He frowned. "I'm right here. You know I always am, don't you?"

Her pulse sped as she took in the muraled walls and high roof, the same as her dream the night she and her father had watched the storm breaking in the far north from the Citadel balcony. As if she was meant to come to this place; as if the gods themselves had guided every step from there to this tunnel, this vault and the power waiting at the end of it, so she could protect it from those who would abuse it. Those who thought themselves new gods and sought to overthrow the true ones.

Power and purpose banded her spine. If the True God Ariadne so trusted was walking beside her in this darkness, and Thorne was on her other side, she would not be afraid. She was born for this.

"I know you're with me," she said, to Thorne and to them.

Something cracked in the gloom, and Cistine jumped; but it was not a trap set off or a flagon shattering somewhere ahead. Thorne had brought a ghostlamp along from Holmlond, and now he broke it open to shed ultramarine light along their path.

She flashed him a grateful smile, and he smirked in return, clipping the ghostlamp onto his belt and drawing his sabers. Cistine followed suit, sword in hand.

"Ready, Wildheart?" Thorne asked.

"Ready, Starchaser."

Steel in hand and heart-to-heart, they entered the vaults.

CHAPTER
FORTY-NINE

TATIANA HAD NEVER been so grateful for three days of walking. She needed that long to acclimate to the notion of battle again, and to find steadiness in the normalcy of this mad quest. No different from wagon raids on the Vingete Vey, no worse than scouting missions or the Izten Torkat or Oadmark or a thousand other dangerous things she'd done for this cabal, for Sillakove Court. She had nothing left to fear, after all. No life to defend within her. If she shattered, she shattered alone.

But she would not. She was stitching herself back together with every step, a tinker and a fixer, a patchwork woman woven of iron threads and fragments sharp enough to cut any enemy who dared lay a hand on her or on her beloved who still lived.

There was no one else she would've rather made this dangerous journey with than steady Ariadne and fierce Quill. They were the two parts of the mountain beneath her feet, the solid stone and the wild hoarfrost, bracing her and pushing her on even if they didn't know about the rage in her, or the sorrow—twin wolves taking turns gnawing on her heart.

Speaking to Mira in Holmlond with Cistine gripping her hand the whole time had been a comfort and a great help, more than she'd expected. She'd left that chamber feeling steadier, less loathing of herself, less like the world owed her a portion of its grief to match her own. But then the fire had kindled while she lay awake their last night in the tower, stretched out beside Quill with her hand on his beating heart, turning from wet rage to a dry, burning fury—and it would not abate. The anger turned outward, away from her own failures, toward the Bloodwights and this war and even toward Pippet and that cruel dagger doomed to take one of Tatiana's loves no matter what she did.

This loss was not Tatiana's fault. It was the Bloodwights, their irreverence for any life that did not serve their wicked purposes. And she couldn't wait to steal something precious from *them*, to make them feel a morsel of the helpless agony they'd inflicted on her when they took Pippet and twisted her and put that choice in Tatiana's hands: Quill's life, or their child's.

The anger carried her step by step up the mountain, burning so hot she wondered if she could melt the snow beneath her boots, if Quill and Ariadne felt the scorch when they walked beside her through the perilous climes to the inner ring. Anything that came toward Kosai Talis to intercept Cistine, if Ashe and Bresnyar or Aden and Kristoff could not stop it, would have to face the three of them. If it came from within, they would resist it first. And Tatiana Dawnstar had enough fire raging within her to burn the entire ancient temple and all its augment-worshipping invaders to cinders.

She had no fear left when they reached the broad cleft Ariadne had spotted from afar during their three-day hike, only searing determination while she and Quill stood-by-side in the divot between mountain slopes and looked up the span toward Kosai Talis. It was a neglected, abandoned relic, ancient ramparts perched on a crop of snow-spattered rock, less formidable than Kalt Hasa or Detlyse Halet. There wasn't even the sense of world-ending decay she'd felt below Siralek. She defied the simple amalgam of stone and snow with a glare, folding her arms. "Now what?"

"Now we wait." Ariadne drummed her fingers on the hilts of the knives belted at her waist. "Stars willing, Cistine and Thorne will enter and escape the vaults by the entrance at the Agerios, and we will have no need to fight."

"The Bloodwights are up there." Quill's voice was shallow, his breaths puffing too quickly. "Do you hear them?"

Tatiana strained, rocking forward on the tips of her toes to stand an inch nearer to the temple. Nothing at first; then an intermittent, crackling *thud* reached her ears, like a fist pummeling clean through stone.

"They're dismantling the temple from within." Indignation rattled Ariadne's voice.

"What does that matter?" Tatiana muttered. "It's nothing but a ruin."

"It's our history. *My* history. I care very much how all these ancient temples have become prisons and fighting arenas, if they haven't been left to decay."

Guilt clawed at Tatiana's throat. It wasn't just this temple Ariadne felt for; it was Nygaten, raided at the beginning of winter for the schematics to help build the siege towers that had taken Stornhaz. It was the *visnprests* and *prestas* slaughtered there because they didn't know how to properly defend themselves. And it was the ones captured when the City of a Thousand Stars fell, and what might still be happening to them...what might happen to Saychelle and Iri if they were caught on their quest.

"You're right," she said, and Quill's brows rose. "They trample over everything the gods hold sacred, everything Valgard stands for. And they deserve to have their heads cut off for it."

"Well, on that cheerful remark." Quill whistled quietly, sending Faer up in a flurry of wings toward the nearest crag. "I'm going to have myself a look around. Send Faer if anything's coming."

Tatiana snagged his hand and yanked him back around to face her, pressing her lips to his in parting, drinking down his breath, his heat, his reckless courage. "Be *careful*, Featherbrain."

"Always am." He nodded to Ariadne and launched himself at the craggy rocks. Nimble and swift as a strike of lightning, he was up the hillside and out of sight.

All was quiet for a time, while Ariadne shifted for a better vantage point and Tatiana paced. It was all she could do; she couldn't bear to look after Quill, to imagine him meeting a *mirothadt* pack or a Bloodwight while he climbed out of her sight. She should've gone with him. Should've watched his back. And yet...

"What did you want to ask me?" Ariadne's question knifed through her raging thoughts, bringing her to a halt.

"I don't know what you're talking about."

Ariadne's brows arched. "You sent Quill off alone to spy on the most powerful enemy we've ever faced. You would only do that if you had something to ask me that wasn't meant for his ears."

Trust Ariadne to see her mind, as usual—the reason she'd done everything in her power to push her away during her last, most desperate drinking binge. Like Quill, Ariadne always stood so close she could practically see through Tatiana. "Do you think children go to Cenowyn or Nimmus?"

Ariadne blinked, both brows rising now. "You know the legends as well as I do. Few people are worthy of eternal rest. You remember what a terror Pippet was even at two years old."

Tatiana couldn't even muster a snort at the thought of Quill's sister, a mischievous and eager shadow plucking feathers from Faer's tail and dropping glass figurines from the cottage attic just to see them burst in prism shards on the ground below. All of it paled in the memory of that same girl's knife plunging into her, ripping her future apart. "I meant the children who don't have the chance to be one or the other. The ones who are never given a choice."

"You mean the ones the Bloodwights take?"

Tatiana shrugged.

"I've asked myself that often, ever since I first met Maleck," Ariadne admitted. "Had he died at fourteen, how would the gods have judged him? A boy corrupted, sent down a path he didn't choose, forced to commit atrocities in a war he never asked to partake in." She leaned her head back on the rock where she reclined, gazing at the faraway temple, sadness stark in her eyes. "What I decided is that the True God I serve is not seeking the smallest cause to cast people through the Sable Gates. No one truly knows, Tati...no one has entered Nimmus or Cenowyn and returned to tell us if one is truly harder to attain than the other. But I believe there's far more mercy in this world and all the ones beyond it than we comprehend. Mercy for boys sent to wars not their choosing. Mercy for those who slip into harms because the weight of life is too great to bear. And mercy for children who never had a choice."

Every word prodded Tatiana's glassy emotions harder and harder until a tear slipped down her cheek; she batted it away, swallowing a curse. She'd never been one for errant crying, but these last weeks had changed her in unexpected ways—perhaps irrevocable ones.

Ariadne shrugged up from the rock and crossed the cleft to lay both hands on her shoulders. "We *will* find Pippet, *Malatanda*. Somehow, we will bring her home. Do not give up that hope yet."

Tatiana nodded, turning her gaze back to the temple high above. She didn't even know what she would say or do if they did save her, if she had to face again the girl who was once like her own sister...who'd killed the child for whom she cried.

She didn't have long to dwell on that; in a shower of gravel, Quill skidded down the hillside to join them, landing lithe and graceful next to Tatiana and straightening, gaze fixed to the east. Faer swooped to his shoulder, talons tight, body flaring forward with a span of his inky wings. The hair rose on the back of Tatiana's neck. "What did you see?"

"I'm not sure." Quill slid his sabers from their sheaths, giving a jerk of his chin toward the horizon. "I don't like the look of those clouds."

Tatiana squinted in the direction he pointed, but she saw nothing out of the ordinary for the mountains at this time of year: ice, snow, a heavy white sky, and a thin bank of stormheads in the far east.

Ariadne stepped up to Tatiana's other side, knives in hand. "Storms don't often roll from east to west."

"Mmhm." Quill prowled along the rock ledge, watching that distant tempest. Shudders skittered down Tatiana's spine, and she drew her sabers as well, blood singing with adrenaline and battle-lust.

Let them come. She was here to fight for her kingdom, her people, their future. And if it began on this hill, with Quill and Ariadne beside her, then so be it.

The enemy had made this war personal. And now they would lose it.

CHAPTER
FIFTY

THE COLD IN Kosai Talis went deeper than mountain frost. If not for the heat that surged whenever Cistine remembered the blast of those spear-like arrows—ballista bolts, Thorne called them—she might've been shaking too wildly to hold her weapons. But somehow the friction of hot and cold brought balance, and in that she found her stride, picking her way through the temple's first long, gloomy hall. Thorne was silent beside her, primed for the release of another weapon somewhere in the dark.

"I don't know why they left the vaults standing." Cistine's voice echoed strangely in the ribbed corridor. "Why not bury the way to the augment entirely?"

"Either they feared instability in the structure would bring it down in time, breaking the flagon and unleashing its contents, or—" Thorne lunged forward, striking an arm out to bar the way, but Cistine had already stopped, catching sight of the thing revealed by the slant of ghostlight ahead: a sheer drop into nothing, a hole across the path that changed the timbre of echoes in the dark. "Or they thought they might need it someday. Which gives us some hope, at least, that the way between here and there is navigable."

"If you have wings, maybe," Cistine muttered. "Or a wind augment."

"Or climbing strength." Thorne nodded to the wall. "Up and across, *Logandir*."

It was a testament to how much she'd overcome in Valgard that climbing unbound over an abyss in the foundation of a temple did not frighten her anymore. She and Thorne scuttled along the wall and dropped on the opposite side, picking up the path again in the dark, only slightly more winded than before. "Do you think they suspected the Bloodwights would come?"

Thorne's armor creaked when he shrugged. "Ariadne believes the gods send premonitions from time to time. It's possible they showed the old Order what waited ahead."

That wasn't difficult to believe when every layer of this place reminded her so strongly of her dreams.

They left the corridor at last, stepping into a broad cavern peppered with archways and columns, ice-rimmed pools, and stalactites dripping into them. Mineral deposits in the stone floor forged a rippling pattern like starlight trails threading into the distant shadows at the cavern's aft. There were glowworms here like the ones in Selv Torfjel, wrapped around those rock colonnades and seeping from the distant roof, painting long stretches of the room in lurid purple, green, and teal. It would've been lovely, were they not creeping under their enemy's feet.

"Go carefully," Thorne warned, and with a swift nod Cistine left the corridor mouth and picked her way into the midst of the mineral deposits framing the floor.

She made it only two steps before the *twang* of a firing mechanism sliced her ears. Thorne's shout of her name disappeared in the echo of shrieking steel and a brush of wind like the Undertaker's scythe cleaving toward her neck. Cistine dove forward and rolled, dove and rolled again when a second weapon gasped alive, and then she ran, not looking back or checking her stride while metal banged and echoed behind her. She flew with all her might to the nearest column in the colonnade, lunged up onto its pedestal in two bounds, and whirled, placing her back to the rock. Clinging to it with both hands, she looked down on the destruction she'd narrowly escaped.

The mineral streaks in the floor were gaps full of glowworms, the stones between them pressure plates. And from those fissures in the rock, steel jaws like bear traps had clamped shut at the weight of her boots, shattering the stone in their mighty bite. If she'd hesitated a moment longer, they would've shattered *her*.

Thorne stood on the other side of them, wide-eyed, chest heaving as if he'd been the one running for his life. Cistine held his gaze until her racing pulse slowed and she could muster enough voice to call out, "Walk on the traps *exactly* where I did."

Jaw tight, he nodded. While he began the agonizing procession from cavern mouth to colonnades, Cistine shuffled around the stone's rounded edge to peer ahead, but there was nothing to suggest what other horrors waited there.

Boots scraped rock, and Thorne vaulted up to join her, bracing his forearm on the column above her head and sheltering her body in the shadow of his while he caught his breath. He radiated heat, the smell of exertion and treated leather wafting from his clothes.

"Isn't this exciting," he deadpanned, and Cistine laughed breathlessly.

"Riveting! We should come here more often."

His thumb brushed her jawline, and he squinted aside into the gloom. "I say we follow the colonnade row for now. It seems safer than the floor."

"Lead on, Chancellor."

He flicked her nose this time, then coiled and leaped to the next pedestal. With a silent prayer, Cistine sprang after him.

The going was quicker along the column bases, circumventing the traps laid into the floor, but it was too easy to last. This respite was simply meant to lull them into a sense of safety; when Cistine landed on the second-to-last pedestal behind Thorne and felt the stone buckle under their weight, heard the resounding *snap* pierce the cavern, she was ready.

The rock gave out beneath their feet, but Cistine was already moving, snatching Thorne by the collar and yanking him away. With the column buckling at its foundations and plunging down sideways, they sprinted across the cavern floor, away from its reach. But the tremble of its quaking loosed stalactites from the ceiling that arrowed down like riving fangs, smashing into the stone floor. Cistine and Thorne separated, whirling and dodging the crumbling column, the falling stalactites, and the mechanisms awakened by the smash of rock and mineral on the floor.

Ballista bolts. Steel traps. It was all a blur of things that wanted to kill them, and Cistine wove into that dance hardly thinking, following Thorne in a wild dash and pattern of leaps over the dangerous floor, sliding under the column's edge just before it finished its descent, then spinning away from the last two stalactites that shuddered free from the high ceiling and smashed apart on either side of them.

Painted in stone dust and burst glowworm grime, Cistine and Thorne huffed and stared at one another.

"Starting to regret coming with me?" Cistine asked.

He straightened slowly with a crooked smile, sliding a hand back through his hair. "You're joking. This is the most fun I've had in months."

She kicked his haunch in passing and plucked the ghostlamp from his belt, holding it up to the path. The old Order, it seemed, was confident the first cavern would be enough to kill anyone who came seeking the augment; or perhaps they'd decided anyone who survived its treachery deserved pity and reprieve. Nothing waited through the next pocket of shadows but the entrance to a second corridor, this one so tight Thorne had to hunch his shoulders to fit inside.

"The Bloodwights would have a much easier time with this," Cistine murmured as they shuffled along. "All those augments in their bodies..."

"I've been wondering about that." Thorne's gloves scraped the rock walls on both sides. "It's not worth wasting a flagon to find out, but I suspect there are elements of the world woven into this rock that would stop an augment from breaking through."

"Like the wall around Stornhaz?" Cistine mused. "No wonder they haven't found these vaults yet. They're using flagons to make things easier, but flagons themselves can't break through." Thorne grunted suddenly, a pained sound quickly silenced, and Cistine began to turn back. "What's wrong?"

"Do *not* stop." His voice knifed the narrow hall.

Chills rippled up her arms. "Thorne, what—?"

"The tunnel is narrowing. I can feel it."

Her pulse pinched in her chest and she raised the ghostlight as high as she could, casting a glow on the way ahead. More shadow. More tunnel.

Another curse, and then Thorne growled, "Go, Cistine, *go now!*"

She burst into a run. Now that she wasn't speaking, she could hear the guttural moan of tremendous pressure descending on the tunnel from above, a trap they hadn't realized they'd sprung unleashing a landslide above, crawling down into the walls. Though she was smaller than Thorne, she felt the weight of the rock closing in, too, the tunnel shrinking around them. Their armor scraped viciously on the stone with every stride.

The fear of being buried alive chased out all common sense. Cistine screamed and barreled forward with all her might, ghostlamp stretched ahead, seeking any glint of hope, any sign the end was near.

There. A flash of wider darkness, the tunnel mouth bowing in ahead of them. She reached back blindly, grabbed Thorne's hand, and dragged him with her; her heart stammered and bucked defiantly when his broad shoulders snagged and his gasps of pain became almost constant.

With a violent roar, the tunnel roof gave way behind them, spilling soil and stone in their wake. Cistine burst into the open, her hand ripping free of Thorne's, plunging her to her knees. She lurched up and spun back to find him caught, hips wedged in the gap, struggling to push free.

Swearing wildly, she gripped his shoulder in one hand and his belt in the other, and with a hard twist and thrust, helped him wrench out. He slid free of the hole just as the largest boulder smashed down where his legs had bucked loose a second before, sealing the tunnel mouth. His momentum drove them both down, and he landed on top of her, flattening her to the rock, his hand barely catching the back of her head in time to spare her a hard impact with the floor. His brow met her collarbone, panicked pants fanning the side of her neck. "Thank you for that."

She wiggled her hands loose to grip his hips. "Are you all right?"

"Just...give me a moment."

She was content to do that, though she feared he could feel the heat radiating from her face in this compromising position. After several moments—what felt like hours, and not entirely unpleasant ones—Thorne rocked back on his heels and pulled her upright. Together they stared at the tunnel behind them.

Utterly sealed. Not a hint of air seeping through.

"You were saying," she whimpered, "about augments not having any power here..."

"Later." Thorne lurched up, offering his hand. "Let's see what we have to conquer still before we search for a way out."

Later. Later. When had that become her perpetual mantra for all things she was too frightened or overwhelmed to deal with yet? All the things she'd delayed would catch up with her eventually; and knowing her luck, it would happen all at once.

But even that thought was meant for later. She scooped up the ghostlamp and turned to stand side-by-side with Thorne, studying their surroundings: a narrower room than the first, but the shadows were deeper, clinging to the hewn rock walls and masking the vaulted ceiling. Whatever lay wrapped within that darkness, no glowworms dared make a home here, and the ghostlight didn't cut far enough to reveal what lay ahead.

But they had no choice, nowhere to go but forward.

"Ready?" Cistine murmured, and Thorne dipped his head. She sidled out, keeping a careful watch for pressure plates or any change in the stone's surface below her feet, ears attuned for the sound of weapons cutting free. She halted only when the ghostlamp's glow painted a ledge before her, and then she raised it high, shedding light across an empty chasm. The walls continued on, but the floor ended in a clean slice—an earth augment's work. Far in the distance, she glimpsed the suggestion of another side. "What now? Do we climb the walls again?"

"Cistine." Thorne's tone was strange—hard, even, and forcibly calm. "Do not take another step. Do not move."

Her heart jolted when she lowered her gaze, but nothing seemed out of the ordinary. Thorne was a shadow at her left, moving into her line of sight several paces away. He crouched, fingertips scraping the stone at level with her boot, and only when she rotated the ghostlamp toward him did she see it: a wire, hair-fine, the exact same shade as the rock, snaking from the wall and across the ledge. She followed it by the glint of ghostlight on its razor-thin edge until it vanished underneath her boots.

Thorne's gloved fingers assessed the line with the lightest touch, tension feathering his jaw. Then he braced his hand on the floor and looked left and right, around at the walls, up at the ceiling. He strode back to the tunnel mouth, scooped up a stone fallen loose from the landslide, and positioned himself to her left again; then, deft and true, he flicked the rock up toward the ceiling.

The echo that returned was not rock on rock; it was rock on steel, loose and whispering.

Cold sweat soaked Cistine's palms, and the ghostlamp wobbled in her hand. "*Thorne...*"

"I'm thinking."

A sob rolled up her throat. There were *knives* up there, steel ready to crash down on their heads if she so much as shifted her weight. And they had no escape, the tunnel sealed at their backs.

She'd brought them both down here to die.

She couldn't even form an apology past the knot of terror lodged in her chest while Thorne returned to the collapsed corridor and grabbed a handful of stones. He flung the first a bit farther, at a different angle, cocking his head at the damning report of stone on blade. Then the second, higher, farther. Then the third.

At the fourth, rock and rock cracked together.

Thorne dusted off his hands, measuring the distance with his gaze from the ledge forward, then from side to side. "Do you trust me, Cistine?"

"You know the answer to that!" Terror made her voice shrill.

"Look at me," he said softly, and she did, angling her body but keeping her boots flat. "I will not let you die here, Wildheart."

Only her lips bitten together kept the sob from escaping now. She nodded, and Thorne took a step back.

"When I say, take your feet off the wire and step toward the ledge."

"But those *blades*—"

"Trust me."

Cistine swallowed her protests and fixed her gaze on him—those earnest blue eyes, that face full of determination—and nodded.

Thorne rocked his weight and settled his stance like a man preparing for a race. "Brace."

She turned and coiled her muscles, focusing on nothing but Thorne's steady presence behind her. Not the blades, not the black chasm below. Just him.

"Move."

Yelling strength down into her shaking muscles, Cistine sprang off the wire. It withdrew in a singing shriek, and the clatter of falling blades filled her ears—dozens of chains stringing free and bolting down toward their heads. Thorne's weight smashed into her from behind, his arm looping her waist, and with a mighty thrust he shoved them both from the ledge.

The rock on their left and right shattered outward and twin battering rams hurtled from the hewn divots in the walls, wicked iron poles bashing together with a *crack* so loud it drove ringing pain into Cistine's skull. She and Thorne slammed into the rams gut-first, driving the wind from them both. Thorne's arm tightened around her, holding her in place against the iron while her hands found purchase of their own.

They hung there for endless, horrifying seconds while blades dropped and bobbed, riving the air just above their heads, so close the tips stroked Cistine's hair. Feet dangling over nothing, a sheer drop to death's embrace, they clung on side-by-side until the blades stopped falling.

At last, Thorne panted, "Up."

Cistine scrambled over the carved edge of the ram, and Thorne lunged up beside her, snagging one of the fallen blades by its chain and stepping up on the crossguard like a foothold. Then he swept her up against him and shoved off of the battering ram's edge.

Their momentum and height sent them careening forward through a hacking forest of steel they could not avoid. Pain erupted along Cistine's limbs, and Thorne's muscles spasmed as the blades whipped through his armor; there was no dodging them, nor the second set of rams that broke through the walls, hurtling toward them while they swung.

Cistine reached up wildly to snag hold of the chain above them, lessening the pressure on Thorne's arm; as one, they put their feet to the battering rams that slammed together and rebounded before them, vaulting up the rounded iron edge and over the top. Then, with a desperate leap, they snagged another bladed chain and hurtled past another set of rams, out from under the space where Thorne's third rock had struck—gliding through empty air to the other side.

The moment her feet grazed the opposite ledge, Cistine pivoted, heel sweeping the rock and metal chain chafing her hand, spinning with her back to Thorne's to scan the darkness behind them while he searched out threats ahead.

Nothing. The cavern fell quiet, the last blade and battering ram rattling silent on their joists.

For a moment, shoulders resting together, they caught their breath. Blood dribbled down Cistine's arms, and Thorne's breaths wheezed slightly. Carefully, she separated her fingers from the chain and turned to wrap his waist, ducking under his arm to look ahead with him; her stomach plunged so steeply she feared she would be sick.

A door was set into the rock before them, strong and iron-banded, thrice-sealed with chain and lock. Impenetrable, by the look of it.

But they had to get through. Because that wild, frantic *thing* hurling itself around her ribcage, that guttural, desperate call, was right on the other side of this door.

Thorne stepped forward first, running his hands along the chains. Cistine moved in his wake, weighing the locks themselves, knocking on the metal. "This feels like ordinary iron. Were they harvesting *Svarkyst* ore yet when these were forged?"

"We're about to find out." Thorne drew a saber. "Pull that chain as taut as you can."

She tugged out the lock as far as it would go, and Thorne rested his blade to the links, pressing lightly. Then he hefted and stroked down.

Sparks spat, and the impact vibrated through Cistine's arms straight into her shoulders. She hissed at the whine of metal on metal, and Thorne's gaze leaped to her.

"I'm all right." Centering her stance, she pulled the lock. "Try again."

It took six blows to the same spot for the links to give; Thorne whooped quietly under his breath when they shattered, and Cistine drew out the next, then the next. They unthreaded the chains, slung them off into the chasm, and put their shoulders to the door.

"On my count." Thorne numbered down from three, and they surged against the wood and iron with all their might, shoving the heavy doors inward with a low, endless grind of metal on rock that crescendoed the cacophony of pain in Cistine's head.

Then it was over. They were through.

The room beyond was so utterly ordinary, it took Cistine completely off guard. No traps to be seen, no hint of a compromised floor or walls set with rams and blades. There was only a simple locked chest in the very center, its banded lid lined with runes.

It was the origin of the call screaming through Cistine's body.

She and Thorne prowled around it, examining it from every edge and angle before they approached. Skin rearing with endless chills, Cistine set the ghostlamp on the lid, shedding light across the markings so she could read them aloud. "*Hval en dermattae kmar hed var.*"

She glanced up at Thorne, and he translated in a voice soft as shadows, "*What is precious comes with a price.*" Blue eyes burning in the gloom, he smoothed his hand across the runes. "If you break this flagon, be certain you're prepared to pay the cost."

Cistine's skin crawled. "We aren't going to use it, just keep it from being abused."

"I know." Thorne motioned her back, and in a dozen strokes, shattered the ancient lock and pried open the chest.

It was not an augment they found inside; it was a flagon pouch, and it too was sealed. She'd never seen a lock like it before—round, barely as wide as her thumb. There was no keyhole, no latch. The seal was all one piece, inscribed with Old Valgardan runes.

The breath rushed out of Thorne, almost in relief. "Impenetrable. The old Order knew how to guard its assets."

Her arm like lead, her heart buzzing with need, Cistine reached into the chest. The moment her fingers encountered the pouch, godlike energy punched through her, a blow so hard it set her rocking back on her heels, all the breath rushing out of her. A ceaseless, screeching current stroked through her body like a pounding surf and flashes of lightning, and she was only dimly aware of Thorne's fingers taking her shoulders to keep her from falling, of his voice shouting her name.

Take defend use come and see come and see COME AND SEE

"No!" Cistine shouted, and the wailing power faltered, the pain in her skull releasing. The cavern swam back into focus, the clench of Thorne's hands on her wounded arms shooting a focusing pain into her body, bringing her back to the room—to him.

"What is it?" he demanded. "What happened, Cistine?"

"It's so gods-forsaken *loud*. I've never felt any augment like this."

Thorne's fingers flexed. "Even with the seal?"

"Even then." Ears ringing, she settled forward again, turning the pouch over in her hands to study the lock. Why was it so *familiar*?

Then it struck her. That pattern of runes, where she'd seen it before: in Stornhaz, below the courthouse.

"The old Order practiced *Gammalkraft* as well as augmentation, didn't they?" she asked slowly. "Before *Gammalkraft* was outlawed."

"So the stories go."

"Except it was used again." She smoothed her finger over the lock. "Just once, by another Order who grew too much of a taste for power."

For a beat, Thorne was silent. Then he took the lock, twisting it toward the ghostlight. His mouth slanted and his brow creased, arriving at the same conclusion she had.

"It's a bloodlock," Cistine whispered. "Just like the rune-lids over the Doors to the Gods."

Thorne's eyes snapped to her face, asking the silent question she did not know the answer to: if *her* blood would open something sealed so long before her time. Had the ritual made the Novacek bloodline the key to *all* doors sealed shut by augmentation and *Gammalkraft*? Did the tie to locks forged by those entwined powers transcend decades, centuries, generations, from the time of this augment's sealing-away until now?

Cistine pressed down against the spectral surge of the call rising once more in her chest. It didn't matter, because she wasn't going to try. The moment this pouch was opened, the flagon was twice as vulnerable to Bloodwight theft, twice as much a threat to their armies and all the kingdoms in the world. As the Key, it was her duty to protect it, not to tamper with it to sate her own curiosity.

She shoved the pouch into her pocket. "We have to find a way out of here."

Thorne frowned at the smooth walls. "This room was not designed to release its inhabitants again. Whoever entered, this was meant to be their end."

"Unless you were right, what you said before...that the Order might've had a contingency in place. A way for someone to take this augment if there was truly a need."

"That's speculation, Cistine. We're here now, and I don't see a way out. This vault was forged to contain, not release."

She didn't see a way, either. But she was learning that often the only path forward was one forged in power, by choice. That was why she was here, after all—what had brought her back to Valgard. Because the war and the Bloodwights seemed so hopeless, a threat beyond surmounting, so she chose to lay contingencies of her own, to map and plot her steps back to the North on her own terms. To return a victor, not a victim.

Cistine Novacek would not fall to ancient traps, nor to Bloodwight plots. She would rise again.

She dipped into her augment pouch, chest tearing with regret at using yet another flagon. But if there was no other way, then she had to do this. She would not be buried alive here while her friends waited above; and she would not subject Thorne to rotting in the darkness with her. "Well, they've never tried to contain *me*."

She smashed the flagon between her hands, freeing the earth augment's power in a crackling halo against her palms. At once, elements of the world woven into the rock itself pushed back, trapping them in a dome of augmented energy; but Cistine did not give way. She shut her eyes and spread her arms, letting the power dance and sing around her, searching for chinks and weakness in the fibers of stone, the places where it buckled, vulnerable to her reach.

Power throbbed in the bones of Kosai Talis. Somewhere above, not within, the world shuddered and trembled, an aftershock spearing all the way down to them.

Something was happening outside.

Fear for her cabal spiked through Cistine, sharp as any armor-piercing steel shaft, and at that pulse of desperation, her power lifted—then punched through. Stone turned to gravel, and a small seam fractured in the wall, letting in a gust of air from beyond.

A tunnel.

"*Logandir*," Thorne breathed.

"I see it," she panted, and aimed her focus toward that tiny crater. It gave a bit more, shuddered a bit wider.

Selv Torfjel.

The heart of all mountains with bloodpaths between, caves and tunnels connecting the Vaszaj Range to the Isetfells and every mountain beyond. But it wasn't only the mountains themselves that were connected; it was Detlyse Halet and Thalma Geris, Kalt Hasa with its broad lower caverns where supply trains came and went, and here: Kosai Talis, bricked over but still part of the chain.

The old temples were built on a web of tunnels, all linked together by an ancient Order more whole and fierce and frightening than even the Bloodwights, joining their places of prayer and practice to the North's beating heart.

"That's our way through," Cistine gasped.

Thorne's hand brushed her spine. "Let me help."

Not trusting herself to speak again, she reached out blindly, hand locking around his, and pushed the power into him so swiftly his body strained and he snarled under his breath; but he did not let go of the strength she gave him, or of her fingers. The power flowed between and from their bodies, hurling itself over and over at that vein in the wall until it widened to a crack, then to a crevice. Then to a wound stricken against the ancient temple's body.

On and on, Cistine and Thorne struck and struck, joined at the hand, joined by the power of the gods. And with every blow, a new sense of purpose jolted through Cistine. Fresh determination. Destiny reborn.

They were getting out of this temple, piercing clean into the heart of the mountains. And then they would bring the Bloodwights to their knees.

CHAPTER FIFTY-ONE

THE VAST EMPTINESS of the Isetfells to the west and the Vaszaj Range to the south spread out beyond Ashe and Bresnyar, a world breathtakingly broad and lonely. But she couldn't appreciate its beauty from her perch on the ledge that made the outermost watchpoint, her dragon curled at her back while they searched the distance for danger.

They'd been silent for hours now; practicing cleaving had been an utter failure their first two days on this boundary line, so they'd given up. If Ashe was distracted before the war camp fell, now she was out of her mind, with no desire for the splitting pain that often came from long sessions winnowing in and out of Bresnyar's sight when she *could* manage it at all.

She needed to be alert for what was to come.

Drawing one leg to her chest, she wrapped both hands around her knee and settled deeper into Bresnyar's side. "Hear anything out there?"

"No," Bresnyar rumbled. "But they're strange, these old temples. When I circled Kalt Hasa to make perch there the night they captured me, I had no sense at all that men lived within its walls until I was inside the cage of their lightning augments." Old anger rocked through Ashe at the thought of anyone caging her dragon, though she hadn't even known him at the time. "I thought it was my grief for Ileria that allowed them to creep up on me in the dark, but now I think it's the way these fortresses are built. Like secrets sprung up from the rock."

"They must be awfully crafty to hide their vaults from *you*."

"Flattery, *Ilyanak*? Are you well?"

Her chuckle cut short, a terrible weight bounding in her throat. "Don't ask me that, Scales."

Bresnyar's only answer was a quiet groan and his head settling on the rock at her side.

They sat that way for some time, unspeaking in their worry for their friends and searching the horizon for danger; then, all at once, the air chilled like a cloud had rolled across the sun, but the light did not change.

Bresnyar's head lifted. His lips peeled back from dagger-sharp teeth, pupils waning to slits. Ashe lurched to her feet and turned a full circle, searching the sky. She saw nothing, felt nothing but that bitter cold racing along her skin. Bresnyar rose behind her, his bass growl sending the tiny shards of stone along the path quaking. In one lunge, he twisted up the mountain to their left, clinging to the peak with his snout angled east.

Ashe brought the starstone close to her mouth to speak without shouting. "What is it? What do you smell?"

Gold glistened across her vision, and for a heartbeat Ashe saw it, too: a dark cloud shooting through a filigreed world. Her vision became her own when Bresnyar dropped back onto the path beside her, shaking out his wings. "Balmond. Moving this way."

Cursing, Ashe drew Odvaya. "I'll hold their attention. You warn Aden and Kristoff."

"If you believe I will *ever* leave you in combat alone again..."

"Bres, you knew this was the plan—we're the first line of defense, we send up the warning beacon! Now *go!*" She struck the flat of her blade on his hide with the last word, spitting sparks, and the dragon snarled and bounded down the ledge. In a deft leap, he was aloft, spearing toward the second pass where Aden and Kristoff took watch.

Alone in silence so thick it thudded against her eardrums, Ashe palmed Odvaya in her right hand. With her left, she drew the flagon Quill had given her in Holmlond. "All right," she hissed toward the still-clear sky, "come and find me."

She crushed the flagon against her armor.

Cold pierced deeper than the threads, wrapping her muscles and freezing her very bones; currents of ice danced along the backs of her teeth, and it took all her effort not to let it burst from her body and turn the trail and cliffs around her to a slick waste.

Seconds marched by. Eerie stillness gripped the air, and Ashe watched the sky, ice pulsing in the fingertips of her gloves, licking at the Atrasat inkings beneath.

Then, gentle as a breath of shadow, the wind began to stir.

Frozen shards flaked from Ashe's armor, sifting onto the snow-lined path. Gray clouds mushroomed above, moving from the east. She gripped Odvaya with all her might as the storm burgeoned, an ink-dark stain against the sky. Then, without warning, a spiral of wind and shadow shattered downward from the cloudbank, slamming into the path several meters above her and annealing into the shape of a man.

A cold wash of dread skittered up Ashe's neck. The breath whispered from her lungs and did not return. She could only watch, sword scraping the cold ground, ears full of the pulse swishing wildly in her chest, as the robed, skull-masked figure straightened from his descending crouch. Her heart hurled itself against her ribs and kicked her lungs back into motion at the sight; not the grotesque wolf mask he wore, covering his features completely, but the flash of braids sliding from his hood.

Her beautiful, braided bastard.

Her Maleck.

The sight of that mask on his face, the animal wariness with which he held himself, spiked fury in Ashe's temples so hard her vision shimmered and swam. She hadn't expected to feel anger at the sight of him. Grief, longing, even love—but not this *rage*. "You need to stop this, Mal! Stop chasing these gods-forsaken augments and come *home*."

He didn't so much as twitch, gave no sign he understood the words. What home *was*.

Ashe took a step toward him. "I know you see me. I know you *know* me. And *you* know I'm not walking off this mountain without you."

He stiffened slightly—not at the words, but because when she moved closer, ice burst from the tips of her boots, fracturing across the path. His braids stirred in an aberrant wind, and Ashe settled on her heels, sword ascending.

Fine. If she had to knock him unconscious and drag him down from this mountain, she would. Like she'd promised Quill—whatever it took.

Coiling like a wildcat, Ashe lunged.

An arc of lightning spewed from Maleck's sleeve and shot toward her, forcing her to feint, her leg catching at an angle on the path and shooting pain into the old wound on her thigh. She buckled down and rolled away from the next slash tearing across the path, a scorching notch carved right where she'd stood a heartbeat before.

He was really trying to hit her.

Screaming with rage, Ashe shot to her feet and charged; again, Maleck flung an augment into her path, fire this time—wielding many at once, just like his brothers did and like no normal augur could. Ashe tucked into a roll between the banner of flames and came up in a crouch, teeth locked together, heat storming her cheeks. He was already so far gone, so much like them.

"Not while I'm still breathing," she hissed, and hurtled in a dead run up the path.

Fire and lightning danced, and she dodged, drawing close and falling back. Every crevice she ducked into and every stone she sheltered behind, Maleck broke apart. But she was wearing him down, she hoped; and she was moving up the trail, closer and closer to his lethal strikes.

Ten meters. Five. Three.

Mustering all her might, she slammed her hand against the mountain face and ripped her palm across it, whipping a sheet of ice between her body and Maleck's next attack. Two more bursts of power, and she'd forged steps up the slippery arc to the very top. She flipped over it, hurtling downward, pommel upraised to slam into the top of Maleck's skull and knock him unconscious.

Without a flinch, he reached up, catching Odvaya in his palm. It did not bite through his flesh; it struck like steel to rock, banging pain into her elbows and shoulders, numbing her fingertips and forearm.

Impervious. Just like any other gods-damned Bloodwight.

Maleck slammed his foot into her stomach, ripping Odvaya from her grasp and flinging her up against the ice wall in one fluid motion. She crumbled to her knees, choking and gasping and spitting blood from her tongue when she staggered upright again. Gods, he *never* hit her that hard, not even when they wrestled and trained.

With a sweep of his arm, Maleck cast Odvaya over the side of the path. Ashe lurched a step after it, a wordless cry wrenching from her lips, a piece of her heart cracking when it spun out and sailed into oblivion. That blade he'd named for courage and unbreaking hearts, for how he saw her...another piece of who he was, who *they* were...

Gone.

Maleck tipped forward in a hunger-drunk crouch, scenting, tasting, *craving* the augment in her armor. He would go mad for it if he was close enough...if she didn't find a way to halt him in his tracks.

With a clench of bloodstained teeth, she bit her glove, ripped it from her hand, and thrust her palm up so hard he coiled back. "*Look at this!*"

Maleck's masked face jerked toward what she was showing him—not the Wingmaiden's brand, but the gash stretching up from it, across the very center of her palm.

"You know what this is," she rasped. "You know what it means."

His right hand twitched...the palm bearing the same mark.

"You've been mine ever since Braggos," she said. "*Valenar.* One heart, one blood, one life. Whatever else I am, I'm *yours.* Do you remember that?"

He stared at her, trembling.

"Say my name." Ashe pushed off the ice and swayed toward him. "Say what I *am* to you."

His reply came at last—not words, but a sideways twitch of his cloak. The glint of an unfamiliar saber drawing from beneath the armored fabric.

Ashe's heart wanted to die right then and there at that answer, that cold and calculative ruthlessness. She'd bared her soul to him, bared the secret he made her keep hidden for her safety, to conceal her from his brothers—and this was how he answered.

But she couldn't fall. Not to him. She would not give the Bloodwights that satisfaction.

Snarling profanely, Ashe freed her offhand dagger, gripped it back against her arm, and leaped. Maleck met her blade for blade.

They dueled in a calamity of steel, her ice cracking across the world around them, building a fragile and glorious palace inside which they fought for love and power, for fury and forgotten things. Those bursts of might were all that kept Ashe ahead of his blows, kept her feet under her, kept her breathing while the pieces of her spirit shattered like these pinnacles of ice giving way under their clashing blades.

With every strike, with every smash of their weapons spitting sparks across her eyes and the holes of his mask, all Ashe could think of was Talheimic rooftops and wine pots and winter festivals. Narrow alleys and bright hazel eyes full of life, and their chests moving in tandem, sharing cold air. A meadow and a forest and ghostplants broken open everywhere, the night they swore their oath and loved one another back to life beneath the churning stars.

She couldn't see his eyes now—dead eyes with life trickling back into them. Couldn't see the man who'd forged the blood vow with her anywhere in this creature that fought to lay hands on the power in her body.

That was all she was to him. A well. A Door to the Gods he wanted to rip open and take from.

The notion awakened a mania that was new and brutal and *terrifying,* and she gave into it, let it flood her with a power no flagon could offer. Bellowing in fury, she hurled herself forward, slamming Maleck backward with their weapons locked at the grips until he struck the wall of ice and could fall back no further.

"Look at me, Maleck!" she roared. *"I'm not afraid of you!"*

He froze. Utterly froze.

His fingers flexed. The sword dipped.

Then a sound burst from him she'd never heard before—a primal roar, a creature's shout of hate and hunger that shook every bone in her body. Maleck dropped his blade, cracked hers aside, and wrapped his fingers around her throat, throwing her flat on her back on the trail so hard all the breath rushed from her lungs. The rest of the augment burst from Ashe's control, and he took some of it, his grip on her throat turning unbearably frigid. Talons of power speared from his fingertips and raked her bare cheek, drawing blood, sending pain singing down the faltering lines of her body.

She was dying, she was *dying* and he wouldn't *stop*—

"*Mal.* Please," she choked with all the breath she had left. "Don't...you *know* me."

His fingers retracted just enough for a tiny trickle of wind to slither into her lungs, pushing the darkness at bay. He bent his head, the wolf's snout raking her cheekbone. Breath rattled out of him—a word, as rough and animal as the rest of him. "*Mereszar.*"

All at once Maleck recoiled, lunged up and staggered away from her, the breeze stirring his filthy braids. Not a natural wind, and not an augmented one either; it was a current kicked up by the beat of wings, carrying with it a ghastly, inhuman shriek.

The Balmond had caught the scent of her blood and circled back.

Maleck stared down at her a second longer. Then he turned away.

"*Darkwind!*" Ashe choked. "Don't walk away from me!"

He froze, trembling violently, fighting the compulsion of that Name and the augment lust, the two natures running deeper than his sane mind. Twin powers tearing him in different directions. Then, with a crack like shattering ice, like thunder, his addiction won over the Name Ashe had thought was unbreakable. In a flash of augmented light, he was gone.

Lying flat on the path, head in shock, heart fit to burst, Ashe struggled to make sense of what he'd done.

He'd fled from her. He'd nearly *killed* her. And he was content to let the Balmond finish the task; they descended toward her bloodied, weakened form, and though she shoved her hands into the blistering cold path and levered herself up, she could not run. There was no shelter to be had. Dazed, dizzy, bleeding, she stared up at the malformed bodies dipping and rising on the wind, spiraling down toward her.

She had to do something. She couldn't die like this.

One inch, then another, she dragged herself toward her fallen dagger. Lifting it was a feat, and tears slid from the corners of her eyes when she rolled back onto her haunches. Arm trembling, she sighted the nearest creature descending quickest toward her. With all her might, she threw.

It wasn't a well-aimed blow. Not a strong one, either. But it was true, and it should have been enough. But the blade struck the creature's hide and bounded off, clattering down the trail.

The beast slammed her into the path. Her head jounced on rock and ice, and pain tore into her shoulder—then burned away with a world-ending roar of rage, and in the darkness behind her closed eyelids she saw herself sprawled on the path, blood pumping from her arm, and the Balmond reeling off her at the slash of talons piercing deep into its hide.

Bresnyar had returned.

In snatches between her vision and his, floating on the edge of dazed oblivion, Ashe watched her dragon massacre through the Balmond. Black ichor painted the mountain face, the ice wall, and the trail on which she lay, struggling not to fall unconscious and to comprehend what she was seeing.

Their hide was impervious to her mortal blade, but not to Bresnyar's teeth and claws, his fire. He shredded this pocket of bloodthirsty hunters in a matter of moments, ripping them from the sky and the pass walls when they tried to skitter free. He was magnificent. Flawless. And once again, she owed him her life.

Barely had the thought slammed through her than Bresnyar's pained cry ripped the sky, jerking Ashe's eyes wide open. One of the Balmond fell on his tail, the naked stripe where Salvotor had chipped away his precious scales, and bore into it with vicious, hooked talons. Blood slapped the path as more scales ripped free. Bresnyar howled and thrashed, slamming the Balmond up against the stone wall, but it clung on like a tick and dug in, shredding scales off, flesh stuck in ropy strands to the undersides.

Agony rammed into Ashe's head, her vision careening white-gold. Gasping, swearing, she rolled to her hands and knees and crawled for her knife. Though it had already proven useless, she would not leave her dragon to fight this battle alone.

Knife in hand again, she staggered up toward the Balmond. She did not bother with the vain hope for soft spots in that armored hide; she crashed full-bodied into the creature, hitting it over and over though she broke no flesh, ripping its clawed hands from Bresnyar's tail and sending both she and it crashing toward the edge of the path.

But she was not afraid. Not when she heard Bresnyar roar her name; not when she saw herself through his eyes, rolling and tussling the Balmond. Not when she knew what would come next.

Bresnyar was on them in a heartbeat, blood fanning from his tail, jaws snapping around the Balmond's body when it rolled on top of Ashe. With a crunch, he spattered gore across the path; then his clawed hand was around Ashe's body, and with one mighty leap and a snap of his wings, he surged from the creviced path and up into a sky blackened with Balmond in flight.

Ashe's eyes watered from more than just the wind when she saw the pack pulling ahead toward the distant ramparts of Kosai Talis. There were so gods-damned *many* of them, so many children corrupted, reforged into these beasts, these unwoundable creatures—

No. Not utterly unwoundable. Not to her dragon.

Ashe shut her eyes against the dizzying shift in color when Bresnyar reached back and deposited her on his spine. Clinging low to his neck, she waited for the pain in her head to pass.

Plans would come from this. She would have to face Quill and tell him she'd failed...if they even survived this battle Maleck had left them to, giving them all up for dead. Giving his own *valenar* up for slaughter.

But Ashe was still alive, with her dragon and the knife in her hand. And in the distance, a whistle floated on the wind, a familiar signal.

There was still a fight to be had. She would not die before it was done.

So Ashe mustered her wits, sent up a prayer, and let Bresnyar turn toward that whistle.

CHAPTER FIFTY-TWO

ADEN KNEW SOMETHING worse was coming when Bresnyar broke off in the midst of telling him about the Balmond approaching. Nostrils flaring, he'd scented the wind back to the south; then, with a hiss of Ashe's name and no other warning, the dragon had taken to the skies—leaving Aden alone, his father already tearing through the pass to raise the alarm with Quill, Tatiana, and Ariadne.

Sabers in his fists, Aden stalked the ledge, turning first south, then east, the way Bresnyar had gone and back again toward the jagged crags and snow-crowned battlements of Kosai Talis. Then back again, toward the thin black stripe fringing the horizon.

The Balmond.

Aden's stomach churned at the thought of facing those abominations again; worse, the notion that perhaps as punishment for Selv Torfjel, the Bloodwights had forged Pippet into one of them. That he might be forced to put his blade through her throat just to end her suffering.

"Not that," he growled to any gods who listened to traitors and Tribunes. "*Not* her."

Harsh, feminine laughter cracked the air behind him. "It's almost amusing...such petty sentiment coming from the Lord of the Blood Hive."

Aden nearly dropped his sabers. That voice—that cold, furious purr—

was as much a part of his nightmares as Deja's vicious touch and Noaam's gloating sneer. And it should've stayed a figment of dreams that woke him sweating in the dark, because the woman speaking should've been dead. He'd *watched* her die.

But when he whirled toward the south again, there she was; a shadow slithering into view, lithe and graceful, the augmented winds parting before her like a veil. Every step predatory, the trained form of a dancer not faded entirely from her killer's body, she planted her feet and laid back her hood.

Aden's breath caught, stumbling over her name. "Nimea."

She inclined on the balls of her feet, a coiling adder seconds away from the venomous strike. "Hello, Aden."

Disbelief socked his gut so hard the words burst from him. "Ashe slew you in the catacombs!"

"She tried." Bitterness coursed through Nimea's words. "But Siralek doesn't let its fighters die easily. One healing augment from a passing guard was all it took, and there I was: alive with what few remained of my loyal friends, and left to become Lady of the Blood Hive. Left to dream day and night of seeing your face again."

Aden's skin prickled. "Come to finish what you started?"

"Arrogant as always, aren't you? Assuming it's all about you." Nimea flipped back the corner of her armored cloak, sliding a serrated dagger from a holster on her thigh. "I'm here for the Key."

Cistine's title on those angry lips turned Aden's blood to ice. "You serve the Bloodwights."

"Oh, aren't you *clever*. What gave it away? The augments in my pouch? The Blood Hive destroyed? Or that I'm standing here, finally *free*, with my knife ready to taste your blood?"

He shook his head as one by one the pieces fell into place. "It was your battle plans laid out in Selv Torfjel. I knew I recognized the strategy, the script. You're one of the *mirothadt*."

"*One of them*," Nimea scoffed. "As ever, you underestimate your opponent. I *lead* them. The Bloodwights needed someone to help lay their battle lines, to form rank and keep order while they hunted augments in this forgotten corner of the kingdom. And who better than the Hive Lady?"

"You always did covet the title."

"You know as well as I...in the Blood Hive, you either led or you were carrion. Of course I wanted the name! And when I had it, I began to dream of something more."

Aden stared at her, horror crashing through him. This specter of Nimmus, his own personal enemy—the one ordering sieges and strikes. The one who'd made the nightmare of Braggos come to pass. "You sent Pippet to that battlefield to lure me away." The words were a breath steaming the frigid air. "You wanted me to survive the ambush in Braggos—to watch them die."

"To know what it's like to live on when all your friends are brutally slaughtered in a melee?" Nimea's lips peeled back from her teeth. "It was just a taste. As is *this*."

She swept aside, and Aden stopped breathing altogether.

He hadn't seen her before, tucked perfectly behind Nimea, moving in tandem with her—a small shadow to the new Lady of the Hive, as she once was to him. He couldn't even summon her name to his lips. But here she was, staring at him through the eyeholes of a bird mask, quivering in her armor, hair stirred by the wind augment she carried.

"Aren't you two going to say hello?" Nimea purred. "Pip, do you know this man?"

Her head cocked, facing toward Aden. She didn't speak.

"Pippet." He cast caution aside and stepped nearer to them. "Look at me. Come...come home."

Her head cocked sharply back the other way. Then she withdrew from him, tucking herself behind Nimea again, who clicked her tongue and laughed. "Contrary little thing, isn't she? She put up quite the fight when Rakel and Devitrius brought her to us. I recognized your threats on her tongue before they muzzled her...I knew *immediately* how this should go."

Aden shifted his focus back to Nimea even while his mind raged, seeking ways to destroy her and bring Pippet down from this mountain. "You're heartless. She's a *child*."

"*I* was a child when they sent me to that place!" Nimea shouted, and Pippet flinched. "Barely seventeen, and the things they did to us there..."

"I sold myself to keep you safe."

"Because you're a soft-hearted fool. You were right...caring for one another's fates was a vow of death in that place. And caring now will be the death of *you*." She dropped back a step, and Pippet advanced, knife drawn from the sheath at her hip. Cold and cruel, she stalked toward him.

He would have feared less, ached less if the mountains had cracked apart at their foundations and sent him plunging to the depths. His student, his sister by all but blood, his guiding star watched him like prey, creeping forward, knife unsheathed.

The knife that went into Tatiana. That had tried to end Quill.

He couldn't draw against her. Not even as she backed him toward the edge of the cleft.

"Pippet, *stop*." He filled the words with all the might and command of their training sessions. "That's enough."

But she didn't heed him. Blade gleaming, she lengthened her stride to a predator's prowl.

"Magnificent, isn't she?" Nimea laughed. "A little Hive Lady, trained by its former Lord. A prodigy prepared to overthrow her mentor."

"Pippet, this is not you."

"It is now, Aden. It's *all* of us."

"No." Heat stamped his eyes. "*No*."

"Let's not kill him, Pippet." Nimea's tone eased into boredom. "Let's just take a piece of him. An eye, perhaps. An ear. His fingers. Have fun with him."

Pippet looked back, something almost pouting in her stance, as if she hated the thought of *not* killing him. Something broke in Aden's chest at that which could never be mended. But he had to try.

"Pippet," he rasped, "*look at me*." She twitched, but didn't turn. "Look at me, little lioness. I'm not afraid of you."

Pippet's head revolved toward him, slow and wobbly, gaze spearing into him through the eyeholes.

"You really think that will be enough to tame her?" Nimea laughed. "She is a *perfect* acolyte. So much energy and stamina. So much fury at a world that kept her locked away for so long. She and I are just the same...let me show you." She sucked her lip between her teeth, and with one short whistle, unleashed Pippet.

She launched herself at Aden, gripping his collar and slamming him flat on his back on the ledge. His head hung backward over oblivion as her fist circled his throat. Her wind dragged the breath from his lungs.

"You should have learned by now to hold on tighter to the things you love, Aden." Nimea's voice descended from a faint opening as he slid down the shaft toward Nimmus. "Otherwise you will always be alone."

He clung to the pinpoint thread of light, to the masked face above him that had saved him so many times from self-hatred, from madness, from giving up. That gave him a reason to drag himself back after Siralek, after he'd stayed behind in Jovadalsa, when he no longer knew who he was or what his future held.

Legacy. What is legacy, Aden?

It was this. She was his.

He swung his arm up, and in one fluid motion, broke Pippet's hold, pushed her backward and shouted, "*I love you!*"

Pippet stumbled back, body coiled tight, staring at him. From beneath the mask, a trembling breath. And she did not strike again.

Nimea's wind slammed into her, thrusting her off the ledge into the chasm below. Aden roared in rage, disbelief, heartbreak, and lunged after her; but his fingers met only empty air. Pippet's own wind carried her away from him, among the craggy cliffs.

He whirled toward Nimea, cursing. "If she's harmed in *any* way—"

"Enough, Aden!" Nimea snapped. "She doesn't want you. She's one of *us*. And after what you just did, I'm going to make her suffer in ways you can *never* imagine."

His throat scorched with emotion, Aden laid a hand to his sabers. "After all this time, this is where ambition leads you? To be a slave to the Bloodwights as you were a slave to the arena? To threaten and hurt *children?*"

Hate slashed through Nimea's eyes. "I don't care for the children your little cabal loves...I'm saving the lives that truly matter. It's been a busy few months, moving back and forth across this kingdom—but worthwhile. We've taken whoever we want for our ranks, however we see fit." She drew her knife and turned it gracefully over her fingers. "We've raided every filthy slaver caravan, every wretched flesh market from here to the Wildwood and back again. The Chancellors would soil themselves if they knew just how many people their laws have *failed*—how many were imprisoned, battered, bought and sold, broken for no just cause. And how desperately those victims hunger for vengeance." Her smile was a flit of yellowed teeth, a cruel wrinkle to her nose. "The perfect conditions for a melee, don't you think, Hive Lord?"

"I am not the Hive Lord anymore. This is not Siralek."

"No, you're right. You're a *Tribune* now." The word sidled between Nimea's gritted teeth. "Well, now that makes you part of the problem, doesn't it? Another broken fragment of a flawed hierarchy that failed the true heart of Valgard. And since this is not Siralek, there are no rules to play by. And you no longer command me."

The knife stilled. With it, Aden stiffened.

"So I can hunt you," Nimea said, "as quickly or as slowly as I want. I can carve into you one piece at a time, beginning by taking everything from you the way you took it all from me. My dreams." She stalked a step toward him. "My future." He retreated an equal pace. "The Tumult." Another graceful, catlike stride. "My *friends*."

His back struck the mountain's face, and Nimea's feral smile broadened to a full and frightening grin.

"They weren't going to bother with Maleck, you know. They thought he was too set in his ways to ever turn back to them. But I proved otherwise, didn't I? That was *my* little game. Taking Ashe's *selvenar* from her like her sponsor took mine from me."

Aden's heart stumbled. Disbelief and fury flushed through him, and Nimea burst into laughter at the contortion of his face. That cold cackle was every scrap of the Blood Hive Aden had fought to walk away from.

"I always hoped you survived so I could have the pleasure of ending you myself, just like this—bit by bit, until you beg for death." She bent toward him, her mouth nearly to his ear. "Maleck's turning was just the first cut. Where shall I make the second?"

A howl of rage burst from Aden's chest, and he swung up his blades, hacking for the sides of her neck. Nimea pirouetted out of reach, a flagon shattering behind her back, a burst of fire screaming around her body and blowing toward him. Aden ducked the fiery onslaught, drawing his blades to meet her charge.

A decade of rage fueled her blows; a decade of remorse hardened his defenses. With every strike of her fire, then the whips of water flying against him when that first augment died, Aden saw the girl she'd once been: a dancer with dreams of becoming a Kanslar Tribune, a girl who'd dined and laughed at his table, grinning with her chin on her fists, listening to Thorne and Saychelle lay out plans for equality among the Courts and women sitting on the Judgement Seat. Of that better world Sillakove still believed in.

But Nimea had taken judgement into her own hands. Blood Hive justice forced her screams, slashing in tandem with blow after blow toward his face, his chest, his torso. Yet through stinging eyes and the calamity of battle raging in his blood, Aden felt a strange calm.

He'd brought this battle upon himself; had brought this fate on Maleck, on Ashe, even on Pippet by betraying the cabal. By failing to save the Tumult from Siralek. By not ensuring Nimea was dead before he'd left that catacomb corridor all those months ago.

The thought of that night hitched his step for one instant, and Nimea, a creature of sand and blood, saw the opportunity. Her watery whip lashed out, snaring his knees and yanking his legs from beneath him, throwing him down; his elbows cracked the stone and sprang his fingers open in a violent spasm, sabers flying from his hands. Nimea scooped up one and crouched on his chest, bringing the blade to rest against his throat; rage rattled her hands so fiercely the edge drew blood.

A distant scream ripped through the painful chill of the air, so achingly familiar it snapped Aden's head around despite the mortal press of the blade against his neck.

Ashe.

Dragonfire spewed into the sky, breaking apart the dark column of flesh—the Balmond. A glint of gold rose, floundered, and rose again through the shadowed flock.

Nimea twisted her hand in Aden's hair and slammed his head back against the rock, driving her weight and his saber tighter against him. "Do you hear her? Do you know what she's suffering? You deserve every scrap of this, you stars-forsaken *bandayo*. This is *nothing* compared to what we faced in Siralek. You sent us to *Nimmus!*"

Aden tore his gaze from the blotted-out horizon back to Nimea's furious face, Bresnyar's bellows and Ashe's cries still ringing in his ears.

She was right. He had done that—he was that man. And weeks ago, he might've dropped his guard and taken this penance as the bitter end. But she was not here just for him. She was here to make *them* suffer. To make his family bleed. And if saving them meant he could not break...

For an instant, he brought their faces back to him in the dark, past the saber's bite, past the strain of Nimea's fingers ripping at his hair.

Pippet's dazzling smile, fists up, ready to fight him. Kristoff's gaze holding his in that cave, an old and undimmed love burning in his eyes. Ashe clinging to him as her world fell apart. Thorne's face when he'd looked at him with utter faith in Holmlond, no fear left. Maleck's embrace, his last farewell of love and sorrow. Quill and Tatiana's matching grins whenever he walked into a room. Cistine's joy when she'd found him in the Chasm. Ariadne's prayers, quiet and steady, forever at his side.

Mira's shoulder, pressed to his in the dark. *You are a good man. You are the one they need now.*

The Hive Lord could lie down and die. But Aden Bloodsinger, Tribune of Spoek, backbone of Sillakove Court, never could. His Chancellor needed him. His kingdom needed him. His cabal needed him to *live*.

The son of the Lion. The son of the Storm. They *needed* him not to break. And for them, he never would.

Roaring his rage, his unfulfilled oaths beating hard and heavy in his blood, Aden grabbed the saber by the blade, twisted it aside, and punched Nimea straight in the throat. Then he swung up and headbutted her with all his might and bucked her from his chest. She tumbled off, gagging and gasping, and Aden wrenched the saber from her hold. He scooped up the second, spun to his knees and slashed toward her, but her water blocked him and shoved him back almost to the ledge before he cut through it, spilling it across the rock.

"*I will never stop hunting you!*" Nimea was still on her knees, blood sliding down her brow, hate shining in her eyes. "I will take *everyone* you love, starting with that little girl. I'll ensure they turn her into a creature so twisted, so deformed, there will be no hope of saving her! And then I'll take the rest of them, one after the other!"

Aden struggled to his feet, staring at her, searching for the girl he once knew in the woman glaring at him across the ledge with murder in her eyes. But there was no trace left; she was the twisted one, and there was no hope of saving her. And he would not become her plaything, stepping into the trap of water crawling across the stone toward her fingertips.

He would not be baited. And he could not break.

So he did not answer to her taunts. He simply faced her fury—and walked backward off the ledge.

Nimea's scream tore out in tandem to the lash of the water whip, but Aden was already beneath her reach, falling straight onto Bresnyar's back, the dragon soaring on toward the faraway entrance to the vaults and Ashe twisting to steady Aden when he landed behind her.

"What happened?" he demanded.

"Maleck." Ashe's eyes avoided his. "I tried."

Dread pooled in Aden's core. If Ashe had failed to bring him back— Ashe, of all people, Maleck's living heart outside his body—what hope did any of them have?

But she did not need to hear him say that, or to know yet that Nimea was alive and this was her vengeance. So Aden squeezed Ashe's shoulder with one hand, gripped his blade in the other, prayed their friends and his father would hold the line until they reached them.

CHAPTER FIFTY-THREE

THORNE HAD THOUGHT the gauntlet of dangers within Kosai Talis was the worst thing he would endure all day. But nothing prepared him to burst through the rock and see his cabal being ravaged by the Balmond. The earth augment's power blew out the side of the temple itself, and he and Cistine slid down the slope, arms and legs spread wide to brace their fall, all the way down toward the crescent of rock where Ariadne, Quill, and Tatiana had stationed themselves; and where Aden, Kristoff, Ashe, and Bresnyar had joined them. They fought for their lives against a beastly chaos of talon and fang and bodies half-human—the Balmond, summoned from the darkest bowels of Nimmus to lay waste to them.

Thorne and Cistine struck the bottom of the slope in a crouch, and Cistine froze for only a moment. Then the earth augment flared out, an attack aimed upward, behind them, at Kosai Talis itself. With a mighty crack, the temple's foundations rendered, rock and ice bending to the Key's will, and the mountain of its perch shook like a ship on storm-tossed waves, throwing Thorne to his knees. The temple walls folded in one after another, screams and howls echoing wherever they slammed down in bursts of gravel, snow, and dust.

The Bloodwights, buried alive—just like she'd done to the *Aeoprast* in Stornhaz. She'd bought them moments to fight, to flee.

Thorne was up, spurred on by the need to protect his cabal, an urge more powerful than the eddies of life and death. Sabers drawn, he lunged into combat, shoving Aden away from a Balmond's talons and hacking down on its gnarled, birdlike ankles with both blades.

They ricocheted off.

Hesitation rooted him in place a heartbeat too long; a second creature smashed into him, throwing him to the ground so hard it drove the breath from his lungs, and his wild backward jab glanced away again. Tatiana dove in from nowhere, tackling the thing off his back, giving him a moment to drag himself up; and when he turned he found her clinging to the creature's thick neck and flailing at it uselessly, but with all her might. The screams plowing from her throat with every blow were as inhuman as the Balmond's bellows shredding the air around them.

Ariadne cried out in agony when a blow to her shoulder popped it audibly from its socket. Beside her, Ashe's face wept from vicious gashes, hairline to jaw. They were fighting, but breaking; the only one who seemed able to rend through the Balmond was Bresnyar, but he bled as well, every stroke of his tail spraying scarlet on the rock. Kristoff and Quill guarded his back to keep the creatures from burying him.

"Get to the edge!" Thorne shouted, and Cistine took up the call, shoving first Aden, then Tatiana toward the bare expanse of rock beneath the shadow of Kosai Talis. She palmed an augment, fire rippling red within the flagon, and Thorne's throat closed at the thought of spending another when they had not even begun to train yet.

But if that alone would spare his friends, then to Nimmus with the rest. He'd raid *mirothadt* camps himself for more if it meant they lived to see tomorrow.

Anything. *Anything* to save them.

Vigor poured into his muscles, and he swung harder, knocking the Balmond away with brute strength, ignoring their shredding talons and teeth, his gaze fixed on the edge of the path he fought to reach. They were closing in, nearer and nearer to freedom—

A roar of pure rage shattered the chilled air. Thorne whirled back toward the mountain just as Cistine did, boots moored to the rock, hair whipped by the winds of their enemy's making.

"Cistine!" Quill shouted. "Stranger, come *on!*"

But she didn't move. She stared back at the temple's crumbled ramparts, at the last tower and corner of the walls not broken by her power; and at the figure posted on that lonely precipice, body cleaving the snow-white and smoke-choked sky like a fang poised to clamp down and shatter flesh and bone, body and spirit. Thorne had never laid eyes on this one before, but he *knew* it was the *Aeoprast*, the creature that had slain the undefeatable Salvotor—one enemy stepping over the corpse of another to strike terror in the heart of Thorne's kingdom.

And now his enemy and his Wildheart stared at one another, nothing but frigid air and the power of the gods separating them, and Thorne could not comprehend what he saw and *felt* in that look crossing the distance.

It was Quill who moved, who had faced this creature in battle before and was not breathtaken by its unholy might. He surged forward, wrapped an arm around Cistine's waist, and with his other hand, broke an augment Thorne hadn't even known he carried. A gulf of wind wrapped around the pair, hurling them away from the mountain.

"Thorne, *go!*" The crack of Kristoff's voice broke the icy shackles of fear around his hands and feet, his heart. He whirled to the others and flagged his arm wildly; they all ran together and leaped onto Bresnyar's back, and though his spine bowed at their landing, he shoved off from the base of Kosai Talis with all his might. Wings snapped, the lingering brush of Quill's wind filling them, and they soared skyward and shot south, leaving the ruined mess of Balmond bodies, furious Bloodwights, and the cold figure of the *Aeoprast* behind.

CHAPTER FIFTY-FOUR

WHEN THE WINDS parted, depositing Cistine and Quill in a sprawl on brittle grass under the Sotefold's familiar shelter, she fell gagging to her knees. Shudders racked her body, her skin so pained to the touch that even Quill's fingers clamping her armor and sitting her back on her haunches burned like fire. She'd given too much, fought too hard even with just a single augment, and her wounded body would not stop shaking.

"Are you all right?" Quill all but shouted in her face. "What in *Nimmus* was that? Why did you *stop?*"

She stared at him, hysteria pounding in her skull. What did he want her to say—what was a princess and savior expected to say? That she was measuring her prey? Challenging the *Aeoprast* with her full face? Staring him down until he begged for mercy?

All noble, all fierce, all rallying. All of it an utter lie.

"I froze," she said, and his eyes widened. "Quill, I just stole from the most powerful, dangerous *being* in Valgard who needs my blood to have *everything* he wants, and I didn't...I didn't stop to really think of what that would mean until I saw him there. I am *nothing* against that. I'm just a princess with a year's training, I—"

"Stranger, stop. Stop. Look at me." Quill took her face in his hands and tilted her head back until their gazes locked. "Look at *me*. When have

I *ever* let the *bandayos* in this kingdom reach you? Where have I been every single time, ever since we met? And Salvotor doesn't count, I wasn't with you outside Jovadalsa."

Reluctant laughter surged from her lips, but the question that escaped after it was honest, trembling. "What if you're not there again? Like you said when we sparred before Selv Torfjel—"

"If you think I'm letting you out of my sight after what you pulled off today..." He shook his head so hard threads of long white hair floated down to brush the old scar on his scalp. "Forget what I said before. I'm always going to be there. You have my swords, my back, every scrap of power I've got from here until it's over. I've faced the *Aeoprast* before, I'll teach you how. All right? Just like the rock top. It's just motions, Cistine. We can do this. Do you trust me?"

Hadn't she always?

Quill smirked at her unsteady nod and released her face to wrap an arm around her shoulders instead, leaning them both back against the nearest tree. "All right. Then we start tomorrow at dawn. I think we could both use a rest tonight."

She leaned her head against him and curled her knees to her chest, resting her hand over her augment pouch and the dark power thrumming inside it. "The others. Do you think—?"

"They'll be here. Thorne led them out." Confident, as if he'd seen it happen even while the winds bore them away from danger.

He would've been a good father.

The thought punched through Cistine so sharply she hurt on his behalf for a pain he did not know was his to feel, because Tatiana hadn't told him yet. And some selfish part of her was glad she hadn't; today, Cistine needed Quill's strength, something solid to lean into.

And lean on him she did, unspeaking and vigilant, listening for the sound of Bresnyar bringing the rest of the cabal to find them.

It was nearly dusk when he finally did, his croaky roar peeling Cistine and Quill up from the cold ground. They jogged to a small clearing among the trees where Bresnyar crashed down, panting and wheezing, and collapsed on his side. The others slid from his back, Ashe tumbling to her knees at the dragon's head and pressing her branded palm to his snout.

Thorne came straight to Quill and Cistine, clapping his friend in an embrace first, then wrapping his arms around Cistine. "Are you all right?"

"Not at all," she choked.

His grip tightened, his face pressing into her hair. But even in his arms, there was no escaping her fear.

Beneath the Sotefold's woven hem of budding branches, the cabal found rest with the coming night and saw to their many, many wounds. None of them had walked away from Kosai Talis unscathed, and every one of those injuries was a separate weight on Cistine's heart. From Quill's bruised sides to Tatiana's torn stitches, Kristoff's ripped armor and Ariadne's dislocated shoulder, Ashe's bloodied face and shoulder and Aden's cut neck, Bresnyar's shredded scales and Thorne's various hurts from the gauntlet—

Not her fault, but her responsibility. They all went to that place for her, and though they'd escaped with their lives, the *Aeoprast's* reckoning roar still echoed in her ears hours later when she sat on the fringes of their close-knit camp, a tiny fire built in the shelter of their bodies by which they could tend their wounds.

Cistine tended nothing. She sat on a log with elbows braced on her knees, rolling the sealed flagon pouch from hand to hand. She wondered what it would look like, the augment within, and what it would feel like to use it—to channel it. Would it be like wielding a single augment, or ten? A hundred, even? Would such an ancient power be her death, or the fulfilment of her entire purpose?

Absently, she brushed her thumb over the lock. How much blood would such a thing demand before it opened?

A new shadow fell against her face, and she peeled her eyes up when Thorne crouched before her. He carried a damp rag in his hand and compassion in his gaze—two things she hadn't realized she needed until he brought them. "May I?" he asked, and when she nodded, he dabbed the edge of the cloth against a cut on her brow. "What does it feel like now that you've held it longer?"

"*Different*," she admitted. "Dark. It reminds me of being inside Cassaida's house in Geitlan, or in the cathedral with the *Aeoprast*."

Her voice shook, and Thorne forsook the rag to cradle her cheek instead. "I'm proud of you for carrying that weight. And for your wisdom not to use it."

She palmed the flagon again and shuddered at the might of its sinister energy slithering like some viscous fluid over her hands. Hastily, she stuffed it into her pouch. "It's not mine to decide. Just mine to protect."

His gaze soft, voice even softer, Thorne kissed her brow and spoke against her hot skin. "You have always been noble. But in moments like these, I realize just how queenly you truly are."

The words warmed her better than a sip of hot tea, and she leaned into his touch when he returned to cleaning the blood from her face. "You were magnificent yourself today. Sometimes I forget what a pair we make, but then we take a battlefield together, whether it's with weapons or words, and I know..."

I know what I want my entire future to be.

The words caught in her throat, and she studied Thorne's lopsided smile, knowing but not *truly* knowing, while he went about his work.

She couldn't wait anymore. Not after what they'd begun today in those vaults when they stole from the Bloodwights. The plan she'd dreamed in the dark of her room in the Citadel, with only her own thoughts and Faer for company, was primed to start now.

She took Thorne's wrist in shaking fingers, bringing his hand to a halt. "I need to ask you something, Starchaser."

His gaze sharpened. "Anything."

A throat cleared above their heads. Aden, grim and stern in the banking firelight, came up on their conversation. "Ashe has something to discuss with us."

Cistine grimaced, swallowing both relief and annoyance, and accepted the hand Thorne offered to draw her to her feet. She would tell him before the night was over.

Gathered around the fire, the cabal looked on the verge of sleep, full of yawns and slow stretches and deep hurts. Ashe alone was bright-eyed, but the grim set to her mouth was hardly comforting. She prodded the fire at Cistine, Thorne, and Aden's arrival, bringing it a bit higher to light their faces. "We all owe our lives to each other today. There's no one here who didn't play a part in getting to and from those vaults alive. I'm grateful for the blood and sweat paid by every person around this fire."

A spark of new warmth beat beneath Cistine's breast. Ashe sounded less like an outcast Warden tonight and more like the commander of the King's Cadre.

"But for everything we gave," Ashe added, "I don't think any of us would be alive if not for Bresnyar. I certainly wouldn't be."

A distinct gust of warm wind stirred the undergrowth, alerting Cistine that the dragon was roosting somewhere in the shadows, listening keenly to every word—as hopeless a gossip as her.

"That's an enormous concern," Ashe went on. "The Balmond are impervious to augments and our weapons. Bresnyar's claws were the only thing that could cleave through them, which is exactly what the Bloodwights want. Their so-called *creations* are something we can't bring down on our own."

"Your thinking?" Ariadne prompted.

Ashe tossed the stick into the fire. "We need more dragons."

Cistine caught her breath, the sound inordinately loud in the dead quiet that followed.

"You mean Oadmarkaic dragons," Tatiana said at last, laying a hand to her gut, "just to be clear."

Ashe nodded. "We need more teeth, more claws. And thanks to men like Salvotor, the dragons in the Three Kingdoms have mostly been hunted out. All the help we can find is in the far north, with the wing legions."

"Aden," Thorne said. "You support this?"

He folded his arms over his muscled torso and held his cousin's gaze. "I do. We're losing this war, *Mavbrat*. We need something to turn the tide, and today we saw a dragon do that. But we can't place the burden of an entire kingdom's salvation on one creature's shoulders."

"Then you should go, Shei," Quill said. "As soon as possible."

"Not just me." Ashe glanced at Kristoff. "I'm going to need someone who knows Oadmark. If there's anything our mission for a peace treaty taught me, it's that going unprepared into a neighboring kingdom is just inviting trouble. Bresnyar can find his old hunting grounds without trouble, and he certainly speaks the language, but he's an exile. I need help from the tribes, and to secure that, I'll need someone familiar with them...someone who can convince them to stand by me. You seem like the right man for the task, Kristoff."

"I can think of none better," Aden agreed.

Gratitude framed Kristoff's smile. "If my Tribune tells me to go, how can I deny him?"

Aden smirked and shook his head. "Don't look at me like that. I'm going with you."

Thorne blinked. "Are you?"

"It's the best choice." Aden's voice was steady, but regret flashed in his eyes. "Nimea is alive, Thorne. I fought her today in the mountains."

Thorne's jaw stiffened, and his throat bobbed. Shock jolted Cistine forward on her seat. "You mean the woman who tried to assassinate Thorne over the summer? The one whose people poisoned Baba Kallah? I thought Ashe killed her in the Blood Hive!"

"So did I." Ashe towed a hand back through her hair. "But apparently it wasn't a mortal blow. And she hasn't let the past die, either."

"She orchestrated Braggos as vengeance against us." Aden's tone hollowed. "And today, she brought Pippet to Kosai Talis to taunt me. To prove this is personal."

The fire popped and sank. Ashe cradled her head in one hand, grinding the heel against her eye, and Tatiana looked away. Quill's arm circled her shoulders, his gaze fixed on the falling embers.

"Nimea will not stop hunting me or using this cabal to break me down," Aden said, "which makes my presence a liability. I can serve best by watching Ashe and my father's backs and lending my sword to theirs." He inclined deeper into the firelight, holding his cousin's gaze with hair-raising ferocity. "You know I wouldn't go if I didn't absolutely believe it was necessary."

"You never do." Thorne's quiet smile, full of faith, brought a stop to Aden's breathing for a moment. "I trust your judgement. You have my leave to go."

Aden nodded, his gaze flicking to Cistine. "I don't know if Pippet truly knew me...if there is any hope of saving her. But if you can reach her before Nimea finishes whatever she's planned..."

"I'll try," Cistine vowed. "I'll do everything I can. For Maleck, too. But you three have to go as soon as possible. Tomorrow at dawn, if Bresnyar's recovered by then."

Ashe's eyes leaped to her, narrowing slightly. "That's an unusual amount of support from you, given you're losing the advantage of Bresnyar in the hunt for Maleck. Assuming that's still your next mission?"

Cistine glanced at Ariadne across the fire and found her friend already watching her. Her face was serene as usual, but her eyes burned, urging Cistine to speak.

"Cistine," Ashe growled. "Are you still looking for Maleck or not?"

"Yes, but..." Rubbing her temples, she let out a long, heavy breath. "There's something I should tell all of you. Something I should've told you back in Holmlond, but I just wanted to reach Kosai Talis before the Bloodwights found the augment."

Kristoff prodded the fire. "You have our ears now."

"When I came back from Talheim, I wasn't completely honest about why," she confessed, and Quill stiffened so abruptly Faer took wing from his shoulder and glided to Tatiana's knee instead. "To help win the war, yes...to fight beside all of you. But not just that." She rolled the words around in her mind, searching for the best way to say them. In the end, she decided a quick yank, like a dislocated bone shifting back into place, would be best. "I came to open one of the Doors to the Gods."

Owlish blinks and tense jaws greeted her words, and awareness crawled up Cistine's spine, a watched feeling that made her skin prickle and wanted to name itself panic when no one spoke. Quill sat straighter; Tatiana folded her hands around her neck and blew her breath out through rounded lips. Aden's brow was low, stormy, a match to his father's. Ashe and Thorne simply stared.

Then she watched the horror sink in, face by face, starting with Thorne.

"Cistine." His voice was harsh with barely-held composure. "That would mean bleeding yourself out on one of them."

"I know, but I can come back. Remember how I saved you after the feast in Stornhaz? How close you were to dying, but you survived? Just because I'm the Key, why should it be any different for me? Who says spilling my blood *has* to end in death? Vandred said it was possible with the right tools. If I had a healing augment, I think I could manage it."

Thorne bent forward, resting his elbows on his knees and pressing his palms together. "There's only one flaw to that strategy: you saved my life with a healing augment. But I would've died anyway if not for the augment Maleck brought you afterward."

Hearing his name spoken brought him close to their fire, as if he were standing at Cistine's back, looking over her shoulder. She wondered what he would say about all of this, about opening a Door again.

"That second one," she said softly. "It was a blood augment."

Grimly, Thorne dipped his head.

And here they were. Back to those augments most coveted and protected by the Bloodwights.

"It's a fairly safe gamble anyone who carried one of *those* from Stornhaz died first in this war," Tatiana said sourly. "The Bloodwights need them to corrupt their child army."

"Without a blood augment, your plan falls apart," Kristoff said. "A healing augment alone is not enough. You must let it go, Cistine."

She chewed the inside of her cheek, looking unhappily at their faces. Thorne's had gone blank; the others were an amalgam of resentment and relief.

A violent gust of wind rocked the trees—then settled again.

"Let's pretend for just a moment that the issue with the blood augment was already resolved," Cistine said, and Quill groaned deep in his throat. "We would need to choose the right Door. The one that would best help our chances."

"Stornhaz," Kristoff said. "You're thinking of retaking the City of a Thousand Stars."

She nodded. "I've retraced the sewers underneath it to the best of my memory, and I thought if we could find Rakel and Devitrius, or speak to Morten about the plans for his siege towers..."

"They would take months to build, even if the entire army put their shoulders to the grindstone," Tatiana argued.

"I know. But now we won't need the siege towers. Not if we have dragons who can carry us over the wall."

Ashe's eyes narrowed. "So that's why you want me to go so badly."

Cistine shrugged. "We need all the help we can find. That's why Saychelle and Iri are searching for the *visnprests* in the west."

"And that's why you wanted *Heimli Nyfadengar*," Tatiana murmured. "Another force, this one from the east."

Cistine smoothed the air with her hand. "I know that's not going to happen. But the dragons alone could be enough to get us to the Door under Stornhaz. You know that, Ashe."

"Know it?" she scoffed. "Cistine, I don't even like *thinking* about retaking the City just to let you bleed on that Door. The longer you dwell on a bad decision, the easier it becomes to make. You start to excuse the risks. I've done it. Baba Kallah and Helga died because of it."

Cistine grimaced. "I hear you."

"I hope you do, because I know you haven't thought this all the way through. If the blood augment doesn't work, what then? What happens if Talheim's sole heir dies for Valgard?"

Cistine turned the betrothal ring around the base of her finger. Ashe's eyes followed the half-conscious, habitual movement—and widened.

"Cistine. Have you lost your *mind*?"

Panic seared through her, and she jerked her thumb from the ring. "Ashe, don't, it's not—"

"You are *not* thinking of marrying Thorne in the middle of this war just to keep the line of succession alive!"

"*Ashe!*" Cistine shrieked, gaze leaping to her *selvenar*. He stared at her, blue eyes wide and full of disbelief, waiting for her to deny it—to deny the very thing she'd planned when she first returned. The secret she'd swallowed back in the war camp when he'd told her how loving her made him fail his kingdom.

When she didn't deny anything, Thorne snapped to his feet and walked away from the fire, into the trees. The darkness between them swallowed him whole. Gritting her teeth, Cistine swung back toward Ashe. "How could you?"

"I didn't think you'd actually be that foolish! It took you and Roz three months to find enough Wardens who don't *hate* Valgard to pull off the first step in this mad scheme of yours, what in God's name makes you think they'd accept a Valgardan as their king?"

"Sooner or later, they must," Kristoff pointed out quietly. "She's marrying him either way, if that ring means anything."

"Let's say Thorne agreed, and for once, everything went right," Tatiana interrupted suddenly. "Would it work, with the Door?"

Ariadne sighed. "Much as I despise the implications..."

"Stop," Ashe growled.

"It's sensible. If we had both augments, and retook the City..."

"Even a flock of dragons won't be enough for that! You're going to need warriors, and in case you'd forgotten, all of *those* want Cistine dead!" Ashe snapped. "They're not going to fight beside her!"

"I'm less worried about what they think and more about what Thorne does." Cistine stood, body a hive of nerves. "I need to talk to him."

"Good luck with that." Quill whistled lowly. "Last time I saw *that* look, Aden went missing for almost five years."

Aden leaned forward to pop Quill on the back of the head. "And you still talk about me as if I'm not here."

That faint furrow of humor petered out when Cistine jogged into the shadows after Thorne.

He was barely out of earshot of their small camp, quartering dry brush over his knee. Plumes of sap-scent riddled the air, reminding Cistine of a different darkness, a different sap altogether. A day just as life-altering as this one. She leaned against a tree and cleared her throat, but Thorne didn't turn. He kept dividing those branches; she wished she could see his face.

"I'm sorry," she said, barely audible over the snapping wood. "I didn't mean for you to hear it like that, if you ever heard it at all. That wasn't the plan."

More breaking. More silence.

"Tell me what you're thinking," she begged.

He snapped another branch in half. "I'm thinking that you're clever, and capable, and the very queen and savior our kingdoms need." He broke both halves into quarters with trembling hands. "And I'm thinking that sometimes you make decisions I can't fathom, that make me feel like I've lost my grip on what we're facing. Back in Hellidom, I would train with Maleck to gain perspective. And since I don't have him now..."

Snap. Cistine winced. "Do you want me to apologize?"

"No, I don't want you to apologize." Thorne hurled down the sticks and turned to face her at last. "Stars, Cistine, I want you to *talk* to me. To discuss things like this before you bring them before a Tribunal. We're betrothed, we're *selvenar*, and yet I find out about your dangerous schemes in front of the entire cabal? I've been less stunned by left hooks to the head! I had no time to prepare, no hope of supporting you when I was reeling like that!" He jerked his chin toward the dim glow of firelight prodding through the undergrowth. "They expect something from me: leadership. Composure. A certain measure of strength. I had none of that tonight, because now I'm grappling with the possibility that you...that *you,* the most important person in my life..."

He dragged his hand down his face, resting it over his mouth. His eyes were fixed on her.

"You want me to take control of your kingdom in the event of your *death*," he said shakily into his palm. "I betrayed my kingdom once for you, and you know how I've struggled with that. And *this* is your answer...to ask me to leave it forever? To become the ruler of a *different* kingdom? What about what I want, Cistine...what of *my* plans?"

Guilt hollowed out the space behind her heart. "I'm sorry. I wanted to tell you that first night in the war camp, but then you said how you felt like a failure for loving me, and I just...Thorne, I couldn't ask this of you. I've been trying to think of another solution!"

Some of the anger drained from his gaze. "But nothing's presented itself."

She bobbed her shoulders weakly. "Not that I've had very much time to think about anything but survival lately."

"True." He crossed the small clearing, offering his hand. When she took it, he drew her close and crushed her to him, one arm looped around her back. His other hand sought the tree behind her, and he leaned them against it, taking some of the weight from his legs. His tremors rocked them both. "I'm sorry I walked away. I was overwhelmed. I'm not used to letting them see that happen anymore."

"And I'm sorry you learned like that. I could've hit Ashe for saying it."

"It wasn't that she said it. It was when you didn't tell her she was wrong."

Her fingertips traced the contours of his chest through his armored shirt, following the hidden patterns of the star maps inked across his skin. "You wouldn't have to be King. My father has plenty of years left to rule...decades, even. You and he and my mother could sort something out in the meantime, some legal adoption, a different heir. This is just a precaution to keep chaos from breaking out if something happens, a contingency in case..."

She couldn't coax the words to her lips. Thorne pressed an unsteady kiss to the top of her head.

A full minute of silence dragged by. Then Cistine added, "You're not going to try and convince me I shouldn't do this, with the Door?"

"I can't...not when Valgard needs those augments. I have to keep those vows to my kingdom and myself. And to you." He drew back at last, one hand still braced on the tree behind her, his gaze searching hers in the weak moonlight. "I'm going to clear you a path and let you do what needs to be done. And as for the rest of it..." A beat of silence. His tongue swiped his lips. "I can't promise to become heir in your stead. But I'm here, Cistine. And we will find a way to save our kingdoms, no matter the cost."

No matter the cost. Even if it might be her life.

She circled Thorne's back with her arms, tucking herself flush against him. "I'm so scared, Thorne."

"I know. So am I." He kissed her temple, her jawline, then her lips. "But you aren't alone, Wildheart. Whatever comes. If you fall, we fall together."

CHAPTER FIFTY-FIVE

ASHE WAS THE only one still awake when Thorne and Cistine returned; the others had fallen asleep quickly after the princess left, heavy with exhaustion from the sacking of Kosai Talis and the realization of what might be coming for Cistine...for all of them. With a kiss to the top of Cistine's head and a nod to Ashe, Thorne went to lie down. Ashe wished she could do the same, sink into the void of slumber and forget the horrors of the day, but no real rest waited there—not when a wolf-skulled figure loomed behind her eyes every time she blinked.

She'd told Quill what she saw, while they passed a tincture back and forth for their wounds. He'd listened in silence, face grave, eyes devoid of their perpetual mirth. Then he'd said simply, "It's all right. It was worth trying. I've got him from here."

She knew he did, and that he understood what she could barely face herself after the day's hard fight. So she sat up by the fire, three weapons around her, her dagger in hand. With its wicked edge, she cleaved a black cloth into strips by firelight, reliving again and again the fight on that mountain path. And not just hers; Aden's, too. This was all happening because of Nimea, because of the mistakes they'd made in the Blood Hive; and for Aden, the years before that.

These inescapable specters. She was so gods-damned *weary* of them.

Armor creaking in the creases, Cistine sank down beside her. Ashe blew out a hard breath. "I'm sorry about before...what I said and how I said it. That wasn't very considerate of your feelings or Thorne's. You just caught me off guard."

"There seems to be plenty of that happening today," Cistine sighed. "It's all right. We talked."

"Did he agree?"

"No. But he promised we'd find a way through this together, no matter what."

"Good At least you still have him."

Ashe tore another strip from the whole. Cistine watched it rend, eyes wide. "What is that?"

"It was a gift someone gave me a long time ago."

"Maleck?"

The cloth ripped audibly this time. Quill mumbled drowsily.

"He tried to kill me today, Cistine." Even now, Ashe could hardly form the words or accept their bitter truth. "I reached him once, I thought I could do it again. He almost took my head for it."

Cistine brushed her knuckles gently along Ashe's spine. "He doesn't know you. Any of us."

"No, he knew me. But he didn't care." The harshest truth of all, the one that made her feel like she'd lost a limb—or worse, a fragment of her heart, the one she'd spent more than half a year learning to stitch back together after Siralek, and Rion, and Talheim. And here she was, just as broken as ever.

"We'll save him, Ashe," Cistine said. "Pippet too. I promise."

"We have to. I don't know what I'll do if..." She broke off, swallowing and scraping her arm over her eyes. "The reason I'm going, it's not just the dragons. Not just Nimea and Pippet, either. If I have to face Maleck again like I did today...Cistine, I'm not going to let myself win that fight. I'm not taking his life. If it came to that..."

She couldn't bring herself to admit it aloud: that if it was her death or his, she would lower her blade. And they could not afford to lose her in this fight any more than she could afford to lose him.

Cistine gazed at her with wide-eyed curiosity. "I know you've cared about him for a long time, but...this is different. What happened between you two while I was gone? What changed?"

At last, someone had dared to ask. Cruel irony that it was today, of all days...as if the gods deemed that secret belonged to the world now. "Has anyone told you about Braggos?"

Cistine pulled her legs into a cross beneath her. "Thorne did, a bit."

"Of course he did. He can't keep secrets from you." Ashe's gaze returned to the dying fire. "You know, he was different afterward. There we were, in the medico's tent, and Aden dragged him in the night before with half his guts spilling out. But by dawn he was off the cot, letting some other poor bastard use it, giving rousing speeches to the wounded." Her smile slipped. "Something changed when I saw him like that. Gods, after that battle, *everything* changed."

She shut her eyes against the memory: the canvas tent humid with blood and sweat, and Thorne rising up among the damned, shirtless and bandaged and fierce as a wounded wolf, leaning on a tent post to steady himself but his voice strong nonetheless. His words echoed across the horrific days from then until now, across the strange, dark spiral her life had become.

Whose kingdom is this? I asked all of you whose kingdom this is!
Ours!
Are you going to let them take it?
Never!
Then this hunt is all of ours! This is our kingdom, this is our hunt...we do not end here. We will not die!

The echo of that shout taken up by the wounded, the sick, the half-dead and dying—by Maleck, levering himself up on his cot, and Quill and Tatiana sitting on the edge of theirs, and by Ashe herself, a whispered prayer more than a battle cry—had given her the strength to go on.

Cistine lurched forward, gripping her shoulder. "Ashe, what were *you* doing in that tent?"

Her jaw snapped so tightly shut that a muscle feathered, and she slowly rocked forward, laying out the finished strips of cloth and picking up the next. Dark reddish strands of hair swept her cheeks and spooled in the corners of her vision like whorls of blood. "An augur broke Maleck's guard." Her right hand formed a loose fist, one knuckle jutting, and she thumped it three times over her chest, just barely to the left of center. "A hairsbreadth to the side, and he would've bled out. He almost did anyway, because I was too wounded to carry him to safety. If Bres hadn't dragged our sorry hides to the medico tent...I don't like thinking what would've happened to us."

But of course she knew. It was that desperation that had broken the last of *her* guard, shattered the walls around her heart utterly in the aftermath, and allowed Maleck to crawl completely inside.

"My fault," she rasped. "He was watching my back, but there were so many gods-damned *mirothadt* there at once, it was like they came just for us. Or just for *me*. Maybe Nimea sent them...I don't know. But *he* should've known better, and he came in after me anyway. And I nearly lost him."

She thumbed her lashes, cursing, then cradled her head in her hands. Cistine scooted nearer and wrapped an arm around her, chin propped on Ashe's shoulder.

They stayed that way for some time, leaning into each other, before Ashe found the words. "It was...after that. Once we recovered enough to realize how close we came to dying, we decided we didn't want to waste another second pretending we belonged to our kingdoms, to the cause...to anything but each other." She flexed her fist again, this time to watch the scar on her palm stretch bright and fade to shadow again. "We forged the *valenar* bond that night. But after that, Maleck started to panic more often. He never wanted me to go anywhere without gloves on. He was terrified his brothers would learn what I was and use me against him. Or kill me just for sport." She scoffed under her breath, passing her thumb along the scar. "Neither of us really thought his weakness would be Aden."

Cistine's hand squeezed tight around her arm. "*Valenar*. I don't even know what to say, I just...wish you'd told me sooner."

"Tell the most famous court gossip in all the kingdoms the one secret

Maleck was desperate to keep? I'm not a fool."

"Debatable, sometimes."

"He asked me to keep it hidden. I honored that."

"I know. I know, and I'm glad you did, but..." Cistine's lips twisted wryly. "That took long enough."

"You're one to talk." Ashe mussed the princess's hair and shoved her away, then looked deep into her eyes. "You know, even when Rion had his hands in things between you and Julian, I've always wanted you to be able to marry for love, not duty. That's all that concerns me."

"It's both right now, and that's all right. That's what it means to be a leader—those things are a part of every choice I have to make. They're two halves of who I am, you know me."

You know me. The words rattled through her chest like blows, and she grimaced, returning to the cloth and dagger, cutting a new seam. "I wanted to ask you...do you know what *Mereszar* means?"

"That's an Old Valgardan word." Cistine dragged her lip between her teeth. "I think it means *fearless.*"

The cloth ripped in Ashe's hands, and this time Quill cursed. They waited for him to fall silent and his snores to rejoin the others; then Ashe let the fabric slide from her hands. Cistine caught it carefully between two fingers, watching it dance on the breeze.

"He gave me this scarf," Ashe said to the silent question in Cistine's eyes, "with Echelon when I left the Den. I've kept it ever since. Used it to stanch the bleeding after we swore the oath, even." She lifted her fingertips to graze the fluttering strip in Cistine's fist. "These are for the cabal, to keep a piece of him with us until we bring him home."

Tears slid down Cistine's cheeks. "Will you help me tie mine on?"

Ashe shifted on her knees, winding the band around Cistine's bicep and knotting it tightly but gently. Cistine stared at the weapons laid out before them. "You're taking Starfall and Stormfury?"

Ashe nodded. "It's just...it's what we do."

Some pledges went beyond words. Some vows were sealed in blood and spoken among the stars, and some people loved in silent gestures, like guarded blades and dark armbands smelling of cedar and charcoal, an oath to wear until the threads fell apart and memory decayed. Or until the world was pieced back together again.

Cistine smiled faintly when Ashe's fingers withdrew at last, leaving the cloth bound around her arm. "Maleck will be glad you had his swords while he was gone."

"I hope he's himself enough to care." Ashe's breath stuttered in harsh beats. "I hate this."

Cistine picked up a second twine of cloth. "So do I."

She banded Ashe's arm with her *valenar's* standard, tying the threefold knot of unbreaking. She didn't speak to the tears that coursed silently down Ashe's cheeks, and that was love, too, the kind that had lived between them ever since Cistine was a child.

So much love given, so much taken away. And tomorrow she and Aden and Kristoff and Bresnyar would leave it all behind and travel into the unknown on a fool's errand for hope from the far north, in the kingdom from which Bresnyar was exiled in shame.

But better the unknown far away than the pain she was certain awaited them in this kingdom, at Nimea or Maleck's hands.

"Are you afraid of what's coming?" Cistine echoed Ashe's wandering thoughts, tying off the knot. "In the north, and...with us?"

Ashe flexed her bicep to test the cord around it. "No, Cistine, I'm not. Am I worried? Yes. But I'm not afraid. We're going to win this war and bring back our people. It's just a matter of time."

A quiet breath passed through Cistine's parted lips. "Maybe I shouldn't, but I always believe you when you say things like that."

Ashe mustered a smile. "Because you know I'm usually right."

Cistine smiled back. "I don't know how you always do it. Ever since I was small, I've seen you go into danger and face battle like you've already won."

Ashe turned to look up through the floating embers to the treetops above, toward the distant stars.

There was really only one way she could face what lay ahead in

Oadmark, what she was leaving behind; the possibility of Cistine bleeding on a Door, of augments unleashed in their full might back into the world, of all the enemies and darkness descending upon them at once.

She did it one step at a time. Just one more.

The wind sighing through the trees seemed to speak a strong, quiet affirmation, whispering an ancient word with its fading breath.

Mereszar.

"You know me, Cistine," Ashe murmured. "Fearless is my name."

EPILOGUE

IT WAS NOTHING. Had become nothing.

Only an empty pit, a ravaging husk full of hunger. Starless night and ice storms and trees and hunger, *hunger*, gnawing and crunching at what was left of flesh and bone and spirit and man.

It glided from the tunnel of winds and hugged the shadows, creeping toward taste toward sating toward relief relief relief

There's only one flaw in that strategy: you saved my life with a healing augment.

Augment augment augment *augment*

Bitter rage and hate and need and want and *deserve*

But I would've died anyway if not for the augment Maleck brought you afterward.

Augment augment Maleck augment Maleck Maleck

Mal. Please.

You know *me.*

It stopped outside the trees outside the light outside of sight and mind and memory.

That second one. It was a blood augment.

It could not move.

Blankets soil steel lavender dresses books hugs smiles emerald eyes hickory hair laughter for the first time since—

Pain blood lightning fire drink drink consume take it it's mine it's mine it's all mine...

It called to wind and shadow, brought them around itself, brought the power into its bones and coiled to strike.

It's a fairly safe gamble anyone who carried one of those from Stornhaz died first in this war. The Bloodwights need them to corrupt their child army.

Pain ripped through it, blood, screaming, pleas and cries, a memory, darkness, figures weeping, brothers battlefields war—

I'm not afraid of you!

Two-colored eyes and braided hair. Steel and snow. Blood and tears. A girl, the woman in the mountains, before the scars, before the pleading, before the—before it became—

Whatever I become

I

am

yours.

It recoiled from the fire, from the words, from the face, from the hands on its hips on its collar pinning it in the snow tongues dancing together fingers digging into its bare back laughter beaches fireside dancing rain in the mountains snow in her hair on her face not blood not ice not augments not *right*—

Without a blood augment, your plan falls apart. A healing augment alone is not enough. You must let it go, Cistine.

It halted. Stared.

In the next, we learn to let you go.

Firelight and gifts and a hand around its elbow and a whisper and a face a girl with a smile whenever she saw it.

I'm not letting you go either—

No name no name it had no name no heart only hunger only need only consuming only

Darkwind.

It lunged backward, swinging up its hands, wind gusting around it, the world blurring by in a pallet of smoky shadows and night and stars as it fled and tumbled out in seconds into thick trees and thick rocks and tall figures robed in night. Stood before them and their dozens of small followers small charges their *corrupt child army.*

One looked at it with her long braids black and brown and laughing eyes cinnamon sticks smirks *try and hit me, Storfir.*

"Ah. There you are, *Allet,*" they said, one voice, many voices, all reaching out to it. "We wondered when you would come home."

It stared at the girl in the bird skull. Stared at her tied to a tree, their weapons drawn around her, creatures huddled on the ground beside her. Ready to be broken. Ready to be forged.

This was making and unmaking. This was abomination this was crafting and forging this was

Balmond.

This was her time they were making her one of *them,* making *her—*

Daisy braids, soup, starlit meadows tracking lessons birds games laughter smiles blood screams

Augment augment hunger need want consume rage

Rage.

Rage.

She did not belong here. Did not belong with them. With it.

With...*him.*

Without the blood augment, your plan falls apart.

Fire lightning ice wind darkness light, stars in a dark sky, stars around on every side, on belts inside cloaks in bodies hands feet heads *hearts*

Heart.

Wild. *Heart.*

There it was. Singing. Calling. Music. Symphony violin piano crescendo—

Augment augment blood augment power it's mine my power my desire my heart my

Wildheart.

Mine.

Hers.

"What are you doing?" its brother hissed as it stepped forward.

With a snap of its arms, the Bloodwight once Named Darkwind called every augment inside it, every flicker of fire and ice and lightning and power screaming in the cavity of what was once a man.

And it unleashed itself against its brothers.

End

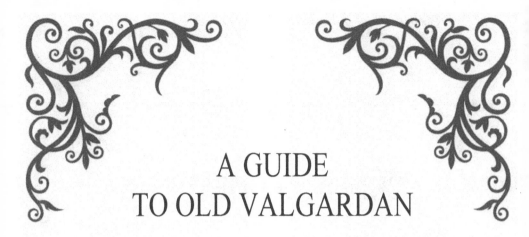

A GUIDE
TO OLD VALGARDAN

Words:

Allatok – Heathen

Slynar – Bitch (roughly)

Bandayo – Bastard (roughly)

Nahdar – Uncle

Allet – Brother

Malat – Sister

Tajall – Infant

Storfir – Big One

Stornjor – Great Love

Yani – Sweet

Sillakove – Starchaser

Selvenar – Blended hearts

Valenar – Blended blood

Phrases:

Hval en dermattae kmar hed var – What is precious comes with a price

ACKNOWLEDGEMENTS

WHAT A WILD ride this book was! Drafting BLOODSINGER was such a unique and challenging experience, and it wouldn't have been possible without a powerful support system behind me!

First, as always, to God. For the inspiration in the cold, dark airport at 4 a.m. when I hit rock bottom and you told me, "Wait. All in My timing." And for giving me the story I love so much when the time WAS right. I'll never stop being thankful You gave me this gift...this story to tell.

To my family, for sticking with me through highest highs and lowest lows. For supporting me and making time for writing sessions and weekend coffee shop dates when I was blasting recklessly through this draft. Thanks for always believing I could do this and making space my whole life to ensure I actually DID.

To JD, my Little Rascal, my love, my life, for taking a mischievous pounce into my life in the middle of editing this book and making me fully realize the future I was, and am, fighting for.

To Miranda and Cassidy, for giving me places to run away to when things got tough, for being my sounding board, my support, my best friends, my soul sisters. These later books were made possible by your unflinching love and unerring support. And I give it all back to you, forever and always.

To Katie and Meaghan, for being the best beta team ever. Thanks for catching all the things that are missed or messy so these books can shine their brightest!

To Maja for making my favorite cover of the whole series, bringing to life exactly what I imagined. You're amazing and you're gonna go so far, kid!

To all my readers, friends, and supporters. There are far too many to name now, which is exactly what makes this journey so magical. To every person who has ever messaged me in excitement, posted about these books, told me how they were touched by them, changed by them...you have a special place in my heart. You help keep me going. You're the reason I do this even when it's so hard.

See you all in the next one! <3

ABOUT THE AUTHOR

Renee Dugan is an Indiana-based YA/NA author who grew up reading fantasy books, chasing stray cats, and writing stories full of dashing heroes and evil masterminds. Now with over a decade of professional editing, administrative work, and writing every spare second under her belt, she has authored *THE CHAOS CIRCUS,* a horror-lite fantasy novel, and *THE STARCHASER SAGA,* an epic high fantasy series. Living with her husband, son, and not-so-stray cats in the magical Midwest, she continues to explore new worlds and spends her time in this one encouraging and helping other writers on their journey to fulfilling their dreams.

Find Renee Dugan online at:
Reneeduganwriting.com
And on social media: @reneeduganwriting